WICKED HARVEST

WICKED HARVEST

ANITRA
LYNN
McLEOD

APHRODISIA
KENSINGTON PUBLISHING CORP.
http://www.kensingtonbooks.com

APHRODISIA BOOKS are published by

Kensington Publishing Corp.
119 West 40th Street
New York, NY 10018

All Kensington titles, imprints, and distributed lines are available at special quantity discounts for bulk purchases for sales promotion, premiums, fund-raising, and educational or institutional use.

Special book excerpts or customized printings can also be created to fit specific needs. For details, write or phone the office of the Kensington Special Sales Manager: Kensington Publishing Corp., 119 West 40th Street, New York, NY 10018. Attn: Special Sales Department. Phone: 1-800-221-2647.

Aphrodisia and the A logo Reg. U.S. Pat. & TM Off.

ISBN-13: 978-0-7582-3533-6
ISBN-10: 0-7582-3533-X

First Trade Paperback Printing: August 2009

10 9 8 7 6 5 4 3 2 1

Printed in the United States of America

To my friends and family,
you know who you are,
thank you, thank you, thank you!

1

Recently shaved, bare-chested, and anointed with *estal* oil, Chur Zenge strode into the Harvest room wearing a pair of ceremonial leggings held together by a wide belt that also nestled a codpiece between his legs. His sharply shined boots boomed against the polished Onic Mountain tile, drowning out the sound of water dancing in the fountains. Garlands of autumn leaves in yellow, crimson, and brown contrasted streamers of flowers—meticulously crafted twines covered the lintels and mantels, flowing down to pool artfully on the floor and around bushels of fresh grains, fruits, and vegetables. Surfaces gleamed and each ceiling crystal glowed, bathing the entire room, even the portraits on the walls, with golden light. The stern faces of those who once held his office glared at Chur as if judging him and deeming him unworthy. Now he saw something else lurking behind their cruel painted eyes.

He sighed and adjusted his ceremonial sword. Whatever anticipation Chur had once felt was now gone after three seasons as the Harvester.

A massive sacrifice table took up the center of the room.

White cloth draped the padded surface so the displays would be more pleasing and command his full attention. The closer he drew to the table, the more conflicting scents overwhelmed him. He'd learned to breathe slowly, through his mouth, so as not to fall under the grip of the pheromone-laced air. Chur didn't know why anyone would want to entice him further as he had no choice but to perform his task. Such devices only agitated his mind and aggravated his primed body.

Following the ancient text of the ritual, Chur approached the north end of the table and considered his first harvest. A deep blue robe of silken *astle* swept over her supine body, and they had taken care to mold the fabric to her high, pointed breasts and down the length of her thighs. Glossy and rich, the sapphire fabric and her pale luminous flesh contrasted her thick black hair. Silver wire twisted through some strands and flowed back over the pillow that cradled her head. He idly wondered how many hours she had lain here motionless as her family members fussed over every detail before finally leaving her alone to wait.

For him.

After preening and posturing the virgin for hours, they left her to him, a man who saw her only as a duty, a ritual to perform, yet this woman had waited and suffered hours of preparation.

As his gaze met hers, he noticed someone had carefully applied tiny blue gemstones to each of her long lashes. When she opened or closed her eyes, the curtain of stones enhanced her wide azure gaze. While he appreciated the effort and the effect, he still felt nothing for the woman behind the elaborate decorations.

Lifting his battle-scarred hands, he cupped her knees and gently parted her thighs. As the fabric slid aside, he noticed a deep crimson edge appear on the sides of the robe, as if to draw his attention to the center of her legs. As if he needed help to find the place he sought. Stifling another sigh of irritation, he slid her forward, placing her left foot against the hilt of his sword and lifting her right foot to his shoulder until her leg was almost straight against his bare chest.

Chur spoke in an ancient tongue. He did not fully understand exactly what he said, as he learned the phrase by rote, but his *paratanist* had roughly translated, "By might of the blade I claim that which belongs to me."

The woman lifted her face and spoke in the same language, "I freely give myself to you." Her gaze held steady with his, but her delicate pink tongue made a nervous swipe against her crimson lips. Perhaps what unsettled her was the scar that ran from his right eye to the upper end of his lip, curling it into a bit of a sinister sneer. He would have smiled to reassure her, but since his previous attempts at friendliness seemed only to frighten the women more, he kept his face carefully neutral.

Chur lowered his hand and tilted the elaborate codpiece aside. His cock was hard and slick with *estal* oil from the ritualistic preparation. He pressed forward and entered her passage easily, as she too had been prepared with the fragrant and soothing oil. Derived from the rare white *estal* flower, found only in the highest slopes of the Onic Mountains, the oil eased his entry but also deadened any tactile sensation; he felt no pleasure, she felt no pain. After burying himself to the hilt, he pulled back, lowered her leg, and helped her from the table.

With bouncing steps and a delighted giggle, his harvest exited the room to seek her family, who would now shower her with gifts and a glorious feast. With the ritual complete, she could now bond with a mate, have children, own property—with one thrust of his penis he made her a fully recognized citizen.

His *paratanist* stepped from an alcove, ceremoniously cleansed his cock, and then applied more *estal* oil. Within a moment, Chur was ready for the next harvest.

Her skin was deep onyx, richer in texture than the most prized Onic timbers, and highlighted by cream-colored fabric that hugged every curve of her lush form. Her hair, dyed red-orange and teased across the pillow below her head, fanned out like the wing of an exotic bird. Tiny slits in the fabric over her large breasts exposed her dark brown nipples. Golden paint in curling filigrees decorated her stiff peaks. As he opened her thighs, he found the same careful detailing all along her ebony legs. Again, he wondered how long she had stayed still for such elaborate preparation when the ritual itself took only moments.

Chur spoke the words and she gave her answer in turn. He buried himself fully, stepped back, and helped her from the table. His *paratanist* cleansed and anointed him again, this time making sure the traces of gold paint were removed from his flesh and clothing.

For the Harvest, all Chur wore was a pair of coarse *mondi* fabric leggings with a large belt to hold his ceremonial sword and the codpiece, and thick boots designed to echo his steps. The booming sound of his boots was supposed to instill fear in men and anticipation in women. Chur didn't know whether they actually had that effect or not; he wore them because he had to.

In accordance with the ritual, his *paratanist* had shaved him clean of any hair, save for his eyebrows and lashes. Where his normally thick black hair covered his scars, the absence of body hair now cast the twisted white shapes in sharp relief against his bronzed skin. He could have them removed, as was the custom of most men, but as the Harvester, his scars practically defined his office. Chur had proved himself superior on the battlefield with the ancient weapons. He couldn't honestly say he wasn't proud of his scars, even the one that twisted his face, for the man who marred him died in the next instant. Chur killed the last Harvester in order to take his place.

An act he now deeply regretted.

As Chur went down the table from north to south, he tried not to let his frustration show. No matter how much attention had gone into offering up the virgins for harvest, he never found any that fully captured his attention. After three seasons and scores of women, he doubted that he would ever find his bondmate during the ritual. He now believed the prophecy to be a ploy to get a man to take an incredible risk; fight to the death to harvest every woman in the land and gain the pride of finding a bondmate. For what man would take such a challenge without the dangling prize of finding his true eternal love along the way?

Disillusioned, Chur continued with his duties despite this realization, for the only way to leave his appointed role was to die on the battlefield during a challenge, and he had not been challenged since he took office, or to retire to the arms of his hard-sought bondmate, which he had not found. Chur realized what the knowledge was behind the cruel painted eyes of his predecessors; they had eventually picked a woman and settled rather than die in battle. Chur refused to claim a woman at random, for he didn't know if she had already chosen someone else. Claiming such a woman as bondmate could cause untold heartache and could not be undone once claimed. He felt trapped and frustrated, betrayed by those who encouraged him to seek out the glory of the Harvester without mentioning the glitches in the flowery prose of the prophecy.

When he'd complained to his *paratanist*, his constant companion offered only that the prophecy was worded vaguely by intent, for what good is a prophecy clearly worded? "Clarity offers no interpretation. A prophecy is cryptic and poetic by design, not default." Such wisdom did not help, but he began to suspect the validity. After three seasons of questioning his ever-present companion, Chur began to understand the reality behind the myth of the Harvester.

The next virgin lay supine on the table, her body almost

completely covered with an artful smatter of fall leaves. All he could see were her cold dark eyes. Her fathomless glare almost stilled him, but he cupped her knees and parted her thighs, causing the tumble of leaves to fall aside. She lifted her head and practically hissed her words before he spoke his.

Chur retreated.

His *paratanist* rushed forward, reminded the virgin of the ritual, covered her with the leaves, and backed away.

Chur stepped forward, parted her thighs, said the words, and the virgin answered correctly at the right time. He harvested her and helped her up. The sound of her running feet amidst the falling leaves conveyed her joy that the ritual was over and she could now move on. Chur imagined her bitter eyes glaring at the ceiling as her family attended her, placing every leaf just so. The virgin had held her tongue, suffering through the ritual to get the prize—total autonomy.

Crude, anachronistic, and downright barbaric, planet Diola clung to the 5,000-season-old ritual of the Harvest. Every autumn, a Harvester, one for all the lands, strode down the sacrifice table, north to south, to cast all the virgins of age into citizenship.

The bawdy tales about the luscious women, the glory of pleasure, and the ultimate securing of a bondmate had fascinated a bright-eyed, lusty young Chur. But now . . . Chur looked down the seemingly endless expanse of table and sighed. Now, he knew, he was only a tool. There was no pleasure, no glory, and apparently no bondmate either.

Hours later, he reached the south end of the table, relieved the ritual was over for another season. He wished to return to his rooms, remove the *estal* oil, have his *paratanist* perform the very last of the ritual, and then sleep for a week. He had a season to consider his next move, but his *paratanist* cleansed and anointed him again.

"There is no other virgin to harvest."

"There is one more." His *paratanist* gracefully climbed up on the table, then arranged herself into a supine pose with her robe hastily thrown around her legs.

Chur gazed down at the figure swaddled in a beige *mondi* robe with a huge cowl hood. He'd never even wondered what sex his *paratanist* was, and now to discover his constant companion was not only a woman but also a virgin he must harvest shocked him immobile. She was the one who shaved his entire body, hardened his cock, and then gently smoothed the oil along the length. When the Harvest was over for another season, it was she who . . .

Once he recovered, he said the first thing that came to mind. "You are not prepared."

"I have prepared myself with the oil."

He shook his head sharply side to side, then realized she could not see him. "I meant that you are not decorated."

After a dismissive sigh, she asked, "Do you need to see more gemstones, fine fabrics, exotic makeup, or smell more rich perfumes?" The hood of the robe hid her face and muffled her voice, but he realized her tone was lyrical, but deep, not overtly feminine, or masculine—no wonder he'd considered his *paratanist* sexless.

Chur reached to move the hood aside but stopped. Once a virgin was presented to him, he could touch only her knees to part them and her feet to place them against his body. According to the ritual, he shouldn't be talking with her at all once she placed herself on the sacrifice table unless he was uttering the sacred words. He wanted to see her face, know her name, and understand how she had become his companion. He had never asked how one became a *paratanist,* and once he completed the ritual she would be gone and he could never speak to her again. It seemed unfair that after three seasons when he could have asked her everything he would suddenly be unable to ask her anything.

His sense of duty overwhelmed his curiosity. He placed his battle-scarred hands on her knees and gently parted her thighs. The rough fabric of the bulky robe clung, keeping most of her legs covered. All he could see were her feet, dirty on the bottom from attending him, and her ankles, slender enough that he could capture both in one hand. If she had been properly prepared for him, the robe would have fallen away when her knees separated. Normally in this situation his *paratanist* would step forward and dart clever hands over the fabric, smoothing the robes to the proper place, but since she was the virgin . . .

Chur didn't know what to do.

By the ritual, he couldn't touch any of her clothing, and he couldn't ask her what to do because she was no longer his guide and companion.

From under the cowl of the robe came a muffled chuckle.

Chur frowned. Was she enjoying this? Had she planned for this, knowing he would be confused and flummoxed? He decided that since she broke the rules by giggling, he'd break the rules by talking. Besides, there was no one here. No one would dare to interrupt the Harvest. He could keep her in this room for as long as he chose to do so.

"Tell me, my *paratanist,* what do I do when the virgin's robe will not part?"

Ever obedient and precise, she answered, "Your *paratanist* is supposed to fix the offering, but since I am also the virgin, I would say we are mired in a conundrum."

"I would say that unique circumstances call for unique solutions." Chur flipped the edge of the robe up, until most of her legs were exposed. She gasped and tried to pull her knees together. "Ah, ah, ah—you cannot move once I have placed you."

She relaxed and he took his time examining the curves of her legs. Her skin was so pale it was almost translucent, milky white and fragile. There were slight bruises on her knees, probably from the hardening ritual if not the meticulous shave, and a reddish brown scar, shaped like a crescent moon, centered on her inner right thigh.

He slid the robe up farther so he could see the color of hair between her legs. His cock twitched when he found her shaved clean. Not only was the *estal* oil wearing off because he could feel a painful throb in his shaft, but the *umer* he'd drunk to keep him aroused yet unable to achieve orgasm was also wearing off because his body ached with a strong need for release. Chur thought perhaps he should hurry and complete the ritual before he violated the most crucial rule of all.

Duty overwhelmed him. He slid her forward and placed her left foot on the hilt of his blade, and the right he lifted until her leg pressed against his bare chest. As he moved forward, she turned her head, causing the hood to fall away.

Chur stopped when he saw her face, for she was much older than the usual virgins were; she had to be at least five seasons older than he was.

Her hair was deep coco-brown with red and gold highlights, but he couldn't tell how long as the length was tucked into the robe. Her almond-shaped eyes were light jade with a starburst of deep indigo imbedded into the iris. Her nose was pert, tilted up at the end, and he immediately thought it was a truculent nose. Her upper lip was fuller than her bottom lip and a soft coral color. For some reason, he thought her nipples, still hidden under the robe, would be the same color. She wore no makeup, no perfumes, nothing to entice or attract, yet Chur felt utterly spellbound.

He fumbled for the words and had to repeat them as his voice cracked. When she flashed him an impish grin, he practically bellowed the words and waited breathlessly for her reply.

She said nothing. She held his gaze with a knowing that he could not continue until she uttered her words.

Chur tilted his head to the side and lifted his eyebrows as if reminding her of her part, which he shouldn't have to do since she knew the ritual by heart. His cock twitched behind the codpiece as he waited. As he opened his mouth to repeat the sacred words, she finally spoke, and even though the phrase sounded a bit different to his ears, he didn't care. He fumbled at the codpiece and practically yanked it off in his hurry to get it aside. With one hard thrust, he buried himself inside her.

And now he knew the oil and drink had worn off for he felt everything—from the slick tight of her passage clinging to his cock to the silken feel of her legs wrapping around his hips to the puff of her moist breath against his chest.

Her moan compelled his. He lowered his hands to her hips, to draw her closer as her legs tightened around him. Her body engulfed his, welcoming and wet, eager and wanton. His body penetrated hers, hot and hard, frantic and passionate. Panting breaths mingled and rose in gasping groans.

Chur violated every aspect of the ritual, but he no longer cared. He needed release. For the first time, he wanted his release within her, not spilled into the ceremonial chalice by her skilled hands.

"Tell me your name," he demanded with a gasping breath, lifting his hand to cup her chin.

"Enovese." She angled up and begged, "Kiss me, Chur."

He knew he shouldn't, but he did anyway. What was one more rule broken when he'd already broken so many? Her lips were firm and ravenous against his. When he opened his mouth, she mimicked him, swirling her tongue to his. He tasted something sweet yet earthy, something he recognized but couldn't name. He didn't care. He wanted her. After an endless line of harvests, Chur wanted Enovese more than he wanted his next breath.

His strokes tightened, intensified, and even though the table was massive, he still managed to sway it when he worked his cock deeper. Enovese met him thrust for thrust. With three strokes and the deliberate spacing of three words, she tightened around him. Her orgasm rippled against his shaft, causing his mounting orgasm to contract his entire body. With one last thrust, he climaxed so intensely he lost his breath and could barely manage to steady his arms against the table so he didn't crush her.

Gasping, he kissed her again; then he realized what he'd tasted in her mouth was a substance that counteracted the *umer* drink that kept him hard but unable to orgasm. In addition, the oil she'd anointed him with the last time certainly wasn't *estal.* He suspected she used the same oil she'd slathered on him after the ceremonial shave. Moreover, if she were able to orgasm, clearly she'd not prepared herself with the correct oil either.

Chur retreated. His frown of suspicion caused Enovese to grin ruefully and sit up.

"Please don't be angry."

"Angry? I've violated every code of the Harvest, yet none of this is my fault. You drugged me."

She shook her head. "I took the impact of the drugs away." Enovese lifted her clever hand and tried to touch him, but he leaned back. She lowered her hand to her lap and pulled her robe down. "Please understand that I had no other choice."

"I would have gladly harvested you like all the others. What do you stand to gain by this?" He could not fathom why anyone would want to compel him to violate the ritual, but she must have a clear purpose in mind for she had waited three seasons to put whatever plan she had into action.

With a soft sigh, she said, "As a *paratanist* I remain chaste and serve the Harvester until I can no longer do so. I help him harvest every woman, yet I am destined to die a virgin." Catching his gaze, she added, "I decided I did not want to die a virgin."

Her answer stunned him. "You decided this without bothering to ask me?" Fury at her high-handedness dissolved into sudden panic. "What happens to the man who dares to harvest a *paratanist*?"

"Death." She shrugged her shoulders so casually it infuriated him.

He grabbed her upper arms and yanked her close. "Do you think this is funny?"

Her solemn gaze met his. "Not at all, Harvester, for my punishment is death as well."

It took a moment to sink in that for their act they both would die. Probably horribly, cut to shreds in some demonic ritualistic way with a cheering audience. "Then why? If death is the only outcome . . ."

"There is a way out for both of us."

He doubted the option would be something desirable since she shifted her gaze and kept her head lowered. "Explain to me this way out."

After a deep breath, she softly said, "To save us both, you must claim me as your bondmate."

His jaw dropped. She had taken ruthless advantage of her position to force him to her own ends and then expected him to claim her for his bondmate? "You want me to swear myself to you for eternity when all I want to do is crush the life out of you with my bare hand?" He clasped one calloused hand to her throat. His massive fist easily encompassed the entire surface of her fragile neck.

With a subtle lowering of her face, Enovese acknowledged that he could snap her neck like a twig. In her calm and soothing voice, she said, "Killing me is another potential solution, but you'll still be killed. Not for harvesting me but for killing me." She met his gaze. Just as he suspected, she did have a truculent nose. Enovese lifted and peered down the sharp edge as if standing well above him when, in fact, she lay sprawled on the table below him.

He released his fist, put his codpiece in place, and stepped back from the table. Even though anger possessed him, he still felt wonderfully relaxed, as if he'd been waiting his whole life for this one spectacular release. For the first time, Chur actually felt the act of penetrating a virgin. In a most perplexing way, Enovese was his first. Not his first virgin or his first harvest, but Enovese was his very first lover.

Chur contemplated her self-satisfied demeanor. "You didn't say the correct phrase, did you?"

Enovese didn't answer, she only shook her head slowly side to side.

"What did you say during the ritual?" When she hesitated, he demanded, "I order you to translate the words for me."

Enovese lifted her truculent nose and boldly squared her face to level with his. Ever precise and obedient, she said, "I said that I gave myself freely to you as your bondmate."

Chur remembered a night before the second Harvest when he'd asked his *paratanist* about the claiming of a bondmate. In her matter-of-fact tone, her face hidden under her hooded robe, she'd informed him that generally men made the claim, but women could too. A virgin could claim the Harvester bondmate during the ritual, but there were no recorded accounts of a virgin taking such a bold step.

Until now.

"And if I refuse your claim?"

A small line appeared over the bridge of her nose when Enovese frowned. "If you make that choice, then we will both die." A small, sad smile turned up the edges of her coral lips. "But at least I will not die a virgin."

2

Enovese resisted the urge to fiddle nervously while waiting for Chur to respond. She'd anticipated confusion and rage but not his withdrawing completely into his own mind. His fury was clear as his facial scar stood out stark white against his flushed face when he clenched his jaw.

Chur stood motionless, as if considering every option. His massive chest, crisscrossed with scars, heaved in and out with his breath. For three seasons, she'd meticulously shaved his entire body free of hair for the Harvest, but she most liked to see his chest covered with thick black hair. Although, when shaved, all his muscles popped, and once she applied the oil, they glistened and flexed, causing a raging heat between her legs.

She could have shaved him with modern implements, but she chose the ancient ceremonial razor because it took longer and she could touch him everywhere twice, once during the shave and again when she applied the oil. Which wasn't technically necessary either, but she had told him it was. For several days after the Harvest she applied more to soothe the itch of the regrowing hair, paying particular attention to his genitals.

When he'd questioned her about her zeal in that area, she informed him that as a Harvester, his penis was his most important asset, and thus by ritual would be kept in the best condition. Such an edict sounded believable to her. When Chur accepted her explanation, she continued to apply oil long after his hair had grown back.

Emboldened by his ignorance, she'd created other rituals designed to keep his most important asset in tip-top shape. Her favorite was the ritual of control. For eight nights, she would tease him to the edge, and for eight nights, she would deny him release. In a daylong ceremony, she would then stroke his tormented cock to a profoundly powerful release. When he found that shattering climax, she found her own, without even a touch to her body.

She'd never worried at her station as *paratanist* until Chur had become the Harvester. When she'd seen him, she knew she wanted him for herself. He stood a foot taller than she did and was wide as a sword from shoulder to shoulder. His midnight black hair was short, shaved almost to his skull for battle. His eyes, the color of the lightest summer sky, had been sharpened with adrenaline from the rush of challenging and killing the last Harvester. The wound that twisted his face had still been raw but did not mar the excitement he exuded. When he bowed formally to her upon introduction, his smile had stolen her heart. Such a smile of joy and anticipation . . . her heart broke when realization set in and he never smiled that way again.

All Harvesters underwent what she called the *realization,* the moment when the reality of the role overtook the fanciful myth. Chur's realization had been profound and painful, coming on sharply during his very first Harvest. After killing the last Harvester, Chur had undergone a hasty preparation ceremony, then found out during the ritual that he felt nothing. All the tall tales of erotic pleasure were false. He could barely feel his own fingers, let alone his cock. His look of shock and betrayal was palpable. From her alcove, a solemn witness to his epiphany, Enovese vowed that she would not die a virgin and Chur would not die in battle.

When they returned to his rooms, questions sprung from his lips so quickly she could barely answer the last before he asked the next.

From that moment, she'd spent all her precious free time researching the exact text of the Harvester prophecy, and all the rules governing her station and his. She became an expert in the ancient language, and unbeknownst to Chur, she often reinterpreted or outright created new rituals. A *paratanist* served the Harvester but didn't normally spend so much time involved in his day-to-day activities as she had; for the most part, her role was important only near the Harvest. Since Chur hadn't known that, Enovese had insinuated herself into his life by designing rituals that needed to be performed on almost a daily basis. To this end, she now occupied a closet off his bedroom as her room.

Preparing him for the actual Harvest never troubled her, for he did not care about the women he harvested, and often complained, loud and long, about how annoying the process was.

"There is no passion, no sensation. I am so numb with drugs and oils that I feel nothing. Even the words I speak I do not understand!" He often paced while he spoke, for Chur was a man who found it difficult to stand still. As best she could, she helped him through this painful time as she had all the others, but never had a Harvester felt so cheated and abused as Chur did.

Given his frustration, she thought for a brief moment that he might be relieved that she'd given him a way out of the role of Harvester, but now, considering his florid face, he didn't seem pleased in the slightest. The only reason he hadn't killed her outright was she reminded him he would only die as a result.

Enovese remained silent and gave Chur a moment to digest the sudden and sweeping change to his station.

"Since I have little choice, I will claim you as my bondmate." Chur met her answering smile with a cruel frown. "But do not think for a moment that I will treat you kindly for what you have done to me. There will be a reckoning, Enovese, and when I am finished with you, I promise you will wish you *had* died a virgin."

His words and the vicious tone of his voice sent cold prickles along her skin. She had not expected or planned for this reaction. She didn't anticipate that he would be profusely grateful, but she'd not expected him to extract revenge either. At a loss as how to respond, she simply nodded.

When he reached for her she wanted to flinch away but forced herself to hold still. Chur pushed the hood of her robe away and pulled her bound hair out, testing the strength and length with his massive hand.

"I did not know it would be this long."

"By my station I am not allowed to cut my hair."

"I don't see why that stopped you. You seem to have no problem interpreting the rules to fit your desires."

His snide comment hurt, but she simply held her tongue. Defending herself or arguing with him would only fuel the flames. To believably pass as bondmates, they would have to convince everyone that their souls had cried out, demanding to be together despite everything. She didn't think they could manage such a masquerade if they bickered constantly.

"Why did you shave . . . down there?" He nodded to her hips.

Enovese stifled a laugh when Chur could not find a word to express his meaning. After his first Harvest, he'd pelted her with questions about the state of most women's cunts. "I did not know a cunt could be so colorful and individual." Enovese had never liked that word, she thought it vulgar and derogatory, but she found it odd that Chur refused to use it with her now after all his questions about the color, shape, and why virgins often decorated their hair with gold dust, paint, or jewels. Never did they shave it off all together, which is why she did. She had wanted to stand apart from the others as much as possible. Her decision had been the right one, for Chur certainly had noticed.

"I shaved my sex to show a kinship with you for you are shaved too."

He nodded and frowned as if he did not believe her.

With a soft sigh, she added, "I also did so for I knew you would notice. For no other woman has shaved her sex for the Harvest. I wanted to stand out."

Now he nodded with acceptance. "Fear not, Enovese, for you have certainly stood out from the rest." He turned his back on her and paced the length of the table.

His boots boomed and echoed, filling the entire room with a chilling drumbeat of fury. Enovese despised those boots, but he only had to wear them for the Harvest. The rest of the season she kept those horrible boots locked up in the sacred chest. Much like her erotic rituals, the sacred chest was another invention. Anything relegated to the sacred chest would reappear only in autumn for the Harvest.

On his second pass, Chur stopped in front of her. "What happens now?"

"We must go to the magistrate and swear out our oaths of bonding. He will question us; then he will perform another ritual, the one of bondmate." Enovese thought of the dress she had painstakingly constructed for the ceremony; emerald green *astle* with hand-sewn water pearls draped across the bodice and spiraled down the floor-length skirt. She couldn't wait for Chur to see her in the revealing dress when all he'd seen her wear was her baggy ceremonial robe.

"And then we can live happily ever after."

His bitter tone chilled her heart, for Chur spoke as if he could never envision them together, let alone happily. Regret crushed down on her, but she was determined to see her plan through, so she kept her tone even, and said, "The bonding ritual is just that—another ritual. You no more have to believe in that than you do the Harvest ritual. If you decide I am not worthy, then I will turn a blind eye as you seek pleasure elsewhere."

Chur uttered a clipped bark of a laugh. "If I am caught in such a dalliance, our lie will be exposed, and we will be in worse trouble than we are now."

Injecting ice into her tone, she said, "Then I humbly suggest that if you decide to take me up on such a generous offer, you do not get caught." Enovese spoke with an air of casualness she did not feel. The thought of Chur entwined with another woman in pleasure tore at her very soul, but she would never let him know how much his happiness meant to her.

Chur eyed her shrewdly. "Do not think for a moment that I will make such a generous offer to you."

It took all her will not to smile, for his possessive tone indicated he did not want to share her with another. A small victory, but still, his dominant attitude was a step in the right direction. Polite and courteous, she said, "I swear that I would never betray you in such a way, Chur. I chose you as my bondmate, and I will honor the vows I make."

He flashed her an annoyed frown. "Forgive me if I do not believe you, Enovese, for you seem to have no problem reinterpreting sacred vows. For surely, a *paratanist* swears to remain celibate, and you clearly broke that vow. Or rather, compelled me to break it for you." After a pause, he lifted her face and delved deeply into her eyes. "Tell me why, after so many seasons serving the Harvester, you decided to pull this stunt on me."

She had anticipated this question and calmly answered, "In

my time I have served three Harvesters. I have witnessed each struggle with the painful and sometimes shameful realization that the prophecy doesn't match the reality. When you realized the truth, it crushed you, for you honestly believed in your role. I knew you would not choose a woman at random, and I did not want to see you die in battle."

Chur uttered a bored sigh.

"And, yes, selfishly I wanted you for myself. As much as I sought to gain you for myself, I genuinely wanted to spare you from your fate. I did not take this course of action lightly. I waited through three Harvests for you to choose, and when you still did not, I gave myself up to you."

His eyes narrowed into dangerous slits. "Do not speak to me as if you have done me a favor. I may have been disillusioned, but at least the choice had been mine. No one forced me into battling for the right of Harvester. But what you have done, Enovese, what you have done is taken the choice of bondmate away from me."

Enovese moved to apologize for she had made the choice for him, but he'd dallied for three seasons and she couldn't wait forever. Before she could speak, he tilted his head to the side and a small smile, lifted up farther on one edge by his scar, cast his face into a mask of speculation.

"Or perhaps you wish to make me think there is no choice."

Confusion caused her to blurt out, "I have given you the choices available. Either we bond or we die. What other choice is there?"

"Yes, as you say, but all the information I have has come from you and your interpretation of the rules. Since I have no independent information, I feel there is nothing compelling me to claim you as my bondmate at this moment."

Her lips parted on a gasp. "But the claim must be made at the time of the ritual."

A mischievous smile lifted his face and touched the deepest

recesses of his eyes. "Then we best not tell anyone." His gaze darted about the vast and empty Harvest room. "I believe it is a secret we can keep for there are no witnesses."

Not in all her planning had Enovese considered this. She could not continue to serve him when she had spoken the words to claim him as bondmate. Just the thought of preparing him for another Harvest chilled her to the very core of her being. "What do you propose? That we act as if this had not happened?"

Chur didn't answer. He ordered her to put her robe back in place and gather her supplies. While she did so, he adjusted his own clothing and strode to the exit. When she hesitated, he snapped his fingers and ordered her to follow him to his rooms.

In her customary ten paces behind, Enovese pattered after him on bare feet, thanking the cowl hood of her ceremonial robe for hiding her face. Hot, angry tears streamed down her cheeks, and terror for her precarious position sent her mind into a spiral of activity. Her incredible gamble had thoroughly backfired. Whatever dreams she'd had of living happily ever after with Chur dissolved into dust.

3

Chur knew Enovese had difficulty keeping up with the pace he set through the maze of hallways, yet he refused to slow. The physical activity helped to dissipate his frustration, but moreover, he wished to punish her, if only in this small way.

Her act astounded him for its audacity, and though she had given him a way out of his dilemma, he refused to feel grateful, for she had taken the choice away from him. He wanted her to know what it was like to have her fate held in his hand and to wonder at what choice he would make for her.

When he finally reached his suite of rooms, he flung the Onic door open so hard slivers of onyx timber embedded into the wall, yet the door bounced off and almost slammed closed.

Tentatively, Enovese pushed the door open and entered.

He followed, then bellowed, "Close it and lock it."

Her hands trembled as she did so.

"Now, my *paratanist*, we will complete the ritual."

Chur stood in the center of his main room and watched Enovese set the stage for the last of the Harvest ceremony.

Colored with rich browns, burnt umber, and the deepest

black, his rooms were simple but lush. The sparse furniture was of the best quality but kept against the walls so that he could use the floor space to practice with the ancient weapons. Only the best lighting crystals lined the ceiling and cast the room with golden light. A ceremonial bathing facility of polished Onic tile and warming crystals took up the entire north wall, and it was there that Enovese meticulously placed the tools she would need. She activated the warming crystals, set the jet of water to the correct temperature, and then approached him.

When she reached out to remove his sword, he gripped her wrist. "Take off your robe."

"But I am supposed—"

"Do you dare to argue with me?"

Her hands shook as she pushed the hood back. She kept her gaze lowered, concentrating fully on prying apart the tiny clasps. Once she'd worked them free, he ordered her to look at him. When she hesitated, he tilted her face up. Confusion and fear caused the indigo starburst in her eyes to darken. A tinge of shame possessed him when he found her terror arousing. For once, he did not feel like a tool wielded by another. For the first time, Chur knew his physical prowess gave him ultimate control over the woman before him.

"Understand me fully, Enovese, you will do as I say and I will only ask once. If you refuse, I will force you to do my bidding. That is a side of me you do not wish to see. Do you understand?"

Her truculent little nose lowered slightly. "I will do as you say without question." Holding his gaze, she opened the robe, slid it off her shoulders, then let the rough fabric pool around her slender ankles.

Just as he suspected, her pert nipples were the exact coral shade of her lips. Turgid and tight against her small but perfectly shaped breasts, her nipples strained toward him, begging him to lower his mouth to taste and feel their pebbled texture.

His gaze swept lower, taking in the soft curve of her belly, the rounded swell of her hips, and that most enticing view of her carefully shaved sex.

To her credit, Enovese did not try to hide from his perusal even when he ordered her to turn and pull her hair away so he could examine the delicate curve of her shoulders down to her high and well-molded buttocks. Her legs were short but in proportion and curvy. When she released her hair, the bound coco-brown length roped down to the middle of her thighs. Those luscious thighs begged his massive hands to grip them, and part them, then plunge between them with one mighty stroke.

His cock twitched below the codpiece. How could he want her again so desperately when he'd had her not long ago? He would blame his reaction on drugs, but whatever drugs or oils she'd used on him would be well and truly gone by now. This was his own physical reaction, and that understanding simultaneously pleased and annoyed him. Chur did not like the idea of her lovely form enslaving him. Perhaps if he had her enough, such a feeling would eventually disappear.

"You may begin."

With an economy of motion, Enovese removed his sword, the codpiece, and the belt that held his leggings to his waist. She dropped to her knees and removed his boots, looking up at him once she set them aside. Her subservient position caused him to twitch when he imagined cupping her chin and guiding her lips to the tip of his cock.

Clearly reading the meaning in his face, Enovese kept her pose. He let her wait for a long breathless moment while he traced his finger along her slightly parted lips, making sure she fully understood his intent. Just when he seemed ready to demand her compliance, he abruptly turned away, striding toward the bathing unit. He didn't bother to see if she followed for he knew she would.

He stood under the jet, allowing the warm water to sluice from the top of his head to the tips of his toes. When he stepped from the stream, Enovese lathered his entire body with fragrant soap that removed all traces of *estal* oil. The rich woody scent also revived his senses, causing any lingering traces of the *umer* to dissipate. As usual, she spent an inordinate amount of time cleansing his genitals. Where once this made sense, for that was where most of the oil was concentrated, he now suspected something else entirely.

"Enough."

No longer able to hide under her ceremonial robe, Enovese blushed and moved to set the soap aside.

"Hand it to me."

Enovese did so and then stood silently, waiting his next order. She no longer dared to question him when he broke the confines of the ritual. For the first time, he was in control and he wanted revenge for all the times she'd tormented him. He would punish her with pleasure, denying her that final release for as long as he could.

While he rinsed off, he had her unbind her hair and then stand under the water. Once she was wet, he had her step forward and he lathered her from head to toe, paying careful attention to her shaved sex. His soap-slick fingers slid easily between the sensitive lips and swirled teasingly against her now-firm nub.

As a Harvester, Chur knew all about that sensitive spot. There was a reason the ritual forbade him to touch a harvest in that powerful, magical place. Mastery over the manipulation of that secret spot could make any woman his slave. Freed of the confines of the rules, Chur delighted in breaking every decree he'd ever learned.

Her lids lowered and her head fell back, exposing the length of her slender neck. A series of soft moans escaped her, reverberating desire down the full of his shaft. Her pleasure radiated out from her and heightened his own. Again, no drugs could cause this effect and knowing that intoxicated him.

Before she could find a sweet release that might compel his, Chur returned her to the water and rinsed her just as carefully as he had lathered her. She said nothing, but the tiniest grunt of frustration clarified her longing. He shut the water off and allowed her to dry him as he did her.

He lifted the bottle of oil and placed a generous dollop in his hands. Mimicking her prior actions, he smoothed his hands together to warm the oil before rubbing it onto her flesh.

Starting at her forehead, he stroked the oil across her elfin face, down her neck, across her slender shoulders, her long and strong arms, and then smoothed his hands along her chest to cup her breasts. Her breath caught on a gasp when he rubbed her nipples between calloused fingers and thumbs.

"I had no idea my punishment would please you so greatly."

Enovese parted her lips as if to speak, but another gentle twist caused her to gasp and forget whatever she had intended to say. He continued to apply the oil down her belly and knelt to cover her legs.

When he looked up, he met her gaze, then urged her legs apart by cupping her inner thighs. Maintaining eye contact, he lowered his face and breathed out, hot and moist, against her sex. Had his rooms not been isolated from the rest of the palace, her moan would have penetrated the walls and caused untold speculation. But they were alone and would be so for as long as he desired; none dared disturb the Harvester after a Harvest.

Keeping his mouth close to her, he softly asked, "Do you have any idea what punishments I intend to inflict on you, Enovese?"

Her beautiful eyes widened, and she shook her head side to side while her tongue slid nervously across her full upper lip.

With a smile, he inched his face closer, then breathed, "I will tease and torment you until you beg me to end your misery."

Her hips tilted forward and before she could speak, he swiped his tongue between the swollen lips of her sex and up to the tight little nub that throbbed against his mouth. A groan of want and need caused her legs to tremble. He pushed her thighs farther apart, encircled her clit with his lips, and then sucked gently as the tip of his tongue flicked slowly back and forth.

On a breathless moan, she begged, "Punish me, Chur, for I have been so terribly wicked."

Flicking his tongue faster, he brought her to the very edge of climax, then ruthlessly stopped and stood. She reached for him and he captured her hands. "I have not even begun to punish you, my succulent servant." He turned her around and continued to rub oil along her back and down the length of her legs. Lifting himself and his hands, he concentrated his attention on her firm buttocks, marveling at the two tiny dimples that dipped on either side of her bottom.

Grasping her hair, he pulled her head back to expose her neck and placed his mouth at the throbbing pulse. With a teasing nip of his teeth, he pressed his body against her and nuzzled his cock between the narrow slit of her bottom. "Tell me, my virgin harvest, that you accept my punishment, no matter what I mete out."

Trembling and breathless, Enovese gasped, "I will do all that you ask to atone for my crimes against you."

Her acquiescence spiraled another wave of heat through his body, and he moved back to slide one slick hand between her cheeks. With soft, swirling pressure, he circled her tight rosebud and worked a slick finger inside. Enovese lost her balance on a swoon and he held her up with a strong arm around her waist as he continued to finger her nether passage.

She gained her footing and relaxed into him. Building intensity by increasing the pace of his thrusts, he lowered his other hand to cup her hairless sex. Slick with her lusty juices, his middle finger slipped easily inside. Working his arms around her in a sideways hug, he managed to thrust his middle fingers into her in a slow, yet building beat.

Enovese lost her balance again, but he caught her and continued to work his massive hands and strong fingers in and out of her most secret and sacred passages. As a Harvester, Chur had never known a woman beyond the ritual of Harvest, and Enovese knew nothing beyond her role as *paratanist*. Virgins both, in a way, Chur thought. He would now act out every wicked fantasy his mind could concoct. He had a season to decide what to do and exploring every inch of his wanton virgin headed the list of what he wanted to do with what might be his last season of life. For he would not claim her as bondmate until he had to. Until then, he would torment, tease, and possess her exquisite form in every way he could imagine.

Lowering his lips to her ear, Chur whispered, "By might of the blade I claim that which belongs to me." He continued to pump his fingers into her welcoming body.

In the same ancient tongue, Enovese gasped, "I freely give myself to you, my bondmate."

He refused her claim and said, "Then you will obey my every desire."

She didn't answer, only nodded, and turned to kiss him.

Kissing was something denied him as the Harvester. Once he knew how intimate kissing was after kissing Enovese during the Harvest ritual, Chur understood why the rules forbid him this singular pleasure. He wanted to kiss Enovese. Kissing her conflicted with his duty, but he didn't care. He had to kiss her again. He captured her lips with his and teased his tongue into her mouth with the same slow stroke he danced with his hands. His cock rode against her slender hip. As desire raced, contracting his body as he neared release, he broke away from her and smiled at her soft groan of frustration. He didn't have the heart to tell her that her torment was just beginning.

He handed her the bottle of oil and commanded her to complete the ritual.

Enovese warmed the oil with her hands, then began at his head, smoothing and working the oil into his skin, gently touching the scar that marred his face. Her fingers kneaded along the muscles of his neck and shoulders, dissipating any lingering tension. As she worked her way down, she left his cock alone, as she always did, until the last. Strong, even strokes along his flesh aroused and yet soothed his exhausted body.

Normally during this ritual Enovese was completely shrouded in her robe, but to see her now, to watch her expressive face, to see desire dilate her pupils and cause her mouth to part in a most suggestive way . . . her arousal nearly pushed him over the edge. She hadn't even touched his shaft.

Once she fully coated him, she knelt beside him to finish, but he turned so she knelt before him.

Her gaze met his briefly, then lowered as she began to work her magic on his throbbing cock. Slick with oil, her slender and oh-so-clever hands encircled his shaft with light pressure that caused the veins to strain, darkening his flesh and contrasting her pale white skin.

Usually during this part of the ritual he did not watch but stood with his eyes closed and his head back so he could fully enjoy the final release. Now, he couldn't take his eyes off her. The light dance of her hands, the way smooth muscles in her arms strained slightly as she increased the pressure, the way her eyes riveted to her task as if he would evaporate if she looked away.

Even and slow, matching the beat of his strained breath, Enovese stroked him, and when his release seemed imminent, she encircled the base of his shaft with a tight ring of forefinger and thumb, then pressed her other thumb to the tip, thus skillfully preventing his release. Once the urge had passed, she continued with her rhythmic strokes. Three times she brought him to the edge, and three times she drew him away. As she built toward the final plunging precipice, her gaze darted to the ceremonial chalice.

"Not this time." Her confused gaze met his and he traced a finger to her lips. "You will be my vessel."

A hot, wanton lust replaced the confusion in her gaze. Enovese steadied his cock with both hands, then slid the sensitive tip across her coral lips. Delicate and pink, her tongue caressed the tip, then slid under to the most sensitive spot where the shaft met the head. Ever so slowly, she sucked him inside the wet heat of her mouth. Her teeth scraped lightly along the top and her tongue stroked softly below as her lips contracted into a tight O that slipped down his length. He swore he saw disappointment flitter across her gaze when she realized she could not draw him fully inside. She surprised him again by using her hands to stroke tandem with her mouth, mimicking the feel of her throat contracted around him.

Every muscle in his body flexed and strained to hold steady against not only the feel of her but also the very vision of her. Enovese held his gaze. Her unbound brown hair spilled down her back richer than the most expensive *astle* and pooled around her legs while her fists eagerly stroked him along with her mouth—his release erupted so cataclysmically she could not have stopped the tide if she tried, but she didn't. Her eyes closed as she sucked hard, taking his climax into herself with a lusty greed that only fueled his orgasm to a far greater height than he'd ever known.

His eyes closed as his head went back, and a tremendous growl rumbled up from his chest and filled the room. Still, she worked her mouth on him, compelling another spasm to shudder through his body. Only then, when she'd drunk him dry, did she release him.

It took him a moment to catch his breath and steady himself. He gazed down at her and found that words utterly escaped him. He lifted her up into his arms and plunged his tongue into her mouth, tasting himself on her, reveling in her answering moan and the way her arms tightened around him as if they belonged wrapped around his shoulders.

He carried her to his bed and placed her in the center, then lay beside her, never breaking the kiss. The oil from their bodies seeped into the fabric, but he didn't care; all he wanted was to kiss her and try to show her without words how greatly she had pleased him.

A part of him still wanted to torment her, to deny her any release, but he found he could not. Chur demanded of Enovese. She had acquiesced, not grudgingly, not by force, but eagerly and wantonly. He had to know why.

Reluctantly, he broke the kiss and pulled back so he could study her face. Tracing his fingers lightly along the bridge of her nose, then down to her mouth, he said, "You enjoyed that."

"Yes."

"Why?" For the life of him, he didn't understand what she got out of his new twist on the old ritual.

"Because I pleased you." Her hands slid along his chest and teased across his nipples. "I could feel your want, your desire, your need. Your pleasure radiated out and into me. The higher I took you, the higher I went until . . ." she trailed off as if searching for the right words, but she stopped and simply looked at him.

After a moment, Chur smiled and asked, "Did you find release without me even touching you?"

Enovese blushed lightly and nodded. "Even before, when we've done the ritual the usual way, I always met your release with my own. I thought the words helped carry me along. Apparently not."

The words. During the ritual when it was time for him to climax, Enovese would ready the chalice and speak three words spaced with deliberately tight strokes that always catapulted him over the edge. She had used those words during the Harvest to push him and herself to climax, but he had no idea that all along she'd found great pleasure in pleasing him.

Even though the long day began to take a toll on him, he found he did not want to sleep, not just yet. Rolling Enovese close, he kissed the tip of her nose, and said, "Tell me how one becomes a *paratanist*."

4

"I was forced to my role with no option of anything else," Enovese explained. Where Harvesters could come from any social class and decided if they wanted to vie for the position, the magistrate picked a *paratanist* at birth by a complicated ritual shrouded in so much mystery she'd still not discovered the details.

As Enovese explained this to Chur, his face darkened. "You never knew your mother or father?"

She shook her head. "Despite what I have read about the process, I cannot believe my parents eagerly handed me to the magistrate shortly after my birth so I could be raised in the *tanist* house." Enovese refused to accept that her mother and father would willingly let her go into a life of servitude. She believed there was something dark in that selection, something deliberately kept hidden, because to expose the truth to the light would destroy the myth. Just as all Harvesters underwent what she called the *realization,* she thought so too did a *paratanist.* The realization came when Enovese understood there was no glory in her role. She was a servant, and her servitude would not end until the day she died. By her very station, she would die a virgin. Enovese had no choice in the matter.

Enraged when she discovered the truth, she vowed that one way or another she would not die a virgin. She had accomplished her goal, but Chur had not claimed her as bondmate. All of her carefully laid plans had ended with Chur boldly demanding her as his bondmate. She knew exactly what she would do when he did. Enovese knew exactly what she would wear when he did. Problem was, Chur refused to acknowledge that he'd even harvested her, let alone stand up and claim her. Enovese didn't know what to do.

By law, by ritual, by the very myth of the Harvester, Chur could stay sequestered in his rooms for a season. By her station, she would be bound to stay there with him. If Chur refused to acknowledge that he'd harvested her, Enovese couldn't claim that he had. With her word against his, Chur would win. What she had to do now was convince him that they belonged together.

He asked what it was like in the *tanist* house and she tried to convey how though women of all ages filled the simple structure, she often felt alone, but more so isolated.

"There were many women, but only the *tanists* were allowed to speak. I was trained not to speak unless spoken to, then to use an economy of words." A memory flooded her mind's eye and she flinched. "I remember one girl stuttered and the *tanist* slapped her face again and again, as if she were determined to slap the stutter out of the terrified girl. The blows only intensified her stutter, and eventually that girl disappeared. I never saw her again. I never asked what happened to her, for a *paratanist* does not question the *tanist*."

"They abused you."

"Not me, not physically, but verbally—" Enovese fell back into that time quoting the endless repetition of her *tanist*'s words, "If careful instructions do not bring the desired result, then physical punishment will." Enovese met his gaze. Chur's eyes of summer sky opened to her. Clouds darted here and there, but below she found acceptance. His upbringing had been very different from hers, but until now, he probably did not understand just how different. Duty burdened him as duty burdened her, but he'd chosen to take on that duty whereas she had not.

"I am not unintelligent, Chur. If my choice is to obey to avoid physical punishment, then I will obey. I read, I studied, and I became the best *paratanist* I could be because that was my wisest choice. The only way I could escape my fate was to embrace my position and then fight from within. I am not impulsive. I am patient. I chose you out of many. I would have chosen you out of few. For Chur, I know in my heart that you are my bondmate."

Enovese realized she spilled her soul out to a man who owed her nothing. Chur had every right to be furious with her, and if he chose to, he could literally destroy her.

Chur held her gaze and frowned. The scar that twisted his face stood stark against the muted light that spilled across his features. "Tell me one thing before I sleep."

Enovese smiled and smoothed the edge of his lip and up along the scar that crossed his face. "Only one?"

"Only one thing." Chur captured her gaze and his powder-blue eyes begged louder than any voice. "Tell me true if you wanted me for me or if you wanted me for I could save you."

With a sigh of understanding, Enovese cupped his face. "I swear that I wanted you as a man. Not as a Harvester, not as a tool to perfect my escape, but as a man, because you, Chur Zenge, you are my bondmate. Even should you decide to cast me aside, I will still claim you as my bondmate in my heart."

Her honesty only troubled him. His gaze lowered and he pulled away. "Do not ask too much of me." After a moment of hesitation, he met her gaze. "I will not claim you as bondmate,

Enovese, for I do not know you beyond what we shared tonight. A singular experience and one I will treasure, but I will not base my heart on one night of sex. For we both know sex weakens the body and spirit."

He said the words by rote, for she had learned them too. The craving for sex was normal, but to indulge only weakened one both physically and mentally. A Harvester and a *paratanist* rose above base desire by the ritual. The fact that they'd both broken the ritual and enjoyed the physical aspects meant only that they were weak. They would overcome such weakness by being dutiful.

Enovese knew that above all else Chur considered his duties. He took his position seriously. He never missed a practice, a function, or a ritual. Chur lived and breathed the role of Harvester. When he felt on shaky ground, he lapsed back into the rigidly defined limits of his duty.

Cupping her hand to his face, Enovese said, "I do not ask you to do anything. I have spoken my claim. You have no obligation to do the same. I ask only that you give me a chance to show you why I have claimed you as my bondmate."

Chur frowned again and rolled onto his back. "Sex will not sway me."

Lifting up so she could look into his eyes, Enovese said, "I have never, nor will I ever, attempt to sway you with sex. By my own volition, I will gladly, eagerly, and most wantonly engage in sex with you, Chur Zenge. If you think I am doing so in order to inveigle you to my whims, then you must stop. If you cannot stop yourself, then ask me to stop. If you cannot manage that, then I humbly suggest that you might actually want me to do whatever it is that I am doing."

Her impassioned speech compelled a sleepy smile. "Yes, my wanton virgin. In the future, I promise that if you are forcing me to do your lusty bidding, I will promptly stop you." He lifted up and kissed the tip of her nose. "Do not think that I'm dismissing you or your concerns. Understand that you have tormented me for seasons with your rituals, I suffered my third Harvest, and my body feels like a wrung-out *harshan*."

Enovese giggled, for a *harshan* was a soft towel used to wipe the sweat from his brow during weapon practice. She nestled down beside him but felt instantly alert when he stiffened.

He said softly, "You will not sleep beside me. You will go to your room." Chur didn't ask, he didn't order, he simply stated his wishes.

Without a word, Enovese left his bed and entered her room. Not even a room, just a closet adjacent to his bedroom. Her narrow bed was cold, but she snuggled into the bedcovers, pulling them over her head. She didn't know if she could ever convince Chur that her feelings were genuine. She didn't know if she could help him overcome his seasons of indoctrination. More than anything, Enovese didn't know how she could continue to be Chur's *paratanist* after confessing her heart.

5

Rich aromas of seared meats and baking breads woke Chur. His *paratanist* created the customary huge morning-after meal and his stomach growled with anticipation. He stretched. Even after a full night of sleep, fatigue crushed his body all the way to his bones. Without lifting his head, he glanced around, but he didn't see Enovese. Relief came with a tinge of guilt; he wasn't sure exactly what he would say when he saw her. A childish part of him wanted things to go back to the way they were, but his logical mind knew they could never go back. His relationship with his *paratanist* would never be the same. She was no longer a nameless servant; she was a woman named Enovese. A woman with the most incredible eyes he'd ever seen.

He rose and showered self-concisely. Was Enovese watching from one of her alcoves? He wondered why such a thought would bother him now when it never had before. When he finished he almost called her out to oil him, for the regrowing hair began to itch unbearably; instead, he slathered himself up. Perversely, he took great care with his genitals, lingering over every touch in case she *was* watching. Her potential surveillance of his act caused a bizarre thrill to harden him fully. He stopped before he lost control, but also he was sore from yesterday; so many harvests had rubbed his cock raw. The oil helped to soothe the hurt, but his touch wasn't nearly as comforting as Enovese's.

He wrapped a black *astle* loincloth around his hips, then ate until his belly almost burst. By the time he finished, Enovese had changed the sheets on his bed. She knew him well. All he would do today was eat and sleep. Chur crawled between fresh linens, flopped onto his back, and dozed.

Hours later, he woke to more cooking aromas. Complex herbs and spices caused his mouth to water. He stretched. When he moved to rise, he noticed Enovese stood at his bedside, still as a statue. The nondescript beige robe covered her, but he pictured her as she had been last night, naked, with her glorious hair unbound and her striking eyes open, passionate, and wanton. He smiled at the image, but his pleasure faded when he noticed she held the ceremonial chalice.

"Explain."

"Last night we did not complete the Harvest ritual."

Her voice reverted to that sexless, emotionless drone of a *paratanist*. Despite his longing for their relationship to return to normal, he enjoyed her real dulcet voice far more than the false tone of her dutiful voice.

Flippantly, he said, "I changed the finale, but we did complete the ritual."

"By the ritual you should have ejaculated into the chalice and I should have taken the cup to the magistrate this morning."

Her informative attitude annoyed him as much as her answer surprised him: Why would the magistrate want that? Several odd images floated in his mind, the worst of which was that the magistrate drank the contents of the chalice. Chur shivered in revulsion. The current magistrate, Ambo Votny, was a short man with a florid face, a bulbous nose, and a distended belly. All Chur knew about Ambo was the man had a jovial attitude from too much drink and an unfortunate habit of picking his nose and then wiping the contents on his trousers. As the Harvester, Chur had attended many formal functions; he could always tell how long Ambo had been there by how many snot swipes decorated his uniform. Repulsion always caused Chur to stand well away from Ambo, for there were times when Ambo would be so inebriated he would wipe his nasal deposits on another.

"For what possible reason would the magistrate want that?"

"I know not why he wants the chalice, only that he does. If I do not deliver the cup to the temple, I will be in violation of my duties." Ever precise and obedient, Enovese answered, then bowed her cowl-covered head.

It was then Chur realized that perhaps Enovese understood that last night should not have happened. Perhaps she too wanted to return to the narrow confines of her role. "If you fail in your duty you will be punished?"

"Yes."

"What if you return the chalice empty?"

After a long pause, Enovese answered, "The magistrate will punish us both."

With a sigh, Chur stood and removed his loincloth, but his mind would not stop gnawing at the question of why the magistrate, or anyone else for that matter, would want such a sample from him. However, once Enovese began to tease and torment his cock with her skilled hands, all thoughts left his mind. Aware of how sore he was, Enovese used feather-light strokes that aroused yet soothed him. Unlike last night, her movements were clinical, ritualistic, and utterly unemotional.

He wanted to push the hood away so he could see her face. He refrained. Perhaps it was for the best that they remained separated by duty. Determined, he closed his eyes and let the pressure mount. Chur forced himself not to think of the hands around his swollen cock as her hands; he thought only that hands other than his teased him. Three tight strokes and three magical words caused him to climax, but not with the intensity of last night. Nothing could compare to how her lips had caressed his shaft or the way her eyes fully captured his attention. Despair tugged at him, for he would probably never experience a climax like that again.

Shrouded in her robe, Enovese rose and bowed to him. She washed her hands, placed the chalice in a Onic box lined with black *astle,* and then left, presumably for the temple on the lower floor.

After he killed the last Harvester, Chur went to the temple for the official inauguration. He remembered a massive room shrouded in heavy fabrics, sparse lighting crystals of azure blue, and a stench of cloyingly sweet herbs. He hadn't paid much attention to the statues and artwork for he was still riled from battle rage. Mainly, he remembered thinking it was odd that such a large room could feel so unbearably small. He felt giant sized, as if he dwarfed the entire palace. He remembered little of what they said or what he signed. He had been relieved when the ceremony was complete and he could leave. Chur simply could not breathe in the temple. Every wall crushed in on him and he barely managed not to run away, let alone stand for his indoctrination.

Alone, he found his rooms lonely for the first time. He showered again, smoothed his itchy skin with a scented lotion rather than the oil, changed his loincloth, and then ate from the warming platters Enovese had left on the table. As always, the food was excellent. She knew exactly what he enjoyed and how he wanted his food prepared; seared crispy skin on the meat and the softest cloud puff of bread, but still . . . something was missing. No matter how much he ate, he did not feel sated.

He practiced with the *dantaratase*, a slender staff as tall as he was, but his movements felt awkward and unbalanced. Reverting to his training, Chur took deep breaths to center his bodyline; yet again, he felt unstable. An agitated unease permeated his entire body causing him to feel uncomfortable within his own skin.

Next, he tried *kintana,* an ancient art of self-defense that used flowing movements to calm the mind and body. After an hour of rigidly focused concentration, he finally found his center. Never had it taken him so long to quiet himself. Almost as soon as he found his calm, he lost most of it when he wondered what was taking Enovese so long.

He thought back to the other Harvests, but he couldn't remember how long it took her to deliver the chalice. Frankly, he couldn't remember because he'd never paid any attention. He had no idea the goblet went somewhere. He thought it was simply ceremonial. The more he thought about why someone would want the contents of that cup, the more agitated he became. What possible things could they learn from his sperm? The first and most obvious was his fertility. Was it in case he impregnated one of his Harvests they could use it as a comparison to determine fatherhood? He shook his head. If he remembered correctly, during his inauguration, some clause forbid him from ever having to suffer sanctions of any sort if a child came of the Harvest ritual. Chur thought they called it *immunity*. He would have to ask his *paratanist*.

As if he summoned her, Enovese entered. She slipped her sandals off and left them by the door.

"I wish to speak to you." Chur paced the length of the main room while Enovese stood statue-still. "Has a Harvester ever produced a child from the Harvest?"

"I know not. I know a virgin has never lodged a claim against a Harvester, but that doesn't mean a Harvester has not fathered a child. However, such an event would be unlikely as *estal* oil is a powerful spermicidal."

Chur considered for a moment, but this information only prompted more questions. "Then why would they offer me immunity if a child came of the Harvest ritual?"

Enovese paused for a moment, and then answered, "The immunity clause is not for you, but for the child. You have no right to make a claim to a child produced during the Harvest."

Again, her answer only prompted more questions to swirl in his mind. Why would they be concerned about such an event if the event were unlikely to occur? A sudden insight caused him to blurt, "At the end, when you prepare me for the chalice, the *estal* oil has been removed."

"Yes." Enovese sounded somewhat bored.

"So it would be a viable sample."

"Yes." She no longer sounded bored but speculative.

Another thought caused the regrowing hair on the back of his neck to stiffen. "You and I, when we broke the ritual, we did not use the oil when we . . ."

Her rigid posture slumped, but she offered him no answer for he had not asked a question.

"Remove your hood and look at me."

With a trembling hand, she pushed the hood back. She met his gaze, appearing both beautiful and tormented.

"Did you try to trick me into impregnating you?"

Shocked by his accusation, she blurted, "No!" Enovese shook her head. "I would never do that to you." Strands of her bound hair caught in the edges of the hood, glistening in the light. Her hair was the most dazzling mix of harvest colors.

"Then why are you crying?"

She wiped the tears away but refused to answer, nor would she meet his gaze. He pelted her with questions, yet she remained steadfast in not answering. Her insubordination infuriated him. In desperation, he threatened her. "I can have you cast out. I could have you exiled to the harsh lands in Rhemna. Barbaric and brutal, I'm told."

Savage and mindless creatures wandered the frozen northern tundra. None went there willingly. Rhemna was a favorite dumping ground for incorrigible criminals who either died quickly or went insane from the neverending ice storms. However, even intimidation would not move her to answer and he didn't think he could hold to his threat, for what if she were already carrying his child? Or was she counting on that? Perhaps Enovese refused to speak for such information would surely help him set a course of action. He decided that the odds of her being in heat on the exact day of the Harvest were unlikely. Moreover, her shock at his accusation had been genuine; whatever her plans, pregnancy wasn't one of them.

"Since you have refused to answer, I will ensure that such an event will not come to pass." He ordered her to step before him and he traced a possessive finger across her tightly compressed lips. "Your mouth has already proved most pleasurable."

Her face betrayed not a flicker of emotion, but anxiety simmered in her eyes. His knowing smile unnerved her and ever-so-slowly, her truculent nose lifted with determination, but the movement did not fool Chur. Her breath was uneven, catching and releasing as sweat began to bead along her forehead.

"Defiant servants must be punished, Enovese. Remember that I told you never to defy me. Since you insist on doing so, I will make you regret your decision." He let the threat hang in the air between them as he considered her from head to toe. The shapeless robe hid every aspect of her form, yet he knew what lay beneath. With a murmur, he ordered her to remove the robe. When she hesitated, he grasped the edge and pulled so sharply the tiny clasps broke. Enovese uttered a gasp of surprise, then quickly shucked the garment before he could damage it further. He had no idea how many robes she had but he didn't care. If she had to run around naked, that was her fault for defying him.

To his surprise, she was not nude below the rough fabric.

She wore a thin shift that hung to her knees. The cut of the garment was simple but enticing in that the weave was thin enough to reveal shadows of her nipples. Extending his hands, he captured the relaxed peaks and twisted until they stood at attention. Her intake of breath lifted her breasts, causing the fabric to tent around her now fully erect nipples. Tracing his fingers around and between her pert breasts, he managed to press the fabric against her belly, thus revealing the shadow of regrowing hair. Lowering his hands to her hips, he pulled the fabric closer to her skin. Against the beige fabric, her hair cast a patch of tawny coco and reddish brown. Stubble caught and pulled in the thin weave.

His heart pulsed in heavy strokes, overheating his body even though all he wore was the loincloth. His cock swelled, pushing against the black *astle* with each thud of his heart. The silken fabric teased his flesh, and the need to possess her again caused his hands to shake as he explored her shift-covered form. Before she could see him quaver and exploit his want, he roughly slipped his hand between her thighs and pushed his fingers into her sex. Her wetness soaked the fabric and allowed a light texture to enhance the thrust of his fingers.

"How wet you are, my *paratanist*. How eager you must be to feel the sting of my wrath." Rocking his hand back and forth, he worked more of his fabric-covered fingers into her swollen sex. He still didn't quite understand why he chose to punish her with pleasure; perhaps so he could indulge himself without regrets for she had forced him into it.

Enovese closed her eyes and her face dipped low, as if she were ashamed of her arousal. Then she followed his movements, angling her hips forward, forcing his hand to ride up high with each stroke. Pleased by her eagerness, he rubbed harder and faster, then realized it was more than sexual pleasure she sought.

With a laugh, he pulled his hand away. "It itches, doesn't it?"

She gritted her teeth and nodded curtly.

Chur knew well that insidious itch of regrowing hair. Nothing really soothed, and scratching the itch only begged more scratching. He felt no pity for her; in fact, he was pleased she suffered the interminable annoyance he had put up with three times over. It was an aggravation he suffered himself at the moment, but the *astle* fabric was far more forgiving than what she wore. As he considered his next move, he thought of ways to increase her torment in that area. On a deep breath, the scents of the food on the table caused his mouth to water, but he wanted a banquet of a different sort.

He had Enovese stand before the table and lower her chest against the surface so her bottom stuck up high. The shift draped over her, offering another erotic hint of curves and shadows that he was compelled to explore. Even though Enovese remained silent, the little noises she made at the back of her throat conveyed a lustful enjoyment and a somewhat fearful expectation. Grasping her bound hair, he molded it along her back until it flowed down between her cheeks. He then moved the edges of the shift up around her hips to expose her legs while keeping her bottom covered. She had beautiful legs. Her muscles were long and strong, the curves of which only enhanced the fragility of her ankles.

"Are you willing to answer my questions?"

She remained mute, so he ordered her to rise on tiptoe so taut muscles drew lines under her flesh. He explored leisurely, taking his time even when she trembled with fatigue. Allowing her to plant her feet flat on the floor elicited a groan of relief that caused him to chuckle wickedly.

Now he turned his attention to her bottom. He pulled her bound hair aside and lifted the shift to expose her backside. Again, he explored this new vision. Bent over as she was, her buttocks formed a heart-shape and caused the dimples to disappear. Her waist seemed impossibly small from this angle. He gripped her hips, marveling in the silky texture of her flesh. As he leaned near, he caught a hint of nervous sweat and saw tiny beads forming along her back. He took another deep breath and found the aroma of her trepidation intoxicating. Lowering his gaze, he decided he did not like her thighs pressed together so tightly, but when he ordered her to part her legs, she refused.

Baffled by her continual defiance, Chur suddenly understood that Enovese *wanted* him to punish her. Something in her needed him to take control and force her to do what she secretly wanted to do anyway. Enovese did not want him to coax her, she wanted his power and authority to overwhelm her and remove her choice. Chur found this difficult to reconcile with what he had learned of her last night. She'd been deeply upset that she'd had no choice in becoming a *paratanist,* but now she wanted him to make choices for her? Or was he really doing that? He wasn't truly forcing her if she honestly wanted him to punish her. He began to wonder just who was in control of this situation, and he had a sneaking suspicion the person in charge wasn't him.

Testing the waters, he grumbled, "I should spank you like a disobedient child."

Her soft groan and a subtle lifting of her bottom was more than an answer, her motion was practically an inducement. Chur had never struck anyone except in battle, and then, only men. Afraid of hurting her, he delivered a tentative slap to her buttock. Her fragile white flesh quivered, but his blow left no mark. She did not react. In quick succession, he slapped her bottom twice, causing a rosy glow to spread. A confusing mix of excitement and shame washed over him when he saw the mark of his hand against her. He wanted to stop, and yet he wanted to continue. He took a deep breath and smacked her again, hard enough to jostle her against the table.

Enovese moaned low, hungry, and lifted her bottom, angling up, presenting herself so that he could see the wetness between her thighs. As he leaned near to inspect her, he could smell and almost taste the alluring aroma of her passion. He realized he did not have to spank her hard, just the quickest flick would blush her skin, flushing the white to pink, exciting her in a way he did not fully understand. As he examined her from all angles, he noticed her pulse pounding in her neck as she panted. She'd shut her eyes tightly and her teeth nibbled at her bottom lip as she held herself steady, awaiting the next slap.

6

When the blow didn't come, Enovese tentatively opened her eyes. Chur stood beside the table. His speculative gaze met hers. His summer-sky eyes penetrated, causing her to feel so vulnerable that she almost looked away, but that would show the truth of her fear. She was terrified that he would understand what she did not. Enovese forced herself to hold his gaze in a desperate bid not to reveal more than she already had.

At first, she'd defied answering his questions, for she did not want to tell him the horrible truth of her station, but then his anger excited her, and when he'd had her bend over the table, she eagerly sought his punishment. She hadn't had anything particular in mind until he offered to spank her. Hot wetness flooded her sex and she'd lifted her bottom in invitation. From the first tentative smack of his calloused hand to her tender flesh, she'd only grown wetter and more aroused. Her nipples pressed into the table so hard she wouldn't be surprised to see dents in the wooden surface when she stood.

With an intense concentration on his face, Chur removed the black loincloth from his hips. His movements were silky, seductive, utterly in control. His penis pulsed with arousal and stood out from his body. He dropped the cloth and wrapped one calloused fist around the base of his shaft. Holding steady, he didn't move his hand up and down as she expected. He gripped himself, then released, several times, as if to thicken his already rigid cock. Veins stood out, darkening the tip, and a shadow of regrowing black hair caused his sack to seem bigger and fuller than ever. The short hairs on his chest and arms enhanced his muscles, shadowing them, making him seem one step up from a wild man.

As her gaze darted to his face, she discovered his eyes had darkened, his lids lowered, giving him a sinister expression that caused another gush of heat between her thighs. His hot gaze darted from her eyes to her mouth. She licked her lips.

One corner of his mouth lifted. "A lovely invitation, but as I said, I already know how pleasurable your mouth is." He stopped teasing himself and moved out of her line of sight.

Enovese stayed still and fought to tame her breath. Her insides churned and she couldn't stop the quiver shivering along her back. Laying facedown on the table with her bottom lifted caused a strange sensation of pleasure. She felt exposed, vulnerable, and yet not knowing what he would do next was undeniably arousing. She did not hear him approach her from behind, but she felt the heat of his body replace the cool breeze that soothed her flushed buttocks. He lifted her hips and placed a pillow between her and the table, then moved back. Still, his body heat increased the warmth until that same heat flooded into her sex.

She squirmed and he ordered her to hold still. For a breathless moment, she held herself steady for another spanking, but then felt his oil-covered hands smoothing along her bottom. He worked the muscles, murmuring for her to relax. Exhaling, she let her body go limp against the table and closed her eyes. Kneading his fingers into her smacked bottom stung slightly, but as he continued, the massage relaxed her to the point she almost fell into a blissful slumber.

Her eyes popped wide when he slipped his hand between her buttocks, probing his thick finger against her taut ring of muscles. The sensation was not new, as he had done so during the end of the Harvest ritual, but now he probed with more intent, as if to open her for something much larger than his finger.

As she pictured him gripping his cock, squeezing and releasing, now she imagined a different objective—as if he were showing her how dangerous a tool he wielded. Preparing her with his fingers was a kindness. At any moment, he could force his prick into her. She had no defense.

Her gasping pants hurt her lungs. She could not catch her breath. Her entire body grew tense with fear, yet he continued to explore her dark cavern. Forcing his knee between her legs, he parted her thighs effortlessly, gaining greater access and making her feel ever more vulnerable.

"Chur, stop, I'll answer your questions."

He did not respond with words, only slid his finger in and out of her secret depth with more deliberate strokes. All at once, she wanted him to cease but also to continue. Shame filled her for she did, indeed, crave to be his servant, knowing only his wants and needs, allowing his desires to dictate hers. But this, this was too much. His thick shaft penetrating her virgin sex without the cushioning of *estal* oil had been painful. She still felt a twinge from the invasion. To even think of his massive cock buried in her virginal ass caused her to clench tightly for such an act seemed impossible. If she couldn't take him fully into her mouth, how would he ever fit there?

Panicked, she tried to lift up and face him to beg for surcease. Chur pressed one massive hand to the small of her back and held her against the table.

With a growling menace, he said, "You had your chance to obey, Enovese. Against my own word, I gave you several chances, yet you continued to defy me. Now you will suffer my punishment."

She well remembered him saying his fury was a side of him she would not wish to see, but regret would not stop the penalty for disobeying him. He cruelly ignored her pleas. The more she begged, the more deliberately he thrust into her. One oil-slicked finger became two. Just when she became accustomed to the invasion, two became three. Pain flared and retreated. Her only defense came when she discovered if she relaxed to the assault, the ache lessened. Once she went limp, to her shock, the dull pain turned to throbbing pleasure. His thrusts caused her sex to gush uncontrollably for that was where she wanted him most. If only she'd told him the truth, he would eagerly plunge himself into her now-rippling passage. At the brink of screaming her regret and acquiescence, Chur stopped all movements.

For a long moment, Enovese waited for him to remove his fingers and plunge his cock into her. The moment spun out, timeless and frightening.

"Move."

Unsure of exactly how he wanted her to move, she held still.

"Ride my hand."

Tentatively, Enovese rocked back. Chur held his hand steady so she could impale herself on his thick fingers. At first she moved reluctantly, but when she realized the power had shifted back to her, her movements became more wanton, willing, and downright desperate. His fingers were no longer enough to fill the need that burned inside. Her thrusts grew frantic. She could well imagine the veins in his arm standing out as he tried to hold steady. When the pillow fell to the floor she barely noticed for she had lifted off the table to better angle her body for the welcomed penetration of his fingers.

On the brink of a shattering orgasm, Chur stilled her movements with a hand pressed to the small of her back. He ordered her to stay still. A desperate groan shook her and she waited for what seemed forever. She knew Chur had moved away, for the lack of his body heat caused a cool breeze to wash along her burning bottom and dripping sex. Behind her, she heard him doing something at the bathing area. Washing his hand, perhaps, she thought. The splash of water stopped. Chur stood beside the table gazing down at her.

Now his eyes were feverishly bright. He shot a stream of oil to his hand, then roughly cupped his sex. One large fist wrapped around the shaft, then slid up and down. Oil slick and pulsing, his cock loomed large, treacherous. Chur groaned as his gaze darted between her lips and her fully exposed bottom.

Watching him tease his cock entranced her. The oil glistened, enhancing the pulsing veins that grew thicker with each stroke. Every muscle in his arm strained, showing off his power, reminding her of his prowess in battle. His breath grew labored, and her breath matched the pace of his. She felt each stroke into her, alternately into her mouth, her sex, or her newly awakened ass.

"Tell me."

Enovese instantly knew what he wanted. Despite the power plays they had explored this night, Chur could not bring himself to force her to do anything against her will. Offering her a choice between pleasuring him with her mouth or bottom, Enovese knew what she wanted, but more so, what he needed. Chur didn't have to compel her, for he had primed her to the point she craved what she once feared. Despite her trepidation, Chur would not hurt her in this final possession of the last of her virginity. Yet, too, she knew, after this, she could never go back. Chur would own her utterly.

In the ancient tongue, she said, "I freely give myself to you." She left off "as my bondmate" for he would balk at that.

Chur shook his head. "Let there be no question, Enovese."

Boldly, she met his gaze and said, "I want you to slide your cock up my ass." Her vulgar words flushed a hot blush across her face, but she refused to look away. She meant what she said. "I'm not afraid anymore. I know you won't hurt me. I'm begging you to finish what you started."

A slight smile lifted the edge of his mouth, softening the twist of the scar that marred his face. He moved out of her line of sight, but she felt his heat rolling out in waves against her behind.

"Open yourself to me." Chur didn't ask, he didn't order, he simply commanded.

Pressing herself against the table, Enovese lifted her hands and spread her buttocks for him. Her action was the final show of her willingness. Wantonly, she exposed herself to him, begging him without words to take her. Desire overwhelmed her fear, and she closed her eyes to focus fully on his ultimate possession.

A pressing insistence settled against her rosebud. The very tip of his cock felt too large. She suddenly changed her mind and let go of her cheeks. Pressing her hands against the table, she leaned up, ready to move away from his thrust. Chur didn't move. His labored breaths puffed against her sweaty back, but he stood statue-still. After a deep breath, Enovese moved back until the swelling knob of his cock once again pressed against her oil-slicked and finger-readied passage. She gasped at the sheer size of him and pulled away, expecting him to press forward, but he did not.

"Move, Enovese. Direct the pace and timing. I will wait for you." His strangled voice conveyed his desire in terms of his need. By his choice, Chur could do any and all he wanted to her, but he found far more pleasure in compliance than coercion.

Trapped between want and fear, Enovese tentatively slid back, trying to ease the thrust of his cock into her. Chur held steady. She could hear and feel his sharp breaths against her back. She knew he exercised every bit of control to hold still. A normal man would have quickly succumbed to his base urges, but not the Harvester, a man well exercised in self-control. Animalistic grunts from the depth of his chest spurred her lust. Working slowly, she finally managed to take the tip of his knob inside. Her passionate gasp startled her and she gripped her hands against the table.

A stream of vulgarities and entreaties in the ancient tongue passed her lips. Knowing he would wait, she explored the delicious breadth of having just the tip of him buried into her tight channel. Fullness pressed all the way across her pelvis, causing her cunt to feel unbearably tight and woefully empty. Alternately cursing and praying, she wiggled her hips in a circle as she gripped the head of his cock and worked more of his shaft inside.

Chur growled and gripped her hips, digging his fingers almost painfully into her flesh. At first, she thought he did so to hold her steady for a thrust. She prepared herself by planting her legs wide against the table. She bit her bottom lip in anticipation; but no, he held on to her in a desperate bid to hang on to his control.

Beads of sweat formed on her upper lip. When she licked the salty moisture, the flavor reminded her of having Chur in her mouth. A deep shudder caused her to grip tightly around him.

"Ah, Enovese." Chur lowered his body against hers, slipping his hand between her legs to tease her sex. "Don't try to take me deeper. Let me feel you climax."

Swirling his fingers around her clit and then around the entrance of her passage caused her ass to clench ever tighter and pull him farther inside. His groan matched hers. Curling closer to her, he breathed into her ear and she turned her head, kissing him sideways. Their tongues danced amid their growls. Enovese muttered lusty words in the ancient tongue.

Chur nipped her lips. "I don't know exactly what you're

saying, but I think I feel the same way." He moved back a bit and thrust gently to the same depth. Repeatedly, he rocked against her while working his finger into her sex.

Enovese angled her body lower, granting him better access and lessening the tight grip she held. Ever so slowly, together they worked almost his entire length inside. He shouted a classic battle cry, gripped her hips, and climaxed so forcefully she felt the gushing tide surge deep within her body. Her orgasm quickly followed, clenching her around him in a rhythmic series of spasms. The sensation was too much for Chur's now overly sensitive cock. He retreated with a yank that left her suddenly empty.

He pressed against her back, kissing the nape of her neck with soft, open-mouth kisses, murmuring, "I'm sorry, it was too tight, and then when you climaxed you felt like a gripping fist. Ah, Enovese." He stood and pulled her with him, turning her to face him. He gazed down at her for the longest moment and she couldn't read his face. Pleasure, yes, but something like confusion lurked in his eyes.

Afraid of the questions he would ask, she stood on her tiptoes and kissed him before he could speak. Clasping his hand, she took him to the bathing unit, removed her shift, and pulled him under the spray with her. After a thorough cleansing, Chur yawned hugely and she drew him to his bed. He smiled, kissed her, then rolled onto his back and promptly fell asleep. His exhaustion would give her one night of reprieve. Tomorrow, he would ask pointed questions and she would have to tell him the truth.

7

Chur woke from an intense dream. His swollen cock tented the fabric of his bed. His balls felt heavy and full. He groaned and rolled to his side. Closing his eyes, he remembered how in the dream he'd been in the training room. Dozens of men sweated and groaned, practicing with a range of weapons, but a group of men circled the tilt-table, a device used to practice balance while fighting one-on-one. The table wobbled while two combatants fought with various handheld weapons, but Chur didn't see any men on the table. Pushing his way through the crowd, he discovered Enovese—facedown, strapped to an edge of the table, with her legs spread wide and her shaved sex exposed. When he glanced around at the men, he discovered all of them were nude, hard, and stroking themselves while looking at Enovese.

Chur felt an overwhelming compulsion to save her, but then realized she was enticing the men with raunchy words in the ancient tongue. Listening intently, he translated a few words and realized she was begging them to take her virginity, encouraging them to fuck her, use her, treat her like a wanton *yondie* who wouldn't even demand payment.

Loban, a husky man with reddish blond hair, a man who never let Chur forget he wanted to be the next Harvester, was the first to approach. His cock was short but thick, jutting out from a nest of dark brown curls. Loban pushed the table so that Enovese's sex was level with his.

Loban fingered her slit until her juice glistened on his hand. "What a sweet virginal cunt." He chuckled as he swirled his fingers around her passage. "This is one virgin sacrifice that will never make it to the Harvest." With pinching fingers, Loban ruthlessly spread her lips apart, then shoved his cock deep inside her body.

Enovese screamed in what he thought was pain but quickly realized was blissful pleasure. Despite her bonds, she circled her hips, encouraging Loban to thrust harder. Using the table for leverage, Loban rocked her on his cock.

"A lusty virgin," Loban exclaimed, casting a knowing wink to Chur. "As the Harvester you must know the thrill of a *yondie* virgin; one of those quaint cunts who wants it so bad but waited just for you." Loban continued to thrust into Enovese, alternately encouraging her and mocking her. Displaying a shocking level of self-control, hours seemed to pass until Loban threw back his head, uttered a battle cry, and climaxed.

Once Loban finished using Enovese, he stepped aside and offered her to the next man in line.

Man after man used her more brutally than the last. No matter how hard or long they pounded her, she demanded more in an insatiable stream of guttural language. A trickle of sperm leaked down her beautiful legs and dripped off her slender ankles. The shape of the stream reminded Chur of one of his scars; a rivulet of pleasure marked her where pain marked him.

Infuriated, Chur pulled a man off her and slapped her behind hard. "You belong to me." He smacked her heart-shaped bottom until a rosy glow spread across her milky pale flesh. Enovese moaned deep from her chest and begged him to strike her harder.

Yanking off his battle gear, Chur was dismayed to discover that he was soft. Someone spun the table so that she could see his flaccid cock. Enovese pouted. The men around him laughed. Denigrating comments that he was no Harvester burned his ears. With a hand cupped to the back of her head, Chur forced himself into her mouth and demanded that she suck him hard.

Enovese willingly wrapped her lips around him. With the timelessness of a dream, he grew stiff so slowly that he could feel each drop of blood filling him, stretching him, making his cock pound with the beat of his heart. When he swelled to the point she began to gag, he pulled out, making a popping noise.

Enovese smiled, licked her lips, tossed back the glorious mane of her hair, and then gave him a lazy wink. The indigo starburst in her eyes glowed as brightly as crystal, hypnotizing him for a moment.

Chur spun the table and centered his cock to the tight ring of her ass. No man had taken her there. She begged him to go fast, to plunge into her, but he refused. He would not be an animal as these other men had been. He would take his pleasure slowly. He would relieve her of the burden of her virginity with grace.

As he pressed forward, he felt the tiny sphincter grudgingly ease around his knob. Tighter than a fist, her passage alternately tried to push him out yet draw him deeper. Bit by bit, he worked himself inside. Enovese swiveled her hips and chanted a slew of vulgar words.

The warriors around him took up the chant, the cadence of their baritone voices matching the thud of his heartbeat. Chur found himself thrusting at the pace their rhythm set. Faster and faster and deeper and deeper he moved. He felt his balls swell and lift, ready to heave a molten stream deep into her beautiful bottom—

He awoke with a jolt. He didn't understand the meaning of the dream, and he did not intend to ask his *paratanist*, not when she was the focus of such a depraved scenario. Chur worried that indulging in sex with Enovese had weakened him, for he'd never had such imaginings before. His handler, Helton Ook, had warned that indulging in the lewd arts could lead to depravity. Helton cautioned Chur to avoid the *yondies* who would likely bed him gratis, but there was always a price to pay. "*Yondies* are not interested in you," Helton said. "They want the Harvester, for bedding such a man elevates their status, allowing them to charge more for their services. Should you impregnate one, your pure standing declines. A Harvester is above simple lust. A Harvester embodies sex by refraining from it."

Helton had also cautioned Chur about the nobles. He warned that both men and women would seek to entice him to their beds. They found Harvesters alluring because of the challenge; by his station, Chur must decline any offers, but if they actually inveigled him, the pride in seducing him gave them a superior status. "And do not think you can indulge them without getting caught. They will only use you if they can have proof of the act."

Chur had not asked Helton to expand on what that proof might entail. During his first official palace gathering, decked out in his most spectacular uniform, Chur found himself on the receiving end of endless proposals. Men, women, and even couples approached him with offers of rich indulgences, guaranteed military positions, even the promise of a daughter in bonding if he would only submit to their pleasure. Politely, Chur had diplomatically declined all offers in such a way as to compliment them for their interest while asserting his duty as the reason he must decline. Somehow, that only increased their desire, but after many such functions the offers lessened into pointed flirting.

Now that he had actually indulged in the lewd arts, he couldn't seem to stop thinking of them. He wanted more. He wished to know Enovese in every way a man could know a woman. He yearned to turn her to every position and taste her every nook and cranny. Feeling her spend on his tongue, fingers, cock . . .

Chur shook his head as if to rid himself of his wayward thoughts. Rather than focus on his training, he'd spent the last two days indulging his lust. No more. He would not become a mindless fiend who only thought of the bulge between his legs.

Determined to regain his focus, Chur tossed aside the bedding and donned his gear. If nothing else, one thing he took away from his dream was that Loban would challenge him for the right of Harvester. Now was not the time to abandon his training. Regardless of what happened with Enovese, Chur would have to survive at least one more challenge. Loban, a novice from the Plete region, had shown such prowess that Helton Ook, Chur's handler, had taken on Loban for instruction. Helton had done so openly; he informed Chur that he must pick a bondmate or ready himself for challenge. Chur would be a fool to let down his guard now. Chur would have to kill Loban in order to have one more chance to pick his bondmate. That final battle was one Chur did not intend to lose.

As he strode to the door, he darted a furtive glance around for Enovese. He did not see her and he did not call her out. The questions he had for her could wait. If she still refused to answer, he would not use sex as a punishment. Not only did sex not chastise because she wanted his possession, but such acts would only serve to weaken him further. Enovese would hold to her duty as his *paratanist* or else he would have no choice but to cast her out. His heart took a dangerous lunge in his chest at the mere thought of dismissing her, but he would be strong, even brutal if he had to be. He would not abandon his duty. He was the Harvester. A lifetime of vicious battles earned him the title and the duty; he would not falter now. He would rather cast Enovese out than let Loban know her as he had. For deep in his heart, Chur knew that if he failed and Loban became the Harvester, Enovese would surely try to work her magic on him.

8

From her alcove off the kitchen, Enovese watched Chur stride from his rooms. Half the night she'd lain awake in her narrow bed trying to determine the best way to tell him the truth of her station. No matter how she tried to cushion the blow, he would never forgive her. His fury at her potentially tricking him into impregnating her would be nothing compared to his rage over this. He would be livid. Chur would never claim her as bond-mate once he knew. A part of her wanted to keep the secret buried, but she could not deceive him, not about something so important to him. The only way she'd been able to fall asleep was when she vowed to confess everything. Only then had slumber come to her. In her dreams, her imagination saw only Chur's understanding and forgiveness—blissful and lovely—but she knew such fancies were only dreams.

When he'd left without even a glance in her direction, she blew out a breath she'd been holding since last evening. Then she quickly took in another for he was not finished with her yet. Resolve, harsh and unyielding, filled his long-legged strides. All she'd gained was another short reprieve.

To distract her churning mind, Enovese removed the food from the table and readied another meal should he break training and come to eat. In a desperate bid to appease him, she cooked his most favorite foods to perfection, even though she doubted that she would see him until nightfall. She knew well that look of determination on his face. Whatever Chur wanted, he would not stop until he gained it.

Chewing at her lower lip, Enovese worried that last night had been too much for him. From her odd need for punishment, his excitement at providing it, her final surrender of the last of her virginity, all of it must have horrified him once he woke to the harsh light of day. She felt both proud and ashamed: proud that she gained what she most desperately wanted, but ashamed that she hadn't really been able to directly ask for her darkest desires. She manipulated him into giving her what she craved. Such trickery was not fair to Chur. And honestly, she did not fully understand her odd lust herself. She'd never fantasized about spankings, for such punishment in the *tanist* house terrified her, but somehow, when he smacked her bottom, the feeling had been one of pleasure. The heat generated across her buttocks spread to her sex. Her position had been one of utter defenselessness, yet somehow the posture filled her with power.

Her training gave her far more sophistication in the lusty arts as compared to Chur. His training focused on how to resist such longings. Her training focused on how to increase those desires and then deny them. When she'd amplified his lust, then offered him an outlet . . . Chur had no defense. Enovese used her skills, her knowledge, and her training to force him to her own ends. She feared she'd driven him away. She could not overcome his indoctrination in a night.

To distract herself, she changed the linens on his bed, washed the bathing unit, restocked the kitchen, and completed all of the myriad details of maintaining his rooms. Servants had once completed these tasks, but she'd convinced Chur to dismiss them. She would minister to his every need. Not only had she wanted to keep him to herself, but doing these mindless tasks also occupied her time while waiting for his return. It also afforded her privacy; she did not want prying eyes looking into her room off his bedroom. Moreover, she did not want anyone opening the sacred chest and discovering the day-to-day record she kept. All her thoughts, dreams, hopes, and fears lay bare within those pages. She would rather suffer the torture of a thousand spikes than suffer the exposure of her secret heart.

Finished with his rooms, she made her way to the library. The hallways she traveled were empty, for almost this entire wing was devoted exclusively to the Harvester and the rituals involved in the Harvest. The library lay at the apex of the wing, so that others could utilize the stacks without interrupting the Harvester.

As a *paratanist*, she had limited access to enjoyment activities, so she spent most of her time in the library. Her station relegated her to text of her rituals and rites. After reading them avidly and endlessly, she felt she could recite them verbatim. Conspicuously absent from the texts were any details of the *paratanist* selection ritual. So far, she'd not found any information regarding that aspect of the Harvest prophecy.

Today, she had a different topic in mind to research; Chur's questions about the sacred chalice had prompted a new avenue for her research. She had performed the ritual many times but had never thought about where the chalice went after or why. Why would the magistrate want a viable sample from the Harvester?

As she entered the library, Enovese saw only the keeper at the main desk and one *tanist* deep in study. She nodded to the keeper, an ancient woman with a severely thin face hidden under a mass of curly gray hair and her skeletal body shrouded under a flowing beige robe. Enovese then made her way to the stacks that held the sacred texts. She pulled down Kipfer's unabridged Harvest text in the ancient language. The book was oversized, heavy, and bound in tooled animal hide. Hefting it to a table in the back, she scanned the table of contents until she found the section dealing with the chalice.

Wading through the verbose and flowery language, she found endless descriptions of the chalice but nothing about where it went after the ritual. Frustrated, she searched through several other texts but found only excruciatingly detailed descriptions of the chalice itself and how to perform the ritual. Enovese toyed with the idea of approaching the *tanist* but decided against such boldness. The *tanist* would likely be annoyed at any interruption and might become suspicious that Enovese asked such pointed questions. The last thing she wanted was to initiate an inquest into her service. Within the texts, Enovese had discovered ghastly descriptions of what constituted an inquisition. Any violation of her duties would end with her public execution. Within moments of questioning Chur, the inquisitor would realize Enovese had grossly violated her station in just about every way possible.

Realizing she had spent longer in the library than she intended, Enovese replaced the texts, then hurried to the storage room to replenish her supplies. Mainly she needed to replace the robe Chur had damaged. She'd barely been able to get the clasps closed this morning. Located underneath the temple, the massive room held extra robes, bottles of *estal* oil, and all the other accoutrements she needed to perform the Harvest rituals.

When she entered, the lighting crystals flickered to life and cast pools of muddy green illumination. She grabbed a new robe, more soothing oil since she and Chur had practically used the entire bottle in two days, and another shift to wear under her robe. She knew she should hurry back to Chur's rooms in case he returned from training early, but her studies compelled her to search through the room. At the back of the crowded and dusty shelves, she found a Onic box that held a chalice. She blew the thick layer of dust off and studied the carving. At first, it appeared as nothing but smooth lines with no meaning. As she removed more dust, she discovered the carving was of two figures entwined in such a way it was impossible to tell where one ended and the other began. Merging and melting, the two figures seemed so inextricably intertwined she couldn't determine the sex of either one. Slipping the deeply carved box under her robe, pressing it against her chest, she then used her satchel of supplies to further hide the bulk of the box. She wasn't sure if taking the box was against the rules, but she didn't want to find out.

9

The dream involving Enovese and Loban was still fresh in his mind when Chur entered the training room. A mix of sweat, wet leather, and a slight hint of blood gave the space a unique odor that Chur found oddly comforting. He spent most of his time here. Divided into sections, each part facilitated training with a specific weapon. More than two dozen men in various forms of combat grunted and groaned.

Chur acknowledged several greetings; then his gaze fell on Loban. Wet with sweat, his reddish blond hair stuck to his skull as he grappled with Helton Ook on the tilt-table. Neither man noticed him as they continued to work with the *avenyet,* a short wooden staff with a slender center that flared out to curved ends, like a double club. Both men wore light leather armor to pad them from blows.

At first sight, one might make the erroneous assumption that Helton, a squat man of advanced seasons, was hopelessly outmatched by the massive Loban. Chur knew differently. Helton was a handler because he knew more about weapons and effective combat moves than any man in the room. Helton was burly with muscles; those that crossed his shoulders were so thick they seemed to swallow his neck. Scars of white and dark maroon crisscrossed his skin as if the gods had put him together from leftovers. Helton's arms seemed too short, his legs too long, his torso too thick, yet Helton moved as if formed of water, fluid and graceful. Only the lines about his eyes and white hair gave hints to Helton's advanced seasons. His wizened eyes of sooty gray missed nothing.

Dodging a blow, Helton acknowledged Chur's presence with a lift of his chin, then snapped his *avenyet* to Loban's midsection. Loban exhaled a gasp of surprise. Helton laughed and said something that Chur could not hear, but he surmised it was a caution for Loban to focus.

Tearing his gaze from Chur, Loban whipped his wet hair aside, causing droplets of sweat to splatter the table; then he steadied his stance. Where the gods formed Helton from scraps, they'd chosen to form Loban of only the highest quality parts. Loban stood almost as tall as Chur, yet his limbs were perfectly proportioned; the span of his arms matched the full of his height. Broad shoulders were square, and a thick neck held up his rounded face. His chest was smooth and tight, his belly layered with muscles. The only fault Chur could find was that Loban's hands seemed a bit too big for his arms, yet this defect gave him excellent control with weapons. Very few scars marred Loban's spectacular form, and they did not stand out for his skin was remarkably pale. He did not bronze like Chur, he only developed tiny bronze blotches. What little body hair Loban had was copper, and when the lighting crystals hit him, Loban glowed, as if the gods had chosen him.

At first glance, Loban's chubby face would cause one to believe him kind, but a long look into his Onic black eyes revealed a fathomless cruelty. When Loban smiled, the cast of his oddly red lips against white teeth gave him the appearance of a predator smeared with the blood of his most recent kill.

Chur had hated the man on sight.

After a season of training with him, Chur found his initial assessment entirely accurate: Loban was evil. Below the dressing of fine physical form lurked a monster.

Chur would rather have anyone but Loban become the next Harvester. Cruel and vicious, Loban often continued to beat his opponents long after they'd surrendered, but never in Helton's presence. Chur had even heard rumors that Loban sought out his conquered opponents after training and raped them as the final degradation.

What Chur considered alarming rumors, probably spread by Loban himself, had become fact when Sterlave, a novice from the Gant region, quietly confessed to Chur that Loban had come to his room, late at night, on the pretext of apologizing for a beating earlier that day. However, once Sterlave granted him entrance, Loban had forced Sterlave to perform an endless series of sexual acts. With his bloodshot gaze cast low, Sterlave whispered, "Loban bragged the entire time about his staying power and honestly, when he finally climaxed, I was too relieved to do anything but curl up and sleep." Chur had urged Sterlave to tell Helton, but Sterlave refused. He'd only told Chur because Chur had noticed fresh blood on the seat of Sterlave's trousers.

Unwilling to traumatize Sterlave further, Chur had sent him on a series of errands that kept him from the training rooms until he healed. Eventually, Sterlave continued in instructions, but he never met Loban's gaze nor would he spar with him. Chur took heart in that the rape, as horrific as it had been, had not kept Sterlave from excelling in his preparations. Over the next season, Sterlave's slender muscles filled out and his prowess grew so rapidly that Helton took him under his wing. Of all the potential challengers, Sterlave would be the one Chur would choose as the next Harvester.

All of this filtered through his mind as Chur performed the

fluid moves of *kintana.* Residual tension from his odd dream melted away as his focus sharpened on training. Even the itch of his regrowing hair faded from his attention as rhythmic breathing helped him center himself, feeling the power inherent in his form.

Helton Ook left off his session with Loban and approached Chur. "I am pleased to see you back at training so soon after the Harvest."

Chur bowed formally.

Leaning near, Helton murmured, "I thought you would not be back. Why did you not choose from this Harvest? I am told the offerings went beyond spectacular."

In a flash, all the virgins exploded in a shimmer of jewels, perfumes, and exotic forms in Chur's mind, but only one stood out: Enovese. Swaddled in her simple robe, her lovely eyes commanding his attention, her voice dreamlike yet powerful, her shaved sex so unique, and then her mouth wanton around his cock . . .

Trying to inject more conviction into his voice than he felt, Chur said, "Amazing as they were, I did not find my bondmate among them."

Helton's fuzzy gray brows drew a sharp line over his sparkling eyes. "Bondmate, pah. Did I not tell you such is the twaddle of poets? One woman is as good as another is. Just pick a pretty one, I said. Not you. And now, by not choosing, you will have to face Loban. He will not wait another season."

Lifting his chest with a deep breath, Chur stood to his full height and asked, "You worry at my ability?"

"Of course not." Helton frowned at him as if to caution him from asking any more stupid questions or he would smack him. "I simply did not want this battle to come to pass. I feel it is a waste, for one of you must die."

Knowing that Helton was the handler for both of them, Chur asked, "Who would you wish to triumph?"

With a sneer of dismissal, Helton deftly avoided answering and said, "I wanted you to pick so that I would not be in the position of setting my two best upon each other."

Before Chur could question him further, Helton clapped his hands and deemed the time had come for work. Smartly, Helton did not allow Chur and Loban to spar together. He set them at opposite ends of the room with other opponents who showed a particular prowess with that style of combat.

Channeling his rage into physical activity helped Chur focus fully on defeating his opponents. He moved through the training with hardly a break between, garnering him several compliments for his stamina. Generally, it took a week to recover from the Harvest, but Chur pushed through the fatigue, almost in an effort to punish himself for indulging in the lewd arts. Several times Helton cautioned him to slow down, but Chur refused. Even Loban grudgingly commented to someone that Chur was a rival to respect, but Chur didn't believe it for a moment. What Loban said and what he felt were often entirely at odds. Loban had no more respect for Chur than Chur had for him. Still, Chur would be a fool to dismiss the threat Loban embodied.

The exhausting day drew to a close and Helton Ook left the training room after issuing the last of his instructions.

Chur returned to the padded mats to cooldown with *kintana.*

Loban joined him and mirrored his every move.

When Chur ignored him, Loban worked his way closer, until the movements of his arms brought him into contact with Chur. With a bored sigh, Chur moved back and continued. Frankly, he thought Loban was acting like an annoying younger brother desperately seeking attention.

Rather than staying put, Loban again moved closer. Realizing that Loban would continue in this vein, Chur bowed formally to him, then left the mats. Feeling pleased with his performance and pleasantly exhausted, Chur was in no mood for any of Loban's games. He wished to return to his rooms, shower, eat, and sleep. Finally, he'd found a way to banish his lusty thoughts.

Loban followed right behind him and asked, "Had enough, mighty Harvester?"

Chur turned so suddenly that Loban stumbled. His heel caught on an edge of the mat and he landed hard on his butt. A few men chuckled, but Chur said nothing. Chur simply considered Loban for a moment, then gave Loban his back—possibly the most insulting action he could take.

"When I am the Harvester, the virgins will know that a man took their virginity, for I will make them bleed."

A hushed silence followed Loban's ugly comment. Chur stopped in his tracks. His gaze fell on Sterlave. A hank of deep brown hair curtained Sterlave's eyes, but shame flicked along the edge of his clenched jaw.

Loban's brutality sickened Chur. During the Harvest, the virgins gave him the gift of their virginity. Chur did not take their innocence and certainly not with a mind of hurting them. He may not have found one that fully captured his attention, but he found all of them beautiful, special, and unique in their own way. Always, he'd harvested them with respect and appreciation. For Loban to spew such a revolting comment, whether he believed it or not, pushed Chur over the edge. He turned and faced Loban.

Sneering, Loban lunged to his feet. "What's wrong, Harvester? Don't you enjoy ripping the virgin cunts?" Loban tossed back his head and laughed. "I know I will!"

Pinning Loban with a piercing gaze, Chur lifted his voice so that all could hear. "The only virgins you will ever know are the men you have raped."

Several gasps followed his bold proclamation. Chur noticed Sterlave wasn't the only man to recoil. Just as he feared, Loban had brutalized more than one of the recruits.

Loban flushed red, and his predatory mouth flapped open and closed.

"What's wrong, challenger?" Chur asked, taking a step toward Loban. "Are you not proud of your forced sodomy?"

Loban flicked an uneasy gaze around the circle of men, several of whom looked quickly away; then his eyes turned icy with contempt. Lifting his hands, Loban said, "Let even one man step forward to confirm your vile accusation, or you have issued a challenge. I will have no choice but to defend my honor."

Chur realized too late that he'd allowed his anger to trap him. If no man stepped forward to confirm Chur's claim, Chur must rescind his comment or face Loban in hand-to-hand combat. The last thing Chur wanted was to publicly humiliate one of Loban's victims. Following the example Helton had set, Chur sidestepped the issue and asked, "How can you defend what you do not have?"

Seething with anger, Loban sputtered, "Apologize, Harvester, or fight."

All day he'd pushed himself to the point of exhaustion whereas Loban had coasted, saving up his energy, probably in the hopes of somehow pushing Chur into a challenge. Loban had succeeded, but Chur vowed he would regret confronting him.

"I will not apologize for speaking the truth." Calmly, Chur removed all of his gear. A formal challenge decreed both combatants fought nude with no weapons but bare hands. Loban's reddish blond brow lifted when he stared openly at Chur's genitals. Black stubble shadowed his balls so his lighter-colored cock appeared enormous even in a flaccid state. Chur let him look, then mockingly asked, "Did you wish to kneel and confess?"

Several men chuckled. Loban flicked his gaze up. His fathomless black eyes narrowed as he bared his teeth. Piece by piece, he stripped off his gear. Placing his too-large hands on his hips, Loban stood absurdly proud of the fact his short but thick cock, nestled in a tuft of dark brown curls, was semihard. Chur wasn't sure exactly what aroused Loban: the idea of fighting or Chur's nudity. It didn't matter. Chur moved to the center of the mats.

When Chur bowed formally, Loban screamed and launched himself, knocking Chur flat. Shouts denigrating Loban as a cheater and fraud filled the air, but Chur had no time to agree as he grappled for advantage. Sweat and oil built up over the day from his brutal workout caused Loban difficulty in grasping Chur. Relatively clean flesh gave Chur an advantage in wrestling Loban to the mat. Only when he worked with Helton had Loban actually pushed himself, and this now gave him an advantage in one way by having more energy but a disadvantage in another way for his skin was easy to grip.

Grasping his shoulders, Chur pinned Loban. Looming over him, Chur whispered, "You will never be the Harvester."

Snarling, Loban said, "You'll never perform again." Loban shot his hand between their bodies, grasped Chur's genitals, and squeezed.

Chur screamed. White-hot pain exploded, blotting out awareness of anything but his traumatized balls. He wanted to cry foul, but he couldn't breathe. He heard a scuffle among the men, those who tried to stop the fight and those who tried to keep it going. When he turned to check on Loban, a fist plowed into his eye. Stunned by the blow, Chur fell back. Loban leapt onto his chest. He punched at his face, splitting his upper lip, causing a gush of blood to fill his mouth. Chur punched Loban in the nose and bucked him off his chest. Still trying to catch his breath, Chur heard someone shout, "He has an *avenyet*!"

A double club smacked into Chur's temple causing stars to dance before his eyes. Chur rolled over to protect his face and head. Loban rained a series of blows to Chur's back. Slipping in and out of consciousness, Chur felt Loban mount his back, and now his cock was hard and pushing against Chur's ass.

Chur wasn't sure who pulled Loban away or where they took him. He didn't care. It took two men to help Chur to his feet. They helped him dress, then left him leaning against the tilt-table. One look at the edge of the table reminded him of the dream and he staggered away. It didn't matter that Loban had cheated. Chur had needed help to subdue him, and thus he had lost. Loban had shamed himself by cheating and by trying to rape Chur in full view of every recruit, but Chur felt just as much disgrace burden his already weighted shoulders.

10

Keeping her head down, Enovese strode through the hallways. Her sandals slapped on the polished floors with a cadence that startled her. Slowing her pace to lessen the noise caused her to feel more self-conscious. As she passed the Harvest room, two servants exited, burdened down with decorations. A mixture of *estal* oil, perfumes, and decorative herbs followed in their wake. She ignored them, but her heart thudded painfully when a palace guard crashed into her. She felt the box slipping and crushed the satchel closer to keep it in position.

"Mind your place you lowly—" He stopped abruptly when he noticed the cut of her robe. The severe angles and color proclaimed her as not just a *paratanist* but also the Harvester's *paratanist.* The guard flinched back as if burned, an expression of terror on his pockmarked face. He darted his gaze around and lowered his voice. "My apologies, *paratanist.*" He offered her a formal bow, which she returned, using the movement to stabilize the box. As she moved away, she considered his dread justified, for her station forbid any to touch her. Even an accidental brush would result in death if witnessed by the right person. Thankfully, they were the only two in the hallway.

Enovese blew out a sharp breath of relief when she entered Chur's rooms.

"Where have you been?"

His demanding bellow startled her, for he'd kept the lights low. When she turned the brightness up, she discovered Chur in the middle of the main room with his face bloody and his battle gear filthy.

As he strode toward her, the stench of sweat overpowered her. Shocked by his battered appearance, she froze. During training, Chur had suffered blows, but never had he returned in such a tattered state. A split in his upper lip oozed, and his eye was swollen and turning black. Several lumps and bumps caused his normally smooth head to appear horribly misshapen.

"I asked where have you been?"

Before she could formulate an answer, he yanked the satchel from her, causing the box to fall on the floor.

Frowning darkly, Chur examined the contents of the bag, then tossed it aside. He pointed to the box. "What is that?"

Enovese snatched it up. "It's a ceremonial chalice box. I wished to examine it to better answer your questions."

For a moment, his brows lifted with curiosity but then lowered. "Why were you hiding it?"

"I'm not sure if it's against the rules—"

Chur cut her off. "You will return the box first thing in the morning without examining it."

Her mouth opened to disagree with him, but she pressed her lips together tightly. Arguing with him when he was in this agitated state would be nothing short of foolish. She bowed her head in acquiescence and placed the box by the door. Yet, already in the back of her mind she was planning a way to examine it no matter what he said. He may have changed his mind, but now that her curiosity had been piqued, she felt compelled to find the answers.

Chur nodded. "There will be no more violations, *paratanist.* We will stay within the limits of our duties. Do you understand?"

Enovese offered a soft yes that apparently didn't appease him for he took one great stride toward her and lifted her face with one grimy hand. He did not push back the hood but simply held her face still.

"Do. You. Understand?" he asked very slowly, enunciating each word.

"I understand, Harvester." Her voice quavered. Never had she been afraid of Chur, but she was now. Something had happened during training. She wanted to know what but didn't dare ask.

Without a word, she helped him remove his gear. She did so gently, for she discovered a multitude of blows that were already darkening into bruises. Twice she witnessed him wince and clench his jaw to stifle a groan. Empathetic tears flowed down her cheeks for never had she seen him so brutalized. Training sessions were supposed to be controlled events using the weapons without inflicting actual damage. Clearly, a fist had caused some of the marks. She had never read of any exercise that involved bare hands.

Dismayed, she followed him to the bathing unit and carefully washed away the grime. Rather than dry him with a towel that might hurt, she chose to flick the water away with a soothing combination of regular oil mixed with a bit of *estal.* She used just enough to deaden some of the pain but not enough to numb him.

Chur sighed with relief.

While he slipped on a loincloth, Enovese prepared a meal and set the table. As per her duty, she stood by his side, fetching anything he required. Her meal would come later, but she doubted she would eat much since her stomach churned with anxiety. Chur ate hugely. She refilled his plate twice and offered him a glass of *soony,* which he refused.

When she offered it a second time, he pushed back from the table with a sigh. "Why do you want me to drink this?"

"The *soony* will further help relieve your physical pain." Brewed from barley and *estal* leaves, the alcoholic drink also imparted a euphoric feeling and somewhat deadened tactile sensations.

Chur eyed the golden liquid suspiciously. "Is it against the rules?"

"No, much like *umer, soony* was developed for the exclusive use of the Harvester." She could cite chapter and verse on how, when, where, and why the drink had been formulated, but the exhaustion in his eyes stopped her. Reverting to her training, she used an economy of words.

Apparently too weary to question her further, he consumed the drink in a few swallows. His hand trembled as he placed the glass on the table. Deeply concerned, for not only his physical state but also his mental state, Enovese had to bite her lips to keep silent. She could not speak unless spoken to, and she found the edict unbearably restrictive.

She poured him another glass of *soony.* This time he sipped it slowly as he leaned back from the table. His summer-sky eyes were bloodshot, clouded with frustration and doubt. He opened his mouth as if to speak but uttered only a long drawn-out sigh. With a shake of his head, he considered his drink, then quickly finished it. Chur stood. Swaying a bit on his feet, he gripped the edge of the table for balance.

Moving instantly to his side, she placed her arm around his waist to help him to his bed.

He nudged her away and snarled, "I can walk on my own."

Enovese bowed and moved back.

With an unsteady gate, Chur staggered to his bed. He collapsed and within moments, snored loudly.

Baffled, Enovese cleared the table, taking a few bites, but the food stuck in her throat and she ended up throwing most of it out. Her gaze darted repeatedly to the box by the door, but she refrained as per Chur's edict. She decided to wait until he either changed his mind or left his rooms. Her mind gnawed endlessly at why he'd had such a change of heart and why he was so battered.

Once she'd prepared the kitchen for his morning meal, she dimmed the crystals and moved to his bedside.

Deep in sleep, his entire body lay limp. Despite his sheer size, Chur appeared vulnerable. His eye was swollen and dark, and more fist-shaped bruises darkened on his face and chest. His dusky mouth, with lips that could be both cruel and kind, was now puffy and crooked. The split in his upper lip grossly exaggerated the scar that often gave him a twisted grin. For the first time, it cast his face ugly, harsh, and frightening.

Lifting her hand, she stroked down the length of the scar and he turned to her touch with a sigh. A lone tear trickled down her face. How could she help him when he refused to tell her what had happened? She pulled the blankets up and tucked them around him.

His fist shot out and grasped her wrist.

Enovese startled back, but he would not let go.

His one good eye opened and peered up at her. With a rumbling growl, Chur said, "He'll only hurt you. If you do this to him, he will use you like a *harshan,* then toss you aside."

Enovese had no idea whom Chur referred to. Who would use her like a sweat towel and toss her aside?

"He is evil. He finds pleasure in inflicting pain. He will destroy you if he succeeds in the challenge."

Suddenly, she knew. Loban Daraspe. In a rush, the fist-shaped bruises, Chur's pain and shame, his desperate desire to cling to his duty, came into full focus. From earlier conversations, she knew Loban had been ready to step in for a season. When Chur first spoke of him, Enovese worried that the threat of Loban might force Chur to choose a bondmate during this last Harvest. When he hadn't, she put her plan into action so that Chur would not have to face Loban in the challenge.

Chur had refused that way out and now, apparently, was regretting his decision. Did he cling to duty thinking that would help him triumph over Loban in the final confrontation? Moreover, she understood in a rush that Chur could not claim her now. He couldn't claim a bondmate until the next Harvest. In order to do that, Chur would have to defeat Loban. His fight with Loban today had put Chur into this temper.

Enovese wanted to reassure him that he would triumph, that she would never engage Loban as she had him, but everything she thought of saying sounded flat inside her head. Words would not lift his spirits. Thinking that actions spoke louder than words ever could, Enovese defiantly pushed her hood back and met Chur's one-eyed gaze.

Chur frowned. "Put your hood—"

Enovese shushed him with a slender finger to his lips.

He grasped her hand, pulling it from his mouth. "How dare you?"

Enovese leaned over and placed her mouth a breath from his.

Chur met her close gaze but said nothing.

Emboldened, Enovese pressed her lips to his, never breaking the intense eye-to-eye contact.

At first, Chur resisted. With a groan of frustration, he cupped the back of her head and kissed her softly. His eye closed when he slipped his tongue between her lips. She tasted the bitterness of *soony,* then the quiet desperation of his need for reassurance.

Pulling back, Enovese whispered to his lips, "I serve only you. I offer myself only to you. You, Chur Zenge, you will not fail, for I will do everything in my power to ensure your success."

Chur shook his head. "You cannot fight my battles for me."

"No, I cannot. But I can prepare you to prevail."

"How can a man of honor triumph over a man who will do anything to win?"

Enovese smiled. "By your honor you will be stronger than any evil. By the might of the blade, you claim all that which belongs to you. You, Chur Zenge, you will vanquish any who is not worthy to become the Harvester."

A befuddled frown lowered Chur's brows. "How can that be if I myself am not worthy?"

Refusing to debate the point, Enovese informed, "You have more honor in you than any man I have ever known."

Chur opened his mouth to speak and Enovese risked his wrath by shushing him with a slender fingertip to his lips.

"You will sleep now." She covered her face with the hood and altered her voice to the sexless intonation of the *paratanist.* "For the prophecy informs that sleep is one of four cornerstones that build the Harvester."

A renewed sense of purpose washed over Chur's face, soothing the worry in his gaze and smoothing away the harshness of his bruises. Within moments, he returned to sleep.

Enovese took the chalice box to her room and placed it in the sacred chest. For now, she would follow Chur's orders, but she would not return the box and risk discovery. Perhaps he would change his mind and they could examine it later, together.

For now, if Chur believed that clinging to duty would ensure his triumph, then Enovese would support him completely. Even though Enovese didn't believe blind obeisance would help, her beliefs didn't matter. Chur believed it, and that's all that mattered. She understood that to reach her own goal of having Chur claim her as bondmate, she had to help him achieve his goal of defending the title of Harvester at least one more time.

11

Chur returned to his training with great vigor. He did not see Loban. Even though he was curious, he did not ask for he almost dreaded the answer. While sparring with Sterlave, Chur complimented him on his focus and Sterlave flashed him a cryptic frown. Later, during the cooldown, Sterlave moved close and said, "You can stop looking for Loban. He will not be back for a while."

Chur's uplifted brows asked the question.

Without any malice, Sterlave said, "Loban got a taste of his own brutality."

Apparently infuriated by Loban cheating during a challenge, several recruits hauled him away and strapped him into the *gannett,* a punishment device that contorted the person into an awkward kneel-bound position. Sterlave had left the room to check on Chur and when he returned, he discovered Vertase brutally raping Loban.

"At first, I simply watched, and there was a part of me that cheered Vertase on because I knew Loban had raped him. But when I felt an urge to rape Loban myself, that's when I knew I had to put a stop to it." Sterlave shook his head as if to chase away the thought. "I was angry, yes, and I wanted revenge, but how could I hold my head up if I became what I loathed?"

Chur clasped a hand to Sterlave's back. "You acted honorably. Brutality begets more brutality."

Sterlave shook off his hand. "You should not have challenged him. It was not your fight."

Bristled, Chur said, "I did not call him out for you. Loban denigrated the role of Harvester."

With a curt nod, Sterlave relented. "I find it odd that having rescued my abuser, I feel freed of him. As you said, my focus is extreme. I am not sure why this is so, but I am pleased I can now move on."

"Does Helton know any of this?"

Sterlave shrugged. "I do not know what Loban told him. But I'm sure you noticed Helton is not here either."

Three days later, Helton and Loban returned to training. Tension was thick, but when Helton did not berate Chur for issuing a challenge, Chur decided the matter closed. Sadly, Loban had not been humbled. If anything, his braggadocio knew no bounds. He was as arrogant and brutal as ever, yet Chur noticed Loban left the training room shortly after Helton. Chur heard no more rumors of rape.

With everything back to normal, Chur was able to fully focus on his training. By the time Chur returned to his rooms each night, he was too exhausted to do anything but shower, eat, and sleep. True to his edict, Enovese held strictly to her obligations. She spoke only when he spoke to her and carefully kept her voice in the neutral *paratanist* drone. It helped him forget what lay below her ceremonial robe. Yet at night, in his dreams, he could not escape the hunger she'd roused in him.

Unbound, his imagination ran wild with fantastic scenarios that always ended in his total possession of her lovely form.

And always, always, her jade green eyes with the indigo starburst penetrated right into his soul, capturing him, ensnaring him, compelling him. Every morning he woke with a painful erection, but he ignored the mounting pressure thinking only that the time drew close for the ritual of control.

At the end of each of the nine cycles of thirty-six days that led up to the time of the Harvest, they would spend the last nine nights engrossed in the ritual of control; eight nights of arousal denied, then a shattering climax on the ninth night. The eight days were hell, but the release on the ninth night was so intense he often couldn't move for hours afterward.

When the first of the nine-night ritual began, Chur engaged in one of the most punishing workouts for fear that he would have no control at all. When he entered his rooms, he was barely able to walk. Enovese helped him out of his gear, bathed him, and then placed him at the table. While he ate, he watched her set the stage for the ritual.

She placed a padded chair with no armrests in the center of the room, facing a wall purposely devoid of any decoration. Beside the chair, she placed a bottle of oil and a cushion upon which she would kneel. Despite his exhaustion, his cock throbbed with anticipation. When he finished eating, he stood.

"We will start the ritual of control," Enovese said.

Did he detect a quaver of anticipation in her voice? He didn't understand why she would be enthusiastic, for in this, Enovese had no pleasure. Then he remembered the end of the Harvest ritual when she'd confessed to climaxing without him even touching her. Did she find release in this ritual too? He opened his mouth to ask, then quickly shut it. There was no point in asking since the answer would not matter. All that mattered was the ritual must be performed and he would have to pray to the gods to keep from climaxing.

As Chur stood beside the chair, Enovese removed his loincloth. Her movements were focused and precise, even when the cloth caught on his stiffening cock. He sat in the chair with his legs parted and allowed her to tie his hands. Thin straps of soft animal hide kept his arms straight against the back of the chair. When he'd questioned her about this in the past, she informed him the bindings reminded him that he had no control but for what he could exercise with his mind. Somehow, the straps only heightened his excitement by giving her complete control over him. His semihard cock grew thicker and she hadn't even started.

Once she had him secured, she bowed formally, then lowered herself to his side. Kneeling on the cushion, she placed a dollop of golden oil in her palm and rubbed her hands together. He felt the heat of her hand before she cupped his balls. When the contact came, his penis twitched, causing a drop of pearly liquid to hang like a teardrop at the tip. His head went back with a rumbling groan from his chest. Softly, she cupped his sack in her hand, stroking with her fingertips until she coated the entire surface with oil.

Lightly, she stroked her fingertips around the base of his shaft. Working her way up, she coated the entire length with oil, yet left the head alone. Chur kept his attention on the blank wall because if he watched her oh-so-clever hand he knew he would not survive for long.

Using the deep breathing of *kintana*, Chur drew in a breath through his nose, then expelled slowly through his mouth. In this way, he could almost exit his body. The sensations lessened, allowing him to enjoy her gentle touch without becoming too aroused.

Wrapping her thumb and forefinger around the base, she slid her fist up, bringing each finger into contact with his shaft as she moved her hand up. Once her entire fist wrapped around his shaft, with the tight ring of forefinger and thumb just below the head, she held her hand still. For a long time, motionless, she simply cupped her fist around him.

His gaze darted to her, but the robe kept her hidden, all he saw was her milky pale hand extended from a sleeve. In his mind's eye he saw her gaze, riveted to her task, her truculent nose lowered, her tongue touching the edge of her fuller upper lip. Had the straps not bound him, he would have damned the rules and removed her hood, but he knew he wouldn't stop there. He would yank the robe off and have her straddle his lap, then lower herself onto him as slowly as she worked her hand.

Ruthlessly, he pushed the image away. He focused again on the blank wall. Alternately squeezing then releasing, she teased until his cock felt painfully thick, on the verge of breaking apart. Her grip changed as her thumb pressed against the most sensitive spot where the shaft met the head. Lifting her fist, her thumb rocked over the tip, wiping away the pearl of moisture, then smoothing the slickness around the head. He had to grip the edge of the chair to refrain from thrusting his hips.

He continued to pull deep breaths through his nose as she moved her hand up and down, ever so slowly, her thumb teasing the head on each upward stroke. He swore he could smell her arousal. She was wet. He wanted to taste her. He wanted to place her in the chair, part her legs, and then bury his tongue in her cunt.

Increasing the pace, she lifted and lowered her hand faster, firming her grip, flicking her thumb over the tip. Despite his best efforts, every muscle in his body tensed, his breathing grew to harsh pants, and the head of his cock darkened and more drops of fluid oozed from the tip. Sensing his imminent climax, Enovese removed her hand. He growled and gripped the chair so tightly the bonds strained against his wrists.

"Breathe deeply, Harvester." Enovese lost her *paratanist* drone as her voice rose with concern.

He tried, but he could not stop alternately panting and groaning. Heaving, his chest hurt and a deep red flush washed over his bronzed flesh. "Help me." He wasn't sure whether he begged for release or surcease. Never had the ritual caused him this much distress.

Enovese shot to her feet. She ran toward her room and returned a moment later with a bottle in her hand. Trembling, she shot a stream of blue lotion to her palm, dropped the bottle, rubbed her hands together, and then quickly smoothed the lotion on his cock.

Instantly, the blood rushed away from his penis. His erection deflated so comically fast he laughed at the sight but also with relief since the urge to climax magically disappeared. His chest lifted with a huge sigh. Enovese soothed the lotion down to his balls and they, too, stopped throbbing. She rubbed lotion all over his chest and legs, and the red flush disappeared.

Shrouded in her robe, her body shook as she dropped to her knees beside him. She lowered her head until her forehead pressed against his thigh. Her flesh felt hot and her trembling breath puffed along his skin in a moist wind. To his shock, he realized she was crying. They had performed this ritual many times but never had his reaction been so painfully intense. Toward the end, he feared that whether he climaxed or not he would die from a lack of air.

"Calm yourself, *paratanist.*" He allowed a brutal tone to vibrate in his voice. A part of him wished to comfort her, but he clung to his duty. Besides, what comfort could he offer her? Moreover, why should he comfort her when he was the one who had to suffer the torment of arousal for eight painful nights?

"We have completed the first phase of the ritual." Enovese straightened away from him and stood. She released the bonds and ran to her room, shutting the door firmly behind her.

Chur grabbed his loincloth off the floor and wrapped it around his hips. He strode to her room and flung the door open. He wasn't sure what he expected, maybe to see her frantically rubbing herself to climax, but Enovese sat in the center of her bed with her hands clasped in her lap. His bold entrance snapped her head up, but the hood shrouded her face.

With two steps, he stood right before her and bellowed, "I did not dismiss you, my *paratanist.*"

She nodded. "What do you require, Harvester?" She tried for the bland voice but missed completely. Her husky tone sounded at once seductive yet tormented.

A thousand requirements flashed in his mind, all of them tawdry and wild, but he said only, "You will set the room to rights."

Enovese darted passed him and he followed. With jerky movements, she placed the chair against the wall, dropped her kneeling cushion on the seat, and then grabbed the two bottles off the floor.

"Tell me, my *paratanist,* are you wet?"

The bottle of oil slipped from her fingers. She bent to retrieve it and his mind flashed on her bending over the table, her bottom rosy from his slaps. He knew he should just go to bed, but he found a surge of energy flowing through him. Perhaps from the odd blue lotion she'd placed upon him. Now that, the blue lotion, was new. She'd never used that on him before. He waited for an answer, but she simply stood still.

"I asked you if you are wet."

Enovese squared her shoulders. "I am wet, Harvester." Again, she could not quite hit that emotionless drone.

"Show me."

For a moment, she stood nonplussed.

Chur pointed to the ritual chair. "Sit."

She followed his order and sat down. She kept her legs together and her hands clasped in her lap.

He thought about his duty and realized as long as he did not touch her he really wasn't breaking any of the rules. He still did not fully understand why the rituals excited her so, but he wished to know just how wet she was. Moreover, he did not want her to find release when he could not. If he must suffer, so must she. Perhaps he'd found a way to punish her with sex after all.

Placing himself cross-legged on the floor before her, he leaned back, balancing himself on his hands as he considered her robe-shrouded form. So bland, so nondescript, the thick *mondi* fabric left everything to his imagination.

"Move forward until your bottom is at the edge of the chair and part your legs."

Enovese slid forward into position. The two edges of the robe overlapped, denying him more than a glimpse of her slender ankles.

"Pull your robe up."

Gripping handfuls of fabric, she slid the robe up, exposing her legs. The fabric bunched around her hips, but she grasped more and pulled until he could see her sex. Short coco-brown stubble patterned a V that drew his attention to coral lips glistening with arousal.

"You are wet."

Enovese turned her head away. Even though he knew he could not see her eyes, he nonetheless ordered her to look at him. Her head turned his direction and he smiled, because he knew she could see him.

"Spread your legs farther apart."

Her breath caught, but she did as he bid. Chur leaned near; almost close enough to taste her. He closed his eyes and took a deep breath of her luscious scent. If the lotion had not been on him, he knew his erection would have returned vigorously. With the lotion blocking the blood flow, he experienced a unique sensation of arousal without any of the typical signs of arousal. Rather than a relentless need for climax driving him, he found he could relax and enjoy every moment.

Enovese, however, was trembling with need. Her lovely sex had grown darker, wetter, and as he blew a whisper breath across her tormented flesh, she uttered a gasp, then a low animalistic groan.

"Finger yourself."

Readjusting the fabric bunched around her hips, she lowered her hand, slid her middle finger down, and buried her finger between slippery lips. Slowly, she slid her finger in and out of her slick passage. Her head rolled back. A shudder trembled through her limbs causing her hand to brush against her clit.

"Not there. You can touch yourself anywhere but there."

She said nothing, but her elongated groan conveyed her frustration. She wanted to climax. If he let her continue, it wouldn't take long for her to reach the edge of the plunging precipice. A part of him wanted to watch her climax, but he also wanted her to suffer. He decided that tonight, they would engage in the ritual of control together. Enovese would wait, and suffer the torments she inflicted on him. He watched her slide her finger around the coral-lipped passage of her cunt until her arousal glistened, coating her entire hand.

"Tell me, my *paratanist,* which do you enjoy more: fingering yourself or me watching you do it?"

Her body strained against the chair. "You watching me." Her tone of voice was stunningly beautiful. He hadn't heard the full richness since his order to return to their duties. He didn't realize how much he missed her true voice until he heard it again.

"Do you want to climax?"

She arched her back and every muscle in her legs went taut. "Yes." She drew out the sound of the *s* until she hissed the letter into a note of pleading.

Lifting her feet to tiptoe, she parted her legs even more so she could get more of her finger inside. The crescent-shaped scar on her upper right thigh smoothed out. She tried to slip a second finger beside the first, but he ordered, "Only one."

Her shoulders slumped, but she followed his command.

He desperately wanted to see her face. He almost ordered her to remove the hood, then hesitated. With nine nights of torment, he didn't want to do everything all at once. Like rare liquor, he would sip slowly and savor every scent, taste, vision, and sound.

"Stop. Pull your hand away."

Her moan was so deep that her torment rumbled through his body. He ordered her to lift her hand, palm out, and when she did, she trembled so violently he felt a surge of pity for her. He picked up the bottle of blue lotion and placed a drop on the tip of her middle finger. He ordered her to spread her lips with her left hand and dab the lotion to her clit.

"Tell me what it feels like."

"My clit is numb."

"No matter how much you rub, you won't be able to climax."

Enovese couldn't even answer; she simply shook her head side to side very slowly.

He chuckled wickedly. "But you can feel blood throbbing in every other bit of your hungry cunt?"

"Chur, please."

"What did you call me?" His voice hardened.

Realizing that she'd slipped, she sputtered, "Harvester, please. I can't stand the ache." Her voice faded to a desperate, begging edge.

He stood and peered down at her. Her spread legs quivered with exhaustion and her shoulders slumped. She looked fragile and broken.

"Now you know how I have suffered. What you feel now is nothing compared to the torment I have known." He grabbed the lotion. "But I promise that you will be intimate with lust denied. Now stand, put your robe to rights."

A bit wobbly, Enovese climbed to her feet, brushed her robe down, and then clenched her hands to fists at her sides.

"Do not tell me that you are angry."

The tension instantly left her fists. "No, Harvester."

"In the past, after each phase of the ritual, you went to your room and pleasured yourself, didn't you?"

She lifted her head and squared her shoulders. "No, Harvester. I waited. On the last night when you found release, I found my own, without even a touch to my body."

He believed her. "Why were you in tears earlier?"

"Because I thought I hurt you. When we do the ritual of control, I experience the depth of your lust. Tonight, the feeling overpowered me, and like you, I could not breathe, and I was terrified."

Now he understood why she found so much pleasure in the rituals. She placed herself within him, mentally, such that she could experience his physical reactions. There was a name for such a thing, but he could not think of what it was. He wished he could do the same to her and feel everything as if he were within her body. He would like to know what it felt like to have his cock slowly penetrate her cunt. He would enjoy feeling both simultaneously.

Lost in the erotic thought, he shook his head, and ordered, "Go to bed, my *paratanist*, but you will leave the door open. I do not wish to hear any—fumbling—in the night."

Enovese bowed and entered her room. Chur put the lotion by his bed. As he crawled between the sheets, he thought of how to increase her distress in the coming nights. There was a delicious irony in the thought that he could torment her by increasing his own torment. However, after his experience tonight, he didn't think he could survive much more.

12

True to his word, Chur conducted his own version of the ritual of control on her each night. His erotic creativity astounded her, and yet he never touched her. Having to perform sexual acts on herself for his amusement drove her body into exhausted arousal.

Throughout the day, her skin sizzled and her cunt (a word she once loathed but now loved) tingled and contracted, as if desperately seeking the girth of Chur's cock. Her longing increased, for she teased his pulsing tool with her oil-slicked hands each night. As she performed her part of the ritual, she could feel his cock swelling painfully, but too, she felt his cock within her. In a flash, she could move her awareness from her body to his, and several times she came very close to orgasm.

She denied herself.

On this the morning of the ninth night, her entire pelvic region felt heavy and constricted, as if all the blood in her body had pooled there and then thickened. As she slid from her bed and pulled on her robe, her thighs slicked smoothly against each other when she walked for she was wet. She had been continuously wet. Copiously and constantly, her sex was slick every hour of the day and night for the last nine.

Her breasts felt swollen and heavy, her nipples chafed from rubbing against her robe, for Chur ordered her not to wear the shift. On the sixth night, when Chur had her open her robe without removing her hood, he'd discovered her tormented nipples.

At first, he had her soothe them with oil, then tug and twist them between her fingers and thumbs. "Lift them up," Chur said. "Cup them with your hands, offer them to me, beg me to suck them."

She'd complied with his order, thanking her hood for hiding her face, for she blushed so deeply her cheeks hurt. Of course, he refused her entreaties, which only aroused her more.

On the seventh night, he had her repeat the actions but added a new twist; rather than using the soothing oil, he had her use pungent oil that at first contact cooled, but as she continued to rub the oil, it warmed, and then became almost painfully hot. Such intensity pushed her right to the edge until Chur allowed her to use the blue lotion to stop the torture.

On the eighth night, he ordered her to her knees before the ritual chair so she could rest her chest upon it. He had her pull her robe up so her bottom was exposed and then ordered her to prepare herself for him. She hesitated, then felt a stream of oil between her cheeks. "Finger your ass with one hand, your cunt with the other."

Trying to balance was unbelievably awkward, but she managed. Chur stalked around her, checking her from every angle, encouraging her as she worked her fingers inside her own body. His words were vulgar, harsh, causing her to feel like a nasty *yondie* indulging a lusty customer. Yet she wasn't ashamed of this image. Just the idea of him paying her to cater to his every whim aroused her. She the servant, he her master. When her breathing altered, and she stood at the brink of climax, Chur ordered her to stop.

Before he would let her go to bed each night he would have her place a dollop of the blue lotion on her clit to prevent orgasm. With only that spot numb, it was as if the rest of her body tried to dissipate the energy, which, of course, it could not. She called it the agony of ecstasy. Her dreams only served to increase the burning in her sex.

Chur's sleep was just as tormented. Since he ordered her to keep her bedroom door open, she could hear him tossing and turning, moaning out thwarted lust deep in the night.

In the midst of all of Chur's demands, she carefully kept to her part of the ritual. She touched him the exact same way each night and put the blue lotion on him only when he demanded it. This gave Chur a tremendous feeling of power and control, which he, in turn, used during his training sessions. One of the reasons she'd developed the ritual of control was she had discovered that Chur took thwarted lust and turned it outward into battle prowess. She honestly believed it helped him focus, and now she had the proof of it. Each night he returned exhausted but pleased with his performance, and ready for the next night of lusty indulgence.

But today, today was the culmination of the ritual. She had no idea what Chur had in mind, but she had her own plans. So far, he had not allowed her to remove her hood. Perhaps he could maintain control only if he did not see her fully exposed. This oddity at first bothered her, as if she were nothing but a body to him, but then she realized the hood afforded her an odd kind of anonymity. Hidden in the shadowed depth, she could more easily indulge Chur's demands while secretly reveling in them.

Normally, she spent the entire ninth day tormenting him, but Chur would not skip even a day of training. The ultimate challenge with Loban weighed heavily on his mind. When he informed her of his decision, she simply bowed, and said, "As you wish, Harvester."

Chur leaned close and whispered, "When I return tonight, we will complete the ritual. Have everything prepared, for I will not want to wait."

His husky tone shot a tingle of electricity across her already sensitive skin, then straight down to her clit. As if he knew, he had her lift her robe and place a bit of the blue lotion upon her sex. He needn't have bothered, for she did not intend to release her pent-up hunger until tonight.

Once he left, Enovese carefully shaved her body free of hair, even her sex. Doing so washed the lotion away and her clit throbbed, demanding attention, which she ignored. She cleaned her hair, then used a scented oil to smooth the wayward strands. She rubbed a fruit-scented lotion onto her flesh. Once her hair dried, she brushed the deep coco-brown length until the red and gold highlights glowed.

Considering her reflection, she longed for cosmetics to enhance the color of her eyes but decided that the lust within the indigo starburst gave her more intensity than any enhancements could. Desire alone intensified the color of not only her eyes but also her lips, her nipples, even her sex. Even though her thighs pressed together, she could see the slick wetness and just the hint of color.

Parting her legs, she now considered her shaved sex. The slender lips were puffy and very dark coral. Her clit poked from a hood of flesh, reminding her of her head emerging from the hood of her robe. Spreading the lips apart with her fingers, her clit stood at attention like a tiny soldier, ready and willing to forge into battle.

Tilting her hips, she could then see the tight entrance of her passage. Slick and wet, she couldn't resist the urge to slide her finger around the taut muscles that stood guard at the entrance.

Grasping at the tiny thrust of her finger, her cunt contracted rhythmically. She had not felt Chur within her passage since the Harvest. Tonight, she vowed, she would feel him stretch that space to the limits. The initial pain of him taking her virginity was long gone. All that remained was a blazing need to feel him plunge into her again.

She teased herself to the edge, then stopped. Her normally pale skin glowed with a flush of excitement. For once, she could look at her body and not worry at the oddly placed scar of the crescent moon on her upper right thigh. She had no recollection of how or why that mark came to be on her pale flesh, and for once, she didn't care. The scar was simply a part of her.

Donning her robe, she then set the stage for the finale. She placed the chair in the center of the main room, placed her kneeling cushion on the floor beside it, and then placed the bottle of soothing oil within reach.

Chur kept the blue lotion and what she dubbed the sensation oil, the one that went from cool to hot, with him. She'd almost laughed at how possessive he was with the blue lotion. Should she wish, she could whip up another batch with ingredients from the kitchen. But again, it gave Chur a profound sense of power that she indulged.

To enhance her own sense of power, she replaced the supple leather straps on the chair with thicker straps. She'd convinced Chur the straps weren't really to hold him; they were strictly ritualistic to help him focus his mental power on resisting the lust she invoked. He had strained against them and had almost broken them, but tonight, even with all his massive power, he would not be able to break free of these straps.

She gave them a sharp snap and hoped he would not notice the switch until it was too late. For tonight, he would be at her mercy.

* * *

Chur returned early from training and his eyes glowed with excitement. As she helped him remove his gear, she discovered he was humming just under his breath, not any song in particular, just a happy buzzing of anticipation. She took her time with him in the shower. He kept sighing impatiently. She shaved his face and longed to shave his genitals, but that wasn't part of the ritual and he would balk—he despised the itching. As she moved around him, she felt her own shaved sex smoothly sliding against the rough fabric of her robe. Enovese didn't care about the discomfort that would come later. She'd gladly suffer anything to have ultimate pleasure tonight.

Chur ate quickly, then shot to his feet. He stood beside the chair so suddenly it was as if he materialized there. With a husky growl, he told her to leave the cleanup for later. Her hood hid her smile; he had never been quite this eager. Truly, his eyes blazed with lust, his breath seemed barely contained by his chest, and his cock pressed fully erect against his loincloth.

"Hurry, my *paratanist*. I am in no mood to wait."

"Yes, Harvester." If anything, she slowed her pace.

He frowned until she knelt beside him; then he gazed down at her with a most wicked smile. Deliberately, she leaned a bit too close as she removed his loincloth. When she let out a sigh that caressed his genitals, Chur took in a sharp hiss of breath and his penis twitched. Once she'd unwrapped the fabric he practically leapt into the chair. He allowed her to secure the bonds. Now she had him exactly where she wanted him.

Enovese began the ritual the normal way by smoothing oil all along his cock and balls. However, once he was at the verge and fully expected to climax, she stopped and stood.

"What are you doing?" Chur regarded her with fury. When she moved to stand before him, his eyes narrowed. "Answer me."

She shook her head.

He yanked at the bonds, and when they didn't give at all, he looked down, then at her. Now his eyes widened with panic. He flexed his arms, causing every muscle to bunch below the dusting of his black body hair. Even his thighs strained, as if to catapult him from the chair. Despite his frantic twisting and straining, he finally realized he could not get free.

"What have you done?" Panting and snarling, Chur bellowed, "You will release me immediately."

In her *paratanist* drone, Enovese said, "When one has willingly entered the trap, one should cease all demands."

"You will regret this."

"Perhaps I will." Enovese carefully pried apart the clasps of her robe; then with her most seductive voice said, "But I assure you that you will not." She pushed her hood back, parted the fabric, and shrugged the robe off her shoulders.

Chur blinked as his gaze roamed over her. He had not seen her face for so long it was as if he saw her for the first time. His lips parted and he mumbled something about forgetting how beautiful she was. He licked his lips when he noticed her shaved sex. Realizing that further resistance was pointless, he relaxed into the chair, but his eyes held a thousand punishments. If he thought such glowering frightened her, he was wrong. Paying for her waywardness in the future was just an added benefit to what she would get now. For he knew as surely as she did that at some point she would have to release him from the chair.

"Tell me, Harvester, do you like what you see?" Enovese turned so he could fully inspect her. Her pampered hair fell to her midcalf and heightened her awareness of her own body. The strands stroked down along her flesh like a thousand soft kisses.

"I would like to see you on your knees sucking my cock."

His aggressive tone and vulgar words only sent another thrill of energy through her. Enovese knelt between his legs with her head hung submissively low. Lifting only her gaze, she met his, and whispered, "As you wish, Harvester."

A look of surprise and confusion darted across his expressive face.

Slowly, Enovese stroked her hands up his legs, enjoying the rough feel of his hair against her soft palms. At his knees, she pressed lightly, pushing them farther apart, sliding her hands up his inner thighs until she reached his cock. Worshipfully, she lifted her head and kissed the tip, sliding the pearl of moisture across her lips.

Chur's lids lowered, turning his gaze smoky as he peered down at her. His nose flared as he took a deep breath, and his lips were tight as he exhaled.

Pulling back, Enovese rubbed her face against the hair on his inner thigh, reveling in the crisp texture, then nuzzled her face to his balls, lifting them with her nose, breathing deeply of the clean smell of his arousal. Extending her tongue, Enovese licked a trail all the way up the length of his shaft. When she reached the most sensitive spot where the shaft met the head, she curled her tongue back and flicked the smooth backside against that spot.

When she looked up, Chur had scrunched his eyes closed and gritted his jaw. His breath pushed out between his teeth. Spreading her lips wide, she took the tip of him into the hot hollow of her mouth. His eyes popped open. His hips thrust forward, pushing more of him into her welcoming mouth. Carefully judging his breathing, she drew him to the edge of climax and stopped.

Chur howled. "Finish. Gods, Enovese, finish!"

She stood and pursed her lips. "Poor Harvester. To be so close to the edge and yet held back." She cupped her breasts, twisted her nipples, and then lowered them close to his mouth. "I beg you, my master, please suck my aching nipples."

A frustrated chuckle escaped him, but he leaned forward

and took a turgid coral peak between his lips. He was not gentle. She didn't want him to be. He sucked hard and then nipped at the pebbled flesh with his teeth. Enovese cupped his head, encouraging him. Rotating her chest, she had him take one nipple, then the other. Each nip and slurp tingled more awareness to her clit. Such a tiny thing swelled to such proportion it became the sole focus of her attention. She wished she could somehow angle her sex up to his face, for if she could, she would beg him to perform the same chewing there. Having him at her mercy excited her, for she knew her capture was fleeting. Soon he would be free and he would make her pay.

Satisfied with his acquiescence, she moved back. Stroking her finger over the wetness on her nipples, she then trailed her hand down, parted her legs, and slid her finger between her pouting lips. Once her finger was slippery wet, she lifted her finger to her mouth and tasted herself. Her desire was salty, reminding her of the way Chur had tasted. She repeatedly teased and tasted.

Mesmerized, Chur watched her tawdry performance, then snarled, "Don't you dare climax."

"No, Harvester. Not without you." Enovese lifted her slick finger to his mouth. "Do you think I'm ready?"

He took a deep breath, then sucked hard at her finger. "You are more than ready, as am I."

She slung her leg over his lap and straddled the chair. Placing her hands on his broad shoulders, Enovese lowered herself to his thighs without taking him inside. Once settled, she used her hands to cup him against her sex, then held his cock steady as she rocked him against her cunt.

"This is not how the ritual should go."

"Do you wish me to stop, Harvester?"

"No!" he said a bit too forcefully. "Please, Enovese, do you wish me to beg? I cannot take any more."

His voice was desperate, tormented, and so plaintive she

knew she'd pushed him far enough. For a brief moment, she regretted her actions. She did not want to hurt Chur, she'd only wanted to bring him pleasure. She wanted him to realize he was a lover not just a mechanical Harvester who mated on command. She hoped by teasing him to the point of no return, he would realize there was nothing wrong with his base desires. She wanted him to explore every sweet or wild fantasy that lurked in his mind.

Lifting up, she angled his cock to the entrance of her cunt and without any teasing, slid down, taking him into her all at once. His gasp matched hers. His mouth took possession of hers, his tongue penetrating between pants.

Knowing that he could not stop now, Enovese released the straps. As if he read her mind, Chur lifted her and strode across the room to the far wall, the one purposely devoid of decoration. Of course, today, the purpose was entirely different than to give him a blank canvas to focus his mind. He pressed her against the wall, better angled her hips, and then thrust into her so hard she almost couldn't breathe. The length of her hair cushioned her against the wall and allowed her to slide up and down easily. His rough body hair stroked along her skin like a thousand biting kisses. His crisp pubic hair against her tender shaved sex and her clit teased with every bouncing thrust. Her tormented clit swelled and became so sensitive she almost couldn't stand any more stimulation. Then the feeling changed, it pushed deeper into her body. She felt surrounded by him, pinned, captured, with no escape possible. But why would she want to escape? In his massive arms, she felt safe. Here, nothing could reach her, not the questions of her origins or the punishment of the *tanists.* In this moment, she was nothing but a lone body and soul clinging to another lone body and soul.

Lost in a haze of desire, Chur growled and nipped at her mouth, his hands gripped so tightly into her buttocks he would leave bruises. She didn't care. When she angled her head to the side, he lowered his mouth to her neck and bit her, pulling and sucking at the skin, marking her. All she could do was cling to his shoulders and murmur her pleasure.

When she was on the verge of orgasm, Chur slowed his thrusts. "Look at me. Look right into my eyes."

Enovese clung to his shoulders with one hand and cupped his face with the other. She fixed her gaze to his and felt penetrated in a different way by the intensity of his summer-sky eyes. He varied the depth and timing of his thrusts while observing her face. Something in her eyes must have beckoned to him, for he knew her climax was imminent.

"Come for me, Enovese. I want to feel you spend on my cock. I want to watch you."

Long denied, the orgasm that tried to find outlet in her flesh now tingled from her extremities drawing to the center of her. Energy built and gathered as it rolled toward her clit. Suddenly that tiny bit of flesh took the influx of power and expanded out, covering her whole body. Her orgasm astounded her and contracted her cunt around Chur so tightly he could no longer thrust at all.

He growled and took several deep breaths through his nose and released them through his mouth. He fought for control and won, but only barely, and not for long.

Clinging to him, she opened her mouth to speak but could only gasp. Chur grit his teeth and brutally thrust into her, causing another orgasm to spasm her whole body in waves. Hot, sticky juice coated his entire groin, giving his pubic hair a new texture against her too-sensitive clit. She slid helpless and breathless while he thrust ever harder and deeper. His hands tangled in her hair, pulling her head back, but he could not stop.

"Tell me whom you belong to."

"You, only you."

He pulled her from the wall, bounced her one last time on his thrusting cock, and then bellowed as he climaxed. The force of his orgasm weakened his arms and legs, and together they slumped to the floor until she lay atop him. Curled to his chest, she lay perfectly still while his cock continued to twitch within her. A hot gush slowly seeped from her and flowed onto him. For a long time, they lay entwined, recovering from the intensity of the frantic mating. All too soon, she felt him pull away from her, not physically, but emotionally. She could not describe this knowing, she simply felt it. Dread caused her to shiver, for she knew what was coming. The time for the pointed questions was at hand. She wanted to run, but there was nowhere to run to, and she could not outrun the truth.

Chur cupped her face and softly asked, "Tell me the truth, Enovese. Did you do this in the hopes of getting pregnant?"

She shook her head and tenderly stroked his facial scar. Tears tumbled from her eyes and splashed against his chest. "You could have sex with me for the rest of your life and still not—" She took a deep breath to bolster herself, then confessed, "I am sterile."

13

Chur didn't know what to say. Her confession rendered him speechless. Her distress was clear, yet he did not know how to comfort her, or even if he should. Her lie of omission struck a fierce chord within his very soul. Above almost everything he expected from a bondmate, children would have to be one of the most important. When he thought of finding his bondmate, one of the primary desires was to have many children with her. Discovering that Enovese was incapable . . .

He'd never told anyone about his dreams beyond the role of Harvester, not even his *paratanist,* for such thoughts seemed less than manly. How could he explain that he sometimes dreamed of holding his own child in his battle-scarred hands? That he wished to watch his child at his bondmate's breast, curl himself around them, and doze peacefully. His world of fighting and battle would be unknown to his children; they would know peace, joy, and the freedom to vie for any position they wished.

All the intense pleasure from his union with Enovese dispersed abruptly. Coldly, he demanded, "How do you know that you are sterile?"

Enovese winced at the harshness of his tone. "Once the magistrate chooses a *paratanist,* they are sterilized."

Her answer appalled him. Without thinking, he muttered, "I don't understand why. You're sworn to celibacy, so what would be the point?"

She gasped at his indifferent tone and lifted herself away from him. Her face was hard with resentment. Raw hurt burned in the depth of her eyes. With a confused shake of her head, more tears tumbled from her, and she quickly wiped them away with the back of her hand. She pushed hard against his chest to get away from him, but he wrapped his arms around her, forcing her to stay atop his body. He did not want her to move away. His cock was still semihard within her and he was not going to withdraw until he was ready.

She struggled briefly, then spoke through gritted teeth, "I know not why the magistrate would sterilize one sworn to celibacy. Now let go of me, Harvester." She squirmed hard enough that his cock fell out of her with a soft plop.

He groaned and released her.

With as much dignity as she could manage, Enovese stood. Her harvest-colored hair was a mess of tangles. Pressing against the wall had tousled the entire length, but she lifted her head and tossed her hair back confidently. Her inner thighs were wet from their lust, and he could see the beginning of fingertip bruises blooming on her hips. He frowned while considering the marks for he hadn't wanted to hurt her. When he looked into her eyes, Enovese tilted her nose up, but tears destroyed her defiant show of pride.

"Stop glaring at my hips. There is no outward evidence of proof. You'll have to take my word that they mutilated me."

He opened his mouth to explain, then abruptly shut it. He'd

been glaring at the bruises, ashamed of his brutality, not searching for confirmation of her sterility. Furious at the idea she'd been trying to get pregnant, the fact that she could not offered him no relief. He hated to admit the truth, even to himself, but there was a part of him that wanted to impregnate her. Such a situation would change everything. Her carrying his child would not change his conflicts. In truth, that situation would only add to them, but he found an intense satisfaction at the mere thought. To understand now, that despite his best efforts, he could never impregnate her infuriated him on a primitive level. Although he wanted to choose his bondmate, he had come to think that Enovese might very well be the one. She alone, without accoutrements, had captured his attention. Now, with this, he knew she could never be his bondmate. The time had come to make sure that she knew the truth as well.

Casting her his best heartless gaze, he tucked his hands behind his head and coldly informed her, "As a Harvester I can have as many children as I wish." Position, intelligence, or possessing a valuable inherited trait dictated the number of offspring a person could have. By virtue of his physical strength and stamina, a Harvester was encouraged to have many children. "Why would I want to bond with a woman who could never give me children?"

Shock widened her beautiful eyes; then they narrowed as she gritted her teeth. After a deep breath, all emotion left her. In her best *paratanist* drone, she said, "You need not tell me what I already know." Enovese yanked her robe off the floor and shook as she pulled it on. She didn't pull the hood over her head, she simply used it to cover the mark on her neck, as if she were ashamed she'd let him put it there.

As he lay on the floor watching her, he understood why she'd been so adamant he claim her bondmate in the Harvest room. By the time he found out the truth, it would be too late to change anything. Anger surged at her trickery, but then compassion for her position tempered his rage. Poor Enovese, trapped in a role not of her choosing and then mutilated so she could never leave her duty. For a brief moment, he considered that she might be lying in order to waylay him into not worrying about impregnating her, but her distress clarified she was telling him a truth she'd rather not confess. He wanted to say he was sorry, to offer her some consolation, but he decided not to. By distancing himself, perhaps Enovese would conclude on her own that he was not her bondmate and thus rescind her claim.

When Enovese took a few steps toward her room, Chur said, "I did not dismiss you."

She faced him but kept her attention on the far wall. Her eyes were glassy and her face was blank. He gazed upon a shell. The real Enovese had departed and left this look-alike behind. His harshness had beaten her spirit away.

"Tell me why you did this tonight."

She shook her head, then flatly said, "What's the point? Now that you know the truth there is nothing I can do."

"I asked you to explain."

She uttered a bitter, broken laugh. "I wanted you to see that sex doesn't weaken the body or the spirit. I wanted to teach this to you for telling you is pointless."

"I don't know about that; I do feel rather weak at the moment." He chuckled as he lay on the floor. He was too tired to even sit up.

Now she looked at him with thinly veiled contempt. Her eyes pinned him with ruthless honesty. "Physically you feel exhausted; but tell me, Harvester, do you feel weak? When you lifted me up, pressed me to the wall, and let desire own you—in that moment you were the strongest you have ever been. You weren't the Harvester, you were Chur Zenge, a man with a heart and a soul. A man who knew exactly what he wanted and took it. From me."

Chur considered. What he'd felt in that moment was almost indescribable—powerful, masterful, and centered within himself. Sex with her was more than just an outlet for his pent-up lust. Sex with Enovese was a defining moment where all the parts of him merged. Unlike the Harvest where the ritual and drugs disconnected him from his body, here, with her, he was fully connected. He felt everything from the masculine thrust of his cock to the tender acceptance of her luscious cunt. Yet she was all he'd ever known. How could he base any decision on his first experience?

At his silence, Enovese lifted a brow. "I wanted you to know that you are more than just a Harvester; that you are a man, and desire is as much a part of you as anything else. You cling to your duty in order to keep those thoughts and feelings at bay. The rules and rituals you live by, the ones that you adhere to so desperately, are there to control you. You say that you want to make your own choice, but falling back, doing what you do, then claiming it is your duty, means you do not have to make choices for they are made for you. Everything from what you eat to what you wear to when you rise and sleep is dictated to you." Her voice rose in volume and her face flushed with anger. "So tell me, Harvester, for a man who insists on making his own choices, why do you cling to a role that entirely prohibits them?"

Her words hit him like a slap to the face. She called him a hypocrite who hid behind the rules for he was too afraid to make his own choices. He did not want to contemplate such a bitter truth. He readied a biting retort, but her snort of derision stopped him.

With a frustrated tone, she said, "Out of all the Harvesters I have served, only you seemed capable of breaking out of the seasons of indoctrination. Only you had a spark, a strength, something I recognized instantly that told me you would be the one to surmount the restrictive rules and become more than just the Harvester. Only you showed as great an intellect as you did physical prowess. You once asked me if I would ever try this on another and my answer was only you. But clearly, I was wrong. You are what you believe. And you firmly believe that you are nothing but the Harvester." Enovese shook her head and looked away, as if ashamed of him.

"How dare you speak to me this way?" Chur found the strength to stand. He would not be spoken to in this fashion by anyone, especially not his servant.

"How dare I?" Utterly unintimidated by him, Enovese approached him and stood almost nose-to-nose. "I dare because nothing short of a verbal thrashing is going to make you see the truth. You don't want to see yourself as a tool, and yet you are because you allow yourself to be. You deride me for breaking the rules and going beyond my role, but I didn't pick this role. The magistrate forced me to become a *paratanist* and then mutilated me on top of it. But at least I chose not to take it lying down. I stood up and made choices. Maybe they were not kind choices for, yes, I tried to make choices for you, but again, you were floundering and unable to decide. I may have tricked you or tried to trick you, but at least I didn't just stand around bemoaning my fate. I took action."

Her tirade left her breathless. Enovese took great gasping breaths in an effort to fight back tears, but she lost the battle. When the first tear fell, she abruptly turned away. Giving him her back. Slapping him with one final insult. He grasped her shoulder and spun her around. There was no fear in her face, only a harsh, bitter fury.

"Go ahead, Harvester. Beat me for my insolence or cast me out to Rhemna. I care not what you do now. For at least you will have finally made a decision." Enovese tilted her truculent nose up.

Rage caused his jaw to clench so tightly he heard his teeth grind together. His fists gripped her upper arms. She winced in pain, yet she did not look away, nor did she apologize. Enovese met his gaze with only determined defiance.

Taking a deep breath, he released her. "You want me to make a decision, then I will. I have decided that you will be my *yondie.* I will use you in whatever way I see fit, and you will comply whether you want to or not." He injected every bit of nasty callousness into his tone that he could muster.

Enovese laughed. Not a giggle or a chuckle but a full-blown, body-shaking laugh with her head tossed back. Rolling her head forward, she met his gaze, and said, "Go ahead and try, Harvester, because as soon as you get close to actually enjoying sex with me, you will relent and cower behind your duty. Just as you did before."

Two could play the nasty game. With a sneer, Chur said, "Not this time. Now that I know you are worthless as a bond-mate, I will have no issues with commanding you to service me."

Her posture stiffened at the insult. A flare of vehemence and hurt blazed in her jade green eyes, then quickly vanished. Dropping into her *paratanist* drone, she said, "As you wish, Harvester." She bowed formally.

Gripping her face in one battle-scarred hand, he said, "My first order is that you will not speak to me in that tone of voice ever again." He shook his head and mocked, "Talk about cowering behind your duty."

Mechanical and cold, Enovese asked, "What tone of voice would you prefer?"

"Use a *yondie* voice. A wanton voice of one who lives only to pleasure me."

Enovese dropped her face submissively, lifting only her eyes, and whispered, "Like this, my master?"

Her voice was deep and rich, pushing every nerve ending from his lips to the tip of his cock. With her voice alone, she aroused him to a shocking degree, but he refused to let it show.

Tracing his finger to her lips, he said, "Very good. Now why don't you put that mouth of yours to work? Get down on your knees and suck my cock." He would make her regret accusing him of not being able to make decisions.

Lifting her brows rather mockingly, Enovese sank to her knees before him and took his flaccid cock into her mouth. Just as in his dream, he felt himself grow hard bit by bit. He literally felt every drop of blood that flowed into his cock. Her tongue swirled over him as he grew harder, her teeth nibbled lightly, her cheeks pulled in a bit as she sucked softly. Enovese kept her eyes open and looking right up into his. He cupped the back of her head, teasing his fingers through her tangled hair, then rubbed the curve of her jaw.

"Very good, my eager *yondie.* You have quite a talent for this." He rocked his hips very slowly, slipping his growing cock over her lips, in and out of the warm wetness of her mouth. "Since I know they didn't train you at the *tanist* house, you must have learned by thinking of sucking my cock. Is that it?"

Without missing a beat, Enovese drew back and nodded yes while running her tongue along the slit at the top of his penis.

"Can you taste yourself on me?"

She executed the same sexy nodding of her head, then flashed him an insolent wink.

Anger had fueled his need to humiliate her, but nothing would humble Enovese. He knew he could say and demand the most vulgar actions and she would comply with that insufferable knowing satisfaction in her eyes. The more he tried to master her, the more fully she would own him. A subtle pang of fear touched him then, for he didn't know if he could continue to treat her this way. Deep inside, the animal part of him wanted to dominate her, force her to act out his most secret desires, but his conscience begged restraint. Standing above her, kneeling in supplication while she worshipped his cock, was a position of absolute power and intense pleasure; however, his position was one of profound responsibility as well. He would have to decide how far to go to get his pleasure without causing her pain.

Chur gave her explicit instructions on exactly how hard he wanted her to suck, when she should tighten her lips, where she should place her hands and how firmly to hold. She obeyed. And always, always, her gaze held his. Exasperated by the amusement in her eyes, he roughly withdrew.

He let her watch him oil his cock. He took his time, working the oil along the length, watching her subconsciously lick her lips. He had her get on her hands and knees. He knelt behind her. She looked back over her shoulder and he ordered her to look down at the floor. She obeyed but not without flashing him a smirk first.

Cupping his large hands to her heart-shaped bottom, he roughly parted her cheeks and placed his cock against the tight ring of her anus. She gasped. Enovese dug her fingertips into the carpet. He knew he'd finally succeeded in removing the mirth from her eyes. With one long, slow stroke, he forced the tip of his cock into her ass. Her head rolled back with her whimper of pleasure.

He knew what she expected. What she wanted. But he was the one making the decisions now. Keeping the head of his cock wedged into the tight sucking heat of her, he then stroked his fist up and down his shaft, masturbating himself into her, using her as his vessel, just as he had on the night of the Harvest. It took a long time for him to climax, and when he did, he stood and walked to the bathing unit. He had no idea if she climaxed or not. He told himself he didn't care. Deliberately, he turned his back on her while he bathed. When he finished, he went to bed without even glancing in her direction.

14

Enovese smoothed the cuffs of Chur's dress uniform so the sleeves of the black jacket fell to the edge of his wrist and the crimson *astle* edging lay flat. Chur stood perfectly still while she fussed over him. He uttered a bored sigh. She knew he despised the official functions, but it was part of his duty to attend. Tonight was Ambo Votny's season celebration. As the current magistrate, Ambo Votny wielded a great deal of power. Anyone of any importance must attend.

The deep shadow black of Chur's uniform enhanced his height and bulk. His thick black hair framed his summer-sky blue eyes, now that it had grown back enough to cover his skull with soft curls. The uniform, composed of a jacket and form-fitting trousers, was utterly black and devoid of decoration but for one slash from his shoulder to his hip. This slash exposed his most fearsome scar, and crimson *astle* edging trimmed the slash, drawing attention to the whiteness of the scar. Earlier, she had meticulously shaved his face free of hair so his facial scar would show, but also shaved the hair around the chest scar.

Once she had the front of the jacket centered, she applied a sticky gel to the edging to hold it against his skin. She supposed the idea was that his scar was a part of his uniform. For military functions, he would wear his ceremonial sword, but not for a season celebration. Ambo had attained the venerable age of seventy seasons. Tonight, all would commemorate Ambo for not only his age but also his contributions as magistrate.

Enovese sighed.

"What?" Chur asked, frowning as he glanced at his uniform. "Didn't you get the stain out?"

At the last function, Ambo had splashed bright purple *immis* on the sleeve. After three hours of careful cleaning, she'd removed the stain. "You look most commanding."

With a subtle lift of his brow, Chur said, "Don't tell me you wish to attend."

Enovese considered. Not that her wishes would matter in the least, for a *paratanist* would be as welcome as food poisoning, but if she could go as Chur's bondmate . . . she sighed and shook her head. "Of course not."

"Good. I would think you mad, for any affair involving Ambo is dull. A gathering in his honor is even more so." Under his breath, Chur muttered, "And I know if he doesn't spill something on me, he will try to wipe snot on me." Chur took a deep breath that lifted his chest. He growled and scratched. "Already it itches."

Enovese brushed his hand away. She didn't want him to destroy the perfect line she'd achieved. Inspired, she retrieved the blue lotion and smoothed it along the scar and the shaved hair. Chur sighed in relief but didn't actually thank her.

"You need not wait up for me."

Once he left, Enovese leaned against the door. For a brief moment, she allowed herself to fantasize about attending the party as Chur's bondmate. She imagined herself at his side, her *astle* dress cut low across her breasts and hugging her waist, then flaring around her hips, flowing all the way to the floor.

Her hair would be up in an elaborate coiffure that would have taken her servant hours to perfect. Chur would not leave her side, so enchanted would he be with her beauty, her poise. Polite banter, soft chitchat, witty repartee would further charm him. He would lean close and whisper to her ear that she was the most beautiful woman in the entire room. Then he would murmer lusts and longings that would necessitate their early departure. Once alone, he would barely be able to control himself long enough to remove her dress and then . . .

With a sigh, she shook her head, causing the hood to brush against her flushed cheeks. Despite her firm belief that Chur would relapse into duty, he hadn't. Now, three entire cycles had passed. He'd kept to his decision to treat her as a *yondie.* He had no problem using her to satisfy his desires and then, without a thought to her needs, he would turn away and go about his business as if she didn't exist. His utter indifference to her pleasure shocked her the first time, but after repeated incidences she felt debased. Where always thoughts of him, her fantasies and desires, had filled her with pleasure and unbearable giddiness, now she knew only shame for her desires, the acts that she performed upon him, and the lust that had always been such a basic part of her—now everything felt ugly. She knew that was his point. Chur wanted to reinforce his edict that she was worthless to him. That he would never claim her as his bondmate. He would use her for his pleasure, then ultimately discard her when the time came.

Despite her mocking or perhaps because of it, Chur made a decision, then ruthlessly stuck to it. He often spoke about the next Harvest and how he would surely find his bondmate this time. As long as he survived the challenge, he knew the woman of his dreams would be among the virgins on the sacrifice table. Every time she thought he'd dug the dagger deep enough, he found a way to plunge it just a bit farther into her heart.

The ritual of control reverted to the original structure she'd created. Chur always checked the straps before sitting. Her movements were mechanical. She no longer relished those nine days. She dreaded them. A part of her wanted to throw it in his face that the ritual had no basis in the prophecy but such might only compel more indifference. She feared that he would laugh and force her to perform anyway. Therefore, she kept her mouth shut and executed the ritual, but she never felt even a brief tingle between her legs.

Chur noticed that where once she flowed with lusty juice she was now almost dry. He didn't care. He used more and more oil. However, she noticed that he was not as hard. Chur went through the motions of using her for his pleasure, but gratification often eluded him. He would suddenly stop and move away, coldly dismissing her. Once, she heard him masturbating below his covers; apparently, his own hand was better than her disinterested form.

Enovese took no satisfaction in knowing this. She longed to return to the honest passion they had shared. To a mutual, reciprocal, wanton lust. She would rather return to celibacy than suffer any more mechanical acts that apparently left both of them disappointed.

With another sigh, she straightened his rooms, then retreated to her bedroom. She opened the sacred chest, thinking that perhaps she would write out the events of the last few days, but tears flowed as soon as she saw the dress. Crumpled in a corner, the emerald green *astle* fabric bunched into a careless mass, as if it, like her heart, huddled with unendurable pain. So much promise had gone into crafting the bonding dress. Not only had she risked discovery by stealing the fabric, but the water pearls, taken a few at a time from the temple, would have resulted in execution had she been caught stealing them from the goddess offerings. Enovese thought the goddess who looked over *paratanists* would have understood. Therefore, she took them despite the risks. She'd painstakingly placed each water pearl across the bodice and spiraled down the skirt. Each night, over the course of three seasons, she'd worked on the dress with visions of bonding with Chur filling her mind.

A surge of anger caused her to yank the dress from the corner. She moved to the kitchen, intent on cutting it to ribbons and throwing it away, but as she lifted a paring knife to the water-soft fabric, she found she could not destroy it. Doing so would be like cutting her own heart from her chest. Instead, she decided to wear the dress one last time before placing it back in the sacred chest forever.

Chur would not return for hours, so she undressed in the kitchen and pulled on the dress. It fit more loosely than before. Chur's indifference caused her appetite to plummet to almost nothing. As she considered herself in the full-length looking glass, she thought the emerald green only highlighted the torment in her eyes. Working her fingers through her hair, she removed the tight braid and smiled at the waves of luscious brown strands that flowed over her shoulders, along the curve of her breasts, almost as if her hair were a cape. She twirled in a circle, fanning her hair out just like the skirt of the dress.

Enovese stared at her reflection for a very long time, committing every detail to memory. For she knew she would never wear this dress again. When she put it away, it would stay there. Letting the costume go would be a concrete symbol of shelving her dreams forever. Despite the pain, she lifted her chin, for she hadn't been a coward. No. She had boldly challenged the confines of her position and strived to make her wildest dreams come true. She had failed, but at least she had tried.

When she heard the main door open her eyes popped wide. She grabbed her robe and pulled it over her shoulders and hair, but it wasn't long enough to cover the flared skirt of the dress. Desperately, she grasped handfuls of silk and bunched it up around her thighs, but now she clearly looked like she was trying to hide something.

"*Paratanist?*" Chur bellowed.

As calmly as she could, Enovese called back, "Yes, Harvester?"

"Come!"

His voice was rough with annoyance. She despised when he ordered her about like a trained animal. He had never done so until lately. Sexual frustration fed his verbal abusiveness.

Peeking around the corner, she saw Chur standing in the middle of the room with a twist of disgust on his face. Something garishly green and yellow splattered the front of his uniform. Nibbling at her lip, she didn't think she could get him to wait for a moment, and there was no way she could assist him and keep the dress hidden.

He bellowed again and she grimaced. In a burst of inspiration, she tucked the dress up between her legs. If she walked slowly, she thought she could keep it hidden. With a shuffling gate, she entered the main room.

Chur frowned. "Stop dragging your feet. Look at what that bumbleton did to my uniform." Chur glanced at the mess and snarled, "Damn drunken idiot slopped an entire bowl of *lete* on me, then had the nerve to tell me I bumped into him."

Enovese didn't bother to ask for a name, it had to be Ambo Votny. Chur despised the man, not that he didn't have good reason since at almost every function Ambo managed to get something on Chur's uniform. The pungent odor of the soup would never fade from the fabric, and the garish color . . . no matter what cleaning magic she performed, the jacket was ruined. What made matters worse was Chur detested *lete*. He called it vomit in a bowl.

Carefully, she pried the sticky fabric off the skin around his scar so it didn't pull any hair. Once she had it free, she then helped him slip the jacket off his shoulders. Chur immediately scratched at the shaved skin.

"Fetch me that blue lotion."

She saw the bottle halfway across the room. Given her predicament, it seemed terribly far away. There was no way she could retrieve it and keep the dress between her thighs. The *astle* slipped against itself and her flesh. Oddly, the sensual feel of the fabric aroused her and only added to her frustration.

When she hesitated, Chur sighed and said, "Never mind. I'm going to have to wash the stench off anyway." He removed his trousers, placed them in her hands with the jacket, and strode toward the bathing unit.

Enovese waddled toward the kitchen thinking that she could quickly change out of the dress while he cleaned up. She'd only made it a few steps.

"What's with you?"

She shrugged. "I know not what you mean."

"Don't take that tone with me," he warned. "You're walking as if toward execution." He scrubbed at his chest yet never took his eyes off her. With a tilt to his head and a frown, he asked, "What's under your robe?"

She ignored him and continued toward the kitchen.

He shut the water off, wrapped a towel around his hips, and stomped toward her. "Don't you dare walk away from me." When he grasped her shoulder and turned her, the entire dress spilled down her legs. The deep green was glaringly bright against the pale beige of her robe. He glared at the fabric, then ordered her to remove her robe.

Enovese placed the ruined uniform on the table and slipped her robe off. She kept her head down because she didn't want to see him laugh. She braced herself for a tirade that never came. Tentatively, she lifted her gaze to Chur. Water droplets rolled from his hair, down his face, his chest, but he simply stood there, staring at her with the most perplexed expression on his face. She opened her mouth to speak and he shook his head, silencing her. He took a step back and continued to let his gaze roam over her. A slow, warm blush worked its way across her face. She closed her eyes, hoping he wouldn't notice.

Chur chuckled. With a rolling murmur, he said, "I have ordered you to perform the most crude acts, yet standing there in a dress causes you to blush."

She said nothing because she didn't fully understand her reaction herself. Perhaps it was wearing her hopes and dreams for his view, or the fear that he would ask pointed questions that would give him further ammunition to harm her. She felt more exposed and vulnerable at this very moment than she ever had. Unable to speak or even meet his gaze, she simply stood and kept her attention on his feet. After a long moment, he moved, and she realized he was walking around her, examining her from all angles. Was he pleased by what he saw or was his low chuckle just the beginning?

After the longest time, Chur sat at the table, as if awaiting a meal. She realized he probably hadn't had time to eat at the celebration, so she removed the ruined uniform and entered the kitchen to prep a quick snack. Little hairs on the back of her neck stiffened when she realized Chur had entered. He didn't say anything, he just watched her prep the food and clean his jacket. When the meal was ready, he followed her to the table and sat. She stood beside the head of the table as per her duty.

Chur asked for a glass of *soony*, which she fetched.

He nodded to the chair closest to him.

Confused, Enovese sat. He had never wanted her to sit with him while he ate.

"Have you eaten?"

"No."

He pushed his plate between them and offered her his fork.

After a moment of hesitation, Enovese accepted. She took a bite, then handed the fork to Chur. In this way, they cleaned the plate. She wondered what was going on now. His attitude was entirely different, and the way he looked at her was baffling. His face betrayed nothing—not joy or anger, just a quiet speculation. He offered to share the *soony* and Enovese took a tiny sip. She had never tried the fermented barley and *estal* drink. Pungent bitterness rolled over her tongue along with tiny bubbles. After a few more swallows warmth flowed from her belly out along her limbs, relaxing every bit of tension. She giggled and instantly clapped a hand over her mouth.

Chur chuckled and pulled her hand away. "It feels good, doesn't it?" He cupped her hand in his.

She nodded. His hand felt big, strong, and warm. Sparks and tingles raced along her body, stiffening her nipples, then dancing down to her hips, teasing across the sensitive flesh between her legs. It had been so long since she felt aroused, but she didn't know if it was the drink or Chur's gentle touch. Three cycles of nothing but harsh, uncaring strokes and cruel indifference made this, this simple handholding, bring a flush of pleasure to her body.

"Where did you get the dress?"

"I made it."

Chur nodded. "Why?"

His tone was gentle, but she didn't trust him. What if she told him the truth and he in turn mocked her, throwing it forever in her face? She pulled her hand from his and stood. Without comment, she cleared the table.

He followed her into the kitchen and watched.

She cleaned up and attempted to dart past him, but he touched her shoulder.

"Wait. There is something else I didn't get to do tonight."

Dread seeped cold along all the warmth the *soony* and his touch had generated. In her mind, she begged that he would not use her tonight, not tonight and not in her beautiful dress, the dress that embodied all her hopes and dreams. She thought if he degraded her in this dress, it would destroy her.

15

The fear in her eyes shocked Chur, for he instantly understood what she thought he meant with his touch and statement. Sex was the last thing on his mind. He removed his hand from her shoulder, and said, "I didn't dance. Do you know how?"

Surprise widened her eyes, then disappointment lowered her gaze. "No."

"I'll show you." He offered his hand. After a moment of hesitation, she slipped her hand to his. Just holding her hand surged pleasure. The last three cycles had been unbearable. He'd decided to treat her like a *yondie* and continued even when he no longer found gratification. The more he tried to distance himself emotionally, by making their encounters strictly about his own pleasure, the more dissatisfactory those encounters became. When he realized Enovese wasn't wet, he at first eased his way with oil, but then found he could not climax. Until then, he never understood how much her pleasure aroused him. He felt locked into his decision. If he changed his mind, he would lose face.

As he ushered Enovese into the main room, he realized he

was still wearing nothing but a towel. He asked her to wait a moment while he changed into a black loincloth. She didn't watch him. In fact, she turned her back as if by looking she might encourage something. He grimaced. Both of them were far too proud. She would never admit she'd goaded him into this, and he would never admit he'd taken it too far. Even in his own heart he wasn't sure what he wanted from her. He could not claim her as his bondmate, but he didn't want to hurt her. If he were honest with himself, he had to admit that he didn't want her to be with another man. He couldn't keep her, and he couldn't let her go. The only thing he knew with certainty was that their current relationship could not continue without destroying them both.

Chur set some music playing, a brightly paced tune of woodwinds and strings, and then bowed to Enovese. She mimicked him. He lifted her hand with his and showed her how the dance worked. Normally, many couples performed the expanding flower petal design of the steps, but it worked well with only two. He also thought the minimal touching would reassure her as to his intentions.

Enovese possessed a natural grace. Her slender limbs, encased in emerald *astle,* flowed smoothly as if born of wind. She innately understood the flirting nature of the dance, how to tip her face just so, how to use the curtain of her hair to advantage. She was stunning. He fumbled more steps than she did simply because he lost track, distracted by her sheer beauty and elegance. The fabric of her dress moved against her with teasing seduction, showing the curve of a breast here, the turn of her hip there, the flash of slender ankles. Enovese had spectacular eyes and devastating hair, but her ankles intrigued him beyond comprehension, because every time he spied them below the flare of the skirt, he thought of grasping them in his fists, parting them, and then . . .

Once the music ended, he played another piece, this one

slower. When he cupped his hand to the small of her back and drew her close, she stiffened and lowered her face. Her panting breath puffed against his chest, arousing him, cautioning him.

"This style is a bit closer, but it's still just a dance."

She relaxed marginally, but he could feel her racing heartbeat. Her reaction reminded him of some of the pre-Harvest women whose parents cajoled them into dancing with him at the Festival of Temptation. They approached him with awe and fear, knowing that he might one day receive the gift of their virginity. Dancing with him was a prelude to that intimacy. Once he swept them onto the dance floor, some giggled, some blushed, but almost all of them were surprised at how delicately he handled them. His massive hands softly touching and his murmured encouragements often caused their first flush of desire and awareness that they were sexual creatures. Enovese was not much different. He had received her virginity and they'd performed a multitude of acts, but there had never been a true seduction. Perhaps that was where he failed. By not giving Enovese the honor of seduction, the honor of pursuit, the honor of allowing her to bloom with his attentions, he denied a basic need. A wry smile crossed his face. She had not done so with him either. She'd placed herself on the sacrifice table leaving him little option. Boldly, she'd staked her claim. He decided the past was past and perhaps, tonight, they could start again.

"You are very graceful, Enovese."

She tilted her face up, surprise washing across her features, then a blush as she lowered her gaze and smiled slightly. He didn't understand her reaction for a moment, but then realized he had not called her by her name for three cycles.

All at once, he was afraid of encouraging her fantasy that they would one day be bondmates, for that would not happen, but clearly, he owed her more than harsh indifference. And what he had seen tonight at Ambo Votny's season celebration had shocked him. He must have answers. His suspicions would remain locked in his mind until he had the truth, even if that truth might destroy the lovely woman in his arms. He needed to slam Ambo up against a wall and shake the truth out of him. Well, he didn't need to do that, but he wanted to, whether Ambo had any answers or not.

Moving Enovese in a tight circle, using his hand at the small of her back to teach her the movements of the dance, surged awareness in his body despite the numbing effects of the *soony.* Her scent surrounded him, intoxicated him, and he lowered his mouth to her ear. He pulled back. Repeatedly he told himself to slow down with her. He tried to imagine this seduction as the ritual of control. Bit by bit he would increase her desire until she wanted him again. Chur couldn't bear the idea of forcing her to his passions even one more time, not unless she wanted him to. At first, it confused him how Enovese relished him forcing her to his wicked lust, then didn't. It took him a while to realize that playing at master and servant aroused her beyond comprehension, whereas forcing her to be a *yondie* who received no pleasure diminished her interest to nothing. His indifference to her pleasure was what had caused the change. He'd taken a gift from her and turned it ugly to drive her away and keep his emotions at bay.

An emotion he didn't recognize stirred deep inside his heart as he danced with her. In the end, he decided that he cared about her, and that wasn't a bad thing. He only cared and there was nothing wrong with that. He couldn't claim her, but perhaps he could ensure the next Harvester could.

Round and round they moved as his mind chewed at this new idea. When the challenge came, and if he defeated Loban, then Sterlave would be the next in line. Sterlave was not only strong but also intelligent; he might be a match for Enovese. Chur doubted that Enovese would enjoy him meddling in her life. She said she would never attempt this again with another Harvester, and that simultaneously pleased and disheartened him. How could he move on knowing that she would be trapped behind her robe, performing an endless line of rituals, sleeping alone and lonely in her narrow bed? Just the thought of it tightened his arms around her.

Enovese stiffened and pushed against his chest. "Please let go. I don't wish to dance anymore."

Chur released her. A thousand apologies hung on his lips, but he only nodded. "Good night, Enovese."

Darting him a suspicious glance, she moved toward her room.

"Enovese?"

She warily faced him.

"Thank you, for tonight." He bowed formally.

Enovese dipped her face in a quick nod of acknowledgment. As she turned away, the barest curve of a smile turned up the edges of her coral lips.

Chur removed his loincloth and slipped into bed. He still wondered why she had the dress, for a *paratanist* would have no need of it, but she'd looked so amazing he hadn't had the heart to grill her to get the answer. At the celebration tonight, there had been hundreds of very wealthy and powerful women. Despite the more elaborate dresses, hairdos, makeup, and jewelry worn by those women, not a one had fully captured his attention. Not like Enovese. For the life of him, he could not understand what Enovese possessed that those other women did not.

However, during the insufferable party tonight, there had been one woman who seized his notice. She had to be at least sixty seasons given the silvering of her hair and the lines that subtly altered the beauty of her face. What had almost stopped his heart was the way her nose tilted up at the tip in a most truculent way. Chur had been discreetly prodding those around him as to the woman's identity when a drunken Ambo dumped the bowl of *lete* on him. Enraged, more by having to leave without the woman's name than the stain, Chur vowed he would discover the identity of the woman who looked so much like Enovese.

16

Enovese woke thinking last night had been a dream. Had she really shared a meal, a drink, and danced with Chur? Her sleepy gaze fell on the bonding dress she'd carefully folded and placed on the sacred trunk. After she'd slipped it off, she hadn't been able to place it inside the chest, not when her fading dream suddenly grew sharp around the edges. She had no idea what was responsible for Chur's change of attitude, but she was glad. Even if the change had been for only one night.

When he'd held her close for the last dance, her body responded to his for the first time in many cycles. Desire grew slowly with each touch and brush of flesh. She'd been able to feel so much of him, for all he wore was the loincloth. The sensuality of her silk-clad skin against his bare skin, rough with dark hair, caused tingles to shiver all over her body. He broke the spell when he'd pressed her fully against him, nuzzling his cock against her belly. She'd frozen in fear. She thought he'd done everything to waylay her into thinking all was not lost only so he could laugh and force her into *yondie* service. Yet when she asked, he let her go, and then thanked her for the evening. In that one moment, he'd stolen her heart all over again. If he played a game with her, it was a very cruel one. She would have to guard her heart and be wary.

As she dressed in her robe, she wondered again at his motives. She did not think for a moment that he had changed his mind about claiming her as his bondmate. He wanted children, and that was the one thing she could not give him. When Enovese lived in the *tanist* house, the only real joy she'd known was when she'd cared for the children. Seasons later, when she discovered she'd been sterilized shortly after birth, her heart had broken despite the fact her celibacy would prevent such an event. Somehow, thinking that she could have children had given her some hope to cling to, but when that last shred of hope dissolved, that's when she decided that she would find a way out of her forced role.

She left her bedroom and found Chur sleeping on his back, the covers tossed to the foot of the bed. He was semihard. Now that his body hair had grown back, he looked sinister, animal, and aggressively male. She had an overwhelming compulsion to wake him up by taking him into her mouth. She stopped and simply stared. How could she think such a thing? He'd used her in a multitude of degrading ways and now, after one night of sweetness, she wanted him again. Perhaps the difference was that the choice was hers, not his. He wouldn't be forcing her to suck his cock; she would be doing it of her own free will. Was that what he was after? Did he wish to return to the time when she would willingly do anything he asked? He'd made it clear he would choose a bondmate during the next Harvest. Perhaps he just wanted to spend the rest of their time together with her eager participation.

A million thoughts and feelings collided in her mind as she fixed his morning meal. By the time she finished, he sat at the table. She served him, then took her place by his side. The morning passed much as usual, and she became convinced last night was just a brief interlude. She helped him don his gear and watched him stride toward the main door. He stopped short and turned to face her.

"Come."

Unlike his tone last night, today his voice rolled with a rumbling seductive edge that shot awareness right to her clit.

Compelled, dreamlike, yet cautious, she moved to his side.

Chur considered her for a moment. His eyes roved over her as if he could see right through her robe. He leaned near, placed his mouth right against her ear, and whispered, "I would very much like to see you in that dress tonight." Leaning back, he added, "But only if you wish to wear it for me." With that, he was gone.

Enovese placed her palm against the door, as if she could actually touch him and know his intent. Absently, she traced the carvings in the Onic wood with her fingertips. As she explored the curves and edges, her eyes tracked her hands and a pattern emerged. It felt and looked familiar. She considered for a very long time, letting this puzzle distract her from the thoughts of what Chur was after. She needed time to decide whether she would do as he asked.

Enovese stepped back and the meaningless lines of the pattern carved into the door resolved into two figures entwined in such a way it was impossible to tell where one ended and the other began. Merging and melting, the two figures seemed so inextricably intertwined she couldn't determine the sex of either one.

Her hand flew to her mouth. She ran to her room, removed the bonding dress from the chest, flung it open, and retrieved the ceremonial chalice box. When she compared it to the door, she discovered the carvings were the same. The door was just on a much larger scale. How had she entered and exited this door a thousand times without even noticing the carving at all?

What did the carving mean? There had to be some significance for it to grace both the Harvester's main door and the ceremonial chalice box. She placed the box on the table and considered it while she ate. Her mind ticked back over the information in the text, but there was nothing there to explain beyond the structure of the goblet itself and the ritual involving it. She considered going to the library to study further, but her last foray into the stacks hadn't yielded anything she didn't already know. She wanted to discuss it with Chur. His perspective would be different. He might see something she did not. He'd been clear about her returning the box, but now that the winds had shifted again he might be more willing.

She considered his request to wear the dress for him again. Perhaps if she did he might be more interested in uncovering the many mysteries of the Harvest prophecy. On the other hand, if he sensed her trying to manipulate him, such might immediately turn his heart cold. She shivered. She would rather do anything than return to the indifferent way he treated her.

Unable to decide, she cleaned up his rooms and took the ruined jacket down to the storage room. She placed it on the repair rack and pressed the service crystal. Once she left, someone would come and replace it. In this way, they never had to see her. This had bothered her when she first started serving the Harvester, but she understood now that her role set her apart from all others who served him. She alone actually touched the Harvester, and that, in turn, made her untouchable. She grabbed another clean robe and a shift for herself, more oil and other supplies, then left.

As she returned to Chur's rooms, she took note of the decorations in the hallway, as if seeing them for the first time. The closer the halls came to his suite, the more the swirling curves of gilded lines resolved, echoing the pattern on the door and box. Again, she had never taken note. She'd walked these halls a thousand times yet never paid attention for she considered it all elaborate decorations. She wondered if anyone else had ever noticed, for the echoing pattern had to have meaning.

No matter how much she would like to solve this mystery, it wouldn't help her decide what she would do tonight. Would she wear her robe or her dress?

Chur went through training with his mind elsewhere. His life became ever more complicated. Where once he only lived and breathed to be the Harvester, now he had to worry at that, but also about who would take his place. In addition, he wondered what basis would he use to choose a mate at the next Harvest, for he had given up all notions of finding a bondmate. Perhaps he would do as Helton suggested and just pick a pretty one. If the woman had already chosen another, that was too bad, for one way or another, this next Harvest would be his last. He worried about his relationship with Enovese, what would become of her, if he could somehow find a Harvester who might take her away from her role for he knew it could not be him. Moreover, overlapping images of Enovese and the elder woman at the party swirled in his mind, causing him terribly dark thoughts of abandonment. Had that woman given up Enovese to gain the trappings of wealth she so happily displayed? All of these thoughts conspired to distract him.

Helton Ook slapped the flat of a blade across his belly with a hearty splat, and bellowed, "Focus!"

Embarrassed by the immediate turning of heads to his direction, Chur centered his attention fully on Helton until the session ended.

Breathless and sweating, Helton sat next to Chur on a bench and said, "You are most inconsistent in your training. One day you focus such I am afraid of you, then the next, you have the attention of a child."

Chur grimaced, for he deserved the reprimand. Helton

would not want to hear the truth of what caused his lapse of attention. Leaning near, Chur asked, "If I have questions that my *paratanist* cannot answer, where am I to turn?"

Bafflement twisted Helton's face. "A *paratanist* is trained in all aspects of the Harvest. What question could you have that a *paratanist* could not answer?"

Afraid of revealing too much, Chur shrugged. "Nothing, but, perhaps I wish to study the prophecy myself."

Helton rolled his eyes. "That is the place of a *paratanist*. You are the Harvester. You are the brawn, the *paratanist* the brain. Such has been so for thousands of seasons."

Frustrated by this nonanswer and still cautious, for if Helton took it in his head to nose around in Chur's affairs . . . Chur simply nodded.

Lifting his head, Helton squinted at the far wall. After a moment, he said, "Well, I suppose there is the tome, but as far as I know there hasn't been a Harvester yet who bothered with it."

Chur's heart raced with excitement. "The tome?"

"During your initiation didn't the magistrate give you a tome wrapped in metal and animal hide?"

Chur thought back to that time in the temple. He remembered reading and signing documents. Heaps of ceremonial gear and weapons had been placed at his feet. Toward the end, when he'd been almost desperate to leave, Ambo had forced Chur's hand on something that grew warm and then placed it in the pile with the gear. Was that the tome? Chur had no idea what happened to it after the ceremony.

With a groan of exhaustion, Helton stood. "Ask your *paratanist* about the tome. There isn't anything in there that isn't already in your *paratanist*'s head, but if that will get you to keep your focus, then by all means, study all evening if you must. Just be ready for me in the morning." Helton clapped a meaty hand to Chur's shoulder and departed.

Now that training was over, Chur allowed his mind to wander to Enovese. Would she wear the dress as he requested? If she did, would he be able to keep his hands off her? The more he pictured her in the form-fitting dress, the less likely he thought he could keep to his plan to slowly seduce her.

An odd quiver of anticipation filled his belly as he opened the main door and entered his rooms.

Enovese wasn't wearing the dress. She wasn't wearing her robe. The only thing she wore was water.

Oblivious to his entrance, for her head was under a stream of water, she continued to bathe. He removed his gear. Settling himself on a padded chair, he simply watched her wash.

Once her hair was wet, she lathered her scalp and worked the foamy bubbles down the length with slender fingers. Her movements, the way she turned her body and tilted her head to caress her tresses, aroused him when he imagined those same motions on his body—her hands and her hair wrapping around him, teasing and soft. He cupped a hand to his cock, stroking himself almost absently as he watched.

Her hands were small and her fingers delicately tapered, but he knew what strength she had in her hands, what magic she could perform with them if she were so inclined. As he watched her hands cup her breasts, twist her coral peaks, and smooth soap along her flesh, he wanted to again feel her hands on him, willingly on him. Not the mechanical necessity of a ritual or those that he demanded, but her oh-so-clever hands working magic because she wanted to.

Even from this distance, he could smell the floral essence of the soap. The sweet scent clashed with the ripe smell of his body. He continued to tease himself, enjoying the mixture of different aromas. He felt dirty, not just with sweat and grime, but also for watching her without her knowledge, and stroking his cock while his hungry gaze ate up every bit of her. He felt nasty for his perversity, but that only excited him more. Defiantly, he pleasured himself and watched her bathe.

Efficiently, she washed her body, but she did linger a bit between her legs, which compelled him to take harder strokes. Her back was to him, but he knew by the way her legs parted and the movements of her arms that she was teasing her sex. Her wet hair flowed down over her back all the way to her calves as if hiding her from his gaze. Bits and flashes of her pale flesh peeked between the darkened strands. He found this vision far more arousing than being able to see her clearly. Imagining her hands at her luscious cunt was far more intriguing than actually witnessing her tease herself. Did she think of him while she slowly worked her hand back and forth, or had he hurt her so deeply she now fantasized about any man *but* him?

Sensing that she was almost finished, with her shower if not a rousing climax, he stood and walked toward her. His pulsing cock pointed at her, seeking, bouncing with his steps, surging an animal lust that he had picked his mate and would now claim her despite her objections. Chur wanted Enovese. He wanted her the way he had cycles ago, wanted her surrender and capitulation. He wanted her wet, moaning, and begging for him. Chur gulped a great breath to fight the rush of overwhelming hunger.

Enovese must have heard him for she gasped and turned, covering herself with her hands. She sputtered something, but he shushed her with a shake of his head and then joined her under the stream. He pointed to the soap in her trembling hand and said, "Help me wash, Enovese."

Eyes round with fear, she simply stared at him. She had helped him wash every night, but she'd had the protection of her robe. Naked, vulnerable, with the sweetness of last night a tiny grain of sand to the horror of three cycles of harshness, she no doubt imagined the worst. He cursed himself a thousand times for putting that terror in her jade eyes. Desperate to turn the tide back, he searched for words to reassure her but found his voice blocked by a lump in his throat.

He lifted and kissed the back of her hand. With his eyes, he tried to convey that he demanded nothing. By his strength and position he could force her, but he discovered too late it gave him no pleasure. Her willing participation, her white-hot desire, that gave him infinite satisfaction. Even if he could speak, he could not find the words to say this, so he simply gazed at her, putting all his honesty and heart into his eyes.

Understanding eased the terror. Cautiously, Enovese turned toward him and smoothed the soap over his chest. His thick hair lathered the soap into a swirl of bubbles that she worked around his chest and his arms. She lifted his arms to scrub at his armpits and then worked down to his hips. When she hesitated, he clasped his hands behind his head. His defenseless posture reassured her. With a darted glance to his face, she lowered herself and washed his legs and feet. Lifting her soapy slick hands, she bravely cupped his sex. Before he could even groan, she stopped.

Enovese stood and moved behind him, washing his back, teasing her hand between his buttocks. Soapy slick, she rocked her hand into the crevasse, dipping low enough to tease his balls. Gently, she removed his hands from his head so she could wash his hair, which she did, working her way around until she faced him again. Pressing close, Enovese angled up until her lips held close to his. Chur stood very still, afraid of making a wrong move. She brushed her lips against his, not in a kiss, but in a teasing stroke. Water wet, her lips rubbed his, arousing and intoxicating. Working the lather into his chest hair, she trailed her hand down, painfully slow, until she grasped his sex. His head rolled back and he closed his eyes.

"Don't close your eyes, look at me."

Her voice was seductively soft, commanding, and compelling.

Chur gazed down at her.

Enovese betrayed no emotion as she held his gaze and worked her soapy slick hand up and down the swollen length of his cock. Alternately gripping and slipping, she eased her fists around him, tugging, pressing him against her belly. Softly, she cupped her lips to his and whispered, "Do you understand now, Harvester, that you need not force me? That I long to please you but only when the choice is mine?"

He nodded, brushing his mouth to hers. "Call me by my name."

Enovese kissed him then. She parted her coral lips, captured his, and teased her tongue against his. With a breath into his mouth, she whispered, "Chur."

She tasted of ambrosia, as did his name on the lush breath of her voice. Chur drank deeply of her taste, scent, and her longing. In a rush, he knew what a fool he had been, for Enovese would do anything to please him. He had but to ask. By forcing her, he destroyed the unique desire inherent within her.

Inflamed, he placed his hands to her buttocks, grasped, and lifted her until she stood on tiptoe. By pulling her close, he pressed his hand-wrapped cock against her belly. Such forced her into an awkward position, but he could not stop. Enovese let go of his prick and lifted her hands to his shoulders. His cock now slid uninhibited against her belly. Enovese angled until his cock dipped low, between her wet thighs; then she clamped them tightly together.

"I have caught you."

He chuckled and nodded, holding her body just as firmly. But then he realized the truth in her words; she had, indeed, caught him. He could not resist her.

Enovese rocked her hips, working his soapy slick cock between her water-slicked thighs, teasing him against the throbbing of her clit and the intense heat of her cunt. Much to his delight, Chur realized soap didn't make her slick, it was lust. For the first time in a long time, Enovese was not only wet, but profusely wet. Wanton. He tossed up a thank you to the god of Harvesters for letting him again know the slick passion of her desire. Yet still, he held still, for he did not want her to think he demanded anything. If he had to scream inside his own head, he would let Enovese dictate the pace and timing of this encounter.

"I want you, Chur." Enovese moved back and forth, rocking him between her legs, riding up high on the curve of his penis to stimulate her clit. She didn't take him inside. Her tightly clamped thighs were soft against his shaft, their pubic hair providing a delicious friction.

Chur lowered his mouth to her ear, and whispered, "I want you, Enovese." He pressed on the small of her back to steady her as they rocked faster and faster. Her wet hair was soft and slick, sliding his hand against her. His cock throbbed and felt so hard it almost hurt. An intense orgasm built within, lifting and tightening his balls against his body. Chur knew he wouldn't last much longer, but he wanted her to climax first. He demanded only that. For he had hurt her so much that he would rather suffer without climax than find release before she did.

Enovese breathed in rapid gasps as she dug her fingertips into his shoulders. She leaned her head back, catching the stream of water with the length of her hair, then leaned forward so the strands teased around their bodies. He imagined if someone saw them from a distance, they would think he embraced a water sprite.

Short, sharp gasps escaped her mouth. Enovese lifted her gaze to his. Her eyes lost focus, her lids barely stayed open, and she blinked in a dreamy slowness. Rocking her hips faster caused her eyes to open wide; then she clamped them shut. A long moan rose from her chest and tumbled out of her luscious lips. Her thighs quivered with the strength of her orgasm.

Her surrender to pleasure compelled his. Wave after wave of sensation rolled from the extremities of his body, gathering strength, only to erupt from his cock. Unable to continue with the smooth rocking pace, he jerked, and clutched at her hips, to steady her as he thrust between her slippery thighs. It was the most wickedly intense orgasm he'd felt in several cycles. Once spent, he held her close, murmuring to her ear, while the water flowed over them. Under the water, holding her tight, he felt reborn.

17

Enovese smiled to herself as she clung to Chur. It seemed she didn't have to worry about what to wear for him after all. A relief filled her, from not only the shattering orgasm, but also that Chur was himself again. Not the vicious master she'd come to hate, but the strong yet gentle man she loved.

He nuzzled her ear and said, "I missed you." His voice came so close to breaking. Longing and apology conveyed without a word. He would never apologize and she didn't expect him to. All she wanted was exactly what she had: a chance to be in his arms and experience the ecstasy of his touch for as long as she could. Because deep down, Enovese knew, even as she embraced him now, she would have to let him go.

Resigned, she kissed his chest. "I've missed you." She tilted her head back. As if she'd asked without words, he brushed his lips to hers in a welcoming kiss. A homecoming kiss that accepted their time together would be short, but it would also be unforgettable. The darkness of the last three cycles faded away as a new brightness emerged.

"There is something—" Enovese began.

"I need your—" Chur said.

Their voices overlapped, and Enovese smiled. "You first."

"Let's talk somewhere other than here."

Tenderly, he helped her dry her hair, then wrapped her in a towel. He dried himself off, dressed in a loincloth, and then offered her one of his shirts to wear. The simple shirt hung to her midthigh, but it was soft and smelled faintly of him. He rolled the sleeves up and kissed the tip of her nose.

He settled at the table and lifted the warming platters to serve himself. When she took her place by his side, he frowned.

"I wish for you to join me."

Touched, Enovese got a plate and sat to the side of him. They ate in silence. When they finished, she rose to clean up, but he asked her to wait. "I need your help."

A flutter of caution caused her belly to tremble. Again, she worried that his motives in treating her kindly were self-serving.

"Do you know anything about a tome?"

She considered for a moment. "The Harvester tome? It's part of your ceremonial gear." She retrieved the heavy book from the sacred chest. The metal and animal hide was dirty from passing through endless Harvester hands. There were a few blood smears on the cover, as several had no doubt received the tome shortly after killing the previous Harvester. When she placed the book before him, Chur turned it this way and that, baffled.

His brows lifted. "Have you read it?"

"No." Enovese realized her tone was defensive. She smiled and said, "I've always wanted to read it, but only the Harvester can open it. In my recollection you are the only Harvester who has ever even asked about it." She turned the book right side up and placed his palm on the cover. The metal clasps that wrapped the tome slid apart.

Chur considered the book, then her. With a grin he asked, "Do we dare?"

Almost too excited for words, Enovese managed, "I dare." She'd always wanted to peek inside to see if it followed the other texts she had access to. However, the book was rather slim, and she'd given up when none of the Harvesters expressed any interest in it. Disappointment crushed her when he flipped it open. Hand-written in a precise but spidery hand, the ink was faded and the pages smelled musty.

Chur let out a dissatisfied sigh. "I guess I expected something grander. And more understandable." He peered closely at the page. "It's almost but not quite our language."

Enovese nodded. "I think it was written at the time when they were moving away from the ancient language. Some of the words are in that language, some more modern, but before they'd standardized spelling." She pointed to a word. "Notice it has double vowels. And some words are spelled phonetically."

"Can you read it?" Chur lifted his gaze to her with a hopeful expression.

"I can. Do you want me to read it to you?"

He nodded and looked away. "I guess what Helton said was true. You are the brain and I am the brawn."

She stroked his forearm to reassure him. "Please don't think there is anything wrong with your brain, Chur. I've spent my life reading ancient texts. Do you think I could lift, let alone swing, an *avenyet*?"

His gaze roamed her form. "You wouldn't need to. A thousand men would eagerly line up to defend you."

His compliment flushed her cheeks. On the tip of her tongue fluttered the urge to say they wouldn't if they knew she was sterile, but she swallowed it. She didn't want to ruin this moment. Settling herself beside him, she began to read, but after a moment Chur stopped her.

"Skip to more interesting parts. I don't wish to hear about the glory of my role again." He rolled his eyes.

She laughed. "It is rather flowery and verbose. Was there something in particular you wanted to know about?"

His eyes darkened. He took her hand and smoothed his fingers between hers, as if he wished to hold her so she didn't bolt upon hearing his words. After clearing his throat, he said, "I wish to know about the *paratanist* selection ritual."

She almost asked why but refrained. It didn't matter if he wanted to know for his own information or if to further appease her by working her from this angle. What mattered was finding the truth. This tome, written between the time of the ancients and now, might contain the answers that had eluded her.

Since there was no table of contents, she had to skim through the text. "It doesn't appear to be organized in any way I can tell. It's almost a stream of consciousness with occasional direct quotes from one of the original texts." After blathering congratulations to the Harvester for attaining his mighty and powerful role, the tome offered practical information, such as how to maintain the ceremonial gear. Rather than leave Chur out, she murmured what each section spoke of and asked him to stop her if there was something of interest to him. He either waved his hand dismissively or shook his head. The small letters strained her vision and gave her a headache. She rubbed her eyes.

"Take a break for a moment." Chur pushed the book away. "You said you had something to tell me."

Enovese darted a glance to the door. "Have you ever noticed the carving on the door?"

"Not really." Chur considered for a moment, squinting and tilting his head. "It looks like two people hugging or . . ."

"Or?" she prompted him.

"Indulging in the lewd arts," he said, flashing her a smirk. "I never noticed an erotic carving graced my door."

"Wait here." She retrieved the chalice box from the chest and handed it to him. "I know you told me to return it, but I was afraid of getting caught."

Chur nodded. He looked a bit irked but not surprised that she refused to follow his direct order. He stroked his fingertips over the box and then lifted it up, comparing it to the door. "They appear to be the same."

"Also, all along the hallway, the gilded paint swirls echo this same pattern."

Chur moved as if to stand, then stopped. "I'll take your word for it." He darted a gaze from the box, the door, then ultimately to her. "Do you know what it means?"

"I was hoping you could tell me."

"You're the brain, not me." When she reprimanded his flippant tone with a frown, he shrugged, and said, "I have no idea. But this"—he touched a particular curve—"looks very familiar." He pushed up the edge of the shirt she wore. On the verge of slapping his hand and telling him to keep his attention off her body, she realized he was only lifting the shirt far enough to expose the scar on her thigh. "See? It's the same shape. Like a crescent moon."

Her mouth popped open. She sat down and compared her scar with the mark on the box. Time and the growth of her body had distorted her scar, but she saw the similarity at once. "You see, there is nothing wrong with your brain. I knew you would notice things I did not."

He only grunted at her compliment and offered her a wry smile. "How did you get the mark?"

"I do not know. From my earliest memories it has always been there." Frowning, considering the box and her scar, she let out a frustrated sigh. "Perhaps it doesn't mean anything. It could be a coincidence."

"I don't think so." Chur took the box from her and placed it on the table. He pulled her shirt down. He carefully considered his words and softly said, "It's a deliberate mark, Enovese, I'm fairly certain it's a brand."

A new and terrible shame flushed her entire body. Trying to control her voice, she asked, "Do you mean someone burned this mark on me?"

With effort, he met her gaze. "When a recruit doesn't perform up to par, they are branded on their forehead and sent home. After the mark heals, the scar darkens and looks much like the mark on your leg."

Tears blurred her gaze. "Will it never end? They take me from my parents, force me to be a servant, sterilize me, and then further mutilate me by burning a mark into my skin?" She didn't want to cry over something that she had no control over, and not in front of him. She was ashamed of what they did to her, but moreover, she feared her ability to deal with it. Once she'd accepted one horror, she discovered another, each more monstrous than the last.

Chur pushed his chair back and gathered her up into his lap. "I am so sorry, Enovese." Cupping his hand to her head, he pressed her face against his chest. "I wish there was something I could do."

Her arms tightened around his shoulders. As she listened to the soothing rhythm of his heartbeat, she thought he could claim her as bondmate and thus rescue her. She could not ask such a grand favor from him. He owed her nothing. She felt in that moment if she did ask, Chur would vow to do so, for honor would compel him to do so. Envisioning their lifetime together, where he would grow resentful, cautioned her to silence. Where once she'd been willing to trick him into claiming her, she found she could not do so now. She understood that deception and force would not bring her what she wanted.

What she wanted was Chur to claim her of his own free will because he loved her.

Chur cuddled her for a long time, his hand idly stroking her hair. He nuzzled the top of her head, murmuring sweet words and placing soft kisses. His strong arms sheltered and protected her. For this moment, she allowed herself the fantasy that he was her bondmate. With Chur at her side, she would be invincible. Together they would find out the truth and make those responsible pay. Almost as soon as she indulged the thought, she dismissed revenge fantasies, for the blame was on a 5,000-season-old prophecy. How could she condemn anyone for edicts written so long ago and faithfully followed to this day?

18

Chur wished he could find the words to comfort Enovese, but no words would erase her pain. The hurt ran too deep. If he could fight her pain with weapons, he could defeat the trauma fully, but all his strength gave him no advantage here.

"Why didn't you say something before?" Her voice rose barely above a whisper.

"About your scar?" He lowered his hand and stroked his fingers over the mark as tenderly as he could. "I guess I didn't really notice until tonight." Now he wished he'd kept his mouth shut. Why did he tell her something that was only bound to hurt her more? Cupping her chin, he tilted her head back, brushing his lips against hers. "It doesn't matter to me, Enovese. That mark doesn't mar your spectacular beauty."

Her brows furrowed and she pulled back. "Do you think I'm upset because the brand makes me ugly?" She pushed against his chest. Her voice rose. "I'm upset because someone burned a mark into me when I was a child!"

He tried to soothe her. "I'm sorry. I didn't mean—I'm trying—" Chur hung his head and took a deep breath before meeting her gaze. "I'm not a poet, Enovese. I don't know the right things to say. I know you are hurt and angry, but I didn't do this to you." He lifted his hands in a supplicating gesture. "I just wanted to comfort you."

All the fury fled from her expression. She stroked a fingertip over his scar. "I'm sorry. I'm not angry with you." She kissed the edge of his mouth. "I'm frustrated and upset. Every time I uncover new information, it only hurts me more. I want to know and yet I don't want to know."

She pulled the book toward her, but Chur pulled it away and closed the cover. The metal bands locked together. He pushed the tome aside. "That's enough of that for tonight."

"But I thought you wanted—"

"I do, but we won't solve the mystery in one night." He sighed and rubbed the tip of her nose with his. "Slow down, Enovese. We have time."

"Not enough."

He sensed a deeper meaning than just time to understand the *paratanist* selection ritual. Sitting very still, he met her gaze. He would not encourage her bondmate fantasy. He wanted her physically and he did care about her. He would move mountains and fight a thousand foes to help her, but he would not bond with a woman who could not give him children. It was that simple and that complicated. Cupping her chin, he said, "We will make the most of the time we have."

Fleeting, down in the depth of her jade green eyes, a shocked sadness flashed, then a resigned acceptance. "We will." She offered him a brave smile that looked entirely forced.

He didn't want to hurt her, but he refused to lie to her. "Do you wish to sleep?"

She shook her head. "My mind is too active. I don't think I could sleep." Curling close, she rested her head on his shoulder. "Tell me about where you came from."

He told her of Ampir, the region of his birth. Ampir lay at the foothills of the Onic Mountains, a rugged and harsh environment. The region was best known for trade in lumber, mined ores, and the flowers and leaves of the *estal* flower. "Most of the people in Ampir look like I do—tall, bronze skin, dark hair, and muscular."

"Even the women?"

"Yes." He chuckled against her head. "Perhaps not as bulky as I, but still, Ampirian women are fearsome warriors. Much taller than you." He caressed her hip and asked, "Where do you come from?" Chur thought she might come from Plete, the same region as Loban, for she had the same coloring.

"I do not wish to talk of me," she said softly. "Tell me more about Ampir."

Chur understood that she might not know her origins because of the complications of the *paratanist* selection ritual. Brushing over his fax pas, he said, "Since the men work in the mountains, the women defend the hearth and home. From youth, everyone learns how to fight and handle weapons. My region takes much pride in that many Harvesters have come from Ampir." He considered for a moment, then added, "Well, male Harvesters. We have never had a female Harvester."

Enovese glanced at him, her uplifted brows asking the question.

He scowled. "They say our women do not possess the softness of beauty. They say that Ampirian women are too harsh in appearance."

Enovese nodded for she understood they selected male Harvesters based on strength and battle prowess; however, they selected female Harvesters based on appearance and the esthetic values of beauty, whatever esthetics were in vogue at the time. Chur always thought male Harvesters had it easier, for their rules didn't change. Strength was easy to define and measure. Physical beauty was far more subjective, if not brutally harsh.

More than one woman had committed suicide over the condemnation that she was too ugly to be a Harvester.

"Did you love a woman there?" Enovese asked.

"No." Chur considered. "In my village, there were many lovely women, but I always knew that I wanted to be the Harvester, so I resisted temptation."

"A Harvester doesn't have to be a virgin."

"No, but he cannot have children. If a woman even raises the issue, the recruiter will look elsewhere. I simply didn't want to take the risk. I knew that my children would come later, when I could provide more for them than just a basic existence in Ampir." As soon as he said it, he wanted to take it back. He felt as if he'd just rubbed salt into her fresh wound.

Before he could sputter an apology, Enovese asked, "After the last Harvest, you will not return to Ampir?"

"No, I will stay here. Helton Ook will leave his post soon and I would like to be a handler." As one of the most popular and famous Harvesters, Chur fielded endless offers of potential military positions, but he most wanted to train recruits. He felt comfortable in the training room. Becoming a handler would let him utilize all the skills he possessed, and he could subtly choose those he felt most qualified for the position. Under his watch, Loban would not have passed the initial selection challenge. He could do little about it now, but once in a position of power as a handler, Chur would have far more control over the recruits. He would ruthlessly weed out the evil, the vicious, or those who did not truly hold to the spirit of the role. As he thought of this, he knew he'd violated his duty, but he honestly felt he held to principle. Chur cared about the Harvest. Despite the realization, the shocking understanding that he felt nothing during the Harvest, he still accepted the gift of virginity with reverence and respect.

Enovese smiled up at him. "I think you would be an excellent handler." She considered, frowned, then cautioned, "You do understand that you cannot tell the recruits the truth of the rituals."

He sighed. "That is the one aspect that troubles me. I remember being furious with Helton for not telling me the truth, but now I understand why he couldn't. He is bound by his role as much as you and I."

They sat in silence for a long time. Chur decided it wasn't an uncomfortable silence but a contemplative one. He thought Enovese might be thinking of what it would be like to serve a new Harvester and hear complaints about him as that Harvester's handler. Would such be torture for her? Knowing that he moved about the palace working, living, bonded, rearing children with another woman.

Would such bother him? Knowing Enovese was within the walls, so close but untouchable. He had a sudden flash of finding her alone, somewhere secluded, pushing her robe up and thrusting into her with crazed lust until a climax rendered them both gasping and breathless. A curious shame possessed him; he had not actually bonded and yet was already contemplating cheating on his mate with his *paratanist*.

His cock twitched against Enovese's hip.

She lowered her hand, pushed aside his loincloth, and teased her fingertips over the hardening flesh. "What are you thinking about? Please tell me this reaction is not from imagining yourself handling recruits."

He laughed. "I was thinking of you. How soft you feel, how sweet you smell." He slid his hand up her shirt and cupped her breast, teasing his thumb across her nipple until it hardened.

She moaned and arched her back, encouraging him without words.

Chur reveled in the honesty of her passion. Enovese held nothing back. Her oh-so-clever hand continued to tease him until he throbbed almost painfully.

She slid off his lap and stood looking at him. Her eyes were dreamy, slightly unfocused. She nibbled at her lower lip, then sat on the table before him, placing her legs on the arms of his chair, leaning back, as if offering herself as a banquet to him.

Just wrapping his hands around her slender ankles caused him to twitch. He caressed his way up her legs, exploring every inch of her. Her every breath and sigh excited him. He slid the shirt up, exposing the full of her legs, and kissed the crescent moon mark on her thigh as if he could erase it and the pain it embodied with his lips.

She sank her fingers into his hair, teasing the strands, stroking his ears, and subtly drawing his head farther up between her legs.

Chur smiled and nibbled her inner thighs. "You are terribly impatient."

"And you love it."

"I do. But you must learn patience, my lovely one." He grasped her ankles, lifting her legs up and apart, then plunged his tongue deep into her passage, sucking and chewing lightly, lifting his mouth to encircle her clit. She was deliciously wet, and her rich passion tasted wonderful. Pressing her legs back, he lowered his hands to her thighs to further open her to his exploration. Another surge pulsed through him when Enovese grasped her own ankles and held herself wide for him.

Constricting bands of pleasure tightened around his body, urging him to take her, but he wanted her to climax first. He wanted her soaking wet with sweat, passion, and dire need. Never again would he take her desire for granted. Teasing her with his fingers drew deeper moans from her, causing her to wriggle restlessly. Unable to hold her legs so widely apart, she let go and lay back with a purr of satisfaction. When he darted a glance up, he discovered she cupped her breasts and twisted her nipples between her fingers and thumbs, using the slick texture of his shirt to enhance her movements.

He took his time exploring her, tasting and licking until he'd discovered every sensitive spot. Her entire sex swelled and turned dark coral. Her clit would push through the folds of flesh for attention but then retreat when he acquiesced. Finding the right blend of soft and hard, slow and fast, proved most engaging. All his efforts pleased Enovese, who twisted and sighed, moaning ancient words of lust and encouragement. When he parted her swollen coral lips, exposing her straining clit, then flicked the rough side of his tongue, then the smooth backside over her clit, she arched her back and climaxed. Her thighs clamped around his head, but he lifted his hands, forced them apart, and continued to tease around her quivering passage. When the initial orgasm retreated, he seized on her clit again.

Enovese lifted up from the table, gasping and trying to push his head away. He refused. She struggled but only angled herself better for his mouth. He sucked her clit between his lips, flicking his tongue over the trembling flesh until another strong series of contractions washed over her.

Chur discovered tremendous satisfaction in pleasing her. His cock swelled and twitched, wanting to know the slick heat and wetness his mouth had created. He stood, pushing the chair back with his legs, then gazed down at her.

Her eyes were half open, her lips softly parted, her skin flushed a delicate pink. Her harvest-colored hair spilled around her head and all over the table in disarray. Some strands were still wet from their shower and contrasted the lighter strands, giving a depth to her tresses, as if her hair were alive.

She lifted her hands to him as if to draw him near.

"Lift your hands above your head." His voice sounded rough with need.

"As if I surrender?"

He nodded.

Enovese teased her hands up her body, molding the fabric to her form. She lifted her hands behind her head, fanning her hair out before finally relaxing them. Her pale limbs contrasted against the darkness of her hair, and her jade eyes sparkled with mischief.

Chur slid her down the table until her bottom rested against the edge. Her eyes widened when he placed her left foot on his hip. He knew she understood what he wished to do. He lifted her right foot until her leg pressed against his bare chest. An odd thrill possessed him for taking the sacrificial pose and using it now. To take the ritual and pervert it for his lust felt madly deviant and unbearably exciting. Just putting her into position twitched his cock, for his body responded automatically. His breathing fell into a steady rhythm. His gaze took in every detail of the sacrifice before him. She was not a virgin, but this was the first time they had come together in mutual passion in over three cycles, so it felt like a first time. The first time he had used the ritual to satisfy his needs.

Chur steadied himself, placing his legs wide, nudging the very tip of his cock to the slick lips of her sex. In the ancient language he said, "By might of the blade I claim that which belongs to me."

"I freely give myself to you." Enovese readied for the plunge by tensing her limbs.

Chur did not move.

Enovese lifted her head, confusion darting across her expressive face. Her lips parted with a sigh of surprise when he eased himself slowly inside. He would not rush. The lips of her sex parted around his cock, gripping him with a wet heat that contrasted the coolness of his shaft still without. An inferno of heat clutched the tip of him, compelling him to thrust, but all his training allowed him to hold steady and enjoy the contrast of sensations.

"Chur, I—"

"Do not speak, Enovese." His gaze fastened on hers. "Feel me. Feel my cock pushing into you, stretching you, possessing you. Feel how cool my cock is compared to your hot cunt. Do you feel this, Enovese?"

She nodded. Her eyelids fluttered as if she could not keep them open.

"Close your eyes, Enovese, and just feel me."

She did as he bid, closing her eyes, rolling her head back, and extending her arms farther above her head. She was such a lovely sacrifice, beautiful in her surrender. Her nipples swelled, tenting the fabric of his shirt, the collar open to expose the delicate length of her neck and the fragility of her collarbone. His oversized shirt only enhanced her tiny form, the vision surging power through him. What she said three cycles ago danced in his mind; that he was a man with desires and needs. He was a man and not a machine to harvest on command. Taking the ritual and turning it to his passions empowered him in a profound way. All his senses opened to capture this moment. Entranced by the vision of penetrating her, he watched as he slowly disappeared within the snug heat of her body. On a deep breath, he could smell and taste her passion. His hands felt rough against the smoothness of her skin. The crispness of his body hair stroked against her.

For a brief moment, he was within her body, feeling himself within her at the same time he felt his cock stretching her cunt. As soon as he captured the sensation, he lost it. But that singular feeling stayed with him as he pressed fully against her, burying himself completely.

Enovese arched her back, tilting her hips, taking just a bit more of him within, giving him another flash of sharing the dual sensation. When he caught Enovese's gaze, the awareness flooded him again. Somehow, locking his gaze to hers helped him access this amazing connection and hang on to it far longer.

Enovese must have felt it too for her eyes went wide, then focused sharply with his. When he tilted his head, questioningly, she nodded, and the sensation grew more complete. He was himself, separate and apart, but he was also her, separate and apart. Erotic and dizzying, he held tightly to her upraised leg yet felt his calloused hands against her flesh as if against his own. The intensity, the connection, grew as they moved slowly, almost dreamlike against each other. Flicking a finger across her clit shot electricity along every nerve in his body. When she cupped her breasts and twisted her nipples, he felt it in her nipples but also his own.

When he looked between their bodies and saw the brand upon her leg with his eyes and her looking through his eyes, he knew then the full of her pain and shame. In a bright blast, he understood all of her emotions about her forced role, her envy at his until she, in turn, saw his role through his eyes. At that moment, they fully exposed themselves to the other and a mutual empathy connected them far beyond the physical. He knew why she wished to bond with him; she knew why he simply could not.

Chur now fully understood how much his treating her like a *yondie* had hurt her emotionally. He'd stripped away her pleasure and degraded her into nothing but a body with conveniently placed holes. Feeling his actions, through her, shamed him in a way no verbal thrashing would. If he could, he would take those three cycles back. Since he couldn't, he showed her through his eyes that he would never hurt her that way again. Once they accepted the emotional gulf between them, their attentions returned to the physical connection.

Breathless, stunned, he rocked deeper, knowing the sensation of his cock and her cunt. An orgasm swept up through her into him and back to her again. Where he thought he would never know a climax as intense as the one he'd experienced within her mouth after the Harvest, it couldn't compare to the concentrated ecstasy that now galvanized his body and hers. Chur experienced all aspects of his orgasm and hers, every sensation in his body and hers in a simultaneous dual conscience. Unable to take any more, he closed his eyes, breaking the conduit, and collapsed against Enovese.

As they lay twined together, an odd emptiness caused a crushing depression. So intense was the loss that tears welled in his eyes. Shocked, embarrassed, he wanted to hide. Below him, Enovese took a shuttered breath. He realized she felt the same loss as he. Chur wrapped her up in his arms and lifted her from the table. He took her to the padded chair in the main room. After he curled her into his lap, they sat twined together, silent in the shock of the aftermath.

Never had Chur known such sensations, such a connection to another. Profound in the moment, it now left him bereft. Drained of both physical and mental energy, all he had left was a swirl of confusing emotions. Pressed against his chest, Enovese cried softly, her tears falling into the mat of his hair, then sliding down his flesh. He could feel each drop and all the emotions behind them, and he wondered if she could feel his.

Chur cupped her chin, lifted her face to his, and kissed her mouth, not with passion but with a deep emotional connection. Enovese kissed him back, clinging to his shoulders, a tormented gasp torn from her lips to puff against his.

He wanted to say a million things but could not form the words. After what they shared, words were no longer adequate. Deep down to his soul, he knew Enovese. He knew her torments, her passions, but most of all, the shocking depth of her unconditional love for him. Enovese loved him. She risked her life to be with him. She would do anything to help him succeed, even if such ran counter to what she wanted. It broke his heart, not only that he did not love her back, but that Enovese now *knew* he did not love her back. Chur wanted to say he was sorry, but how did one apologize for not having the same feelings?

"Enovese, I—"

She shushed him with a lingering kiss. When she drew back, she caught his gaze. "I knew the truth before tonight. I think, deep in my heart, I have always known that you would never feel the same for me." Tenderly, she brushed away his tears, then stroked the scar along his face. "I am not angry, Chur, for now I do understand how much you care."

Again, she expressed her love by letting him off the hook with a gracious spirit. "Enovese, I can promise you one thing; I will do everything I can to help you uncover the truth about the *paratanist* selection ritual. It's not much, but—"

"It's enough." Enovese untwined herself from his lap and offered her hand. "You must sleep, for more training awaits you come morning."

Chur cupped her hand and stood, placing a kiss in the center of her palm. "Is there anything I can do?"

Her lips parted with an automatic dismissal but then closed as she glanced away, considering. "I ask only one thing."

He waited, willing to grant her anything she asked.

She took a deep breath and caught his gaze. "For the time we have left, until the next Harvest, I ask only that you be with me."

His confusion must have been evident.

"With me as if we are bondmates."

He wanted to say no. He wanted to caution her that such would only hurt her in the end, when the fantasy must end, when he must choose another during the next Harvest. However, in her eyes he saw that she understood such was only an indulgence. Perhaps, he thought, such would give her the strength to move on with another when he was gone. Despite his reservations, Chur nodded his agreement and took her to his bed where they slept twined together pretending they would be this way forever.

19

Enovese woke wrapped in Chur's arms. For a moment, she reveled in the sensation that she was his bondmate and in her rightful place. Reality intruded when she knew she must rise, prepare his meal, his gear, and send him off for another day of training so that he could win the challenge and thus choose another. Refusing to worry over the future, Enovese rose determined to enjoy what she had now.

As she performed her chores, she thought back to last night and the connection she'd shared with Chur. Alone, she'd split her attention between her body and his, but not where she could feel both simultaneously. When she had looked into his eyes a line of energy flowed between them. Shocking yet powerful, wonderful, and then terribly painful when the connection abruptly ended. She had touched something ethereal only to be dumped unceremoniously to the ground. She grieved for the loss and then for the knowledge she had gained. She now knew Chur did not love her, but she also felt within him a hidden emotion, something that Chur seemed oblivious to, something that she herself did not understand. He had so thoroughly convinced himself that he could never love her that he believed it a truth. Below that conviction hid something deeper than the care he willingly expressed.

As soon as she placed the food on the table, Chur sat up in bed, stretched, and smiled at her, a deliciously sensual smile, filled with a thousand lusty promises that tingled awareness all the way down to her toes. His tousled black hair only added to his untamed appeal. He flung the covers back, exposing his muscular body and his semihard state. With a crook of his finger he called her to his side, then pulled her into his bed, masterfully turning her to her back so he could peer down at her with his summer-sky eyes.

Expecting a kiss, she tilted her face up, but Chur only glanced down at her, his eyes searching as he asked, "What happened last night?"

"I do not know." Sneaking a kiss from him, she then fell back and said, "As I told you, I've been able to place my awareness within you but not into my body and yours simultaneously."

Chur nodded; then his lips descended to capture hers in a kiss that expressed desire, care, and unbridled passion all at once. He pulled back, considering her. "I do not think we should do that again."

Enovese wanted to ask why but she knew: The unbelievable ecstasy of the connection hurt too much when broken. Softly, she said, "I did not cause it to happen, so I don't know how to control it."

His brows lowered. "I think it came from me. I felt brief flashes; then I looked into your eyes and something clicked, locked, and then the energy flowed both ways." He kissed her again, gently easing his way between her legs.

"Perhaps the position helped the phenomena to occur." Enovese wrapped her legs around his hips drawing him up until his cock rested against her slick sex.

A deep chuckle rumbled his chest against her, causing his prick to tease between her lips and awaken her clit.

"What?" she asked.

He nipped her nose. "I like this way of discussion." He lifted his hips, sliding his cock into her with one long, slow plunge, and sighed. "I think, from now on, we should have all our talks this way."

His full submersion elicited a purr, and she tightened her legs and the inner muscles of her passage. "It would make it far more difficult to argue."

For a time they simply rocked together, keeping their gazes locked. She could feel sparks of the connection, but nothing clicked and locked like last night. This was softer, a fragile thread, wrapping and tugging, not binding.

"Why do you think the position had something to do with it?" Chur asked, rolling his hips around to better angle his thrusts.

Enovese raised and lowered her hips, stroking her clit against his crisp pubic hair. Lost in the rising pleasure, she had difficulty answering his question. "Because I think your body undergoes a change for the Harvest ritual. To perform it without all the oils and drugs might open your mind to such a connection."

As the pacing of his thrusts increased, he punctuated each thrust with a word of his answer. "That . . . could . . . explain . . ." Chur was too busy kissing her to finish his answer.

Her body sizzled with heat as they worked against each other. Beads of sweat caused them to slip and slide, and all conversation was lost between kisses and gasping growls. This was the first time she had felt Chur on top of her, the first time they had shared his bed in this way, and even though he balanced his weight on his elbows, his massive body pinning her aroused her on a new level. Captured and held below him, she felt vulnerable and small but very safe and protected.

Chur increased the pace, his mouth seeking out her ear. Hot and moist, he breathed, "Talk to me in the ancient language."

Enovese urged him on with every lusty word she knew. The old language had a melodic fluidity that lent itself to such salacious pleadings. She knew he did not understand but half of what she said, but the tone, her gasping delivery between his powerful thrusts, clarified the meaning.

Between ragged breaths, Chur echoed some of the words, placing them at the end of his driving thrusts, catapulting her to delirious rapture. Lifting up so he balanced on his hands, Chur pounded into her with all his strength and an ever-building speed. She thought from a distance his movements would appear brutal but for the way she wrapped her legs around him, urging him on with every bit of strength she possessed. She wanted to feel all of his masculine power expending into her, filling her, pressing her into the softness of his bed.

She stroked her hands up through the thick, dark hair of his chest, now wet with sweat, to cup his shoulders. Sweat plastered his hair to his face, and he flicked it back impatiently without missing a beat. He kept his eyes closed, perhaps to guard against what had happened last night. An animalistic snarl darted across his lips. In the ancient tongue, he ordered her to climax, surprising her with his command of the language.

His wicked thrusts rubbed his pubic hair hard against her clit, causing a delicious orgasm to tighten her around him, her cunt gripping his cock, compelling his orgasm to shudder his body against her. With one last lunge and a snarled cry, he collapsed on her for a brief second. His weight was such she could not breathe, but she wrapped her arms around him, holding him, reveling in the brief moment of fusing flesh and her utter and willing submission to him.

Angling up on his elbows, he took his weight from her. He chuckled at her gasping indrawn breath. Kissing her softly, he said, "I didn't mean to crush you."

"Your weight felt wonderful but longer than that . . ." Her voice trailed off when she locked her gaze on his. That tingling awareness, weak threads of the full connection, simmered between them and his eyes went wide.

She thought he would look away, but he simply held her gaze, exploring the sensation, as did she. This wasn't as deep as last night; a weaker connection, but still she could feel fringes of his physical body and lightly touch his mind. She knew his satisfaction at having pleased her and the relief of his release, but then his pain that no matter how many times he found his release within her, he could never impregnate her. As this last darted into her awareness her eyes went wide, causing him to frown, but still, he didn't break the fragile connection.

Softly, he said, "I am sorry. That is not something I would have told you, but this, this phenomena as you called it, doesn't give me much choice."

Enovese touched his face. "I am not angry, it's how you feel, and I understand." For just as she knew this truth from him, he could now feel how much she wished for the same thing, that she too believed it was the only issue holding them away from each other.

Bit by bit the connection fell apart until they were simply gazing into each other's eyes.

Chur rolled to his side, snuggling her against him as he drew the covers over their cooling bodies.

Toying with his chest hair, tracing her finger along the shaved scar, Enovese said, "If we linger much longer, I'm afraid you will be late for training."

Chur laughed. "I think I've already had my workout for the day."

Nibbling his ear, she said, "I humbly suggest, Harvester, that you do not tell that to your handler."

"That would not do." Chur kissed the tip of her nose and rolled out of bed.

She followed him to the table. Once she served him from the warming platters she stood at his side.

Chur frowned. "No more of that, Enovese. If we are to play at bondmates, I expect you to share my table as well as my bed."

Delighted, Enovese joined him and they ate in silence. Afterward she moved to the bathing unit, but he declined saying he did not have time. She helped him don his gear.

At the door, he cupped her chin, placed a kiss to her lips, and murmured, "I will not be late."

Before he could move away, she captured his face with both her hands, kissed him deeply, then asked, "Is there anything you would like me to have ready for you?"

Chur considered her for a moment, then whispered against her lips, "Surprise me."

As she cleaned and set his rooms to rights, she considered how she could surprise him tonight. A giddy thrill caused her skin to tingle, and a cool shower didn't quash her wayward thoughts.

What Chur had said about his place of birth, Ampir, and the particulars of the selection of female Harvesters set her mind to a new path of research: Who set the values of beauty, and by whom were the candidates judged?

Donning her robe, Enovese went to the library and delved into the stacks. Since her entire training focused on serving the male Harvester, she'd never bothered to read anything about the female Harvester prophecy. Now, to her surprise, she discovered major differences, in not only the selection but also the preparation.

Recruiters scoured the regions hunting for women of surpassing beauty, but they also culled women who had competed in a local contest based wholly on their physical allure. From these regional contests, or the recruiters' own whimsical selection, those chosen would be taken to the palace to compete in another contest where they were expected to display not only beauty but skills such as singing, playing an instrument, composing poetry, or dance. From this contest, a panel of judges, composed of the magistrate and others in high authority, would select a winner to harvest the males who came of age.

A female Harvester must compete in the palace contest every ninth cycle to retain her title. Rarely did a female Harvester serve more than two seasons before another replaced her, for the peculiars and particulars of beauty were ever changing. Since recorded history, only one female Harvester had kept her title for five seasons. Arianda Rostvaika had done so by reinventing herself for each contest and displaying a wealth of skills in music, dance, and poetry. Her reign had come to end when she abruptly withdrew from the palace contest during what would have been her sixth season. Despite her diligent search, Enovese could find no explanation for Arianda's hasty abandonment of her role or what had happened to her afterward.

Where Chur must compete in the challenge, a contest based solely on physical prowess, this woman had held her own against those younger than she by possessing surpassing beauty, grace, and a multitude of skills.

As Enovese read further, she agreed with Chur that a male Harvester had things much easier in that his skills could be quantified and measured. How exactly did one distill beauty and the comely arts into a definable measurement? For the first time, Enovese found comfort in her misery at her position; yes, the male and female Harvesters vied for their role of their own free will, but that didn't mean the rules were more pleasant or agreeable.

Recognizing the duality of the male and female Harvester roles, Enovese searched for the female equivalent to the ceremonial chalice. She found the answer but also found it perplexing, raising far more questions than it answered. After the Harvest, a female Harvester retired to her rooms where her *paratanist* inserted a thick cylinder into her passage, pleasured her to climax, then she slept with the device buried deep within. Come morning, her *paratanist* would pleasure her again, remove the device, and then deliver it to the magistrate. There was no information on what happened to it at that point. Again, she wondered why they would want such samples from the Harvesters? And what exactly was the sample from the female Harvester? If they took the male Harvester's sperm, then they would take the female Harvester's . . .

"Eggs."

When Enovese realized she spoke aloud, she darted a quick gaze about the stacks. Relief washed over her when none noticed. Relaxing the rules around Chur was beginning to affect her in public, and that simply wouldn't do. One mistake could bring a multitude of troubles down on her head.

Enovese replaced the books and exited the library but doubled back and headed in the direction of the female Harvester's suite of rooms. She didn't think the guards, if there were any stationed, would notice she did not belong there, for the only difference between her robe and a male *paratanist*'s robe was a notch cut into the hood. The V was the only mark that indicated she was female. As she worked her way down the halls, she noticed the same golden filigree paint slowly resolving into the twined figures that graced Chur's door and the chalice box.

The door to the Harvest room was closed. Darting her gaze up and down the hall, Enovese didn't see anyone, so she reached out and pushed on one of the double swinging doors. She had only a brief glimpse inside before a guard turned the corner and strode in her direction. Enovese turned away from the Harvest room and moved toward the guard, hoping the door would swing closed before the guard noticed.

Behind her, she heard him mumble something; then she heard a bang and a loud click. He'd just locked the door. Disappointed, Enovese continued up the hallway away from him.

Once she rounded the corner she looked back and discovered the guard stood in front of the Harvest room doors. She wondered why. What was in there that needed to be guarded?

As she returned to Chur's suite of rooms, she passed by his Harvest room. No guard but the door was firmly locked. What needed to be protected in there? She mentally compared the male and female rooms, and realized the only difference was that where Chur's had a massive table for the sacrifices, the female room had pallets on the floor, which made sense for the ease of the Harvest. Each male sacrifice would lay supine on a pallet with *umer* keeping him erect so the female Harvester could lower herself upon his shaft.

Paintings of the previous Harvesters lined both rooms, but Enovese didn't have enough time to study those in the female's room. She desperately wanted to see the paintings of Arianda Rostvaika. What would such a compelling woman look like? And what happened to her after she abandoned her role? Had she left for a bondmate? From what Enovese had read in the stacks, female Harvesters rarely selected their mates from the sacrifices. Most ended up bonded to men in high authority. Ambo Votny had bonded to a female Harvester named Litha Emmel. She remembered this for Chur had attended the mourning rites for Litha during his first season as Harvester. Enovese had never seen Litha but heard she was a delicate beauty from the Gant region. Litha had died in her sleep at a bare forty-six seasons of age. Enovese remembered the event for it was the first time Ambo had spilled something on Chur's dress uniform. From that moment on, Chur had a strong dislike for Ambo. For not only the stain but also that Ambo had seemed oddly jocular at his bondmate's mourning rites. Chur said Ambo had not been outright jolly, but he drank as if it were a celebration and not a time for bereavement.

A million questions swirled in her mind as Enovese entered Chur's rooms. Chur sat at the table hunched over the tome. His face was a mask of annoyance as he squinted at the text. When he heard her enter, he looked up and the frustration fell away into genuine pleasure as he smiled.

"I cannot tell you how pleased I am to see you." Wet black hair clung to his head, and a few drops of water traced down his chest. Drops caught in his chest hair and sparkled like crystals.

Enovese pushed her hood back and echoed his smile. "I'm sorry I wasn't here to help you wash."

"As am I." His grin turned deliciously wicked. "However, I did notice cleaning up is far faster without you but not nearly as enjoyable." Chur pushed the chair back, stood, and opened his arms to her.

Touched by his welcome, Enovese practically ran into his embrace. As she pressed her cheek to his chest, she smelled lingering traces of soap. All her questions and concerns melted away in his arms. For a long moment, they simply clung to each other until a rumble from Chur's belly caused both of them to laugh.

"Clearly my stomach has missed you as well."

Enovese moved to start the evening meal. Chur surprised her by following and insisting he wanted to help.

"Bondmates share the chores, do they not?"

She nodded and fought to suppress her joy. Despite how strange it felt to have him working beside her, it also pleased her that he had every intention of holding to the agreement to live as bondmates. However, his culinary skills left much to be desired. He handled the slim knives like weapons, attacking the food rather than preparing it.

She stilled his hand. "Cut even pieces so the meat will cook evenly." She moved his hand over the raw *aket* showing him how to cube it rather than shred it. "*Aket* is very tender and easily ripped apart. See how a slow, smooth stroke of the blade keeps the chunks intact?"

Chur nodded. "I guess too many years of training have ruined me for the kitchen. Or perhaps I am thinking of Loban while I work."

"Did something happen during training?" Enovese readied the *vacsear*.

"Nothing beyond the usual."

Enovese sensed a hesitance in his tone and then noticed he again attacked the *aket*. "If you do not wish to discuss your training, then—"

"It's not that." Chur cut her off, then slowed his movements. "I am concerned that Loban will not be the only one to issue a challenge."

Enovese considered. Usually the recruits battled amongst themselves to determine who would issue the formal challenge, but that did not prevent several from doing so. "Do you think Loban is compelling these recruits to challenge you?"

"That is exactly what I think. If I must fight several before Loban, then he will have a distinct advantage when his turn comes."

Enovese placed the cubed *aket* into the *vacsear*. As the machine drew the air out it seared all sides of the meat simultaneously. "Isn't Loban generally disliked by the recruits?" she asked, for she wondered why any of them would help Loban in his scheme.

"That is what I thought." Chur washed the knife and cutting surface. "It is not to their advantage to issue a formal challenge, for if they lose they will die. To challenge amongst themselves only results in a bit of damaged pride, not death."

Enovese turned the food out into the warming platters. Chur helped her carry everything to the table. As they ate, Enovese speculated about what would compel the recruits to do something so foolish. "It is as if they wish to kill themselves by your hand."

Chur abruptly stopped chewing and cast her a shrewd glance. He finished his mouthful and thoughtfully said, "Better death than disgrace."

It was one of many credos that recruits learned by rote, but it was also one of the most powerful. "But there is no disgrace in being a recruit."

Chur sighed. "No disgrace, but for those at the lower end there isn't anything for them beyond the training room. Only the top recruits become palace guards. For the lower ranks, all that awaits them are menial palace jobs or a position in the palace army. They are discouraged from bonding, and if they do, they are allowed only one child."

Enovese had never considered what happened to the recruits who didn't advance. "Do they not have the option of returning to their homelands?" She always thought they returned to their regions with some glory for having gotten into the Harvester training.

"No, once they accept the position of recruit, they can never leave the palace, unless they are banished."

"With a brand upon their forehead."

Chur gave a grim nod.

"With so little to look forward to, I do not think it would take much persuasion to convince them to challenge you. From their point of view, they have nothing to lose. Death at your hand would carry more honor than a lowly position."

Chur lifted his brows. "But who is doing the persuading?"

Enovese mimicked him. "You already know the answer to that."

Chur considered the food on his plate. "The one with the most to gain: Loban Daraspe."

20

Chur entered the training room early and stationed himself in a central location so he could observe without being obvious. Recruits came in small groups and warmed up before engaging in mock battles. He noticed several pushed harder than the others did, almost as if they were desperate to advance. It wasn't unusual for recruits to train hard, but these men exuded a frantic air. His critical eyes noted their strengths and their weaknesses. None would be a match for him. Some were strong but lacked dexterity. Others were dexterous but lacked raw power. No matter how hard they trained, they simply wouldn't improve much beyond their current skill level. It was despicable for someone to convince them otherwise.

Loban entered and Chur watched without drawing attention to himself. At some point during the day, Loban engaged each of the strugglers, as Chur decided to call them, in a sparring event. On the surface, Loban appeared to be helping them improve, but Loban had never shown such generosity before. Loban had always taken pleasure in defeating the raw recruits, but now he took pains to coach them.

For his own evil ends, Chur thought, but he knew if he openly accused Loban of treachery, then Chur would again be issuing a minor challenge. Such would only encourage Loban and perhaps give credence to whatever tale he told to motivate the recruits. As Chur watched, he noticed Helton observing Loban as well, and he wondered if Loban merely put on an act to please his handler. Perhaps Helton had instructed Loban to spend more time with the recruits to assess their strengths and weaknesses. Chur refused to jump to any conclusions. He would wait and observe.

After a brief cooldown, Loban exited the training rooms with Helton at his side. As casually as possible, Chur moved near Phavage Nerys. Phavage was extremely tall and slender, possessing more speed than strength. His hair was stark white, and his eyes were a luminous pink that were indicative of his region of Ries. At one time, the Ries region was famous for supplying female Harvesters, but white hair and pink eyes had fallen out of fashion. Chur knew there wasn't a single male Harvester from the Ries region. Riesian women were ethereal and lovely, but their men didn't possess the physical form to rise over the men from harsher regions. Six of the nine cycles plunged Ries into darkness, which gave its residents exceptional eyesight and pale complexions but little else.

Phavage cast Chur a dubious glance as he grunted his way through a solo practice with the *dantaratase*. Phavage twisted and thrust the tall staff with marked precision. Droplets of sweat splattered to the floor, but Phavage deftly avoided slipping by planting his long, skinny feet firmly to the aged wood. Chur admired his skill but knew his finesse with one weapon would not help him during a formal challenge.

"Why do you watch me, Harvester?" Phavage continued to twirl the staff with his slender white hands.

"I admire your technique."

Pink eyes narrowed to angry red slits. "You hope to intimidate me." With a flick of his wrist, Phavage snapped the staff vertical and tapped the floor with a sharp *thunk*.

"Only if you are intimidated by one who watches." Chur met Phavage's glare without malice.

Tendrils of white hair brushed narrow shoulders when Phavage tilted his head. "You have lost your standing, Harvester. Even your handler seeks to destroy you."

Chur digested this information. Would Loban claim the orders had come from Helton himself? Such a claim would bolster Loban's position that he wasn't instigating the mass challenge but simply following orders.

Phavage smirked. "You had three seasons to choose, but your arrogance held sway."

Chur lifted his brows. "Arrogance did not give me the strength to defeat any challengers, of which there was none. Do you think your righteous indignation will allow you to triumph?"

Phavage's eyes went wide. Perhaps he was just now realizing that arrogant or not, Chur wasn't going down easily. Phavage lifted his chin. "You are not special, Harvester, and this season there will be challengers, and you will lose. Not by one hand but by many hands. Together, we will weaken you and overcome your arrogance and your strength."

Chur's chuckle wiped the smirk off Phavage's face. "Many hands to weaken me so Loban can emerge victorious. Have you not considered that he is using you as fodder? Loban encourages you to challenge me for it helps him. If he was secure in his ability, he would not need your assistance to defeat me."

Confusion twisted Phavage's features into a mask. "Loban? He will not challenge you this season."

Before Chur could question him further, Phavage turned on his heel and placed the *dantaratase* against the wall. If this scheme wasn't enacted by Loban to win the challenge, then who would be the ultimate challenger? When Chur looked up, he gazed into golden eyes flecked with brown. Sterlave flicked back a hank of deep brown hair. A look of regret mingled with determination said it all.

Sweat poured off Sterlave as he trained with the *avenyet* against three opponents. His muscles bulged causing his veins to stand out as he twirled and defended himself against all three attackers. Fluid, dance-like movements allowed Sterlave to deflect an attack by one opponent, then launch a counterattack on another. As Chur watched, he suddenly realized Sterlave was not a raw recruit anymore. In the last few cycles, Sterlave had transformed into an extremely strong and dexterous fighter.

A sinking feeling gripped Chur as he left the training room. Sterlave would be a match for him now. If a handful of other challengers first weakened him, Sterlave would have no problem finishing him off. Even without the others, Sterlave possessed the drive and fortitude to launch a brutal challenge all on his own.

Had Chur been so wrapped up in his problems that he hadn't noticed the shifting winds? All along, he'd been preparing himself to face Loban, a man he had no problem killing. Chur did not feel the same about Sterlave, a man he actually liked. Since the challenge was to the death, Chur would have no choice. He considered, then rejected the idea of talking Sterlave out of the challenge, for what waited for him? If Chur convinced Sterlave and the others to wait one season, that Chur was determined to choose from this year's Harvest, the role of Harvester would likely fall to Loban. Sterlave would have to wait another season and then challenge Loban. There was no benefit to Sterlave in waiting.

The bigger question was why Loban had unofficially withdrawn from the challenge. Orchestrating this group effort had come from someone, and if not Loban, then who? Sterlave didn't seem to possess the maliciousness this scheme required, but perhaps the rape had had a profound effect upon him. Sterlave might be more willing to confront Chur rather than his rapist.

Questions surged through Chur's mind as he entered his rooms. His thoughts quieted when he spied Enovese at the table with the tome open before her. Tears shimmered in her eyes, but she hurriedly blinked them away. She trembled as she stood and moved toward him to help him remove his gear.

"What's wrong, Enovese?"

She shook her head and drew him to the bathing unit. Silently, she washed him and refused to answer his questions or even meet his gaze. All through prepping the meal and eating, she kept her head lowered, a posture not of pain but shame.

When she rose to remove the dishes he pulled the tome to him and peered at the words. Frustrated by his inability to read, he glared harder at the pages, but it didn't help.

Enovese entered and her eyes went round with horror. She tried to pull the book away from him, but he placed one massive hand on the open pages. "Even if you managed to take it away, I would simply take it back."

She let go and slumped into the chair next to his.

"Tell me what you discovered."

She shook her head in refusal.

He repeated his command with a stronger tone.

On a deep breath she said, "I know where I came from."

He thought the knowledge would please her but apparently not. What had she discovered about the *paratanist* selection ritual that would cause her such shame? He pushed the tome to her and demanded she read the passage to him.

Her hands trembled as she pulled the book toward her. Tears gathered in her eyes and slid down her cheeks as her lips quivered. She started to read, then stopped on a gasping breath.

"Stop." Chur pushed the tome aside. He wanted to know, but Enovese was so upset it was cruel to force her. "Come here."

When he opened his arms, she curled up in his lap and buried her face against his chest. He murmured soothing words as he stroked her hair. Again, he wished he could help her, but he simply didn't know how. Words of comfort felt forced and flat; only his touches seemed to reassure her. He lifted her with ease and took her to their bed. When his large fingers fumbled at the tiny clasps of her robe, she offered him a small smile and undid them. She slipped the rough fabric off and climbed into bed. Chur removed his loincloth and joined her.

Enovese spooned up to him. He traced idle patterns on her shoulder until she surrendered to sleep. Too many concerns kept him from joining her in slumber. Questions about the upcoming challenge filled his mind. He had no choice but to fight any and all who wished to confront him. Unlike Loban, Chur could not simply withdraw. Either Chur defended his position or he would die. If Loban was not behind the mass challenges, who was? Sterlave just didn't seem capable of such a plan, but moreover he would have no pull with the other recruits. They would not seek to help him, for they would gain nothing in return. Such was true of Loban as well. Helping him would serve no purpose to the recruits.

A terrible foreboding filled Chur's belly when he realized the only one who could enact such a plan would be Helton Ook. As a handler, Helton could influence the recruits and convince them such a move was to their benefit. Could Helton have decided that Chur would never choose a bondmate and getting rid of him was the only option? Why would Helton care about how long a Harvester chose to remain the Harvester? What would removing Chur do for Helton? Helton had to gain something from this scenario, but Chur couldn't summon a single answer. He gnawed at the question until sleep finally pulled him down to darkness.

Chur woke with his semihard cock planted between Enovese's lush lips. He grew harder as she mouthed him, using her hands to further tease his sensitive flesh. He glanced down but found her eyes closed as she focused to her task. Coral-colored lips slipped slowly from the tip to encompass the head. Her hands, soft and smooth, gripped his shaft in tormenting pleasure. Once he was fully rigid, she lifted up and straddled his hips, rocking her slick sex against him. Her movements were graceful and precise, but she kept her eyes firmly closed, lost in pure sensation.

When he reached for her, she pressed his hands back beside his head, forcing surrender. Even though he had the power to flip her and do as he wished, he indulged her. Chur would never consider himself submissive, but if Enovese wished to command him for this moment, he was willing. He closed his eyes and kept his hands flat to the bed, palms open to the ceiling. With the absence of sight, he allowed his awareness to flood into his other senses.

Her body smelled of passion, spicy and rich; as he took a deep breath, he could almost taste her unique essence. Chur felt the wet heat of her sex sliding against his cock. Enovese was so deliciously slick she coated him after three languorous passes. Gods torment him, but he wanted to taste her. He wanted to suck at the source of her lusty scent and know it deep into his mouth, deep into his lungs.

When she leaned over him, he felt pebbled nipples pressed to his flesh, then her lips to his. Firm, ravenous, like the first kiss they shared, Enovese teased her tongue to his. Her mouth tasted sleepy sweet.

He lifted his hands to pull her closer, but she pushed his hands back to the bed. His growl caused her to smile against his mouth. Now that he was unable to touch her, he found he desperately wanted to. He wanted to cup the back of her head and hold her while he plundered her mouth. He longed to tangle his fingers in her harvest-colored hair and feel the strands tickle across his chest. He wanted to grasp her hips and rock her against him, then lift her up so he could plunge inside. To stop himself from doing any of those things, he clasped his hands together and put them behind his head.

He felt her smile as she kissed him; then she lowered her mouth to his ear. Enovese did not speak but only moaned, very low and deep, right to his ear. Her panting breath, moist and warm, aroused him further, and his penis twitched against her belly. Every muscle in his body went taut as he tried to keep his hands behind his head. Her lusty moans increased as she snuggled her tummy to his penis, sliding it this way and that, tormenting him with the promise of her soft skin. Sliding her hips up allowed her to stroke him with her pubic hair. The contrast between her smooth belly and textured hair caused him to groan and clutch his hands to fists.

He wanted to be inside her.

Only his skill in resisting, learned from the ritual of control, permitted him to stay passive. Anticipation lifted him higher. Expectation always made that final release shattering. The only way he could resist was by reminding himself that every bit of torment would be repaid a thousand-fold when he climaxed.

Enovese lifted her upper body away from his and teased her braided hair along his face, his neck, his nipples, then down to his shaft. She used the tufted end like a brush, stroking his length, then around and around the tip. His pulse pounded in his ears and caused his cock to bounce with each thud of his heart. If he could not touch her, he damn well would look at her, but when he opened his eyes, she cast her gaze down and lowered her face.

"Enovese?" He refused to lay passive when it was clear she was avoiding his gaze and had been doing so since last night. He cupped her chin, but she kept her eyes closed and shook her head, then pressed his hands back.

"No." He captured her wrists. "Something's wrong and I want you to tell me what."

She struggled briefly. "I will, but please, let me have this first."

He wanted to demand his way, but her plaintive whisper silenced him. If the hurt inside her could be soothed with a morning of sweet indulgence, he would gladly give her this. Chur placed his hands behind his head.

Enovese slid off him, turned away, and then straddled his hips with her back to him. Placing her hands against his knees, leaning forward, she lowered herself until just the tip of him waited at her passage. She held this arrangement for a long time, allowing Chur to gaze at her heart-shaped bottom and enjoy this new position. He found the lack of eye contact took away his feelings of intimacy. He thought that might be her desire; she did not wish the conduit, that amazing phenomena of connection, to occur, for if it did, what she held secret would be laid bare.

Longing to complete their union caused him to twitch, and she slid slowly down until she engulfed him completely. Her facing away altered the angle of her passage, gripping him tighter along the underside of his shaft, putting pressure at the most sensitive spot where the head joined the shaft. As she settled herself, snuggling his penis within, the walls of her clenched him in a unique way.

Enovese did not move, and Chur allowed his gaze to roam over her gently rounded shoulders, to the narrow nip of her waist, then down to her bottom. With her weight on his hips, her fanny became more heart-shaped, and the two dimples on either side deepened. He wanted to trace his finger along them and then the split between her cheeks so he could slip his finger inside her tight nether passage. Keeping his hands to himself became ever more difficult. When she began to rock her hips forward and back, it was almost impossible. She didn't lift and thrust, but rocked to and fro, as if she danced upon him. Her subtle movements rolled his cock inside her, her passage clutching and sliding, clenching then releasing.

As much as Chur found this novel sensation enticing, he deeply missed being able to see her face. When caught in the ecstasy of the moment, Enovese's expression conveyed such rapture it heightened his own. In this position, he could only watch the delicate motions of her muscles below her milky pale flesh, but as she continued her luscious dance, her head went back, causing her braided hair to swing in a mesmerizing loop that mimicked her hips. Round and round in tiny rings she circled his cock. Her moans deepened and he could just barely hear her whispered murmurs of lusty ancient words. Her hands lifted from his knees and stroked up along her outer thighs to capture her breasts. He could not see, but he knew she had cupped them and tweaked the nipples to full attention. She then drew her lithe limbs above her head, arching her back, as if in surrender to a powerful god, with he the altar upon which she offered her sacrifice. Lifting her hands caused her weight to shift, driving her more fully onto him. Never had he been so deeply within her.

Just when he thought he could stand no more of her delicious torture, Enovese lowered her back to his chest. Once settled, she pushed his legs apart so hers were between his as she lay on top, like a laying-down hug with his chest to her back. He lifted his knees so he could cradle her against him while she moved her hips in tiny circles.

"Touch me, Chur."

She didn't have to ask twice. Like a starving man offered a lush banquet, he didn't know where to start. First, he traced his fingertips across her face, stroking her truculent nose, her high and proud cheekbones, and then her mouth. Since he could not see her, he let his hands become his eyes. He traced her lips, feeling how full her upper lip was as compared to the bottom.

"You have a most intriguing mouth, Enovese. Everything

you feel you express with the movement of your lips." Her slow smile teased his fingertips, causing him a burst of satisfaction. "Ah, see there? It pleases you that I've noticed. Did you know your lips are the same coral color as your nipples?"

A ripple of laughter escaped her. "I had not noticed."

Chur trailed his fingertips to her proud chin, then cupped, turning her head so that he could kiss her. She kept her eyes closed, but he plundered his tongue deeply inside. He pulled back and whispered to her ear, "Your mouth tastes of lust with secrets locked behind a tormented smile."

Before she could speak, he shushed her, then caressed her neck, her shoulders, then cupped her breasts. Calloused fingers and thumbs encircled her nipples, twisting to bloom them into turgid awareness. Her hips snuggled down, nestling his cock, as he continued to tug lightly at her pert breasts. "I long to take each peak into my mouth so that I can bite and suck and chew."

A rock of her hips conveyed her longing, but her gasp at his sharper twist made clear her lust. "Ah, see, you like soft, then hard. You revel in rough touches followed by gentle. You are such a perplexing creature, my succulent servant."

"I live only to serve you, my wanton master." Enovese twined her hands in his hair.

With a thrust, he chuckled wickedly to her ear. "Now that is a lie, Enovese. You live for pleasure. You take all you know as a *paratanist* and use your knowledge in a quest for gratification."

She tensed at the mention of her title.

Chur soothed her with strokes along her waist to the small roundness of her belly. Tracing his finger along the gentle slope to tease her belly button elicited a giggle. He marveled how far they had come in their lovemaking. This was not a frantic joining but a languorous exploration. His only regret was he could not see her face. The loss of that intimate contact spurred him to find another way to establish their connection.

Placing his hands flat, he smoothed down to cup her hips.

His hands spanned almost her entire hipbones, reminding him how delicate she was but also how large he was. There was tremendous power in his form. His strength was unmatched in combat, but here with her fragile form clasped in his hands, he knew his own tenderness. Taming his muscle for sensual exploration gave him great pleasure. He possessed the power to force her, but quelling his needs to meet hers was intensely erotic. Chur held her hips steady as he thrust at a leisurely pace, dancing below her, letting her feel his penis move within the grasping heat of her sex.

Enovese sighed and trailed her hands along his arms, her fingertips tracing the movement of his muscles below the hair and skin. Her grip tightened when he thrust deeper, pulling her hips down as he moved his up. Lifting his legs around her, straddling her as she lay above, gave him more leverage, allowing him to move deeper. With her legs clasped together, he could only tease one finger between, but her sex was wet, her clit stiff and straining to feel his touch. Lightly, he stroked his finger to match his thrusts. Enovese placed her hand over his in an effort to compel him to press harder.

He nipped her ear and whispered, "I love how you can tease me endlessly but turn most greedy when I attempt to torment you."

She uttered a strained laugh. "As the Harvester, you are trained in denial where I am not."

"Then I will have to instruct you." He kissed her cheek. "First, take deep breaths through your nose and release them slowly from your pursed lips." He lifted his hand to her chest to feel her lungs expand. "Very good." He then touched her face. "Tighten your mouth more so you are pushing the breath out." After several minutes, she had mastered the *kintana* breathing technique. "You are a most apt pupil. Now, keep that pace while I torment you."

Chur slid his finger between her legs with a feather-light stroke. When she began to pant, he reminded her to keep her breathing rate steady. After several minutes, her body relaxed and he now continued his gentle thrusts. He synchronized his breathing to hers, and together they went higher into a dizzying fervor. Increasing his pace and the pressure against her clit caused their breathing to deepen because she tightened around him, gripping him firmly, rolling her hips in small circles as he thrust.

Enovese tried to part her thighs, but he kept her firmly nestled between his powerful legs. His hand at her hip and that between her legs controlled her movements. A rush of power possessed him, for in this moment she belonged to him. Enovese, soft and smooth, writhed against his hard and hairy body with a need for release. He controlled when and how he would bestow that upon her.

"Feel the awareness of your whole body, Enovese, not just in your clit, not just in the grasping greediness of your slick sex, but all over your skin. Feel the need in your nipples, in your mouth, down to the tips of your toes pointed and ready to plunge into climax."

Enovese growled. So base and animal was her demanding snarl that her lust spilled into him. For all his ability to wait and enjoy the anticipation, he lost control. Chur cupped her chin, drawing her head back. He plunged his tongue to her mouth and she met his invasion with wild abandon.

Breathless, he pulled back. "You try my resistance. How dare you seek to break my focus?" Blaming her for his own lack of control excited him and her.

With a whimper, Enovese sought out his mouth and kissed him with crazed need. "Please, Chur, my flesh burns, my lungs cannot take another breath, my—"

His massive hands lowered to her hips, grasped, and held

her steady for his mighty thrust. Her howl spurred him on. "Now, my wanton, feel the power of my body. Feel the aggressive invasion of my cock." Chur gave a brutal thrust while forcing her hips down.

Enovese grasped handfuls of his hair and bayed her surrender.

"Tell me you want more," Chur demanded. He didn't need to hear the truth spoken aloud, but he wanted to hear her pleas for her willingness aroused him beyond all comprehension.

"I want everything you can give."

He gave another rough thrust. "Is that what you want?"

"Yes." Enovese stretched the word into a hiss of demand.

Bouncing her upon him, he growled to her ear, then asked, "Deep, hard, ruthless—Is that what you want?"

"Gods, yes." She could barely say the words as she clutched her hands to his, helping him to hold her hips steady for his merciless thrusts.

"Finger yourself. I want to feel you spend on my cock."

His permission, his demand, encouraged Enovese to slip her hand between her clamped thighs and press as hard as she could.

Chur pressed his thighs tight so she could only work one slender finger between her swollen lips. Her frustration lifted up in the form of a moan and the desperate swivel of her hips.

"Torment upon torment, my servant, that's what you have done to me."

"I beg you, please, let me—"

Chur didn't allow her to finish. He parted his legs, then hers, and placed his hand over hers. With her thighs parted, he forced her hand to stroke with sharp pressure, up and down the full of her split sex. "Feel my shaft within you. Feel how swollen your lips and how rigid your clit. Feel my hand master yours."

Enovese struggled to breathe deep and steady as he had taught her, but she lost her battle. Her climax gathered in a taut expression of her muscles. Her legs went rigid, then her arms, her hips, her neck, and her back as she lifted away from him.

Chur rubbed their joined hands faster over her clit. Enovese climaxed with a rush of breath. Her whole body went tight, curling in; then as the orgasm reverberated, she quivered and shook upon him, her body going loose. Her surrender spurred his. Plunging hard and deep, he lost all control.

With her hands to his thighs, Enovese encouraged his maniacal movements. Low, deep, luscious, her voice and the ancient words further drove him to wild abandon. A madman possessed, Chur captured her hips and forced her to take every lift of his hips. Undaunted, Enovese angled back and captured his mouth, kissing him between growling encouragements.

"You torment, you tease, you range from sweet to nasty, you drive me to distraction, and then you take all I can give." He climaxed on a kiss, his body heaving into her with full possession. In that moment, Chur knew he would never let another man know her as he had. He would rather die a thousand deaths than allow any to possess Enovese. The realization shocked him, for he no longer cared about her ability to have children. There was more to a bondmate than that. Together, they would find a way to overcome any trial. With her, he was strong. Without her, he would be nothing.

Once he caught his breath and the last tingles of his climax faded, he embraced her, turning her so that she faced him.

"I claim you, Enovese."

Her eyes opened with hope, but then a desperate fear darkened the indigo starburst.

Chur discovered the hurt she denied. His eyes widened, then watered. Devastated, he could not speak. He shook his head side to side in denial.

Enovese nodded once, then fell to his embrace.

Her tears mirrored his. Her torment reflected and deepened his. Repeatedly, she murmured that she was sorry, so sorry, that she could not find the words to tell him, for as she discovered the reality of her position as a *paratanist* she uncovered the ugly truth behind his role as the Harvester.

21

Buried in a rambling description of combat rules and Harvest rituals, Enovese discovered the elusive truth. The man who had written the Harvester tome had tossed the information onto the page as if it were the most widely known fact. She had read the passage over and over, unable to comprehend. Then horror filled her. Shame. Disgrace. In the midst of her descent into repulsion, she thought of Chur and how such would affect him. More than anything, she suddenly wished she did not know the truth, for Chur would find out. Once their gazes locked and the threads between them intensified, he would know everything.

Enovese had avoided meeting his gaze for as long as she could, but when he'd spoken that he claimed her, such joyous surprise caused her to look right into his eyes—in a rush he knew. Devastation stamped harsh lines across his face, twisting his scar, curling his lips back, and causing his head to shake in denial.

"It isn't true." He drew harsh breaths through his nose and blew them out between clenched teeth. In this way, he managed to control himself and blink back his tears. Part of the code he lived by prohibited him from such an emotional display. She would never condemn him for his feelings, but he would criticize himself.

Enovese simply looked into his eyes and shook her head. "I wish it wasn't true, but you know, deep down, that it is." She twined her hand to his and he yanked his away as if repulsed by her touch. Automatically, her spine stiffened. "I didn't do this to myself."

His eyes widened with surprise, as if he'd just realized this wasn't all about him. He took her hand in his. "I was afraid you wouldn't want to touch me."

She gripped his hand. "None of this is your fault. You are as blameless as I."

Chur lifted her hand to his mouth and placed a kiss in the center of her palm. Enovese found the gesture intimate, erotic, and brimming with acceptance. He was genuinely afraid she would reject him when she was convinced he would reject her. Trapped by circumstances beyond their control, they sat silently for a moment, reconciling their feelings.

"How can this be?" Chur asked. "It is the most revolting situation I have ever heard." He rolled his head back and glared at the ceiling. "No wonder they hid it away. If not for that ancient tome . . ." Chur drifted off; then hope filled his summer-sky eyes. "Perhaps that is what they did before, in the time of the ancients, but not now. Our people would not do something so barbaric."

Enovese took a moment to consider her words. "For all the advancements of our culture, most of our rituals come directly from the time of the ancients. Harsh, brutal, barbaric—the rituals have survived the test of time for they are traditions that have served our people well. As much as this information sickens us both, it does answer all the questions we've pondered."

Chur glared at her. "How can you speak of this with such a lack of disgust?"

Enovese felt her face harden with a severity she made no effort to hide. "I am a *paratanist*. I am no less horrified than you are, but I have several times over encountered ugly truths that shook me to the core. And in this, I've had more time to consider the information." She smoothed her finger along his chest scar. "Beyond that I realize there is little I can do to change what is."

Chur touched her face, smoothing away the hard lines. "I admire you, Enovese. I do not think there is another woman who is as strong as you."

Enovese blushed a bit and lowered her face demurely. "You compliment me greatly." Chur could not have given her higher praise.

Cupping her chin, he lifted her face and placed a kiss on the tip of her nose. After a series of sweet kisses, he drew back and asked her to translate the exact passage for him.

Enovese closed her eyes and visualized the text. The words danced in her mind's eye in spidery script and maroon ink, the color of which reminded her of dried blood. "The issue of the male and female Harvesters is combined, and all viables are placed within a *tanist* host. At term, the *tanist* is sacrificed, the viable is branded, sterilized, and placed in the training house."

Enovese shuddered. They didn't even call her a child but a viable. Worse, she wasn't actually born but ripped from a *tanist* during the *paratanist* selection ritual. As they pulled her forth, the *tanist* bled to death. Enovese knew if she remained a *paratanist*, she would one day become a *tanist* and suffer the same fate. Her dream to have children would transpire but in a most horrific way.

At long last she now knew exactly where she came from. Her parents hadn't given her into a life of servitude, for they had never known she existed. Her parents were Harvesters who were oblivious as to what happened with the products of the Harvest. This thought caused her to look at Chur. In his eyes she could see that he wondered how many children he had produced. His horror was born from the life he had inadvertently bestowed them. The life of a *paratanist* was one of silence, rituals, and ultimately a chilling death if they were female.

"How many children have come from my three Harvests?" Chur asked the question to the air for he didn't look at her.

"I know not. It would depend on how many ova the female Harvester produced."

Chur frowned. "Is it not but one when a woman is in heat?"

Enovese had considered this, but after reading about the rituals the female Harvester underwent before the Harvest, she suspected part of it was to enhance her fertility. "As you and I engage to torment you, to deny you release so you are at your most potent, I believe they do the same to her. With oils and drugs they could force her body to produce many ova."

His face twisted with pain. "There could be dozens." With the delicate threads of the conduit, she saw him picturing his children learning to speak and walk only to embrace a life of servitude. He envisioned them coming of age and then a *tanist* forcing a ceremonial robe over their heads. "Gods save me, but this would explain why I must sign the immunity clause. I have no right to claim a child produced during the Harvest. I thought it was for children a sacrifice might have, but now I know that I released my rights to all those children they took from me. I can't claim them now. I can't save them from their fates."

Chur dropped his weary head into one massive hand. His body shuddered and his chest heaved. Desolation rolled off him in waves that broke her heart. Moving to his side, Enovese embraced him, resting her head against his arm. She searched her mind to find something to offer him solace but came up woefully empty.

By right, by law, Chur could do nothing to help the children he produced during his time as the Harvester. Most devastating for him was knowing that even if he could pluck them from the *tanist* house, he could not repair the damage inflicted upon them during the *paratanist* selection ritual. Branded, sterilized—they would be forever lost to him. Deep in her heart, Enovese knew how much Chur wanted children. He wanted them to carry the glory of his name, but he also longed to protect them, to give them a better life than what he had known. To discover his children would one day become as she . . . No words would soothe such a hurt.

"There must be something I can do." His gaze met hers with so much hope her heart splintered even more that she could not think of anything. His face fell when he realized the truth. They could do nothing. Even if they somehow managed to determine which children were Chur's, and then extricated them from the *tanist* house, where would they take them? There was nowhere safe. No civilized land would accept them. The frozen tundra of Rhemna would welcome them only to crush them in its icy grip.

Chur flung the covers back and left the warmth of their bed. He paced. With great strides, he ate up the distance, then turned sharply on his heel to repeat the path. The muscles in his body bunched and flexed. Black hair streamed from his head in a dark wind. The dusting of hair along his body caught and flickered the crystal light. Beautiful, powerful, and dangerous, Chur moved like a deadly animal desperate to find the path of his prey. His nostrils flared as if he sought the scent. A shiver traced her spine, for in such a state Chur would not be civil. He would not be rational. Rhythmically, he clenched and released his hands, and Enovese knew he would use his massive fists with deadly intent. Even now he moved them as if they clutched the throat of the responsible party.

Enovese watched him pace for a long time. She knew the movement would help him calm and return to a more rational state. For surely he would realize, just as she had, that there was no one person to blame. The rituals were to blame. The traditions were to blame. Even the magistrate himself was bound by ancient laws that none had dared to question in thousands and thousands of seasons.

"Perhaps the time has come."

Chur spun on his heel and faced her. "Do not think I'm training today. In this mood, I might kill one of the recruits in blind rage."

"I do not think you should train today." Enovese rose from the bed and felt a flush of pride at his feral look. Anger aroused him and intensified his base needs. Now that he had calmed a bit, he vacillated between wanting to fight and wanting to fuck. "I think perhaps the time has come for someone to question the customs of our people. I think that someone is you."

Chur barked a bitter laugh. "I am the strongest man in all the realm, but I cannot fight everyone."

Standing near enough that she could feel his breath upon her breasts, Enovese stroked her hand across his brow. "This will not be a physical fight. You will use your mind, not your muscles."

He captured her wrist. "My brain is not my strong suit."

With a lift of her brows, Enovese said, "Do not hold yourself in low esteem, for where you know not, I do."

A wicked smile lifted his mouth as understanding brightened his gaze. "You would be the brains behind the brawn."

"If I could, I would stand and condemn them as mindless fools who blindly follow traditions, but who would listen to me? A *paratanist* does not speak unless spoken to, and even then they would not hear my words. But you? You are the Harvester." Enovese traced the mighty scars that marred his magnificent body. "By your title, you command influence. They will not only hear you, but they will listen."

A frown drew lines across his forehead. "I am but one Harvester in a long line of many."

"You are the most celebrated Harvester in hundreds of seasons. The elite name their children after you. Men aspire to be you. Women desire to bed you." She paused and grinned. "Perhaps some of the men, too, but the fact remains that you have far more persuasion than any Harvester since Esslean of Plete."

Part of Chur's training included learning about the Harvesters before him. Esslean of Plete was renown for his changes to the selection and training of Harvesters. Rather than a haphazard system of conflicts within each region, Esslean created a more efficient way to gather recruits and then instituted the rules by which they battled for supremacy. Esslean of Plete was the first official handler. Chur now worked under the Esslean training rules and regulations, often called the *Esslean code of conduct.*

"Esslean is a prime example that changes can occur, but not overnight and not easily, but change is not impossible." Enovese touched one finger to Chur's mouth. "Change starts with one voice."

With a pucker, Chur kissed the tip of her finger and then drew her hand to cover his heart. "What if my one voice is not loud enough?"

Enovese considered. "Let your voice be the first drop of rain against their dry tradition. Another will join. And another. So many drops will deluge them until they are flooded. They will have no choice but to adjust or drown. I believe they will change if only to protect their positions. Your voice will be the first rumble that starts a torrential storm. For if others comprehend what we know . . ."

Chur cast his gaze over her shoulder. "You once cautioned me that if I became a handler, I could not tell a future Harvester the truth of the Harvest. How is this any different?"

Enovese heard Chur's belly rumble and moved to start his morning meal. "It is a nasty trick to make a man think he will find erotic pleasure in the Harvest ritual, but to steal his progeny? That is entirely different. It is not a simple deception, it is a gross violation."

Chur leaned against the doorway, watching her cook, remarking that perhaps she should always work in the nude.

"Dangerous, depending on what I'm making." She selected some fruit and set him to work preparing them.

"Even had you known the truth about your lack of tactile sensation during the Harvest ritual, you still would have fought for the right, for there are great benefits, yet never would you have agreed to give away your children."

"No, that I would not have agreed to." Tension flared along the edge of his jaw as he trimmed the hard husk of the *nicla* to expose the red–orange flesh inside. "But even if I tell the truth I know, who would believe me? The only proof I have is a tome written in a language few understand anymore."

With a sigh, Enovese said, "And I doubt they will accept my translation. More likely they would take the book, destroy it, and then dispose of us both."

"Then we are right back where we were before."

Enovese considered and rejected several ideas. "We will need proof other than the Harvester tome."

A frown lowered his brows. "Yes, but proof from where? Clearly they've removed any mention of this from all the other texts, or you would have found out long before now."

Enovese set the table and they sat down. She picked at her food, too distracted to eat, but Chur ate heartily.

With a wry frown, he said, "I am not truly hungry but for my training I must. How would it look at the Festival of Temptation if my uniform hung on me?" A burst of inspiration lit his face.

When Enovese looked deep into Chur's eyes, she saw a vision of herself, much older, yet still beautiful. "You see me in the future?" Such a thought filled her with hope. Even after all of this, did he intend to claim her?

"At Ambo's season party, I saw a woman and I thought perhaps she was your mother. I didn't tell you for she was wealthy beyond measure and I worried that she had sold you."

Her heart leaped in her chest. "To look that much like me she must be my mother, which means she was a Harvester. What was her name?" Excitement caused her hands to tremble and she set her utensils aside.

"I was trying to find out when Ambo dumped *lete* on me." Chur rolled his eyes. "If I didn't know better I would swear he did it on purpose."

"He couldn't have known what you were thinking."

"I know. I just detest the man. He seems to impede my steps in everything I do."

Enovese thought Chur had good reason to dislike Ambo for not only his attacks on his uniform but also his despicable conduct during his bondmate's mourning rites. "You must find out who this woman is." Enovese considered her plate, then pushed it aside. "She could be the proof we need."

"What does she prove exactly?"

"That *paratanists* come from Harvesters. The idea that parents willing to give their children away is a myth to hide the despicable truth. With the tome and this woman we have enough proof to at least get people to consider what we say."

"We?" He lifted his brows. "Now you intend to stand beside me? And exactly where, when, and how do you propose I break this information?"

"I haven't figured that out yet."

With a sigh of frustration, Chur stood from the table. He

paced. His moves weren't as vigorous. He set a contemplative tempo. Enovese cleared the table and then sat upon their bed. She wanted to stay out of his way but also she enjoyed watching him move. For a large man, he possessed incredible grace.

"What is to prevent them from killing me? As popular as you seem to think I am, there wouldn't be anything to stop them from disposing of me."

Using the deep breathing Chur had taught her, Enovese calmed her mind and body. "There must be a way and we will find it."

"You will find it." Chur caught her gaze as he paced. "For one thing is certain: I must win the challenge. I cannot make a stand when my position is precarious, as it is now. And if I do not survive . . . well, then, my problems are over."

It took several deep breaths to dampen her anger. "Stop speaking to me of defeat. If you die your problems are not over, for your children will still exist in a world of horror."

He gritted his teeth. "You are right and I am sorry." He caught her gaze and the harsh lines of his face softened. "Ah, Enovese, I did not even think of you." With three strides, he was at her side and sat next to her on the bed. "I am a selfish man." He wrapped his arm around her waist and pulled her close. When she failed to correct his self-assessment, he asked, "Forgive me?"

"Yes." She forgave him for focusing on himself and his children, because when she had first read the passage, she instantly thought only of herself. Her concern for Chur had come later. Her concern for the population of Diola had come only recently.

"I swear that I will do everything in my power to change what is, even if it costs me my life. Better death than disgrace." He squeezed her tighter. "If I know this and fail to act, I have dishonored myself greatly. And as you said, my voice will be but the first."

Enovese had known for a long time that she loved Chur, but now, she admired him. He was more than the Harvester, more than a man; in her eyes, he was a hero. She loved and deeply respected him. He would fight for change, no matter what it cost him personally. He put the greater good above himself. Deep down in her heart, she knew she would have to make such a sacrifice herself.

When she looked to the future, she no longer saw a happy ending to their relationship, not as she once had. She now realized she had been painfully naïve to think that Chur could whisk her away from the constraints of her position as a *paratanist*. She intended to stand with him and give a voice to all those who could not speak, for if she remained silent, she, like Chur, would dishonor herself greatly.

As she sat beside Chur, idly tracing her finger along the thick hair on his thigh, she worried at the details. Determining the timing of the revelation was critical. It had to be a time when Chur had a captive audience. She pushed the problem to the back of her mind for now because they had other goals to accomplish first.

"I think I should go to training today." Chur stood. "Missing even one day could show weakness." He flashed her a smile, but she realized it was more a baring of his teeth. "I wish to terrify them and make them strongly consider challenging me."

Enovese helped him wash then don his gear. "The Festival of Temptation starts in ten nights. Try to keep your face clear of bruises, but be sure to inflict them on the recruits."

Shock turned his blue eyes dark.

"Do not look at me like that. I don't want you to hurt them but mark them. If you stride in unmarked while they stumble in battered, it boosts your myth as the mighty, untouchable Harvester. You know the Festival of Temptation is all about appearances."

Two cycles before the Harvest, all the Harvest participants engaged in the Festival of Temptation where the sacrifices, the current Harvester, and the recruits attended an elaborate celebration in their honor. The virgins showed off their beauty, the Harvester could decide if one would suit for bonding, and the recruits might see a woman worth issuing a challenge to the death. The current magistrate, his staff, and all palace dignitaries would also attend. Among them would be the woman Chur had seen.

"You think I should deliver this information there?" Chur shrugged his way into the cross-strap harness of his chest plate.

Enovese adjusted the straps to fit snuggly but not tight over his shoulders. "No, I think you should terrify them in the training room and at the Festival. You should stride into the ballroom as if all are there to admire you."

With a chuckle, Chur stood taller. "I should be a horrifying monster barely contained by my finery."

Enovese nodded and adjusted the thick animal hide that cupped his left shoulder. For the Festival, he would wear his dress uniform and his ceremonial sword. Heavy and jewel encrusted, the weapon enhanced his size, and she noticed whenever he wore the sword he walked harder, his face turned harsher, and his eyes glowed with a ruthless entitlement. A similar change overcame him when he wore the blade for the Harvest.

Enovese imagined a sacrifice seeing Chur for the first time at the Festival of Temptation. Would they feel a rush of fear followed by a quivering anticipation? During the Festival, his black hair brushed the collar of his uniform. The soft curls framed his face, highlighting the summer-sky blue of his eyes and white twist of his scar. Deep black fabric contrasted the red piping that framed his chest scar. Would such a vision frighten or intrigue a young woman?

Not all the virgins attended the Festival, so many saw Chur for the first time during the Harvest. How did they take his shaved head and chest, his partial nudity, muscles coated in oil, and eyes gleaming from arousal denied?

"Enovese?"

Chur's voice pulled her from her thoughts. "I was thinking what a woman would feel upon seeing you for the first time at the Festival."

"Terror." He responded with a definitive air. "I'm so much bigger than they are. I'm convinced they think I will manhandle them like a brute." A wry smile lifted his lips. "But when I dance with them, the terror gives way to surprise that I am gentle."

Enovese remembered dancing with him and her own astonishment at not only his grace but also his tender touch. "Perhaps that dichotomy is what has led to your popularity: the brute with the benevolent nature."

Her praise caused him to roll his eyes and remark, "You would do well as a poet, Enovese. For one who can turn monster to man is a master of words."

"You say that you are no poet, but you, too, have a way with words." His statement sparked an idea that merged with the problems at the back of her mind. She would do well to read what the poets had written about Chur Zenge. Insight into his myth might yield an answer to their dilemma. She needed to find a way to exploit his myth to his benefit.

Chur sighed and tilted her face to his. "I see the wheels spinning in your mind." He kissed her cheek. "I will leave you to your thoughts."

Before he could turn away, Enovese captured his face in her hands and kissed his mouth. He deepened the kiss, pulling her against his armor-clad body. Muscle, animal hide, and metal pressed into her yielding form, reassuring her with his strength. As he pulled away, Enovese feared their time together grew short.

22

Chur breathed a sigh of relief that the ritual of control was over for another night. He stood on his private balcony, nude, hard, looking over the meticulously manicured lands surrounding the palace. As the time of the Harvest drew close, the garden below swelled with bounty. Fruits and vegetables rambled over the ground or high upon trellises, slowly growing in the fading light. From his vantage point, they appeared as tiny houses, fit for only the wee people. The image lifted a smile that turned to a grimace. Nightmares of his children in cribs, crying for comfort and ruthlessly ignored, filled his slumber with cold terror.

He turned his gaze to the fields where grains nodded and bounced on the light breeze that carried wisps of salt and fish from the Valry Sea. He found the scent soothing, for the essence of the sea made him think of renewal and rebirth. Even when the cold came and gripped the land in icy tufts of snow, the smell of the Valry offered a promise that life would come to the land again.

Tandalsul, the twin suns, had just dipped below the Onic

Mountains, almost perfectly aligned into a cleft between two peaks known as the Temptation crevasse. Tomorrow night, the suns would nestle directly between the mounds, heralding the start of the Festival of Temptation. Whoever had designed the palace had placed the Harvester rooms in alignment to view that moment. As the suns descended, they cast the clouds in reddish purple, an oddly angry color amid so much serene beauty.

Chur's body ached from brutal training sessions and his mind jumbled with too many thoughts. Enovese's torment only added to the pounding in his head, as if he had too much blood to be contained within his flesh. She had offered the blue lotion, but he'd declined. Somehow, the familiar punishment soothed him for such was a basic part of his duty. A sigh escaped him as he thought back to the words Enovese had flung in anger cycles ago, accusing him of cowering behind duty for he feared making his own decisions. He found himself clinging to duty again. Much like the torment of lust denied, focusing his mind to his responsibilities soothed with well-known constraints.

Simultaneous feelings of anger, fear, and disgust paced his every moment. From his dreams to his waking moments, he had no respite. During training, his focus had been so sharp as to render him a brutal machine. He took down any who faced him with vicious efficiency but such was borne of fear. For the first time, Chur didn't believe he would prevail at the challenge. Sterlave seemed to grow ever more powerful and dangerous. His muscles bulged, his eyes narrowed, his movements were both fluid and deadly. Dueling during mock battles had left them at a draw, for neither could seem to gain advantage over the other. It pained Chur to be at odds with a man he genuinely respected and even cared for. The only solace he gained was that Sterlave's gaze reflected the same fearful determination.

Anger often gripped Chur when he returned to his rooms,

for he felt he'd gained nothing during his training. Helton had been curiously absent. When Helton did make an appearance, he clung close to Loban and focused all his attention there. Chur found his behavior odd because Loban had unofficially withdrawn from the challenge. Chur consoled himself with the thought Helton perhaps did not wish to take a side between him and Sterlave. However, such a thought did not soothe the sting of Helton's abandonment. Usually, Chur could not shake Helton during the last few cycles before the Harvest. Now, he could barely catch his gaze for a brief acknowledgment before Helton twisted away, giving Chur his back. Helton's behavior only reinforced that he had turned against Chur. What had Chur done to alienate Helton? Had his questions about the rituals irked Helton for Chur had dared to broach into *paratanist* territory? Chur now realized he should have kept his concerns to himself. A Harvester was brawn not brains, brute strength not mental finesse. Perhaps what angered Helton the most was that he believed Chur should have chosen a bondmate from the last Harvest. In not doing so, Chur had inadvertently ruined Helton's plans, whatever they may be.

As he shared time with Enovese, he discovered a profound feeling of disgust ate away at his pride. Putting an end to the *paratanist* selection ritual consumed Enovese. She worked tirelessly in an effort to find a way to inform others without destroying everyone in the process. She seemed oblivious to what such a revelation would cost her. She shrugged it off, willing to cast herself into the ceremonial fires if it would bring forth change. His disgust came when he realized he did not feel the same. He had sworn to her he would do anything—death before disgrace—but now he wanted to take his impassioned words back. He wished he did not know the truth. He wanted Enovese to let go, forget, so that he, too, could attempt to distance himself from the horrible situation. Disgust borne of fear for he did not think he had the power to fight against an ancient and terrifying ritual. Duty beckoned to him, for he should not worry at the outcome of the rituals. He wished his heart would grow calloused, uncaring, so that uncertainties over what he could not change would release him from anguish. He could not save his children. He did not believe he had the fortitude to fight a powerful and faceless enemy, for how did one battle the ancients and their rituals? Chur had always felt powerful in his form and his position, but now he felt utterly impotent, and such disgusted him.

A tap against the glass pulled him from his thoughts. Enovese motioned him inside for his evening meal. Usually he ate before the ritual of control, but his growling belly helped distract him from climax. He'd retreated to the balcony to escape the luscious scent of Enovese. The ritual stimulated her, making her wet, infusing her robe with an aroma of passion. Her natural perfume added another layer of torment to his aroused state. If nightmares about his children didn't distress him, dreams of Enovese did. They had agreed that during the ritual they would not share a bed, for after the first night he'd awoken with her in his arms, his stiff cock seeking the wetness between her legs. Tonight was his last night of agony, for tomorrow, after the Festival of Temptation, Enovese would bring him to a shattering climax.

Chur couldn't wait for release, but he wasn't looking forward to the Festival. He found the entire affair tedious. Virgins batting their lashes, engaging in coy conversations that often left him more irritated than intrigued. They often gossiped about people and schemes he knew nothing about. Frankly, he did not think the young ladies knew much about them either, for his simplest question left them baffled. Chur suspected their parents put them up to dropping names to impress him with their connections, thus making them appear more desirous as mates. The frustration he felt during the Harvest possessed him during the Festival. None interested him. Not once had he gazed upon a sacrifice and known deep in his heart that she was the one he'd longed for.

Until Enovese.

He startled at the thought and placed his hands against the cool stone railing. Without any enhancements, Enovese had commanded his attention during not only the Harvest but also all the time since. Beyond her stunning beauty, her thoughts and beliefs held him in a trance. She was brave. She was bold. She saw what she wanted and would do all in her power to achieve her goals. When he'd thrown blocks in her path, she either plowed through them or climbed over them. Driven by forces he deeply admired, Enovese refused to accept the limits of her position.

While they were making love he'd boldly laid his claim to her, for he could not bear the thought of another man knowing her as he had, but now, he realized, his feelings went far deeper than simple sexual possession. Somehow, Chur had fallen in love with Enovese. The feeling came over him so inexorably he had no idea how it had started or when the tide had turned, he only knew the truth of it down to his soul. Enovese swore he was her bondmate, that she would have no other, and now he felt the same way.

Chur turned and looked through the glass. Beyond his ghostly reflection, Enovese sat at the table, reading over the tome, waiting for him. Tendrils of harvest-colored hair spilled out of the braid at the back of her neck and teased around her face, which was dipped low in concentration. With a delicate dab of her fingertip to her tongue, she turned the page.

Entranced, he simply watched her for a moment, drawing his gaze along her pursed lips, the upturn of her nose, and the little line that formed between her brows. Enovese never sat idle. Even when he'd caught her sitting motionless, he could see her mind working. She would not rest until she had found a solution. She had no qualms about sacrificing herself, but she would not allow him to be hurt. Another pang of disgust ate away at his pride for she should not worry over him when he did enough of that himself. As much as he wanted to put an end to the revolting practice, he did not want to forfeit all he'd worked so hard to obtain.

On the brink of retiring from the fighting arena, he wanted the rest of his life to be nothing but lazy days of decadence. He could choose from a multitude of undemanding military positions and then work himself into a political position if he desired. However, if he decried the ancients and their traditions, they would kill him or cast him out. Where Enovese proudly declared she would forfeit her life for change, he simply wasn't willing to go that far. He'd worked diligently his entire life to obtain his position, and he didn't want to throw everything away.

Selfish, he knew, but it was the truth. Chur did not know how to tell Enovese because he couldn't stomach watching how her gaze, with eyes that always shined with pride, would look to him then. The fire-bright love that filled her eyes would turn cold, coloring her indigo starburst to ashes. She would claim him a coward. Knowing her as he did, he believed that she would still love him, but she would no longer respect him. He discovered her opinion of him deeply mattered to him.

Chur did not want the weight of the world upon his shoulders. He wanted the life he'd fought so ruthlessly to obtain. Petulant as a child, he felt cheated anew. Bad enough the Harvest ritual was not as tales would tell, but now to face this situation not of his making made him want to rail how unfair it all was.

Over his shoulder, he looked to Enovese and a new burst of shame caused him to turn away and gaze toward Ampir, nestled at the base of the Onic Mountains. Circumstances beyond her control gripped Enovese, but she did not cry or protest what was; no, she simply accepted and pushed to change them.

He admired her anew for her fortitude. She was much stronger than he was; but also, he admitted, she had far less to lose.

He berated himself for his uncharitable thought. Who was he to decide her sacrifice was worth less than his was?

Wind rippled against his flesh, cold and moist, filled with the promise of rain. He shivered. Below the refreshing cool air came the knowledge that the Harvest slouched closer, like a beast that would consume him utterly. Win or lose, he knew his life would never be the same. He could not go back. He must go forward. Whether he went onward as a coward or hero was entirely up to him.

As he opened the glass door and entered, Enovese glanced up and a smile bloomed her face to touchingly beautiful. He saw himself reflected in her eyes as a strong, powerful, driven man. Acceptance, respect, and love glowed from the very core of her being and flowed toward him.

In that moment, all his fears dissolved. He would be her hero. Even if in doing so he must forfeit his life, for he could do nothing less for the woman he loved.

"Shave my whole chest. The uniform will fit better if you do." Chur stood near the table, his face already shaved, his naked body waiting for the next step of preparation for the Festival of Temptation.

Enovese paused with lather in one hand and the ceremonial razor in the other. Playfully, she smeared blue froth across his belly, then dipped her hand to his genitals.

Laughing, he drew her hand up. "I said my chest."

She frowned. "Since I'm shaving you, I might as well—"

"No." He kept his voice firm but smiled nonetheless. Enovese had a fascination for shaving his sex. He found sensations stronger when freed of hair, but the damn itching wasn't worth the increased pleasure. "Only my chest. But if you want me to shave you . . ." he trailed off and dipped his gaze to her hips.

Hidden in the depths of her robe, Enovese sashayed her hips with an enticing wiggle. "Perhaps you are too late."

A growl rumbled from his chest. He loved when she shaved, exposing all of her charms to his gaze. A lack of hair sensitized her skin so that even the barest whisper caused her intense pleasure. When he chewed her naked flesh, she writhed below him, her breath gasping and wild, her head tossing with ecstasy, tangling the length of her lustrous hair. With nothing to bar his contact, he could take all of her essence into his mouth, slicking her silk across his teeth and tongue. If he must choose a way to die, drowning in her arousal would be his first choice.

"You are lucky I'm going to the Festival of Temptation this evening. Otherwise, I would yank your robe up and inspect you myself." He offered her his most lustful leer. "A most thorough inspection."

"Lucky is not the word I would use." Enovese palmed another bit of foam and smoothed it around his chest hair. Swirling the puffs of blue into black strands, she worked up a solid lather, then carefully swiped the razor across his skin. What she wielded could only be classified as a weapon, but her delicate touch slicked the hair away with the barest brush against his flesh. In between flicks of her wrist, she cleaned the blade on a *harshan* tossed over her shoulder.

His breath tensed, as it always did, when she neared his nipple. Expertly, she circled the puckered flesh, whisking the hair away.

"You always hold your breath as if I will slice your nipple off." She glanced at his face, then dipped her head, swiping her tongue across his nipple. His quick intake of breath caused her to laugh. "I would never hurt you, Chur."

"I know." He sensed she meant more than just hurting him with the blade. After she deftly removed the hair around the other nipple, he released a tense breath. "Do you imagine you would be relaxed if I held such a weapon to your breast?"

"I would be most tense," she said, her eyes going wide. "For I would wonder how I had grown hair there." She flashed him a pert grin, then flicked another patch of hair away.

He waited until she drew the blade back to wipe it off before he laughed. "What about your sex? Would you be relaxed if I were to shave you there?"

With a purse of her lips, she considered. "Perhaps not. I've seen how you are with the kitchen knives." When he reached for her, she danced back with a delightful giggle. "Now hold still so I can finish. You are supposed to be there soon."

"I plan to make an entrance." He lowered his hands to his sides. "You are most playful this evening." He suspected her humor sprang from a need to bolster his spirits. She knew how much he loathed official functions. Her joyful banter had the desired effect, for he did feel less cranky and more able to cope with the tedium that awaited him.

"At least now you do not have such a nasty sneer on your face." She kissed his chin. "You are far more handsome when you grin."

"Are you sure you wish for me to be handsome? What if I entrance some powerful woman and she decides she must keep me for herself?" He asked it in jest, but a look of deep concentration caused Enovese's brows to lower as she removed the last of his chest hair.

"A situation such as that would be to your advantage."

Her words stunned him, for she wasn't teasing. Her posture and the cast of her face were intently serious. Before he could ask what she meant, she turned away to place the *harshan* and blade on the table. She retrieved a water-filled bowl and wiped the remains of foam and hair off with a soft sponge. After she dried him, she smoothed the soothing blue lotion over the shaved area and he breathed a sigh of relief. His urge to itch instantly faded. When she finished, he captured her wrist and drew her close.

"Explain."

She lowered her face. "Nothing. We will talk of it later."

A touch of his finger to her chin raised her head. "I wish to talk of it now."

She sighed softly, then said, "A powerful woman wields influence."

"So? Enovese, I said it in jest. I have no desire for any woman but you."

Pleasure and sorrow mingled in her gaze. Her heart beat fast against his palm as he held her wrist. Her lips parted to speak, but she pressed them together, as if to desperately hold back the truth from spilling out. He knew only one way to release the tension from her mouth.

He kissed her.

She resisted for only a brief moment, then allowed his tongue to tease her lips apart. After a thorough, soul-searing kiss, Chur released her. "Now, tell me what scheme is turning the wheels in your mind."

A worried frown cast her countenance into a mask of regret, but she softly said, "If you were to bond with a powerful woman, then you, by association, would wield even more influence." Enovese drew back and took a deep breath. "Her position would protect you when you confess the truth of the *paratanist* selection ritual."

His heart skipped a beat, then pounded at his temples. After everything he'd gone through to get to the point where he wanted to claim her, she no longer wanted him to do so. Frustration compelled him to grasp her shoulders and yank her against his nude body. "I have already chosen a powerful woman. I have chosen you." He didn't give her a chance to speak. Chur lifted her bottom, pulling her up, forcing her to twine her robe-clad legs around his hips. His mouth descended on hers with possessive intent. He plundered, he pillaged, he penetrated. His tongue mimicked what he wished to do with his straining penis. A need for release suddenly possessed him with profound passion. Pressing her against the table, he tugged her robe up, determined to have his needs met.

Enovese struggled, pushing against his shoulders. She stopped his quest by locking her knees together and gently reminding him they had to wait until after the Festival.

He retreated. His breath was so harsh and heavy, each pull of air hurt his lungs. Eight nights of torment only added to all the emotions of the past few days. Everything bundled up into a burst of fear, anger, desperation, despair, disgust, and inescapable desire. Trapped in his role with so much weight on his shoulders, he slumped and turned away. He drew deep breaths through his nose and released them through tightly drawn lips.

He felt her hand, so small and warm, against his back. She did not speak but conveyed her sympathy with a touch. He hated her in that moment. Hated her for understanding how longing ruled him and cast him an animal. Hated how she forgave him for his base actions. In the same breath, he loved her for accepting his outburst, her cool ability to remind him of his duty. He wanted to curse and cherish her in the same breath. He faced her and kissed the palm of her hand.

Without a word, she climbed off the table and handed him his trousers. He yanked them on, wincing as he fastened them over his straining cock. Enovese knelt and slipped on his socks and boots. She hesitated for a moment, looking up at him. He traced a trembling fingertip to her lips and murmured, "Don't tempt me."

Rising slowly, Enovese held his gaze. "Do you think denial is easier for me?" She helped him slip on the jacket of his uniform. "Do you honestly think my body doesn't burn and ache each and every time I am near you?" With a sharp yank, she aligned the sleeves and then centered the slash over his scar.

Chur stood motionless and silent while she applied the

sticky gel that would hold the crimson trim against his skin. He didn't answer because she already knew that he had thought it was easier for her. Why he felt this way he did not know, but the truth of his opinion remained. Glancing down at her flushed face and flashing eyes, he suddenly realized she craved release as much as he did.

Enovese lifted the ceremonial blade from the table. She parted the flap on the left of his jacket and fastened the sword to a loop on his trousers. He instantly stood taller. A curious tingling rush flowed from the gem-encrusted metal touching every part of his body with strength.

Once she had the blade settled, she stepped back and assessed him critically. "Lean forward."

He bowed from the waist. She ran her fingers through his hair, breaking up the semi-wet strands, teasing his onyx locks over his ears so they brushed the edge of his jacket collar. With her so close, he could smell her arousal. He took a deep sniff to hold the essence in his mind until he returned. When he did return tonight, he would lose himself in her scent.

Enovese lifted a sleek metal cup from the table and offered it to him. *Umer.* He knew without tasting for a burnt wood odor wafted from the brown liquid. Reluctantly, he consumed the vile substance and set the cup aside. From the tip of his tongue all the way to his belly warmed on contact. His erection swelled painfully; then he lost all sensation. It was curious how *umer* kept him aroused yet all he could feel was an odd heaviness in his genitals. He wouldn't be able to orgasm for hours. A scowl etched lines so deeply on his face he could feel each furrow.

When he glanced at Enovese, her lips trembled as she compressed them. Concerned, he reached for her only to realize she was holding back laughter, not tears. When her mirth erupted, she clapped a hand over her mouth and turned away. Her back shook with suppressed giggles.

"What do you find so funny?" Her moods changed as swiftly as a battle on the tilt-table.

"I'm sorry, Chur, but your face, the way you grimace when you drink the *umer*—" she cut herself off.

He shook his head and turned her to face him. When she finally braved a look at his face, he flashed her a smarmy smile, which only caused her to laugh harder. Joining her, he let a cleansing chuckle wash away his tension as he embraced Enovese.

"You should go." Enovese reluctantly stepped back.

Chur cupped her chin. "Will you do me a favor?"

She nodded.

"Wear the green dress for me, and wear your hair down."

She lowered her face demurely. "As you wish, Harvester." A flash of devilish delight filled her gaze when she tilted her face up. "Do you wish for me to shave my sex as well?"

Desire shimmered along his nerves, causing his desensitized cock to twitch. How Enovese could counteract the *umer* with such a suggestive question was beyond him. Afraid his voice would be nothing but a growl, he simply nodded, then turned away before he lost control again. With his head held high, his shoulders straight, and his terribly hard penis tenting his pants, Chur strode to the Festival of Temptation.

23

Enovese gave Chur a few minutes to clear the main hallway, then pulled her hood up, covering her face. She slipped her sandals on and then cracked open the carved Onic door. She pressed her ear to the gap and listened for a few moments.

Silence.

She left his rooms. With her head bowed, she walked with processional steps toward the temple. While the revelers celebrated with food and drink, she would kneel and pray. At least she hoped that's what the guards would think.

As she passed through the heavy fabric that covered the arched entrance to the temple, she took a deep breath and held it for as long as she could. An acolyte shrouded in a white robe turned toward her, then quickly turned away, placing a bundle of leaves in a large brazier.

A waft of aromatic herbs caused her to waver on her feet. She kept her breathing shallow in an effort to avoid the effects of the smoke. She'd learned long ago the piles of smoldering plants provided much more than fragrance. Breathing deeply long enough caused odd effects including auditory and visual hallucinations. Once, she truly believed the ancients blessed her. She felt their hands upon her head, sanctioning her, compelling her to accept any sacrifice they demanded. Days later, she realized what had happened and took great care when in the temple.

Kneeling before the goddess of *paratanists,* Enovese touched her forehead to the warm floor tiles. She took another deep breath since the air here was free of smoke. If any saw her, they would find her pose one of utter obeisance, but she just wanted a few sips of clean air. Once she realized the acolyte had left, she rose and slipped behind the statue. A wall of draped fabrics gave way to a door. Covering her hand with the sleeve of her robe, she tried the knob and it turned easily. She cracked it open and listened at the gap. Shimmering blends of voices, music, and hard-soled shoes against Onic tile murmured out of the darkness.

Enovese entered the small anteroom and closed the door behind her. She was careful not to touch the knob on either side with her bare hands. The oils on her hands would mark the shiny metal and she did not want anyone to know she had been in here. The room was a storage space for herbs, oils, and other temple offerings. Enovese had acquired the fabric and water pearls for her bonding dress from here. As she made her way to the back, the sounds of the party grew louder. Hoisting herself up between the shelving and the wall, she climbed into a narrow cleft, an air duct carved into the rock that linked the temple to the great hall where the Festival took place.

As she crawled along, using her elbows to drag herself forward, Enovese could hear voices more distinctly and the lowest stirrings of music. When she reached the end of the stone tunnel, she pressed against the decorative grill and peered down.

A swirl of colors against black flooring stunned her eyes. From her vantage point, they seemed a mass of flowers floating on a dark sea. Each color denoted a family line, and the intensity of the color designated social rank. Only the most elite wore vivid colors, the landed gentry wore pastels, the members of the military wore grays, members of the religious sect wore white, and servants wore browns. Her eyes found Chur quickly, for he was the only one dressed in black. Only the past or present Harvesters wore black. Crimson piping elevated him as the current Harvester, for only the empress wore red.

The empress, dressed all in crimson, sat upon her throne. She held her head high, black hair twined elaborately with gems, but her eyes seemed weary. Her consort's intricate seat sat empty. He had died under mysterious circumstances two seasons ago, and despite intense pressure, she had refused to choose another. Enovese had thought it most tragically romantic for surely, the Empress Clathia had deeply loved her consort.

As Enovese watched, she saw a brief flicker of joy cross Clathia's face and realized the lady watched her daughter, also dressed all in crimson, dance with Chur. Sudden tears blurred her gaze, and Enovese understood Clathia's reaction for they were beautiful together. Chur rested his hand delicately against Kasmiri's lower back, guiding her in the dance. He took care to move lightly so he did not disturb her sophisticated coiffure that spiraled her black hair into a cone on the top of her head. Kasmiri's skin glowed tawny gold and her strong, angular face tilted slightly as she gazed at Chur with nothing short of enchantment.

When the dance ended, Chur bowed politely, but when he attempted to turn away, Kasmiri placed her hand against his forearm, effectively stopping him. He turned to her. Kasmiri said something that Chur couldn't hear for he leaned close. Standing on tiptoe, Kasmiri spoke close to his ear. Luscious lips of crimson rolled the words from her mouth. Concern and then shock washed over his features. When he pulled back, Kasmiri nodded, then walked away.

Enovese couldn't help but notice that Chur watched Kasmiri until she exited the great hall. Chur shook his head and ran his hand through his hair. He stood alone on the dance floor until the music started again and another sacrifice was ushered into his arms. As Chur danced with this new young lady, his gaze kept darting to the hallway Kasmiri had exited.

Enovese frowned. Did he wish to follow her? Why? What had she said to him before she floated away, her hips rolling seductively in shimmering blood red *astle*? Enovese had inadvertently discovered this hideaway when she stole the green fabric for her dress—someone had left it as an offering, and judging by the intensity of the green, it was a member of the elite—but not once had she seen Chur cast even a lightly interested gaze upon one of the virgins. His reaction to the daughter of the empress was unique and startling. Enovese knew she should return to his rooms to ready for the finale of the ritual of control, but the drama unfolding below riveted her.

Her earlier words to Chur, that a powerful woman would serve him well as a bondmate, replayed in her mind. Was Kasmiri the answer to their problems? Could Enovese release him from his claim and push him into the arms of another woman? If Chur chose Kasmiri during the Harvest, his claim could not be denied, and the empress would throw a decadent bonding ceremony. In that moment, with the ears and eyes of all the most powerful in the Onic Empire in attendance . . . Enovese couldn't imagine a more perfect opportunity.

Enovese believed the empress would not allow any harm to befall her daughter's consort, and if Clathia knew the horrid truth, she would not let the practice continue. Enovese knew the way to appeal to Clathia was to appeal to her as a mother. If Chur compelled her to think of her daughter, she would understand.

Envisioning the moment with ideal clarity, Enovese did not see herself present. What would happen to her? Even if Chur called her forth as proof, along with her mother, what would they do with her afterward? A shiver of revulsion clutched her heart when she imagined herself becoming a servant to Chur and his chosen. She shook the vision away. Chur would not allow that. But how much power would he wield as consort to the future empress? Would he command enough influence to protect her? At best, she would have a life in the *tanist* house, teaching those who would come after her. Heaven alone would have to forfend her from ending up a *tanist* swelled with viables.

Rather than dwelling on a future she had little control over, Enovese turned her attention back to the great hall, seeking out the woman she had seen in Chur's mind. It took a long time to locate her for her dress was black, blending into the darkness of the Onic tiled floor. Enovese knew the woman was her mother, for her hair was the same color and her skin was just as pale. Her mother sat on a high-backed chair so alone in the swirling sea of people. She lifted a crystal goblet to her lips and drank deeply of whatever liquid it held. When a beige-clad servant offered to refill her cup, Enovese noticed her mother's hand trembled when she held out her goblet.

Concern for a woman she honestly didn't know caused Enovese's blood to pulse hard in her ears. Clearly, she was drinking and quite heavily, too, because no sooner had the servant filled her cup when she drained it again. What tormented her mother so?

"She knows."

Enovese clapped a hand to her mouth when she realized she spoke aloud. Was that what crushed her mother's spirit? She knew the horrible truth and felt powerless to act? If such were true, she might choose to stand with her and Chur in an effort to change the ritual.

When Enovese searched the room for Chur, she couldn't find him. She wondered if he had followed Kasmiri and jealousy surged, but she pushed the feeling away. She trusted Chur. No man on the planet had as much self-control as he did. His absence caused panic, for if he returned to his rooms and didn't find her waiting he would be livid. He was expecting the conclusion of the ritual of control and she wanted that release as much, if not more, than he did.

Wriggling backward, Enovese struggled to keep her robe from bunching up around her hips. It took far longer to extricate herself from the narrow stone tunnel than it did to enter. She scraped her knee when she dropped down along the shelves and wall but barely noticed as she shook the dust off her robe. At the door, she again covered her hand with her sleeve and listened intently before leaving the anteroom.

Striding quickly along the hallways without going so fast as to draw attention to herself, Enovese returned to Chur's rooms and tentatively pushed open the door. A sigh escaped her when she discovered he hadn't arrived. She pushed her hood back and released the clasps of her robe. Sliding the rough fabric off her shoulders, she yanked off her shift and unbound her hair.

She placed a mirror before the chair they used for the ritual and then carefully shaved her sex. Since she was pressed for time, she used the modern tool that tingled vibrations along her too-sensitive flesh as it removed her hair. She stroked the tool along her legs, then brushed up the mess and moved to the bathing unit.

To dampen her ardor, she deliberately turned the jet to a much cooler temperature and plunged under the spray. Her nipples peaked and she gasped at the shock of cold water against her hot skin. Efficiently she washed her hair and body, then dried off and soothed oil over her shaved sex. When she caught herself lingering between her legs, she uttered a sharp groan and stopped.

Rushing, she towel-dried her hair as best she could, then retrieved the green dress from the sacred chest and pulled it on.

She grabbed the oil and the blue lotion, and placed them by the chair. Once she had everything set, she stood gasping in the center of the room. She laughed. Here she was rushing about when she probably had hours before he arrived. Relieved, she grabbed the tome and settled into the couch to wait for Chur's return.

A warm press of lips to her ankle woke her. When she blinked the sleep from her eyes, she discovered Chur, on his knees, kissing his way up her leg.

"Did I wake you?" His voice rumbled low yet playful.

"In a most pleasant way."

He had turned the crystals low. A golden glow barely made him visible. A clash of different perfumes wafted from his uniform, but below she found his spicy masculine essence. She set the tome aside and reached for him, but he motioned her back.

"I am performing an inspection. A most thorough inspection." He continued to press soft kisses along her leg, nipping his teeth to sensitive places, caressing her tingling skin with his calloused hands. "You have beautiful skin, Enovese. So pale and fragile, reminding me of winter's crystal covering, where if one dares to touch, the crystals melt away."

She dissolved under his poetic words and sensual strokes. Chur didn't rush. He lingered and loved every part of her limbs from ankle to knee, then performed the same teasing inspection of her other leg. When he came to the scrape, she tensed, but he only kissed lightly. He pushed the skirt of her dress up, but not too far, when she wanted to yank the entire costume off. Truly, he had far more patience than she did.

Holding her gaze, he pressed a kiss to each knee and then cupped the tender skin behind. Confident and controlled, he parted her legs, letting the green *astle* slick between her spread thighs. Breathlessly, she waited for him to work his way up, but he only flashed her a wicked smile and lifted her leg again.

"Do you have any idea what part of your body intrigues me most?"

She shook her head, for she doubted he would name the part pulsing and quivering below her skirt.

Sliding his hand down, he cupped her ankle. "Slender ankles that seem too slim to support such a strong woman." Teasing his teeth and tongue around each ankle sent her into a spiral of anticipation. "When we danced I lost my steps because flashes of your ankles distracted me. I wanted to grasp them, like this." He wrapped one massive hand around each of her ankles. "Then part them wide, like this." He spread her legs as wide as the span of his arms.

He held her open and exposed, but his gaze never wavered from hers. Soft summer-sky blue turned smoky and penetrating. She realized even if he looked between her thighs all he would see was the fabric of her dress. Heat from her sex, trapped by the tight weave of pooled *astle,* built the temperature until she was convinced the fabric would ignite.

Drawing her legs together, he balanced her ankles on his shoulders, then slid her down the couch. Her skirt bunched around her hips but still didn't draw high enough to expose her to his gaze. He moved forward so her calves dangled over his back. His uniform felt rough in comparison to her dress, adding a new layer of sensation as he nuzzled her inner thigh.

With a wicked smile, he rubbed his face along her thigh and stopped at the juncture of her legs. "I have heard the term pleading eyes, but yours, Enovese, your eyes are beseeching." His voice puffed a moist breath against the fabric, increasing the temperature of her slick sex.

She could imagine how she looked to him then, with her legs trembling, her breath catching with anticipation, her eyes begging him to please, please, please release the heat from her sex.

"If my eyes don't compel you, could I entreat you with my voice?"

A sinful chuckle moved more warmth against her, causing her to clench her legs, dragging him a bit closer, but not close enough.

"It is your greedy groans and plaintive whimpers that inveigle me most."

He lifted her legs from his shoulders, parting them so he could ease between. He lowered his head and nuzzled his nose into the folds of fabric, seeking out her twitching nub. He knew when he located her clit, for she released a gasp and wriggled closer. His hands to her hips stilled her while he persisted in moving the fabric aside until only one layer barred him from direct contact.

Darting her a glance, he nipped her clit with his teeth, but before she could react, he sucked the pulsing flesh into his mouth. Hot, wet, his seductive mouth pushed her right to the edge, but *astle* blocked the full sensation. Release hovered just beyond her grasp.

She bit back a scream when he stopped. She had thought he would be so aroused that he would not linger, but again, he exercised legendary control. Enovese realized she wanted more than just a shattering release. She wanted to taste him and feel his body atop hers. She wanted to merge with him, clasp him fully, intimately. Terrifying emotions simmered within her heart, and she shut her eyes to block him from discovering the truth: Enovese loved Chur so much she decided that she had to let him go. It was the only way to protect him and give him the power to find his children.

"Thank you, Enovese."

Startled that he had connected to her thoughts, her eyes went wide, and she fumbled for an explanation.

"For wearing the dress, letting your hair fall free, and shaving your luscious sex." He drew the fabric away and placed the sweetest, softest kiss to her mound. "So wanton and wet, so slick and sweet, ah, Enovese, I could happily drown."

Reverently, he closed his eyes and his velvet tongue worked between her swollen lips, then around and around the hood of flesh that cradled her clit.

She grasped his head, twining her fingers in his shadow black hair, tracing her fingertips to his powerful jaw. Hours since her careful shave, his emerging beard rasped and tingled her flesh. Gently, he sucked her clit between his lips, forcing the hood back, exposing her utterly to the ministrations of his probing tongue. Ecstasy consumed her in flames of hunger.

"I wanted to tease you, then have you climax as I plunged within your silken heat; but now, I want to taste your pleasure." With a nipping flick, he drew her to the edge of the plunging precipice. "I want to savor your orgasm. I want to drink every drop of your delight." He met her gaze with concentrated lust filling his eyes. "And then, I will do it all over again when I plunge my cock into you."

His tone and the thrust of his words allowed her to actually feel that moment when his shaft penetrated, possessing her utterly. Her passage contracted around the idea of his penis. With words alone, he ruled her body in ways she barely understood.

"After so many nights of denial, I will work my shaft so deeply into you that you will not know where I end and you begin."

Words escaped her as her breath caught in her chest. She couldn't think straight with her body twitching and straining. His words and the cast of his gaze enthralled her, for she knew he would delay his orgasm until he'd reduced her to a mass of lustful flesh. She would suffer delicious torture at his expert touch.

Masterful and secure, Chur slid his hand up her leg and teased his massive finger against her. "Greedy and grasping," he said, tracing his fingertip around the muscles of her quivering passage. "Would you enjoy my finger plunging into you?" Holding his finger ready, he waited for her reply.

Unable to speak, she nodded.

With inexorable intent, Chur slid his finger into her. His gaze never wavered from her face. Her muscles contracted around his digit, then clutched with dire need. He twisted his hand, twirling his finger deep inside, causing her to gush to the point she knew she would leave a stain against her dress. She didn't care. Lifting her hips, she met his thrusting finger with wild abandon. As she neared the edge of climax, he slowed his pace and lowered his lips to her clit.

Sucking, biting, rasping his tongue along her sensitized flesh as he fingered deep into her, Enovese thrashed in an effort to push over the barrier. Chur forced a second finger inside her, curling them, pressing up against her passage, teasing a secret spot that caused her to go rigid when she hit the edge.

Freefall.

Plunging over the precipice, her physical form reduced to sensation, she dove into light that blinded her to blackness. Consumed with fire, heat that burned yet soothed, Enovese lost consciousness. All she knew in that blissful moment was pure, unadulterated paradise.

Reluctantly, she blinked her way back to reality.

Chur waited, between her legs, rapt with attention.

When she looked at him, he smiled the most satisfied, prideful smile she had ever seen. His smirk lifted the edge of his scar, sculpting his face to dangerously handsome. Confidence that bordered on arrogance exuded from him as he stood, and the twinkle in his gaze said he wasn't finished with her yet. Her heart pounded with raw excitement. Recently released from eight nights of torment, his possessive manner still compelled her nipples to harden and her clit to twitch anew.

He stood over her for a moment, enjoying her disheveled state. He offered his hand and she clasped it. Chur pulled her to her feet, spilling the emerald *astle* down from her hips. Her legs wobbled. He wrapped his massive arms around her, pulling her against his solid form. Clutching his shoulders, she pressed her face against his jacket, feeling delicate, fragile, and gloriously feminine. She reveled in this side of him, this triumphant side where he found the most intense satisfaction in her pleasure.

"You are stunning when orgasm possesses you, Enovese." He trailed his fingers through her hair. "Such rapture causes you to glow."

Such an image caused her to laugh. "At one point I thought I would burst into flames."

He chuckled and nestled her close, pressing his erection into her belly.

Irritation caused her to pull back a bit. "How can you stand any more denial? Why are you not crazed with need?" She worried that she wasn't as desirable as she thought, certainly not enough to inspire the same insatiable lust he created in her.

Tilting his face as he considered her, he traced her lips with his fingertip, speculative and sensual. "I just took your words to heart, that you crave that stunning moment of ecstasy as much as I do. I thought I was being quite the diligent lover to allow you to go first."

A sudden understanding flashed. "How kind of you, mighty Harvester." She batted her lashes, then whispered, "A dose of *umer* also helps."

He chuckled as he pressed his forehead to hers. "I can never fool you for long."

With his face so close, she tried to smell the *umer* on his breath but caught only her scent on him when he kissed her.

Dueling tongues plunged together and rapture held her captive again. Tightening her grip, she realized she didn't want to let him go, not now, not ever. Everything she dreamed of was within her grasp. Chur wanted to bond to her and not because she'd tricked him or he felt obligated. He wanted her because he loved her. He hadn't spoken the words, but she felt the shift in his emotions. Now, she was thinking of sacrificing everything to protect him. To help him help his children. To give him the path to change thousands of years of indoctrination. She had started this process with selfish intent, caring only about herself, but now all she could think of was Chur.

He fumbled with the fasteners on her dress. He broke the kiss in order to mumble, "I can wield a mighty sword, yet I'm undone by simple clasps."

With a step back, she deftly removed the dress. Emerald *astle* pooled around her. Teasingly, she lifted her legs, then stopped, flashing him her ankles.

"Wicked *yondie,*" he murmured, trading his gaze from her feet to her face. "I never should have told you my weakness."

"Should I tell you one of mine?" she asked as she removed his jacket and traced her hands along his chest. "I am most fascinated by your body hair." When he lowered his brows, she continued, "I enjoy shaving you free, then the rough edge as your hair returns, then the thick mat that covers so generously I can scarce see your skin. Such reminds me of the gardens that go from fallow to bursting and back again."

"Poetical *yondie,*" he murmured, preening under her sensual strokes.

She sunk to her knees before him to remove his boots but realized he had already done so. When she glanced up, Chur stepped closer, waggling his brows suggestively. Her hand trembled as she undid his trousers, not from fear but from unbearable anticipation. His engorged cock bounced once freed and pulsed as she slid his trousers down and off. Looming above her nude, hard, every muscle in his chest bulging, Enovese lifted up and placed her mouth tentatively close. He waited breathless, his eyes blazing and impatient.

"Do you have any idea what else intrigues me about your body?" she asked, letting her moist breath waft along his shaft. His tortured groan appeased her. Apparently, his *umer*-induced self-control wavered.

"Tell me, but tell me fast for the *umer* has worn off."

With a wicked smile, she stroked her hands up his legs and cupped his muscular buttocks. "I love the taste of you." Drawing him forward, she wrapped her lips around his dewy tip and drew him into the hot hollow of her mouth. Salty and earthy, she rolled his luscious taste over her tongue, reveling in the texture of his silky hard cock.

His buttocks tensed as he fought for control.

Swirling her tongue round and round, she held him steady with her hands. Quite suddenly, he stepped back, yanking out of her mouth with a pop. He pulled her to her feet and lifted her into his arms. He strode to the chair they used for the ritual of control and sat down, facing the mirror.

As he turned her in his lap, facing her toward the mirror, draping her legs to the outside of his, he said, "I know why that mirror is here, you used it to shave your lovely sex." Parting his legs caused hers to part wider. His erection pressed hot and hard against her bottom. "Now I will use it to watch my shaft slide into you."

He lifted her up and pressed the tip against her slick passage. Ever so slowly, he lowered her, his eyes riveted to the mirror. Entranced, she watched too. Glossy lips parted around his cock, welcoming him inside, stretching to accommodate his girth. Straining veins along his shaft and the dark dusting of hair caused his cock to look sinister as it invaded her exposed sex. To see him plunging into her heightened the sensation of feeling him do so. Eight nights of painful denial, longing to know him this way again, were suddenly over. When he filled her fully they gasped simultaneously.

"Kiss me, Enovese."

She turned her head and kissed him over her shoulder, tasting her passion on his lips, twining her hands in his thick hair. His hands stroked her, teasing her nipples, cupping her breasts, as if he had never touched her before. A slight trembling in his fingertips expressed eight nights of craving. It pleased her to know he was as frustrated as she was, but her satisfaction diminished when he did not thrust. He simply held her and caressed her, driving her into a flurry of need. When she attempted to move, he nipped her shoulder and ordered her to hold still.

"Now it is my turn, Enovese. I will drag things out for as long as I please." Her growl of frustration elicited a chuckle. "Your aggravation is only fueling my determination."

"Why?" She tried to keep her voice even, but the one-word question came out as a petulant whine.

Catching her gaze in the mirror, he said, "I want you to stop thinking of sacrificing yourself for me."

His words stunned her and clarified his motivations. Increasing her anticipation opened the conduit between their thoughts. She scrambled for an answer.

"You need not speak, for I do not need an explanation. I can see the reason in your eyes. You love me. You believe you are doing the noble thing in releasing me from my claim, but the decision is mine."

"You claimed me in the heat of passion—"

"I have laid my claim to you." He cut her off with tender words. "I am a man of my word and I have no intention of going back on my claim. Nor will I release you from the claim you made to me. Do you understand?"

She shook her head. "Kasmiri, the daughter of the empress, could help you retrieve your children."

His laugh shook him within her, shocking her for it was so out of place during such a heated debate. He didn't ask how she knew Kasmiri was at the Festival of Temptation. He'd probably read the truth in her eyes.

Chur met her gaze in the glass. "Kasmiri wouldn't care, Enovese. She is the most spoiled woman-child I have yet encountered. Do you know what she asked of me tonight? She wanted a private showing of my skills." His disgusted frown conveyed how he felt about that. "Kasmiri is no tender sacrifice ready to bestow her virginity to the Harvester. Kasmiri is ruthless, calculating, and unbearably calloused. She stole my ceremonial sword and is holding it hostage until I agree to claim her at the Harvest."

Enovese gasped. She had thought Kasmiri would be a perfect bondmate for Chur, but not if she were attempting to force his hand. With a wince, Enovese realized she had done the exact same thing by tricking Chur into harvesting her. She had only compounded her error in trying to force him to a new path without any consideration for his feelings in the matter. Her guilty gaze met his.

Chur nodded. "You once tossed angry words at me that I hid behind my duty from fear of decisions, but now that I've staked my claim, you wish me to retreat." He sighed and nestled her hips firmly against his. "As you once said, I am a man. A man with needs and desires. I have a right to decide what is best for me." With a string of open-mouthed kisses along her neck and shoulder, he said, "What is best for me is choosing a woman who loves me for me, and that woman is you."

His words touched her romantic and tender heart, washing away any lingering doubts about his intentions. He forgave her for her actions and loved her despite her trickery. Still, he had not said the words she so longed to hear, but such didn't matter. Words were not as strong as actions. Tonight had not been about mastering her, or proving his staying power, or delaying his gratification. Tonight had been about showing her without words that he put her before himself. What she had been thinking of doing was along the same lines, but the difference was, she wasn't allowing him the right to choose for himself. She had no right to push him in the direction she thought best. He was smart enough to decide that for himself.

Tilting her head back, she kissed him, conveying to him without words how much she loved him. Abandoning her plans vexed her practical mind, but her heart and soul soared with gratitude. As she felt him moving within her, her passion changed from a demanding need for release to a softer longing to share their passion in this most intimate way.

Chur slid forward on the chair and parted his legs farther so that he could more easily see their coupled bodies. "Do you see how we are joined?"

Enovese cast her gaze to the glass. She could barely discern where he ended and she began, for they had merged into one.

"That is what I want, not only for tonight but for a lifetime. Not sex, Enovese, but our bodies and souls inextricably united in pleasure and acceptance." Rolling his hips as he rocked her caused gentle friction inside her passage. He teased his hand along her belly to cup her mound, slipping a finger between her lips to stroke her clit. "I want to feel you surround me, I want to know the heat of your depths, the scope of your need, the pinnacle of your passion, for within all of that is you welcoming me. That is you giving yourself to me as I give myself to you." He took a deep breath and met her gaze. "Please tell me you understand."

How could he think he did not command the power of a poet? His words were beautiful, and the plaintive honesty in his eyes compelled her to whisper, "I understand. I am so sorry for what I've done."

Chur slid back on the chair, wrapping his arms around her, holding her tightly against him. "No apologies. I do not need or want them." He lowered his head to rub his cheek against hers as their gazes held within the glass. "We have many problems to overcome, Enovese. We will not solve them overnight and certainly not if we are at odds with one another. Working together, joined fully as we are now, will give us the strength to prevail."

She placed her arms over his, deepening the hug. Enovese thought they complemented one another perfectly. She was pale where he was bronze. She was slender where muscles rippled him. Beyond their physical forms, they meshed well, for he was a man of action where she was a woman of contemplation. He was impulsive where she was pragmatic. Together, they balanced.

Time passed but she was unaware for he trapped her attention in the mirror. His intense gaze stroked her without a touch, building her passion, igniting a fire along her flesh, and awakening a new and powerful connection. This bond was more than sex, far more than love. In the past, their thoughts had connected, but this was a sharing of souls. The intimacy was both frightening and magnificent.

Rolling slowly, from the tips of her toes and tips of her fingers, pleasure drew strength as it pulsed toward her sex. Her breath grew unsteady. Her body undulated from within but not with a frantic need to reach the peak of climax. This was a languorous dance she yielded to, allowing the pleasure to build and possess her utterly.

24

Tandalsul filled his rooms with bright light and Chur awoke with renewed confidence. He and Enovese moved through the morning routine with the ease of lifelong companions. Last night had caused profound changes in his psyche. A murmur in the back of his mind kept him connected to her, allowing him to tap into her feelings and thoughts. At first it worried him, this new connection, for the idea of her perpetually in his mind was intimidating, but he found he could suppress the intensity by turning his attention elsewhere. If he wished, he could block her access and she the same. They could limit the depth of the intimacy if they chose.

While she dressed him, he turned his awareness to her and discovered how much she enjoyed gearing him up for training.

Enovese laughed, her bare breasts bouncing. "I can feel you exploring my mind, Chur. Remember this is a dual connection." She caressed his arm. "I thoroughly enjoy transforming you from a man to a warrior. A fearsome intensity radiates from you that I find very arousing."

"Perhaps the change is not from the gear but the fact that a beautiful, naked woman is dressing me."

Enovese tightened the last strap on his chest plate. "You should go now before this naked woman decides to train you in a completely different way." She slipped visions of herself lashing him to the bed and then using him as she wished right into his mind.

He tossed back his head and laughed. "I would thoroughly enjoy your instructions."

After a lingering kiss good-bye, Chur strode to the training rooms. He discovered he no longer cared who was scheming or why. Such thoughts only distracted him, and he vowed to keep his focus on increasing his strength and dexterity. He moved through his routine, pushing himself beyond his perceived limits, reaching for excellence, reveling in the sweat that saturated his gear.

All the grunting, groaning, and smacking of weapons stopped abruptly as every man's attention turned to the diminutive woman in the doorway. Dressed in the drab brown of a servant, the woman kept her delicate head lowered, her wisps of brown hair hiding her face. Every man simply stared, for none but men entered this hallowed chamber. What stunned them more was that a belt of crimson proclaimed her a servant of the empress.

A chill of foreboding shivered down Chur's spine.

Helton approached the woman and respectfully inquired about her business. Despite the crushing silence, Chur could not hear her response for her voice was too high-pitched. Helton scratched his head and turned, flicking his fingers impatiently at Chur.

A thousand bricks landed in his gut. With heavy steps, Chur joined them at the doorway, fully aware of every man's attention on him. He didn't even speculate what they were thinking. Such a situation was unheard of. Why would the empress send her servant to the training rooms, and what did she want with him?

"The empress requests an audience with you." Helton flashed him a scowl of suspicion. "Have you any idea why?"

Chur shrugged. If Helton could keep his secrets closed, then Chur felt he had every right to do the same.

Bulky armor and muscular forearms impeded Helton from crossing his arms, but his mistrust came across crystal clear. Helton wanted to pelt Chur with a thousand questions, but Helton had lost his chance when he dismissed Chur cycles ago.

Helton continued to consider Chur with a sullen expression, thinking his silence would compel Chur to speak.

A perverse pleasure at thwarting his mentor, who had dared to abandon him, caused Chur to lift himself through the chest and steady his stance. He simply considered Helton and awaited his permission. By his duty, Chur could not move from this spot until Helton discharged him.

Grumbling, Helton dismissed and insulted Chur with a flick of his fingers. Helton turned his back on Chur so fast he left a wind in his wake. It did little to cool Chur's fury. Absorbing the now open disdain of his mentor took tremendous strength. No mortal blow could wound as deeply as his handler's contempt. One way or another, Chur vowed to make Helton regret his actions.

The *serbred* nodded and turned on her heel, her barefoot steps gliding along the hallways as Chur followed three paces behind. He didn't speak. She would only repeat the request of her mistress.

A baggy dress of dark brown proclaimed her station as a servant; her brown hair exactly matching the color proclaimed her a *serbred*. Bred for passivity and obedience, their family lines went back to the time of the ancients. All *serbreds* had pale skin, brown hair and eyes, and extremely short stature. The *serbred* Chur followed barely stood to his waist.

They would speak but only to repeat their instructions. "My lady, the Empress, requests an audience with Chur Zenge."

That is all she would say. Chur followed her delicate steps for so long he grew annoyed. He wanted to toss the plodding servant over his shoulder and make haste to the Throne of the Empress. As a part of the palace guard, Chur knew every nook and cranny of the palace, and certainly where the empress sat in residence.

Then again, perhaps he shouldn't wish to hurry for he did not know what the empress wanted. Chur doubted it was something good. He was fairly certain she had found his ceremonial sword in her daughter's possession. Would Clathia demand an explanation, or insist Chur claim Kasmiri at the Harvest? Chur wouldn't put it past Kasmiri to devise such a clever plot. Kasmiri knew what she was doing when she stole his blade. After their dance, Chur had stepped close to hear her over the cacophony when she'd deftly removed his sword and walked away, hiding it in the voluminous folds of her dress. By the time he'd followed, she had hidden it. Her smile of triumph dissolved when Chur flatly refused to barter his integrity. Kasmiri was livid that Chur wasn't enamored of her charms. Apparently "no" was a word the young woman was not used to hearing.

When they reached the throne room, the *serbred* pulled the door curtain back and then lifted her hand, directing him inside. Chur entered. A blood red carpet stretched across the floor to a raised dais. Empress Clathia sat upon an elaborately carved Onic throne. The back of the chair loomed over her, easily twice her height, yet she did not seem small upon such a massive chair.

Clad in crimson, her elaborate bodysuit covered every bit of her skin but for her hands and face. Judging by the texture and the loops around the waist of the garment, the empress had been climbing *galbol* trees for sport. Rich red contrasted her tawny brown flesh and highlighted her piercing eyes. Long strands of rich black hair flowed down around her face and curled around her heavy breasts. Chur didn't know how many seasons had touched the empress because she had the proud carriage of an ancient but the smooth face of a sacrifice. More than beautiful, Clathia was commanding and utterly intimidating.

With a tilt of her chin, the empress bid him approach.

His heart pounded as he advanced.

A line of palace guards stood on either side of the carpet that led to her throne. Chur saw a few familiar faces, but they looked through him, seeing him but not acknowledging him. Everything in the room was immaculate and perfect, the air smelled of night-blooming flowers. He took a deep breath and his own rank smell hit him. He felt like a noxious weed infiltrating a pristine flowerbed.

When he reached the dais, he dropped to one knee and bowed his head. Protocol demanded he not speak until she gave him permission. A thousand thoughts rolled through his mind causing his heart rate to increase. He calmed himself with deep breaths.

He heard a snap of fingers and then the pounding march of two dozen feet exiting the room. Clathia had dismissed her guard. Fresh sweat beaded along his forehead and trickled down his neck. Drawing each breath grew more difficult for the air grew heavy and thick. His neck and knee began to ache.

"You may stand, Harvester." Her cultured voice was low and strong, but a subtle humor lurked below.

"Thank you, my lady." Chur drew to his feet and stood at attention. Up close, he discovered two barely perceptible lines bracketed her mouth, indicating she smiled often. When he turned his attention to her eyes, he was startled to discover they were not black but a deep golden brown. A terrible sadness simmered in the depths. Once she had smiled so much it marked her face but not for a long time.

"Beside me is an empty chair."

Startled, Chur glanced at the throne for her consort. A swath of black *astle* covered the seat as if in mourning. Perhaps all his worry was over nothing. Clathia might wish him to discover the truth behind her consort's mysterious death. Such was not within the scope of his duties, but if she asked, he would comply. His interactions with the empress were limited, but he'd always admired her ability to wield tremendous power with gentle compassion.

Clathia's hand trembled as she stroked the arm of the empty throne. She did not have to say how much she missed her consort.

Chur lowered his face respectfully, acknowledging her pain without words. Empathy filled him, for he would be devastated if he lost Enovese.

"For two seasons I have kept a lonesome vigil at my throne and in my bed." A weary loneliness muddied her golden eyes.

A buzz of anxiety coiled around his gut, for he doubted the empress discussed such things without good reason. Another thousand bricks joined those already weighing down his belly. Chur had no idea what she wished him to say, so he held his tongue.

With a flick of her wrist, Clathia removed the swath of black fabric. His ceremonial sword lay on the seat of the consort throne. Gems glittered and polished metal gleamed. Enovese kept all his gear clean, but someone had spent hours meticulously cleaning the sword.

When his gaze met hers, accusation sharpened the muddy brown to sparkling gold. He held perfectly still, for looking away or fidgeting would convey his anxiety. Had her daughter placed the blade there to implicate him in the death of her mother's consort?

Clathia's eyes narrowed and her brows lowered as she considered him. "How bold you are, Chur Zenge, to lay claim to the empress herself."

He did his best not to react, but his confusion must have shown in his face. His blade placed there was not an implication of guilt but a proclamation of intent. He could not have been more shocked if the empress transformed into a thousand butterflies.

Clathia frowned, mirroring his puzzlement.

They stood at impasse for a long moment.

Understanding washed over her face and she released her rigid posture with a sigh. "You did not place the sword here."

"No, my lady."

A delicate pink blushed her cheeks as she gritted her teeth.

Chur wasn't certain, but he thought the empress had been rather delighted at the idea of him audaciously laying claim to her. To discover he had no such intentions crushed her tender notions. An apology filled his mouth, but he chose not to speak for his words would offer no comfort.

He knew her daughter, Kasmiri, was responsible for this very cruel prank. He understood why Kasmiri wished to hurt him, but why would she lash out at him at the expense of her own mother? Kasmiri struck him as a spoiled woman-child, but to display such hostility toward her mother was appalling.

"Who placed your sword upon my consort's throne?"

Chur swallowed hard for her intelligent eyes had already surmised that he knew precisely who had done the deed. Lying would not serve him well but tact might. "My lady, I cannot say who placed it there, but the last person to possess my blade was your daughter."

Crimson lips parted with shock. "You intend to lay claim to

Kasmiri?" Clathia was not pleased with the notion. Fury stiffened her body, causing her hands to grip white on the arms of her throne.

"No, my lady."

"Then why did you give her the sword?"

"I did not give Kasmiri my blade."

"Explain." She tapped her nails impatiently against the carved Onic wood of her throne.

"After our dance, she leaned close to speak to me and removed the sword." He discreetly left out the part where Kasmiri said he could have it back once he'd demonstrated his prowess privately.

"What did she ask of you?"

Trapped, Chur struggled to answer. He did not want to malign Kasmiri or hurt her mother with the truth that her daughter maliciously schemed to possess him. "Kasmiri expressed an interest in having me claim her at the Harvest."

Clathia laughed as if she'd been holding back for years. "You are more than a warrior, noble Chur Zenge. You are a smooth diplomat." Her shrewd gaze assessed him. "Kasmiri does not express an interest, she demands, but you are kind to place the truth in the most flattering terms."

For the first time in the presence of the empress, Chur relaxed. She was a wise woman who knew well the impulses of those around her, especially her daughter. However, Clathia's speculative gaze sparked a new twist of apprehension. She examined him in a leisurely but entirely possessive manner.

Crimson fabric clung to her lush form when she rose. The bodysuit left little to the imagination. She moved with the sensuality of an exorbitantly priced *yondie*. Chur had to tilt his head back to meet her gaze as she stood several steps above him. She turned and the fabric caressed her rounded bottom when she bent over to retrieve the blade. He wondered if she and her consort had played erotic games like he and Enovese.

Would any man dare to spank the bottom of the empress even if she asked? Surprised at the turn of his thoughts, he looked away but not before she noticed the direction of his gaze. He wanted to offer an apology, but Clathia did not seem angry but pleased. He was not the first man she had caught examining her. She wore her beauty like a weapon, for she knew exactly what power it granted her.

Holding the sword in her hands, she descended the steps of the dais until she stood one step above him, her face level with his. He couldn't help but examine her anew. Her lips were full, and a slight nip in her upper lip gave a decidedly bow shape to her mouth. Tiny lines that echoed her laugh lines radiated around her eyes. Her hands were small with palms lighter than the rest of her skin, but her slender hands conveyed strength and delicate power. Up close, she was even more stunning, causing him to take a deep breath. Her perfume entranced him, bringing to mind a lush garden in full bloom. Embarrassed, he wanted to step back to protect her from his stench.

Her teeth flashed white against her crimson lips when she smiled. "You are an impressive man, Chur Zenge. Rare is the warrior with the eloquence of a diplomat."

When she offered out the blade, he took it and placed it on his belt. It jarred with his filthy appearance, but it pleased him to have it returned. Relief filled him that despite Kasmiri's machinations, she had not succeeded in harming him or her mother.

A jolt galvanized him when Clathia placed her hand on his shoulder.

"Your strength is most beguiling." Her low and intimate voice caressed his ears as her hand trailed down his arm to cup his bicep. "I am not surprised my daughter would seek to possess you by any means necessary."

He had undergone detailed protocol instructions, but he did not recall how one was to deal with a blatant come-on by the empress. He plunged back to the awkward stance he had as a young man in Ampir. When the women of his village flirted with him, he simply stood silently uncomfortable, clinging to his dreams to escape the longing in his loins. In all honesty, he found the empress most appealing, but his heart and soul belonged to Enovese. While he appreciated Clathia's magnificence, he had no desire to sample her charms, but how did one rebuff the empress without incurring her wrath?

Tactfully, he said, "You flatter me, my lady."

She laughed with delightful joy. "I seek not to compliment you but to convey to you my interest." With a graceful step, she joined him on the red carpet, tilting her face up to meet his gaze. "I find you fascinating, Chur Zenge. There has never been a Harvester with such an intriguing combination of physical power and sharp intellect." Caressing the length of his arm, she added, "All of that wrapped up in a delightfully handsome package."

Sweat trickled along his back. "You flatter me, my lady."

"Strip."

Her one-word command brooked no argument. Chur carefully removed all his gear, piling it before her feet. Nude and dirty, he cast his clothing aside without pretense, but he kept his face lowered. Sweat gathered in his armpits and trickled down his sides.

Clathia stroked his chest. "I would like to see you when your hair has grown back." She explored the smoothly shaven area, then the parts still thick with hair. Her touch implied ownership, as if he were nothing more than a meat animal she considered purchasing. "You defy the perception of grunting brutality that embodies most Harvesters."

Terrified at the turn this audience had taken, Chur simply repeated, "You flatter me, my lady."

With slow and deliberate intent, Clathia lowered her hand and cupped his sex, gauging his reaction by keeping her attention on his face. Her hand was cool against his heated flesh. He held his breath, trying not to panic. Shame caused him to slump and turn his head to the side, away from her probing gaze, which only caused her to chuckle and stroke more firmly. Deep inside his chest burbled a scream of fury that no one should touch him this way without his consent. He held the torment locked behind gritted teeth for he could not reprimand the empress. He allowed anger to replace his shame, for this was not his fault. Even the strongest man in the realm could not raise a hand to this woman. With a deep breath, he stood tall again, turning his attention to the connection with Enovese, but it flickered weakly as a sputtering crystal.

"Relax, mighty Harvester," Clathia crooned to his ear, standing on tiptoe to reach. Her breath smelled of sweet wine and her breast pressed against his arm. "I only wish to examine my consort."

His heart raced for he did not wish to be her consort. He wanted to wrap his hands around Kasmiri's neck and throttle the life out of her for setting him up. A new thought pressed in his mind, that Clathia and her daughter competed against each other. Each trying to take what the other wanted. Where Kasmiri used her youth, beauty, and a viciously clever mind, Clathia used her experience, beauty, and the absolute power of her position.

Skillfully, Clathia continued to rub and stroke, but no matter how adept her technique, she could not summon the same burning lust as Enovese. When he remained flaccid her touch turned groping, tugging his hairs hard enough to pull some free. He tried not to wince.

When Clathia realized that no amount of stimulation would harden him, she yanked her hand back and then slapped him so hard his head whipped to the side.

Stunned, he took the blow without any outward reaction. Her eyes blazed. Her face turned red with frustration. Her breath puffed against the sweat of his face and chest, cooling him despite her heated fury.

"I am not some virginal sacrifice flattering you to seek your approval. I am the empress. With a flick of my finger I could have you castrated for your impertinence."

Chur bowed his head. He did not know what to say or do. He stood statue-still. If he could summon an erection to please the empress, he would, but his body flatly refused to respond. Panic was not an arousing emotion.

"I care not that you are sterile. Such information compelled me to consider choosing you as my consort, for I do not want any more children, but I will not accept a man who is impotent without drugs or oils."

Her words rolled over him, nipping and biting, destroying a part of him with shocking finality. He dismissed the claim of impotency forthwith. Chur did not need drugs or oils to achieve or maintain an erection. Enovese could command such a reaction with just a glance, the tilt of her nose, or the flash of her ankles. Just because the empress could not stimulate him to hardness didn't mean he was impotent. However, her audacious claim that he was sterile confounded him. How would the empress know such a thing?

"I am sterile?" he asked, thinking she must know with certainty to bandy the information about so blithely.

"Of course." With a disgusted sigh, she wiped her hand along her bodysuit as if touching him rendered her filthy. "Why do you think the magistrate and your handler conspire to unseat you as the Harvester?"

His head spun. Ambo Votny and Helton Ook had united to set up multiple challengers. In one fell swoop, the information explained all of the questions plaguing him. Helton had turned on him because he wasn't living up to his full duties as the Harvester. Which meant that Ambo, Helton, and even the empress herself knew what happened with the Harvester issue. They knew all about the despicable *paratanist* selection ritual.

A new and more terrible thought invaded his mind; he and Enovese should have surmised this, for if the empress had no qualms about breeding servants, she would not hesitate to breed *paratanists*. The secret they had uncovered was only a secret to the masses, not to the elite.

Chur clung to the one good thing that came of this startling information; if he was sterile, he had not produced any children. As much as he'd wanted children, he hadn't wanted to subject any to the harsh brutality of life in the *tanist* house.

Clathia must have noticed his relief. "Why does this information please you?" Her glare sharpened as she assessed him. Her voice dripped with snide rebuff when she speculated that "No dalliances with the elite will return to haunt you."

It took a moment for him to process that she thought he was pleased he could not have impregnated any of his conquests. He did not doubt that some of the elite would have told tales of seducing him that were utterly false.

Calmly, he said, "I am the Harvester, my lady. I do not dally with any, for physical intimacy is against my sworn duty."

She scoffed. "I have heard tales of the recruits turning to one another for pleasure. Perhaps that is why my touch does not arouse; my hand is too soft." Clathia spun on her heel and ascended the dais. At a table tucked beside the throne, she lifted a crystal decanter and poured a cup of wine. She sipped, glaring at him over the rim. Her inability to arouse him infuriated her for he doubted she'd ever encountered such resistance. Most men would stiffen at the sight of her in the body-hugging outfit.

He wanted to say his lack of interest was not because of her soft hand but her cold heart. Clinging to tact, he met her flashing gaze and said, "I am trained to resist temptation. My lack of response is a tribute to my teachings, not an indication of your appeal."

Somewhat mollified, Clathia took another sip. A resigned smirk turned her harsh face beautiful again. "You are indeed a fine diplomat." She inclined her head in the direction of his gear. "Dress." She sat upon her throne, cradling her glass as she watched him don his gear. "A Harvester may choose among the most beautiful young women in all the realm, but you have rejected them all. Your handler refused to speculate, but I believe you have shrewdly waited for a sacrifice who possesses power. Perhaps my daughter Kasmiri is of interest."

Chur could not think of a sacrifice he wanted less than Kasmiri. He'd rather castrate himself with a rusty blade than be saddled with such a vacuous narcissist. Moreover, he did not believe the empress wanted him to select her daughter. He firmly believed Clathia wanted him to favor her over her daughter. Rather than submitting himself as consort to the empress, he'd rather die on the battlefield. He wanted but one woman. He wanted Enovese. He would not settle for a lesser bondmate than the one who had fully captured his heart and soul.

Once he had dressed, he faced the empress. "By my duty I am burdened with many restraints. I spend my life learning the art of battle and I put my life on the line to defend my position. I embody sex, yet I must abstain from any physical pleasure. The only right I have is the absolute right to choose my mate, and that is not a decision I take lightly."

"Warrior, diplomat, and a romantic. How charming." Clathia saluted him with her glass. "By the prophecy you will find your bondmate during the Harvest." A mocking laugh erupted as she shook her head. "Perhaps you are not as intelligent as I thought."

Tension crept into his muscles. He'd had enough of her crude seduction and her insults. The high respect he once held for the empress had reduced to a low tolerance. He wished she would just finish and dismiss him.

"Let me enlighten you, mighty Harvester. There is no eternal bondmate. Such is a myth crafted by the poets. You should have chosen at last Harvest, for you will not make it to the next Harvest." She drew her fingertip along the rim of her glass and flashed him an arch smile. "Well, not without my help."

Chur almost laughed. She was as clever and manipulative as her daughter. Everything before this moment meant little. All of it—from the consort claim, to the stripping, to the groping—was to unbalance him. Throwing him into turmoil made him more pliable for when she asked for what she truly wanted.

Narrowing her eyes and tilting her head, Clathia said, "At the Festival of Temptation you spoke to a woman, Arianda Rostvaika, who was once a Harvester."

Chur nodded, keeping his face carefully neutral. Clathia was intelligent, but it was unlikely she knew the woman was Enovese's mother. To Clathia, Enovese did not have a name or a mother; she was only a *paratanist*.

Clathia lowered her voice and said, "I want you to kill Arianda Rostvaika."

25

Chur was late. Enovese tried to keep her attention on the Harvester tome, but the squiggly handwriting and anxiety over Chur conspired against her. Repeatedly, she tried to connect to his mind, but an odd whooshing sound, like waves upon the shore of the Valry Sea, blocked her access. She nibbled her lower lip, consumed with the idea he laid injured and unconscious.

When he finally entered, she shot from her chair, bashing her leg into the table. A demand for an explanation died in her throat when she saw his face. Smudges of darkness hollowed his eyes. His normally proud posture slumped with defeat. Bronze skin streaked with dirt and sweat looked sunken and pale.

Silently, she moved to his side and removed his gear. She detached his ceremonial sword without comment. His normally ripe after-training scent was more pungent, mixing exhaustion with anxiety and a nasty tinge of fear. She noted no external bruises, but his spirit had taken a terrible blow. Respecting his privacy and knowing that he would speak when ready, Enovese made no further attempts to probe his mind.

At the bathing unit, he touched the collar of her robe, and she removed it. Together, they washed, lingering and exploring. Chur drew her into his arms and simply held her as water streamed over their entwined bodies. Where she had always found such strength in him, he now took that from her. He clung to her as if she could buoy him from everything without their tiny world within. She felt no fear. She could be strong when he was weak, for he would be strong when she was weak. Wrapping her arms around him, she held him, cradling him against her, conveying power and compassion with her embrace.

After bathing and eating, she drew him to his bed. She placed him on his belly and massaged him with soothing oils. No matter how deftly she worked, he only tensed more.

She climbed off him and asked, "What can I do?"

"Nothing," he mumbled into the pillow. With a sigh, he rolled over and faced her. "I am trapped, Enovese, and as hard as I try, I cannot find an escape."

For such a strong man he seemed terribly defenseless. He had yet to open his thoughts to her and she realized he was not hiding something. He was protecting her from something. Whatever happened gnawed at him and he was afraid of hurting her with the truth. He would not let her see it, nor would he speak of it. However, keeping her in the dark wouldn't help.

She placed her hand on his leg. "You must tell me what happened today. Remember last night you said that only together could we triumph." Her mind flashed on their bodies so deeply entwined that she could not discern where one ended and the other began. Much like the carving on the door. A flash of insight caused her to understand what the carving conveyed; two becoming one, two becoming stronger as one than in their separate halves. She did not think the ancients meant for it to apply to her and Chur but to the issue of the two Harvesters. Did the ancients somehow revere *paratanists* as the definitive joining of the ultimate male and female counterparts?

After considering her hand upon his leg, he offered, "I was summoned by the empress today. She . . ." Chur trailed off and cast his face down. His handsome features turned stoic and harsh.

Enovese waited for him to continue, but he simply shook his head. It took great strength to set her frustration aside. She desperately wanted to know but pushing Chur would only cause him to withdraw. What had the empress done to him? She remembered him saying Kasmiri had his sword, but tonight when he'd returned, the blade was on his belt. Her stomach sank. What had he done to get it back?

Summer-sky eyes met hers, touching her with a tender vulnerability. Slowly, he opened the connection and showed her exactly what happened. She lived each moment as if it had happened to her. Enovese felt his shock at Clathia thinking he'd issued a claim to her, to his shame when the empress ordered him to strip, to his horror when she groped him. Her emotions surged, blending confusion, repulsion, and embarrassment. Now she understood why he'd held back, for if he'd hit her with everything all at once, she would have collapsed from the onslaught. Even with him trickling the information to her gradually, she still jerked with each new revelation, then the final crushing truth: He must kill her mother or die during the challenge.

His words, that he felt trapped without escape, now made perfect sense. He must either murder her mother or die in challenge. Two choices faced him, and neither was acceptable. More damaging was that she had berated him for not being able to make decisions. Her harsh condemnation haunted her now.

Enovese did not want her mother to die, but she did not want Chur to die. Speechless, she simply looked at him.

"I did not expect you to offer a solution." Chur moved away and rolled off the bed. "I have already made my decision." He stood looking down at her. "I will not kill to protect myself. I would rather die honorably than commit such a foul act."

Her heart skipped a beat, then pounded ruthlessly in her chest. "Did you tell the empress that?" she asked, for he'd closed her off from the final moments of his time with Clathia.

He turned his back on her.

"Chur?"

His chest lifted with his breath, tensing every muscle all the way to his calves. Nude, he was beautiful in his strength and power. Oil glistened along his body from her attempt to soothe him, but now it cast his form sleek and dangerous. He moved away from the bed, pacing across the floor. She didn't know what to say. She cringed at asking him anything more for a part of her did not want to know. She could not ask him to kill her mother, yet she did not want him to die. How could they solve such an impossible situation?

Horrified, Enovese realized she did not know her mother and her mother did not know her. Forced to choose, Enovese would pick Chur. Her stomach revolted that she even considered dismissing her mother's life. What kind of a foul being was she to even think of killing the woman herself just to protect Chur? Gasping, Enovese pushed the thought away. How could she even contemplate murdering her own mother to protect Chur? Was she so desperate to possess him she would destroy any who stood in her way, even her own mother?

Enovese watched him pace, her brow knitted in concentration. Turning her mind from the horror of her thoughts, she moved to matters that were more practical. "Why does Clathia wish death upon Arianda?"

Chur missed not a step in his pacing. "I know not."

His tone only aggravated her for she sensed that he did know but refused to share. "I cannot make a decision if I do not understand all the facts."

Chur spun on his heel and faced her. "You do not need to make a decision. The choice is mine and I choose not to become an assassin for the empress."

His eyes blazed, searing her with intensity. He had not asked her for a solution, but she was the brain where he was the brawn. A wave of new anger surged inside her breast for again, she had no choice in the matter. Her life seemed ever determined by outside forces that cared nothing for her.

Chur pulled back his still-damp hair and blew out a tense breath. "I honestly do not know why Clathia wants Arianda dead only that she does. If I knew, I would tell you. But not for you to decide if she is deserving of death. Whatever Arianda has done is none of my concern."

Enovese understood that Chur could not cast himself into the role of judge over another. Dispensing death without battle was not within him. Softly, she asked, "Why would the empress demand this of you? She has hundreds of dedicated servants and a multitude of palace guards who literally worship her."

Chur stopped pacing. "I thought on that most of today and all I can think is that she wishes to have something over me. Some secret that she can wield against me when I am no longer the Harvester. Perhaps she has a place for me carefully thought out, a position where I would be her puppet."

Political intrigues were not what Enovese studied, but she understood enough of the struggles between the elite to know they always sought power over one another. Every dance, every dinner, every tiny gesture could become a bargaining point. She doubted the empress would act rashly in choosing Chur. Clathia had weighed and measured people within her power and selected Chur over them all. The question was why. What did Chur possess that the empress wanted?

"I see the wheels turning in your mind, Enovese." Chur's tone was cautionary.

Irritation showed in hers when she said, "Do you expect me to stop thinking merely because you have made up your mind?" She let out a tense breath. "You and I both know I have no power to force you to do anything. Clearly, I have no choice in the matter, so at least let me have my thoughts." She turned her head away, hiding her face behind the curtain of her hair. She felt his body sink into the bed beside her, but she refused to look at him. He pulled back her hair, draping it over her shoulder.

"I do not wish to fight with you, Enovese." He slid his fingertips along the back of her arm. "We have so little time left. I would rather spend those moments in almost any way other than surly silence or heated bickering."

Reminding her of that simple fact drained all the fight right out of her. She turned and lifted her face to his. "I do not want to fight with you either." Pressing her lips to his, she kissed him softly, then drew back. "But I honestly cannot give up. My whole life has been a series of choices made by others and forced on me. This is no different. If I give up now, if I do not put all I have learned to task and struggle to find a solution . . ." she trailed off and strove to find the right words. "Giving up now would make my whole life pointless."

Chur nodded, sympathetic to her reasons, but determination stamped clear lines across his face. "I wish you to understand that nothing you say will sway me to murder a woman I have no grudge against. Clathia's rancor is not mine." He twined his fingers with hers. "I long loathed being a tool wielded by the prophecy, but I will not become a tool wielded by the empress. For committing such an act would enslave me to her. Do you comprehend why I simply will not do this?"

"Of course I do." She gripped his hand. "But do you see that I do not want you to die for your nobility?"

"There is no other way."

It frustrated her that a man who rose to greatness by fighting his way to the top would suddenly give up without any fight at all. If she didn't know him better, she would think he wanted to die.

"What happened in the last moments with Clathia? Why would you not show that to me?" Enovese hoped against hope that something in that last exchange would give her the sliver of an idea on how to change this predicament.

"Because she made matters very clear. If I did not follow her wishes, I would not live past the challenge. I spared you from the ugliness in her tone. Clathia is beautiful but more ruthless and cunning than any I have ever met. To defy her demand is to condemn myself to death."

"Death before dishonor." Her voice sounded hollow to her own ears. Every recruit knew well that code, and surely the empress knew the inculcation of the recruits. A new and more dangerous thought crossed her mind. "What if that is the point, that Clathia knew you would refuse such a dishonorable act and thus willingly die in the challenge?"

Chur frowned, his scar twisting his lip. "What would she stand to gain by revealing the betrayal of Helton and Ambo? I can do nothing against either man, and they set the scheme into motion long before Clathia got wind of it. She is just using their machinations to her own ends."

Staring at their joined hands, she again thought of the carving on the door and chalice box. Two figures blending, becoming one, rising above the chaos below. "If you did kill Arianda, that means the empress has the power to alter the challenge. She could thwart the plans of Helton and Ambo. How exactly would she do that? One word to them and they rescind a plan it took them cycles to enact?" Enovese shook her head. "I do not think the empress has any say in the structure of the challenge."

Casting a gaze to the Harvester tome on the table, Chur pursed his lips, then glanced back to her. "Then why the summoning and all those ridiculous actions?"

Enlightenment hit. "Because either way you die."

Chur's uplifted brows asked the question.

"Even if you did as she asked and killed Arianda, you would then die in the challenge that she cannot change. If you did not do as she asked, you still die and thus can tell none of her plans. Perhaps she thought she could use you to kill for her and then have you disposed of later. Either way you are silenced."

"Dead men tell no tales."

"Precisely." Enovese nodded solemnly. Clathia was indeed a most crafty opponent. Another thought invaded her mind for she remembered witnessing Arianda drinking heavily at the Festival of Temptation. Perhaps her mother's binge had another reason other than Enovese's assumption that Arianda knew the truth of the *paratanist* selection ritual. Perhaps Arianda knew her days were numbered.

"At the Festival, when you spoke to Arianda, what did you perceive about her state of mind?"

"She seemed sullen and somber. When I remarked to her that we wore the same color, she laughed bitterly and said something about casting the vines to shadow. Before I could ask for an explanation, she glared at the empress and stormed out."

"Casting the vines to shadow?" Mentally, Enovese searched through all the texts she'd read but came up empty. She had never heard or read the phrase before. Picturing a vine cast to shadow, she then understood. "When you cast a vine to shadow it withers and dies."

"True, yet how are she and I like vines?"

"Because you bear fruit."

Confusion twisted his face.

"Arianda knows about the *paratanist* selection ritual. She knows that you and she are vines that provide fruit to perpetuate the *paratanist* class. Once they have harvested all they can, they cast you to shadow for they have no further need of you." Enovese thought that was why only Harvesters wore black.

With a shake of his head, Chur disagreed. "Prior Harvesters are not killed. They often rank high among the elite. They are encouraged to have many children." A pained expression tightened his jaw.

She knew he thought simultaneously of how he'd once thrown that bit of information in her face to hurt her and Clathia's startling revelation that he was sterile. Enovese agreed with Chur's assessment that the truth was both a blessing and a curse: a blessing that he had no children in the *tanist* house and a curse that he could never have any. Chur shrugged the thought away, and out of respect for his pain Enovese chose not to comment.

"Do not laugh at my ignorance, but until I read it in your mind I did not know that various colors indicated rank. I guess I never noticed. If I had, I would have made some connections much earlier." Idly, he traced patterns in her hair that streamed across the bedcovers. "So how then are Harvesters cast to shadow? It must be more than our color of black."

Puzzled, Enovese let her mind focus on the patterns Chur teased within her hair. She had discovered long ago that thinking indirectly often led to a direct answer. She thought of patterns, layers, shadows, and rank designated by color. Enovese let her attention wander and Chur respectfully held his tongue. She felt him within her mind, marveling at her thought process. Her mind felt chaotic to him where she found his mind carefully regimented.

Murmuring almost to herself, Enovese said, "We know very little about Arianda's life after her time as Harvester. Five seasons she held the title, then suddenly withdrew. The question is why. Did she find out what happened to her issue? Did she find a bondmate? If she did, how many children did Arianda produce, and what happened to them? There is a reason for her actions, just as there is a reason for Clathia's wrath."

Chur grunted a short breath of frustration. "It matters little, Enovese. We concern ourselves with knowledge that will not help us."

Stilling his hand by placing hers atop, she forced him to look at her. "Knowledge is power, Chur. Uncovering the details brings focus to the overall picture. Everyone moves within this world motivated by their desires but bound by the laws and rituals of the ancients. It is not about discovering one man or one woman's truth, for their truth may be another's lie. What we must accomplish is the unveiling of the truth behind our culture."

He smiled then, lightening the chains around her heart. "You are very wise, Enovese. When I touch your mind I am in awe of the information stored there, and the connections you make that utterly elude me."

She preened under his praise, for he was the only person who had ever complimented her. Even the *tanists,* when she had performed well, offered no praise but only a surcease of verbal abuse. She thanked him with a lingering kiss.

"So tell me, my wise and beautiful bondmate, what will we do?"

Pleasure surged again for he did not call her his *paratanist,* but his bondmate. He elevated her status to match his.

"The empress, Ambo, and Helton play a cruel losing game with your life. I think you should play the game back, but with far more skill. If devious machinations and promises that hold no value are the ground rules, then you would do well to do the same."

She sensed an immediate reluctance from Chur. He met her gaze with consternation. "I am not suited to games of intrigue.

Again, I did not even know rank was designated by color or I would have realized your mother was a Harvester." He condemned himself an idiot for not knowing a fact she took for granted.

Enovese cupped his chin rather sharply. "How would you know such a thing unless you'd been told? I will not suffer you belittling yourself. For I finally understand the carving that graces your door." She turned his face to look at the oversized Onic door. "Two figures entwine, they become one, stronger than each alone, and they rise above the chaos." She turned his face back to her. "Just as you astutely surmised, we are stronger together. When we merge, we enhance one another and become profoundly powerful. The connection that we share, our ability to slip into each other's minds, is not common. I believe it is a unique phenomenon. That is the one skill we possess that the other players in this game do not. They have more political sway and they have more minuscule details, but we have the power of two."

"Stronger together than apart." He clasped her hand. "I exchange my power with the strength of your heart."

"You are a poet." Before she became lost in the pleasure of his touch, she turned her attention back to practical matters. "When, where, and how does Clathia expect you to kill Arianda?"

Chuckling wickedly, Chur pulled her against his chest and rolled over on his back, taking her with him. Her hair, still damp from their earlier shower, covered her back and trailed onto him. When she shivered, he yanked the bedcover over them. Simmering heat from his form infused her almost instantly.

"Better?" Chur asked.

"Much."

Snuggling her close, he kissed her nose, and said, "Since this season is the season of Kasmiri's sacrifice, the empress is throwing an elaborate party at the beginning of the Harvest cycle. I think by royal decree everyone in the palace must either attend or at least celebrate her daughter's sacrifice. Clathia impressed upon me that this party would outshine the Festival of Temptation. No expense would be spared to provide her daughter with the most grand pre-Harvest party ever thrown."

"I thought it was customary to celebrate after the sacrifice?"

"Yes, but the empress wishes to commemorate the occasion before and after."

Enovese rolled her eyes. "The elite spend an obscene amount on celebrations."

"After my audience with Clathia today, I do not think she honestly cares about her daughter's Harvest. I believe the party is strictly a cover for Arianda's demise."

She kissed his forehead. "You do have a mind for intrigues."

"I'm quite astute at grasping the obvious." Before she could reprimand him, he continued, "Clathia wants me to poison Arianda's drink."

"That's all?" Enovese scowled.

"Isn't that enough?"

"I find it very odd, for anyone could slip poison into her drink."

"Have we not already determined that Clathia picked me because either way I am silenced?"

"Yes, but still." Enovese left off the new questions swirling in her mind. "Where are you to get this poison?"

"Clathia will give it to me before the party."

"That is unfortunate. I will have no chance to analyze it and perhaps determine exactly what it is." Not an expert by any means, Enovese still knew enough about herbs and oils that she could probably make an educated guess.

"Does it matter? As long as it's deadly, Clathia has met her objective."

"What if it isn't poison?" Enovese arched her brow. "What

if the substance doesn't kill Arianda but causes some other harm?"

"You ask too many questions." Chur growled and hugged her hard. "Touching your mind gives me a headache."

Enovese decided to leave off any further pondering and turned her attention to the delicious man below her. All wonderfully hard and masculine.

A bright smile lifted Chur's face for he had read her thoughts. "Oh, I absolutely agree that we should turn our attention away from intrigues and focus on the lewd arts." Cupping his hands to her bottom, he pulled her up and teased his sex against hers.

"I believe this explains why men do not make good spies." She nestled down until she felt his tip press against her passage. "Men are too easily distracted by pleasures of the flesh."

"Then don't let me distract you." With a devious grin, Chur thrust up, penetrating her in one smooth motion. "Please continue with your questions."

His sudden possession stole her breath along with her thoughts. Chur deliberately flashed erotic images directly into her mind. She shivered. Each position, each lusty montage, caused a profound reaction. Her sex gushed and clenched. Her nipples tightened. Despite her efforts to control her breathing, she could not. Gasping, she clutched his shoulders as he rocked into her with lazy grace.

Twining his hands into her hair, he pulled her head back and bit along her neck. Chuckling, he placed his mouth to her ear and asked, "What, no more questions?"

Rising up by placing her hands against his chest, Enovese looked directly into his eyes. "Two can play this game." Deliberately, she flashed her own erotic images into his mind.

Chur twitched within her.

Rolling her hips as she rode atop him, Enovese trailed her fingers along his chest and tweaked his nipples.

He lost his carefully controlled breathing. Before she knew what he was up to, he lifted her off him and placed her face down on the bed. Her unbound hair spilled around her body. He yanked her hips up, lifting her to her knees, exposing her bottom.

"Naughty woman." Playfully, he smacked her buttocks.

Heat spread along her flesh, exacerbating the heat within her sex. Without thought, she arched her back, lifting her backside to receive his slaps. Excitement grew for she had read his musings earlier where he wondered if the empress played such games with her consort.

Each clap of his hand to her bottom sent her senses reeling, increasing the fire building within. Damp tresses flicked along her flesh, cooling her flashes of warmth.

Kneeling beside her on the bed, Chur continued to smack her bottom with carefully timed and delivered strokes.

Blazing desire surged along her nerves. This time he did not punish her in the truest sense of the word but used the actions to enhance her pleasure. Enovese loved him more for understanding her odd arousal in this most wicked act. Spankings in the *tanist* house were horribly brutal. No pleasure manifested during those beatings. With Chur, it was playful, erotic, delicious, and above all welcomed. For if he thought for a moment he hurt her or she was afraid, he would stop. What excited her was the heat generated by his gentle slaps. Chur tapped her bottom until a rosy glow infused her flesh. He parted her trembling legs and centered himself.

Thick, hard, insistent, he pressed against her quivering core. She moaned and lowered her head while lifting her bottom. A grander invitation she could not give. Chur accepted and plunged swiftly into her. His moan mingled with hers. He punctuated each full thrust with a lovely slap when he withdrew.

"Ah, Enovese, you possess me fully."

Chur dug his fingertips into the meat of her hips. Plunging deep, he rode her until she collapsed against the bed. Following her down, he continued to stroke, filling her mind with lusty images as his body acted them out. Enovese made no effort to resist. When her orgasm rippled her around him, encompassing him, he bayed and parted her legs wider, to thrust deeper. Chur lost control and the last of the images faded away when he climaxed. He dropped his full weight on her for only a moment. Wrapping his arms around her, he rolled over onto his back, taking her with him.

As he fell asleep, cradling her in his embrace, Enovese kept her thoughts positive. Once sleep claimed him, she couldn't escape pressing fears that their time together drew short. Outside forces would pull him away from her no matter how she struggled to keep him near.

26

Clathia held to her word that her daughter's pre-Harvest party would rival the Festival of Temptation. Frankly, Chur thought it surpassed the Harvest itself. He had never witnessed such decadence. Huge tables were laden with exotic foods from all over the Onic Empire. On closer inspection, he realized some of the serving platters were men or women covered with treats. As the guests ate, they revealed more of their nude bodies. Servants had decorated every nook and cranny of the great hall with gleaming fruits, vegetables, and bundles of ripening grain. What he thought at first were statues turned out to be painted servants who carefully held their poses. He wasn't sure but he thought they were supposed to be a depiction of Clathia's family line. Against one wall, Clathia had arranged a miniature tableau of the sacrifice table complete with several virgins. Chur kept his distance. No matter what the empress might want, he refused to demonstrate for her guests. Just the thought turned his stomach.

A servant approached, offering him a tray of drinks, which he declined. After his discussions with Enovese, he decided not to eat or drink anything. If Clathia sought to poison a guest, she might also try to impart euphoric feelings to her guests by drugging the food. Enovese filled his belly before he left his rooms. Mentally, he reached out to connect to her but couldn't. They had been testing their conduit but couldn't decide if distance impeded the link or if some other factor did.

Dancers moved about the hall, displaying their acrobatic skills and entertaining the attendees. Chur was surprised at not only their abilities but also their mode of dress. Most were nude, or near nude, and several dancers engaged in simulated sex acts as they danced. The entire theme of the celebration was inherently erotic. He felt distinctly uncomfortable. When he looked back at the mock sacrifice table, he discovered several guests "playing" at Harvester. They would approach a sacrifice, lower their trousers, and then plow away. He noticed several women trading places with the virgins so they could "play" at sacrifice. Not only were they doing it wrong but also they mocked a sacred ritual. When he checked around, he was relieved to discover he wasn't the only one who thought the display unseemly. Several other guests, male and female, shook their heads and moved away.

Chur considered the people around him. Now that he understood how colors designated rank, he noticed far more intense shades at this party than at the Festival of Temptation. Deep jewel tones of blue, green, yellow, orange, indigo, and purple swirled before his eyes. Men and women wore their family colors with pride and sought to outdo one another in design and decoration. One woman in blinding yellow had a jewel-encrusted hat that was so heavy she had difficulty keeping her head up. So far, she hadn't moved from one of the reclining couches scattered about the hall. Other members of the elite wore see-through outfits that boldly displayed their breasts, buttocks, or genitals. Quickly, he realized there were two distinctly different types of attendees: those who willingly embraced the lewd decadence, and those who tolerated but refused to participate.

Clathia darted about her guests, smiling, laughing, touching a shoulder here and straightening a lapel there. She seemed utterly within her element, for despite the party's purported purpose, clearly Clathia sought to show off herself. Her blaring crimson dress drew every eye, for she was the only one wearing red. The jewel-encrusted garment dipped dangerously low across her shoulders, nipped in at her waist, hugged her hips, and then flared out and down to the floor. So long was the skirt that guests had to take great care not to step on the train. As Clathia maneuvered toward him, Chur struggled to keep a scowl off his face. Again, her beauty struck him, but the calculating coldness in her eyes chilled him to the bone.

"Mighty Harvester, how good of you to attend." Clathia leaned close as if to speak privately, but instead she slipped a vial into his hand. Like mother like daughter, he thought. Kasmiri used the same move to swipe his sword. Flashing him an arch smile, Clathia turned on her heel and swept away, swirling night-blooming flowers in her wake. His gaze followed her through the crowd, then turned to the liquid-filled vial. Small, slender, crafted of delicate blue glass, the tiny thing felt weighty and chilly in his palm. He shivered. Scanning the crowd for Arianda, he didn't see her. For that matter, he had not spied Kasmiri either. Perhaps the subject of the party wished to make an entrance.

After a discussion with Enovese, Chur decided not to keep the poison on his person just in case Clathia had some other vicious plot in mind, like accusing him of trying to murder her. He placed it at the base of a lush plant, tucking it into a corner where few guests ventured. A few swipes with his fingers covered the vial with moss. Looking without being obvious, he didn't think anyone paid him any notice. Too many other bizarre entertainments held their attention.

When he moved back into the throng of people, an older, slender, and slightly tipsy man dressed in crisp orange approached him. Bright orange clashed with his yellowish skin tone and oddly ginger hair.

Enovese educated him with a basic understanding of the rank associated with colors. He knew the intensity of the orange indicated this man was a high member of his family line. Those below him, his brothers and sisters, for example, would wear increasingly softer shades of orange. His children would wear the same shade as he. The man bowed in a modified military greeting, which Chur returned. He introduced himself as Rier Dalep and then went on at length about his daughter, who would be among the sacrifices at the Harvest.

Rier's praise crafted his daughter a paragon of all things feminine. Chur nodded politely. Thinking back to the Festival of Temptation, he remembered a sallow-faced girl in orange with big brown eyes and a mouth that never closed once during their dance. The girl had babbled incessantly about her father and that if Chur were to select her, he would have an excellent life among the nobles. "Why, you would not even have to lift a finger for we have many servants," the girl gushed. Simpering her face up, she added, "And I would be a most willing partner in your bed." Chur forced a smile at the girl, refraining from comment, and then moved on to his next dance. He couldn't remember exactly what she had said her father did, not that such information mattered. He asked Rier a few inane questions to fain interest, then disengaged himself from the conversation, citing the many other guests he must meet.

Repeatedly, he had similar conversations with other nobles hoping to inveigle his interest in their daughters. He'd had a slew of such discussions during the Festival, but apparently they were eager to have a second chance. Oddly, this time, they were far more discreet. He surmised it was because they suspected the party was to push Chur into choosing the daughter of the empress. Since the nobles could not compete with the riches of the empress, this time they focused on the pliable nature of their daughters. More than once he heard, "My daughter's temperament is sweet and demure, not fiery and headstrong." Honestly, Chur thought they did their children no favors. Describing them as doormats for his mighty feet was not as attractive as they might think. What man wanted a spineless child for his bondmate? Luckily, though, only a handful of the elite had daughters who were ready for this Harvest.

A series of tiny bells began to ring, growing in volume as ever-larger bells chimed. The crystals dimmed. A spotlight fell on the entry to the great hall. Red carpet rolled into the room like a giant tongue. A flutter of wings filled the doorway as several bird handlers released a mass of tiny red birds. Streamers of red floated down from the ceiling with crimson flower petals. A powerful blast of perfumed fog wafted through the door and over the crowd. Chur tried desperately not to laugh. Kasmiri was making the epitome of a grand entrance. A booming processional replaced the tinkling bells.

Once the fog swirled away, several gasps filled the air, his among them. They gasped not at the production but at what the daughter of the empress wore. From her jaunty hat, to her jacket and trousers, to the delicate boots on her feet, velvet black trimmed with crimson covered Kasmiri—colors relegated to the current Harvester. Chur's heart slammed painfully in his chest. Was Kasmiri laying claim to him by wearing his colors? She had no right to do so. Furious at this trick, he whipped his head about for the empress.

At the back of the hall, Clathia stood on a dais, clearly having launched herself from her throne. Her mouth was agape and her eyes wide. She strained forward as if she wanted to launch herself across the room. When her shocked face resolved into twisted fury, Chur turned his attention back to the doorway.

Arianda entered right behind Kasmiri. As a prior Harvester, Arianda wore black without the crimson trim, but her dress matched Kasmiri's suit in cut and style, almost as if they wished to present themselves as a couple. When Kasmiri clasped Arianda's hand, she confirmed his thoughts. Kasmiri wasn't wearing his colors but Arianda's color mixed with her own crimson. Kasmiri's eyes glowed with triumph where Arianda's twinkled with a malicious kind of satisfaction.

Speculative murmurs burbled through the crowd. Heads turned from the spectacle in the doorway to Clathia and back again. Snatches of conversation filled his ears. They labeled Kasmiri rebellious, willful, perverted, and Arianda faired no better. People were most vicious about her age as compared to Kasmiri's for over forty seasons separated them. Now he understood why the empress wanted Arianda dead. The woman had an unnatural relationship with her daughter.

Head high and her whole body prepared for a confrontation, Kasmiri strode into the room, dragging Arianda with her. Where Kasmiri seemed not only ready for an altercation but welcomed it, Arianda's bravado evaporated under the blistering glare of many condemning eyes, but with a deep breath, she straightened her shoulders and entered. To the casual observer it would appear that Kasmiri was leading this charge, but Chur saw beneath what Arianda hoped to project; all her hesitancy was an act. Clearly, Arianda was pulling Kasmiri's strings.

Same-sex liaisons were not unheard of or strictly prohibited, but everyone in the Onic Empire knew how Clathia felt about such relationships. Chur's understanding was clarified by Clathia's nasty comment, that her hand was too soft as compared to the recruits, and the repulsed look on her face when she accused him of being more interested in men than women. The fact that her daughter sought out a woman rather than a man devastated Clathia and prompted her murder plot. If Kasmiri held to her preference for women, the line of empress ended with her, for

Clathia had no other daughters. Power in the Onic Empire was matriarchal, from mother to daughter. If Kasmiri refused to breed, the line ended with her. A problem that weighed so heavily on Clathia she would kill to change what she couldn't discuss away. Chur now understood Clathia's reasons, but eliminating Arianda wouldn't solve the problem. Such a vile act would only drive a wedge between them and prompt Kasmiri to select another woman.

After the initial shock faded away, guests returned to eating, drinking, and making a more subdued merry. Several people cast surreptitious glances to the empress, as if seeking permission to return to the unfettered joviality.

Clathia wore serenity like a mask upon her face, but fury sparkled in her golden brown eyes. She regally descended the steps of the dais. Her even pace reminded him of a hunter with prey in its sight. As if grain parted by the wind, guests drifted aside, leaving a path from mother to daughter. Anticipation hung in the air with the last traces of perfumed fog.

With perfect form, Clathia approached, then embraced her daughter, careful not to disturb the jeweled hat upon her head. Confusion narrowed Kasmiri's gaze as she let go of Arianda's hand to return the hug. For all her pretentiousness, Kasmiri was terribly young, playing an adult game well but not with as much skill as her mother. Kasmiri had anticipated a scene with screaming and recriminations, but Clathia would not fuel the mouths of the gossipmongers.

Clathia stepped back. "How daring of you to wear such an imaginative outfit." She smiled broadly, giving life to the lines in her tawny face, but mirth never touched her eyes. "Did you design it yourself?"

"Arianda helped me," Kasmiri offered churlishly, still hoping to provoke her mother's wrath.

Silky smooth, Clathia swiveled her head to face Arianda. "You have excellent taste. How charming of you to suggest my daughter break with boring old tradition." Despite the jovial tone, there was no escaping the pointed jab behind her words.

Arianda swallowed hard but lifted her truculent nose, reminding him of Enovese. "Some traditions serve no purpose but to enforce conformity." Arianda bowed politely to the empress but under her breath added, "While others have their roots in evil."

Chur understood at once that this was not a battle between mother and daughter, but between empress and former Harvester. Kasmiri was simply the fulcrum on which each woman pivoted for position.

Clathia dismissed Arianda's cryptic remark with a clap of her hands and a call for drinks. Servants flooded the hall. Their bland brown robes were a startling contrast to so much finery. When one appeared at her side, lacquered crimson fingertips plucked up a slender crystal glass filled with blood red wine. Clathia encouraged all her guests to do the same. Anticipating a toast, the elite scrambled to comply. Chur selected a glass and cupped it in his palm.

"To my daughter!" Clathia's voice filled the hall. "Long may she live; long may she bring glory and riches to the Onic Empire."

Everyone lifted his or her glass, echoing, "Long may she live!" and then drank.

Chur did the same but only pressed the cup to his lips without swallowing.

Arianda sipped from her cup and then passed it to Kasmiri, who downed it in one swallow.

Clathia's mask slipped almost imperceptibly, but she filled the crack with another feral smile. "Let us celebrate the cusp of my daughter's transformation from child to woman." With that, swift music wafted through the hall. Satisfied that the drama was over, guests returned to dining, drinking, and dancing.

Kasmiri turned her back on her mother, linked her arm through Arianda's, then headed for the tables laden with treats.

Clathia suppressed a snarl as she turned to Chur.

"Honor me with a dance, Harvester." She snapped her fingers. A servant dutifully appeared with a tray. They deposited their glasses.

Chur placed his hand at the small of Clathia's back. Heat from her flesh surged through the fabric, warming his palm and saturating the air around her with night-blooming flowers. When he went to capture her hand with his, she forced his hand to her waist. Clathia cupped his shoulders and drew him close. Swaying in time to the music, she shimmied her body along his. He fought to put some distance between them. She maneuvered closer with each step. Plastered against him in the most unseemly way, Chur struggled to keep his disgust under control. He knew the empress had no interest in him physically. She sought only to use him.

Lifting her head very close to his, Clathia whispered, "You cannot do as I asked for Arianda is sharing her food and drink with my daughter. I will not take the risk."

Relief threatened to drop him to his knees. Since Clathia did not know of his decision, he said, "Such seems most wise, my lady."

Clathia drew back. "Call me Clathia."

"As you wish, Clathia." He'd call her anything to escape further intrigues. He longed for the evening to end so he could return to Enovese. After she helped him remove his uniform and washed away the sticky gel that held the slashed fabric to his skin, they would tumble together in his bed, surrendering to dizzying passion. That moment seemed ages away. Reluctantly, he turned his focus back to Clathia.

Arching her brow, she cast her gaze to her daughter and Chur did the same. Arianda and Kasmiri put on quite a show.

Clinging to one another, laughing, feeding each other—they did everything short of copulating. Chur couldn't wait to ask Enovese what she thought of this display. Why would Arianda deliberately seek to incur Clathia's wrath? It would be one thing if Arianda showed up with a woman as her companion, but why, of all the women in the Empire, would Arianda select the daughter of the empress? He shook his head, convinced that he would never fully understand the machinations of others.

"Disgusting, isn't she?" Clathia asked, misinterpreting his shaking head. "You can understand now why I wish to rid my daughter of such an evil influence."

Chur refused to comment. He had never explored his personal feelings about same-sex relationships. Loban's raping of the recruits infuriated him for rape was not a mutual joining. If two men or two women agreed to the liaison, he couldn't see why anyone else would care. He certainly didn't. His early thought, like mother like daughter, flashed through his mind. Had Enovese ever been attracted to another woman like her mother clearly was? If everyone wore shapeless robes in the *tanist* house, he didn't see how such was possible. Yet still, he didn't want to picture Enovese in anyone's arms but his.

Clathia uttered a deceptively soft sigh. "There is only one solution. You must claim Kasmiri at the Harvest."

Her tranquil words hung between them while a million thoughts raced through his mind. How dare she suggest such a thing as if he were in complete accord with her wishes. Her treatment of him as a servant who lived only to do her bidding incensed him. He wanted to grasp her upper arms and shake her until her coiled hair untangled, her eyes rolled back in her head, and her teeth rattled together. All the while he wanted to scream in her face that she was nothing but a ruthless bitch who was so enchanted with herself she could not see beyond her own pathetic desires. Rather than brutalizing the empress, which would end in immediate execution, Chur calmed himself with some *kintana* breathing.

He realized he could boldly lie to Clathia and say that he would, but when he didn't the fallout would lead only to misery for him and Enovese. His deception might end in exile. He'd rather deal with her wrath now.

"Respectfully, I decline. As I told you before, the only right I have is the absolute right to select my bondmate. Kasmiri is a lovely young woman"—he almost choked on the words—"but she is not the woman for me."

Her intense gaze snapped back to him. At first her eyes went wide, honestly shocked that he dared to disagree with her, but then they narrowed. Outraged, she sputtered, "I will not tolerate your insolence. You are my subject and you will do as I command."

Chur spun her sharply for the dance, dipped her back over his arm, and then pulled her close. "I am your loyal and faithful subject, but I will not offer an eternal bond to a woman I do not love." With a nod of his chin to Kasmiri and Arianda, who still clung to one another, he added, "And clearly, she is not in love with me."

"Love does not matter in a match like this. You will be consort to the future empress."

"She seems more interested in another."

"She's young and confused!" When several heads turned their direction, Clathia flashed a smile as if nothing were amiss and then lowered her voice. "Once selected I know her attention will turn fully to you. Remove Arianda's influence and Kasmiri will recognize her duty."

"While I appreciate your conviction that I could woo any woman, including your headstrong daughter, I must keep true to my duty to myself."

Clathia tilted her head in consideration. "You have already selected another woman."

Refusing to confirm or deny, he shrugged and promptly changed the subject. "I cannot claim any woman if I do not survive the challenge."

Clathia startled at his words. When she looked up into his face, he saw the truth flickering in her gaze: She had no say in the challenge. Her prior claim that she would ensure he would not survive if he did not kill Arianda was an empty threat. Even if she could manipulate Helton or Ambo, she still had no direct influence over the challenge. She knew it and now he'd confirmed his suspicions. Much to his surprise, the icy sheen melted from the empress. A touching vulnerability softened her features. Clathia was not a monster, she was only a woman determined to protect her daughter and ensure the future succession of her family line. In that moment, he felt for her.

Soothing his voice to a low murmur, he offered, "You are strong, Clathia. Manipulation and murder will not serve you well in this crisis. If I could help you, I would, but even if I did as you asked, I cannot father children."

Clathia tossed her head, "There are ways other than traditional methods."

Apparently, even his sterility wouldn't get him out of his mess. Calmly, he continued, "Do you think I am the kind of man who would force my attentions on your daughter? Would you allow any man to subject your child to such brutality?"

Tears gathered in her eyes and he thought he had finally touched her heart, her mother's heart, but Clathia blinked the moisture away. Below his hand, her spine stiffened. Her chin lifted regally high.

"I would rather her forcibly plowed than allow her to remain fallow." Her callous words clashed with the last dulcet notes of music. With the dance over, Clathia moved out of his embrace. "Heed my words well, Harvester. If you survive the challenge, I expect you to claim my daughter. Dare you choose another, I will destroy not you but your chosen."

27

The last cycle before the challenge zinged past swift as lightning. Chur had returned from Kasmiri's pre-Harvest party with a vile of poison and the ruthless edict of the empress. Enovese bothered not with words to soothe him but obliterated all thought with physical contact. Rather than frustrating him with continual questions and speculation, she kept her whirling wheels of thought to herself. When Chur touched her mind, he found only calm, as if water untouched by wind or tides. She didn't fool him for a moment, yet he too wanted their last days to be peaceful.

Each night after his brutal training session they would bathe, eat, and then wallow in passion. Chur surprised her with his need for physical contact but not necessarily sex. More often than not, he would simply wrap her in his arms and spend the entire evening kissing her. Amazed, she reveled in his ability to kiss in endless ways. From short nips to a smoothing of lips to open-mouth dueling of tongues; his inventiveness never failed to excite.

Despite their efforts to remain positive, in the shadow of

night, Chur would toss and turn, his tormented groans ripping her from sleep's embrace. In his dreams, he lashed out against unseen enemies, vowing to destroy them, willing to die to protect his eternal bondmate. Enovese moved to the far side of the bed to avoid his flailing arms. Hurt burned deep inside, for she knew his conflict was over protecting her. He'd shared with her the exact conversation with the empress. Either Chur laid claim to Kasmiri or Clathia would destroy his chosen.

Held far under the water of the calm Enovese projected lurked a deep-seated rage. They had worked so diligently to be together, yet something thwarted them at every turn. If she believed in fate, she would think it held some personal grudge against her, but Enovese believed she made her own fate.

Refusing to give up, she readied his rooms for the transition to new Harvester. This she did when Chur was training, for he might worry she anticipated failure. She did not. One way or another, she would not serve the new Harvester. Removing the traces of her living within Chur's rooms took very little time for she had few personal possessions. Mainly she removed the bed from the closet and returned it to her tiny room down the hall.

She hadn't spent any time in her area in almost three seasons. Everything, from carpet to bare walls was the same creamy beige, as bland as her nondescript robe. Since her room was adjacent to the Harvester's suite, it had no windows and only cheap lighting crystals of muddy green. It was more cell than room. Just stepping foot within the cramped space depressed her. She cleaned the layer of dust off everything so that it appeared lived-in, placed the folding bed along the wall, and practically lunged for the door. One way or another, she would never enter that prison again.

Despite her efforts, Chur noticed the changes. He didn't comment. She didn't probe his mind. They moved through the last few days projecting so much positive thoughts to the other that maintaining the optimism grew tedious.

On this, the last day before the challenge, there would be no punishing training session for Chur. He slept in, holding her so tightly in his arms she had difficulty breathing. She clung to him, welcoming every moment, taking and locking the sensation of his massive body, his heat, and his unique scent into her consciousness. When he woke, he groaned and rolled to his back, pulling her on top of him. He grasped the end of her braided hair and worked the strands free, draping her tresses over their entwined bodies.

"Such beautiful harvest-colored hair." He rained kisses along her cheek to her neck, then to her shoulder. "Several times I've fantasized of being bound by your hair."

Playfully, she wrapped a hank around his wrist. "Long as my hair is, I think it is still too short to fully bind you for my pleasure."

He laughed and then flashed an image to her mind: her straddled across his hips as her hair swirled around her head, lengthening in the wind until impossibly long. Tendrils lashed out, binding his wrists and ankles. Once she captured him, she began to dance upon him, lifting her face to the sky with her neck beautifully arched, her eyes closed, her mouth moving as if in prayer. Magnificently lovely and profoundly erotic, the picture he painted aroused her, for in his mind, he saw her as devastatingly stunning.

"You are stunning, not just in my thoughts but in my eyes." Cupping the back of her head, he drew her close, brushing his lips to hers with reverent attention. "You are a goddess, Enovese."

In his arms, she felt like a goddess. Cherished and treasured, respected and loved. "If only I had the powers that went with the position."

"Hmm," he murmured, "but would you bestow your favors on a mere mortal such as me?"

"You are no mere mortal." She teased her hands along his

bulging muscles. "I would steal you away from this corporeal realm to live with me in *Jarasine*."

"I thought the gods were formless in *Jarasine*, that they only took form in the mortal realm?" He kissed her nose. "I would not want to be without form. I take too much joy in the physical."

"I had not thought of that." Enovese traced his scar. "But who knows how the gods find pleasure? Perhaps the merging is more intense without a body."

"Perhaps." Working his hand down, he swirled his fingertips along the curve of her breast. Her throaty moan elicited a satisfied smile. "But I have no desire to find out. I rather like my body merging with yours."

And there it was.

Regardless of all their efforts to refrain from discussing the truth, reality popped up anyway.

Chur did not want to die.

Enovese couldn't bear to lose him.

He closed his eyes. He continued to stroke her, but his movements were no longer fluid but erratic. She stilled his hand by pressing close. They lay together for a long time, not moving, not talking, simply waiting for the sharp ache to abate.

"If I fail the challenge, I want you to try again."

They'd had this argument before. She had no desire to rehash her position so she said nothing.

Chur ensnared her gaze with fierce determination. "I don't want you to give up."

"I could say the same to you."

A frown twisted his features. "I intend to win, but should I fail, I cannot bear the thought of you being used in the *paratanist* selection ritual."

This was his greatest fear. Several times, she caught flashes of his perception of the ritual. Chur saw her belly swelled with issue, a gleaming knife descending, ripping the screaming innocent from a bloody mass that was once her body. When the acolytes finished with her, Chur envisioned them tossing her aside, like a worthless *harshan,* with her limbs in a heap, her tresses tangled and as lifeless as her blood-drained form. So vividly did he picture this, when she first witnessed the impression, she rushed to the basin to vomit.

"I do not intend to become a part of that ritual." She tossed her head, moving her gaze away from his, but not quickly enough. He'd caught the thread of her thought and followed it into her mind, unraveling her intention despite her efforts to block him.

"Where is it?" Rolling her off, he untangled himself from her hair, climbed out of bed, and stormed into the kitchen.

She followed, watching him yank open every cabinet and drawer. She knew exactly what he was looking for. He wouldn't find it.

Frustrated by his fruitless search, he strode to her, grasped her shoulders, and demanded, "Tell me where you hid the vial."

"No."

Sinking his fingertips into her upper arms, he shook her, not violently, just enough to frighten her. When she struggled, he let go.

"What you are planning is not a solution, Enovese. How dare you accuse me of giving up when you are considering killing yourself?"

She didn't deny the accusation. She didn't bother to defend her decision either. For at least the final choice would be utterly hers.

"Do you think it pleases me that you would rather be dead than without me?" His expression changed from confusion to disgust. "You are the strongest woman I have ever known. How can you be so weak to even think of suicide?"

Her shoulders stiffened with his insult. Ruthlessly, she pushed his vision of the *paratanist* selection ritual into his mind.

He winced.

"With that looming in my future do you deny me the option of a peaceful exit?" She didn't want to hurt him, but he had to understand why she had settled on this if all else failed. "I have suffered a lifetime of other people's choices. I want the last one to be mine."

His torment showed in every powerful line of his form. He appreciated her reasons yet elected to fight her anyway. "You don't know what's in the vial Clathia gave me. You said yourself it might cause some harm other than death."

"I said that before I'd had a chance to examine the contents. I assure you, the liquid is deadly." One drop to her lips would result in instant painless death.

"The only assurance I want is that you will not consume that vile liquid." He observed her eyes with a desperate hope she would reveal the hiding place.

"Do you wish for me to lie to you?" Drawing near, she stood close enough to feel his heat. She tilted her face, capturing his gaze. "I could swear to you that I won't, but one look in my eyes and you will know that I am lying."

Disappointment clouded his summer-sky gaze. "Give me the vial. I will destroy it."

Enovese stepped back but kept her head high. Her withdrawal caused the temperature around her to plummet, puckering her flesh, tightening her nipples. She hoped the reaction would distract him, which it did, but only for a moment. Tenacious, he refused to allow her to divert his attention. He moved close, too close, enveloping her within his heat, his embrace. Wrapping his powerful arms around her, he maneuvered her close, lowered his head, and whispered directly to her ear.

"I cannot draw strength from you if you give up. Please do not vex me with this now, not when I need you most."

His plaintive words broke her heart. Bolstering his spirit

loomed most important in her mind. Without her positive strength, he had little chance to triumph in the challenge. As she clung to him, she tried to uncover another solution. There were a million ways to die. The poison was only the kindest resolution. She remembered his possessiveness with the soothing blue lotion and thought that if she just gave the vial to him he might feel mollified. A new and terrible thought occurred to her: What if Chur decided all was lost and consumed the poison himself? She shivered uncontrollably and wrapped her arms around his waist. Now she understood exactly how terrified Chur was. She realized her motives went beyond selfish, they were entirely narcissistic, because she thought only of ending her own pain and not what pain she inflicted on others by her actions. She'd felt justified for the only one who cared about her was Chur, and if he were gone . . .

Withdrawing from his embrace, she retrieved the poison from the sacred chest. She held it out to him and marveled again at how cold and heavy the vial felt in her palm. If she didn't know better, she would swear some supernatural element was at play.

He placed his palm over hers. Despite the heat of their hands, the vial remained chilly.

"Several times we have faced insurmountable odds and we have triumphed. Don't give up now."

She didn't want to argue with him. She wanted him to pour the poison away so that the option would no longer be available to her. In the same breath, she wanted to clutch to this last hope if all else were lost. She realized her own arrogance that she trusted herself with the decision but not Chur.

"Take it away." She lifted her arm, pushing the vial into his grasp.

Chur placed it on the counter and hugged her. "Each new day brings new challenges but also new solutions. Promise me that you will always greet each morning awaiting the revelation of answers. For nothing is set in stone. I thought that I could never want you as my bondmate, but now I can envision no other. What if you had given up when I refused you then? We would not be here having this argument now. Do you see how situations change?"

She nodded, rubbing her face against his chest, some smooth patches and some hairy. Tomorrow, she would shave him free of hair in preparation for the challenge. She had given little thought beyond that moment and she didn't want to dwell on it now.

Chur leaned back just enough so she could look up. "I'm not going to destroy the vial, for it would be a pointless act. If you wished, I have no doubt you could fashion another batch, what I want is your promise that you will not use the contents on yourself."

"I won't." From the depth of her heart, she swore that she wouldn't and she meant every word she uttered. He connected to her mind and read her thoughts about him making that horrific choice. With that, he understood her change of heart. "I'm sorry I even—"

He cut her off with a quick kiss. "Believe me, I understand why such a thought would cross your mind." He scooped her up into his arms and carried her back to bed. Once he had her settled in the sheets, he retrieved her hairbrush and slid into bed beside her. "Today should be about us."

Warily, she eyed the hairbrush. Exactly what did he intend to do? Paddle her, penetrate her, or some other perverted passion she had not yet envisioned?

With a waggle of his eyebrows, he placed her on her back and brushed her hair around her body, looping tresses around her breasts, smoothing strands along her belly to her hips and thighs as if decorating her. She became his canvas. A rich blend of sensations, from the rough of his fingertips, to the stiff bristles of the brush, to the smooth stroke of her hair, aroused every bit of her flesh.

Leaning back, balanced on one arm, he considered her for a moment. Tousled black hair slipped down, covering his eyes, and he tossed the sleep-clumped strands back. His gaze roamed over her, lingering, seeking, almost as profound as an actual touch. Reaching out, he moved a few strands around her breast, teased her nipple to a turgid pucker with the stiff bristles of the brush, and then leaned back to consider the effect.

"Exquisite." He was in no hurry. He wanted one last day to worship her with everything from his touch, to his gaze, to his heated words. "You respond as if new, as if never once touched. Each time I caress you my contact is like a virgin Harvest."

When tears slipped out the edges of her eyes, he wiped them away. He didn't ask or probe her mind for an explanation. He accepted. Lying here on his bed, nude, vulnerable, she was a sacrifice to him. This day was their last day. What came after this they had little control over; terror struck her, a raw, painful need to clasp him, draw him over her, compel him to plunge within so she could know him one last time.

"We have all the time in the world, Enovese. Today is endless."

How she wanted that to be true. She wanted *Tandalsul* to hang steady in the sky, keeping the night from descending. If the world stood still, tomorrow would never come. More tears leaked. She tried desperately to stop, but fear overwhelmed the passion he'd evoked. In her mind, she pictured the vial of poison sitting on the kitchen counter. As much as she tried to move away from such destructive thoughts, she couldn't stop.

Chur stretched out beside her and kissed the tears away. He rolled her to her side, nestling her along him, wrapping her up with powerful arms and burning heat. "Tell me what I can do."

"Make love to me. No teasing, no waiting." She knew he

wanted to torment her all day long and end with a final passionate joining, but she couldn't wait. A need to feel him inside, similar to what she felt during the ritual of control, pulsed in her limbs.

Chur lifted her leg around his hip as he slipped his cock against her slick sex. He cupped her chin, compelling her to look at him. Beautiful eyes met hers. Eyes filled with care and concern. Eyes that effortlessly opened the connection between them.

As he penetrated, his lids lowered, his nostrils flared, and he took a sharp breath. In that blissful moment, she felt her body and his. She knew his pleasure of her slick honey heat enveloping his throbbing cock.

He flashed a satisfied smile. "Words cannot express how wonderful you feel."

With a kiss, she returned his smile. "Luckily, we don't need words."

He stroked his hands all over her body, gliding, using the strands of her hair to smooth his tender touch. Sensual and searing, his contact only heightened her senses as the conduit flared with intensity.

Threads flowed between them but suddenly grew taut, pulling them tightly together, binding them. A blast of bright light exploded in her mind, blinding her.

She gasped, clutching Chur in panic. His arms tightened around her and she realized the light blinded him as well.

"Enovese?" His voice sounded terribly far away.

"I'm here," she responded, barely able to hear herself.

White light blazed then pulsed with their heartbeats, causing a trembling effect. Chur rolled on top of her and his weight pushed her into the bed, not crushing her but comforting her. More than feeling his actual touch, she felt pressure, slight pressure, which grew less substantial until she felt nothing at all.

"Chur?"

No response and she couldn't hear her own voice. She contracted her limbs but felt neither him nor her own body. In a timeless swirl of luminous white, she floated, insubstantial and disconnected. Soon even her thoughts faded away.

Cocooned in a dream, she awoke to a regular *lub-dub, lub-dub,* and realized she heard her own heartbeat. Then she heard and felt her breathing. Slow, even breaths filled her lungs and released. Curling her toes caused sensation to return to her limbs. Chur was still above her, nestled between her legs, his cock still buried deep within.

"Enovese?" Groggy, he stirred, clasping her tightly and thrusting once. "Ah, you are there. I lost you for a moment."

"Me too." Blinking several times caused the light to retreat. When she looked up, she caught Chur's face. So handsome, he astounded her. His eyes glowed, his black hair shone as the mass of careless curls softened his angular face, his lips curved into a wicked and compelling grin. The scar that had always marred his attractive features seemed softer and less menacing.

When his eyes went wide, she surmised he saw similar changes to her appearance. "Your eyes are . . . brighter, your skin luminescent, and your hair is literally glowing. I've always found you beautiful, but now you are ethereal. A real-life goddess in my arms."

Even his voice sounded different—richer, more commanding, with a resonating timber that shivered her spine. Was it all a trick of the blinding light, or had they undergone some profound change?

"I don't know." Chur blinked at his own answer, for her question registered to him without her asking it.

Where the connection once simmered in the back of their minds, it now took the forefront. When she tried to shield her thoughts from him, she discovered she couldn't. All of his memories flashed before her eyes and she felt them as if they were hers. She knew he could feel hers the same way. Panicked, she tried to push him off, but he captured her wrists before she could even begin to wriggle out from under him.

"Enovese, stop. I don't know what's going on but panicking won't help." Soothing her with his voice, he drew his face very close. "Somehow we've changed the connection again. You're right there in my mind. I couldn't shut you out if I wanted to. But there has to be a reason for this. It must be a good thing."

Such intense intimacy overwhelmed her. All her thoughts and memories were now his and vice versa. "I'm afraid. What happens if one of us . . ."

"Dies," he finished softly. "I don't know. The only thing I know is that I don't feel anything evil in this. Do you?"

"No, it just feels overwhelming."

Rubbing his nose against hers, he lowered his lips until he kissed her. A smile twisted his mouth against hers for he read her thought about what a talent he had for kissing. Parting his lips, he probed hers with his tongue, prying them open, slipping his tongue inside. Gods, he tasted like ambrosia. Twining her hands to his head, she lifted her hips, clasping him with deep inner muscles. Rocking above her at just the right pace, his cock swelled and she could feel how his balls throbbed with a need for release.

She merged her thoughts with his, moving to give him the greatest pleasure as he did the same. All without a word. Thoughts flowed between them with effortless grace, each adjusting, twisting, and moaning to please the other. A deep satisfaction flooded her mind and body until the orgasm tingled her toes, tightened her limbs, and tumbled her over the edge, with Chur right there with her. More than just a simple flush of pleasure, this went beyond animal gratification and into something just short of divine.

Replete in the afterglow, they clung together. This time was different from every other encounter in that there was no striving to push over the edge. Effortlessly, the pleasure flowed through them, embraced them, twining them in the bright light of ecstasy. And for a time, *Tandalsul* hung motionless in the sky, giving them a day without end.

28

Alone on a square platform, elevated in the center of the training room, with lighting crystals blazing down upon his bald head and nude body, Chur stood ready for the first challenger.

Phavage Nerys strode up the steps to face him. His white hair fluffed around his skull like silken chaff. A body of translucent skin glowed oddly vulnerable. A moment of pity swamped Chur before he hardened his heart. This was to the death. This was to claim Enovese. He had not asked to battle a man one step up from a boy, but he would kill any who dared to stand in his way.

Pink eyes narrowed to red slits as he approached with a *dantaratase,* Phavage's most skilled weapon of choice.

A recruit handed Chur the same weapon. He moved to the center of the platform. Tapping it twice, he grasped the slender staff with both hands, crouched into position, and waited.

Around them, the crowd of recruits hushed. Somewhere out there Chur knew Helton Ook looked on, waiting for his demise. Chur vowed he would never taste that victory. He too felt the eyes of Loban Daraspe but dismissed him as a cowardly fool easily manipulated by others. Most importantly, he felt Enovese in his mind, right there with him. He knew she waited in his rooms and he tasted her concern. Chur would block her from this horror if he could, but they no longer had that option. The blinding white light had forever changed them and their connection. Still, he sensed nothing evil in this bold power. In truth, he drew strength from her, pulled her insight and potency to him, as he never could before.

Phavage tapped the staff twice, crouched, and then circled.

Warily, they slunk around each other.

Phavage lunged as if to drive the staff into Chur's heart, but he whipped his staff up, thwarting the blow. The shock wave caused Phavage to reverberate. Fear widened his pink eyes. Chur knew that look. Pure terror swept over his pale form when he realized as skilled as he was, he was no match for Chur.

"Tell me again about my arrogance."

Phavage retreated, dread evident in the quiver that shook his form. His pale genitals, nestled in wisps of white hair, shrived until they all but disappeared. Blue veins ran like fragile rivers under translucent flesh.

Chur took advantage and whirled his *dantaratase* over his head as he flung the end of the staff toward Phavage. His blow struck his fragile head. Crimson exploded, fanning out like an inglorious cape. Phavage hit the platform with a dull thud. Blood pooled around his crushed skull.

Ambo Votny strode importantly onto the fighting ring. Rotund, he bent over with difficulty and reluctantly pronounced Phavage dead. Casting Chur a disgusted glance as he exited the platform, Ambo picked his nose and wiped it on his trousers. Recruits were called forth to remove the body. A maroon streak marked Phavage's sad exit. Another recruit swabbed up the mess, but a dark stain remained. Regret touched Chur for a moment, but again he pushed it away with Enovese's help. Such horrible tragedy was not his fault. He had no choice but to kill or be killed.

No mercy, no quarter, no second thoughts.

Chur flung his bloody *dantaratase* away.

"Who else dares to challenge me?" Extending to his full height, he glared into the crowd of recruits. Enovese's careful shave removed all his hair, leaving him an oil-glistening monster of muscle. He flexed, reminding all comers that he was no weakling.

A murmur rose then quickly ended when Onya Ritlin strode up with an *avenyet* clasped in his burnished fists.

Black as Onic timber, Onya's golden brown eyes, nestled in his dark face, were reminiscent of the empress, but Chur again pushed any thoughts aside. Onya selected the *avenyet,* for again, it was his most skilled weapon.

A recruit handed Chur a double-edged club and he grasped it in the center, feeling the weight distribute along his arm. Twisting the club with intent, Chur didn't wait for Onya to advance. He attacked in a roundhouse swing.

A mistake.

Defensively, Onya ducked and landed a blow to Chur's chest, knocking the wind out of him. Staggering back, Chur dropped to his knees, faking a greater blow than what he'd sustained.

Onya rushed him, lifting his club high to bash Chur's head, but Chur flung up his *avenyet,* catching Onya in the chin, flinging his head back.

When Onya toppled to the floor, Chur pounced and bashed his head in with both ends of the club. Blood splattered all over his body, the oil allowing it to drip like rain back to the floor. Enovese cringed away; Chur regretted her revulsion but knew she understood this was his life. This was the challenge.

Ambo again pronounced the man dead. Recruits dragged him away and cleaned up the mess.

Splattered in gore, grinning, Chur boldly called, "Who is next to die?"

Two other recruits took the platform, both falling dead within moments of facing him. He took a blow or two but nothing damaging. Perhaps now Ambo, Helton, and the other conspirators realized the plan was better in theory than execution. Too, touching Enovese lifted him, increasing his speed and power. She wasn't a fighter by any means, but somehow just having her there with him maximized all his abilities.

A murmur went through the crowd when no other recruit stepped forward. Chur squinted, trying to see through the crystal glare, but all he could discern were indistinct shadow shapes of men. Easily his eyes picked out the blubbery silhouette of Ambo and decided the massive lump next to him must be Helton.

After a flurry of discussion, where Chur could just barely detect the denigrating tone of Helton Ook, another recruit stepped forward.

Ard Dren.

Golden hair, green eyes, and built much like Helton Ook, Ard was a mass of mismatched parts. His arms were too long, his legs too short, his torso oddly feminine while his shoulders bunched with muscles that swallowed his neck. Ard had been in the training house for three years. He'd always managed to run just short of glory. Now he stepped forward with a *cirvant*, a curved sword as long as his forearm. The *cirvant* was highly polished with a razor edge. In a talented hand, the weapon could slice a man to ribbons, killing him before he hit the ground.

Ard possessed that talented hand.

A recruit handed Chur the same weapon. Hefting the short sword, familiar with the weight, but knowing he wasn't as skilled as Ard revealed the first chink in his armor. Doubt crumbled a corner of his wall of certainty. Before the tremor caused a catastrophic failure, Enovese was there, pushing mortar into the cracks, filling his misgivings with her conviction. Buoyed, Chur swung the weapon in a looping arc and took the center of the platform.

Choosing the weapon was an advantage the challenger had, but Chur had the advantage of choosing his posture. In this case, he wisely chose defense.

Smirking, swinging the *cirvant* in wide arcs, Ard circled Chur like a hungry dog. Ard lunged, snagged a shallow thrust to Chur's upper arm, and then withdrew before Chur could react.

Blood oozed.

Twice more Ard pricked his arms, clearly determined to drain him slowly.

In the background, Chur heard Helton's gruff voice encouraging Ard to finish him quickly. Twirling, Ard slashed across Chur's chest. Blood washed down from the cut, cooling his body. The shock dropped Chur to his knees.

When Ard played to the crowd with a chuckling lift of his weapon-clad hand, Chur thrust out, stabbing Ard in the lower back, deep enough to damage his kidney.

Furious, Ard swung around. Wild and unfocused, his blow swept over Chur's ducked head.

Chur stood and sliced his *cirvant* in a series of carefully placed arcs. Where Ard wanted to humble Chur by slicing him slowly, Chur took Helton's words to heart; he aimed to finish as fast as possible.

Blood spurted along several major arteries.

Ard wobbled. He cast his green eyes down, stunned, dismayed, and then cast his gaze to Chur.

Ard collapsed. A crimson pool spread around him. At least in his last moments he wore the color of the empress.

Chur stood over him.

"Finish me."

Chur plunged the blade deep into Ard's heart, killing him instantly. Enovese cringed, but he assured her his action was the kindest cut of all. To leave Ard alive and bleeding was malicious for they would wait for him to exsanguinate. A quick, painless death was the last compassionate gift Chur could give.

Ambo again ascended the platform, pronounced Ard dead, cast Chur a furious snarl, and then dissolved into shadow as recruits removed the body.

Another discussion between Helton and the recruits ensued as Chur stood bleeding. His arm and chest thrummed with pain and the trickle of blood began to fuddle his mind. He'd thought the cuts shallow, but on second consideration, he realized they were deep enough to cause a steady flow of blood. His connection to Enovese grew tenuous. A wave of panic ensued.

Bright as the light that blinded them, Enovese pushed to his mind, whispering, *I'm here, I'm here.*

Chur answered, *I feel you.*

Strength galvanized his form.

"If there are no more challengers the magistrate must call an end to the challenge."

After a hushed debate, Sterlave ascended the steps.

Chur had hoped that he would not have to face a man he genuinely cared about, a man he honestly thought would be a valid contender for Harvester. He shot a glare in the direction of what he thought was Helton. How dare he manipulate this honorable man into a challenge for his own end?

Sterlave entered the platform without a weapon. He had chosen to fight bare handed.

No wonder Helton was furious. His oil and blood coating gave Chur a distinct advantage. As an experienced fighter, Sterlave understood this. What would prompt him to wrestle at a disadvantage?

Chur took a neutral position in the center of the platform with his feet shoulder-width apart, his hands open and ready.

Sterlave mimicked the stance.

They nodded and the match began.

Sterlave executed an offensive takedown by lowering his head and shoulder, and charging toward Chur.

Chur created an angle and drove across his hips, knocking him sideways. Using his forward momentum, Chur hooked his leg to Sterlave's, tripping him back.

On the way down, Sterlave attempted to grasp Chur's hand but only caught his wrist. Chur broke the hold by rotating his arm. He grasped Sterlave's hand. Following him down, Chur rolled him over and pushed his arm up to the middle of his back.

Sterlave growled.

Lowering his head, Chur whispered, "You should not have challenged me."

"I didn't have a choice." Sterlave lifted his hips, trying to buck Chur off, but Chur had him locked down. "Just finish me."

In that hushed plea, Chur understood Sterlave had witnessed Helton's behavior and knew what was going on, but he was powerless to stop the mass challenge. Sterlave took no pride in fighting a wounded man, a man cheated, but he also couldn't refuse Helton's order to enter the platform. To refuse was to exhibit cowardice.

Releasing his hold, Chur stood.

Sterlave took to his feet, blinking confusion.

A rumble erupted. Above the rabble, Chur heard Helton's voice encouraging Sterlave to take advantage.

Eyeing each other, Chur and Sterlave ignored the crowd and circled around each other.

Plunging his head into Chur's chest, Sterlave executed another takedown move but held back and asked, "Why did you release me?"

Grasping his shoulder, as if to take him down, Chur said, "I don't want to kill you."

"Then I have no choice but to kill you."

Grappling, they fought for advantage.

Regret caused Chur to give quarter when he knew he shouldn't.

Lament caused Sterlave to do the same.

Sluggish, time passed as the crowd around them grew restless.

Clearly, neither man had his heart in killing mode.

Chur realized the more he dragged the battle out, the more his blood loss drained his energy. He labored for breath, and what air he drew tasted of copper and sweat. He didn't want to kill Sterlave, but he had no choice.

With an aggressive step-in, Sterlave sought advantage, pinning Chur down, wrapping his arm around his neck, squeezing until Chur's vision swam gray.

Bucking his hips, struggling to break the hold, Chur lost his connection to Enovese.

Like a vise, Sterlave's arm crushed his neck, blocking blood flow, jamming his gasping breaths. How cruel that in his kindness he would taste defeat.

A rush of white light enveloped his body. Chur found a well of power. Bucking Sterlave off, he rolled him over and wrapped his arm around his neck. Squeezing, Chur blocked his breathing until Sterlave moved no more.

Even though he'd won, Chur took no pride in the accomplishment. He slid off Sterlave's lifeless form and stood. Ambo ascended the platform, pronounced Sterlave dead, and then allowed the recruits to carry him away.

"Call an end to this now."

Reluctantly, Ambo decreed the challenge finished. Ambo moved to grasp Chur's hand, to proclaim him victorious, but Chur shoved his hand away.

"You are a man without honor."

Ambo sneered. Chur no longer cared. His connection to Enovese snapped. He stomped off the platform. As he strode nude to his rooms, thinking only of Enovese, he heard only a dead whoosh of emptiness.

Blood, gore, and sweat dripped off his form as dread consumed his heart. No matter how focused, he could not connect to her.

Alarm quickened his steps.

Shoving open the carved Onic door, Chur stopped dead in his tracks.

Enovese lay in a collapsed heap in the middle of his rooms.

Legs and arms akimbo, she resembled a broken doll tossed aside by an uncaring child. So similar to what he imagined she would look after the *paratanist* selection ritual.

He panicked.

"No, no, no!" Chur rushed toward her pale and fragile form.

Cupping her up, pulling her nude body to him, he hefted her lifeless corpse into his arms. Her eyes were open, unfocused, dead. Trapping a scream in his throat, Chur placed his mouth to hers.

Breathing life to her, he crushed her close, begging repeatedly, "I love you. Don't leave me. I love you."

29

Bathed in white, Enovese floated.

She gave all of her life, her power, and her essence to Chur to ensure he won the challenge.

Drained, she collapsed.

In the last moments, she tasted his antagonism, his reluctance to kill a man he admired, but Enovese pushed all her being to him in an effort to help him triumph. When she gave the last of herself, she had no idea if he won or lost. She committed herself to him knowing that she had drained herself beyond the point of no return.

Death embraced her, taking her away from the mortal realm.

30

Terrified that she would kill herself if he lost, Chur had no idea she would sacrifice herself to ensure he won.

Clutching her lifeless body, he cast his gaze about his rooms. Enovese had laid out his gear, the *umer,* the *estal* oil, and all the accoutrements for his Harvest ritual. After a challenge, she would give him a viscous drink that would revive his senses, his strength. Locating the bottle, he poured half into a cup, then placed it to her lips.

"Drink."

Honey thick, the drink spilled beyond her lips.

Chur again pushed his breath to her.

Enovese remained dead in his arms.

Sinking down, clasping her close, he fell to the floor, breathing his life to her lips. Imagining the white light, he called it forth, begging the brightness to enshrine their bodies.

When nothing happened, he breathed harder into her body, inflating her lungs with his breath.

Enovese laid mute, eyes wide and lifeless.

Lifting his face to the heavens, Chur begged, "Take me instead. Let her live!"

Pressing his lips over hers, he breathed into her again.

Nothing mattered to him but having her back. He could not go on without Enovese. How malicious of him to drain her for the challenge. He didn't know how he'd had so much strength, but now he did. Enovese channeled her life force to him. Chur drained her to win. He killed a man he respected by draining the woman he loved. Desperate, Chur breathed into her body, imploring the light to consume him.

"I will do anything you ask if you will just bring her back."

Brilliant, blinding brightness consumed Chur's form. Still cradling Enovese, Chur blinked into the glare.

"Tell me, Harvester, do you wish to save yourself or her?"

Chur didn't hesitate. "Her."

"Do you love her?" the sexless voice asked mockingly.

"More than my next breath. I will give my life for her."

"Then drink," the sexless voice encouraged, casting light unto the vial of poison.

Hesitating, Chur grasped Enovese close. "Bring her back first."

A chuckle reverberated through his mind, his rooms. "Drink and I will bring her back."

Chur let Enovese slide from his arms. He approached the vial, cupped it to his palm, uncapped the bottle, and lifted the pale blue glass to his lips. Casting his gaze back to Enovese, he tilted the vial and let the cold liquid flow down his throat.

As he gasped with the pain of death, Enovese gasped with life. Turning to her, desperate to tell her everything, Chur died.

31

Dirty light wrenched her back to the mortal realm. Enovese resisted for the clean bright light was warm, comforting, and pure. She did not want to return to a life of struggle and pain. Only thoughts of Chur compelled her to go back. She would suffer anything to be with him. When she blinked open her eyes, she saw Chur standing near the kitchen, consuming the vial of poison.

"No!" The one word strangled out of her throat as she coughed up traces of Chur's reviving drink. She scrambled to her feet as he fell to his knees.

His mouth moved without sound.

He collapsed.

Her heart shattered into countless shards. Tears blurred her vision. Why would he consume the poison when he'd begged her never to take such a dark option?

Dropping next to him, she ripped the glowing vial out of his hand. When she found it empty, she threw it against the wall. Thick blue glass bounced off and skittered across the floor.

"Chur?" Cradling his head, she lowered her lips to his, determined to taste the poison and join him in death. She probed his mouth with her tongue and tasted not bitterness but the sweetest ambrosia.

Chur gasped, pulling her breath from her lungs.

Elated, she called his name over and over, kissing his lips, his strong jaw, his sweaty brow. She touched his neck to make sure her senses had not deceived her. A strong, steady heartbeat pulsed under her fingertips. When he wrapped her up in the power of his arms and crushed her to his chest, she released the tears simmering in her eyes. Oil and dried blood smeared her body and assaulted her nose, but she didn't care. He was alive. He was kissing her. He was holding her. He was murmuring her name.

And he was glowing.

"Chur?" She struggled to move back, to see him more clearly, but he refused to release her.

"I don't want to let you go." He inhaled her scent and grasped handfuls of her hair, turning her head to better angle his possession of her mouth. In between passionate kisses, he murmured, "I know I'm glowing because I can feel power surging along my nerves."

Reaching out with her mind to his, she had barely touched the surface before she abruptly withdrew.

"Enovese?"

"Too much, too intense, I—I've never felt anything so superior." That wasn't the right word but she couldn't verbalize exactly how overpowered and insignificant she felt when she connected. "Almost as if I touched the mind of . . . a god."

Chur uttered a laugh that was more demonic than divine. "I am not a god." He released her from his embrace.

As she leaned back, her breath caught in her throat. Golden light shimmered just below his flesh. His beauty caused her eyes to water. No scar marred his form. All the cuts and bruises from the challenge disappeared. Even the blood and sweat vanished. When she looked down, she still had streaks of both on her body, but he was clean, as if he had just stepped from the Valry Sea. Leaning near, she inhaled his essence and was relieved to discover his familiar masculine scent, but she found a new fragrance, something arousing and compelling. The perfume made her want to throw herself at his feet in obeisance, or fall to her back and part her thighs.

"Why are you looking at me like that?" Chur stood and offered her a hand up.

Trembling, she clasped his hand. A shock flashed across her skin, tingling her blood, flooding her sex with sudden arousal.

His brows lifted at her reaction.

"You're beautiful."

A wry smile twisted his face. Without the scar to lift his upper lip, it was a grin of intriguing sensuality. "I can't imagine that trading in death has improved my features."

Enovese drew him to the mirror.

His jaw dropped. "My scars. All of my scars are gone." He traced his hand along his chest and face. Leaning near to the mirror, he examined himself with more horror than wonder. "What happened to my eyes?"

Summer-sky blue had deepened to a crystal azure that gleamed with frightful intensity. When he turned them on her, she lowered her head automatically. She wasn't even aware she had done so until after she completed the motion.

He cupped his hand to her chin and tilted her face, but she kept her eyes downcast.

"Look at me."

Lifting her gaze to his, she almost swooned. She felt utterly exposed and terribly unworthy to stand in his presence. An acolyte should be properly anointed, not naked and befouled with blood and sweat.

"Why do you cower away from me?"

Even his voice had changed. It was deeper, richer, and painfully arousing, and Enovese knew that even his whisper would command authority. His presence struck her mute. When he glowered with frustration, she panicked and tried to fling herself to the floor in supplication.

Chur grasped her shoulders and commanded her to speak.

Mustering her strength, reminding herself that he was still the Chur she loved, she whispered, "I want to drop to my knees and either worship you or take you into my mouth. Perhaps both."

A booming laugh filled the room. "I'd prefer the latter."

When she moved to comply, he chuckled and stopped her. "Not now, Enovese. We must ready for the Harvest."

A new terror tingled her flesh. Now that he had changed so profoundly, perhaps his thoughts had changed as well. Would he claim her now that he was a god? If this miraculous change could wipe away his scars, it surely could repair his infertility. A god could have any woman. A god could have many women. A god did not have to settle for only one woman. She longed to probe his mind, but her earlier experience frightened her from even trying.

Chur turned his attention to the accoutrements she had placed upon the table. "I think we can dispense with the reviving drink." He flexed his golden muscles in a slow-motion wave of masculine power that shivered her with attraction. "I believe I have been fully revived."

She nodded. Even though she had performed this ritual many times, the particulars escaped her. His presence was far too distracting and she could not think straight.

Chur sensed her hesitancy. "First, we bathe."

He strode to the unit. Every muscle in his body moved in sensual concert. At once, she couldn't wait to touch him but then feared to do so. He seemed larger than he had before.

Powerful, dangerous, and arousing—he was the ultimate male. Perhaps, she thought, he was a god of war and sex, for that's what he embodied. How dare she, a lowly servant, dare to touch a god?

"Come." He crooked his finger and her knees threatened to give way, but she moved to his side with sheer determination.

Trembling, she set the water to the right temperature. As he wetted himself, she smoothed the soap between her hands, building the lather. Every sense heightened. She noticed the luxurious feel of the soap, the pop of bubbles against her flesh, even the woodsy scent smelled stronger.

He lowered his head so she could reach.

Her first contact caused her sex to gush anew.

Touching him was sublime.

Smooth and silky as *astle,* his skin compelled her to explore. She marveled in every plane of his skull, the shape of his ears, the power of his neck and shoulders.

A low chuckle rumbled through his chest as he rinsed the soap from his face. "Ah, Enovese, your moans of pure pleasure are most arousing."

She hadn't even been aware of making any noise but realized she *oohed* and *ahhed* as she washed him. "I can't help myself. Touching you is like touching . . ."

"A god." He waggled his brows. "But I assure you, I am very much a man." He placed her soapy slick hand around his straining cock.

Her eyes rolled back at the jolt of sizzling pleasure.

Heavy and thick, his shaft pulsed, causing her mouth and sex to water. Licking her lips, she drew her other hand along him, not cleaning him so much as increasing his ardor. She wanted him desperately. If she could not have him within her soon, she thought she would implode upon herself and dwindle into a puff that a strong breeze would sweep away.

"As much as I am enjoying this, I think we will be late if we linger." He pulled her hands from his sex.

A groan of pure frustration reverberated in her chest.

He shushed her gently and began to soap her body. "My sweat and blood mark you, so I should clean you." He intoned the words as if prophecy. She tried not to hear the trace of mockery in his tone, but she did. He humored her. He belittled her attraction. He was fully aware of his power and made light of her attraction to it. She wanted to resist his allure, but her frail human body could not.

His soapy strokes were like liquid sex. Each part he touched sprang to awareness. Swaying on her feet, she transcended beyond her physical self. She hovered on the edge of a profound orgasm but could not push over since he did not want her to. Lost in golden clouds of ecstasy, she reached for a higher plane and came close to touching *Jarasine.* On the verge of parting the veil to the misty world of the gods, she plummeted back to Diola and found herself wrapped in a towel.

Lost in a daze of lust, she had to rely on Chur to prompt her through the rest of the preparation ritual. She oiled him, determined to keep her focus, but again she uttered mewling pleasure groans as her hands slicked along his muscles. When she knelt to cover his legs, she couldn't help but part her lips and slide them worshipfully across his cock. Pearls of moisture tingled her tongue with delicious magic. She wanted to drink his climax.

"I am hard enough," Chur said, stepping back.

His withdrawal was like a slap in the face.

He plucked the *umer* off the table and consumed it with one mighty swallow. A grimace curled his lips. "Gah, it still tastes like burnt wood." He dropped the cup to the table, then handed her the slender bottle of *estal* oil.

His attitude was strictly professional. Again, her heart lurched.

From his posture to his words smacked of duty and nothing else. Her lips upon his cock didn't seem to even arouse him. He'd pulled away without any regret. After everything she had done, to help him, to protect him, even giving her very life for him—her sacrifices meant nothing. He had ascended. No matter what he said, he was a god. She was nothing but a sterile mortal, a lowly servant. A *paratanist* created from a horrific ritual that left her too damaged to be a bondmate to a man, let alone a god.

Pride stiffened her spine even as she knelt before him. She refused to beg or remind him of his impassioned words. Drizzling the golden *estal* oil to her palm, she coated his cock with rhythmic clinical movements. When she finished, she stood, recapped the oil, and placed it on the table. Unceremoniously, she wiped her hands on a *harshan,* then tossed the towel aside.

He frowned.

Ignoring his alluring intensity, she helped him don his leggings, his wide belt, and his ceremonial sword with swift, mechanical movements. Last, and most reluctantly, she helped him slip on his booming footwear. Her revulsion for those horrible boots helped her distance herself from his potent appeal.

Once she had dressed him, she stood, and immediately turned away. She couldn't bear to look at him. In his eyes, she feared she would find pity, confusion, or a mocking indulgence. She could not read his mind, but surely he could tap hers without her knowledge. Gods did things like that. They took advantage of mortals and used them to their own ends.

Determined to cling to her role without any demand upon him, Enovese shrouded herself in her baggy robe. Rough fabric chafed her flesh after his silken touch, but she ignored the assault. She vowed she would play her role to the bitter end. Covering her face with the cowl hood, she placed her bag of accoutrements around her waist and lifted her hand to the door, directing him to precede her for she must walk ten paces behind.

Chur stomped to the carved Onic door.

His boots boomed, echoing in the small space of his rooms.

She cringed. Gritting her teeth, she moved to follow.

He flung the door open hard enough to imbed the black wood into the wall.

She did not react.

Glowing golden, Chur strode down the hall as if he owned the entire palace. In a way, he did. For she intuitively knew no weapon could harm him, and any woman he turned his attentions on would instantly fall at his feet. He would enter the Harvest room and have his pick of any virgin there. Broken in form, he would not select her.

Meekly, she took double-time steps to keep up with his massive strides.

He bothered not to look back to see if she followed for he knew she would. Such was her station to serve the Harvester.

Two palace guards blocked the double hung doors to the Harvest room. Despite years of training, they gasped when they saw Chur. Both recovered quickly. They grasped the massive handles and pulled the doors open.

Chur strode into the elaborately decorated room. Since this was the harvest for Kasmiri, the servants had spared no expense in ornamentation. More gleaming fruits and vegetables littered the floor than ever before. Garlands sagged with a profusion of leaves and autumn flowers. Rather than water in the fountains, red wine splashed in garish spurts, reminding her of horrid battle wounds.

She slipped in behind him before the doors closed. Moving to her alcove, she pressed her back into the wall. Cold and hard, just like her future. Anger flushed the chill from her bones. Why had he ascended when she'd made just as many sacrifices?

Had he known all along the poison would have this effect? When she examined the contents, she determined it was a simple concentration of a deadly herb, but there was something odd about the coolness and weight of the bottle.

Chur stopped to consider the portraits of the prior Harvesters. Enovese thought they had captured only harsh brutality, for not a one smiled. Each man looked ready to leap from the wall snarling and waving a weapon. None was as perfectly formed or as beautiful as Chur. She wondered what his portrait would look like, but his portrait would go up only when he selected a bondmate.

What if he decided to continue as the Harvester? No mortal man could best him, and if he didn't age . . . the entire structure of the Harvest prophecy would change forever. Now that he knew the secret of the chalice, he would not allow that practice to continue. *Paratanists* would eventually disappear. Who would serve the Harvesters? Her stomach roiled, for she knew Chur would demand she remain as his *paratanist* until she could no longer do so. Then what would he do with her? Fury and fear danced hand and hand in her mind. Knowing she had no choice, she huddled in her alcove.

Chur turned his attention to the long sacrifice table. The virgins lay perfectly still, shrouded in their gaudy finery, each trying to outdo the other. Kasmiri caught her eye, for she was the only one dressed in a blaze of crimson and diamonds. Even though it was against the rules, servants had given Kasmiri a bit more space than the other girls had, probably so she would stand out even more. Not that she needed any assistance there. Glittering gems encrusted every inch of her robe and the pillow below her head. Kasmiri glared at the ceiling with profound boredom. She was one of those sacrifices who just couldn't wait for the ritual to end.

Enovese considered the other virgins and some looked more irritated than Kasmiri, but others had rapture in their eyes.

They believed in the transcending power of the ritual. Still others appeared nervous yet hopeful. Usually those who had that peculiar combination wanted Chur to select them. She imaged her face, under her robe, had that tense but optimistic blend.

As Chur adjusted his ceremonial sword and approached the first sacrifice, her last hope that he would choose her evaporated.

32

Chur gazed down at the first sacrifice. Sallow faced with enormous brown eyes, her bright orange robe clashed with her ginger hair. He remembered her as the chatty girl from the Festival of Temptation. He also remembered her father from Kasmiri's party. Following form, her father offered her up as an easily manipulated doormat that would do as he wished, if only he would claim her. When she looked up at him, her mouth parted with wonder, but she quickly lowered her gaze. The reaction caused him to grimace. Enovese had a similar response. He thought the odd glow to his skin was disconcerting, but it seemed to have lessened into a burnished radiance. When she flitted her gaze up and down again, he realized it was not fear for she was not cowering; she was in awe of him.

Suddenly, all of Enovese's reactions clarified.

"*Paratanist!*" he bellowed, calling her forth.

She appeared at his side.

Her cowl hood covered her face, but he could tell she kept her head lowered nonetheless. A tender part of his heart splintered. He had not even tried to console her before leaving his rooms. So wrapped up in his own startling transformation, he never considered what this change meant for her. Slipping to her mind as easily as slipping a blade to his belt, he instantly knew her fear that he would no longer want her. That he would continue to be the Harvester for endless seasons. That he would force her to serve him while he lived the life of an indulged god.

He realized he could change the scope of the prophecy forever. The choice was up to him. As much as the power appealed to him, he did not want to shoulder the burden.

Lifting his hands, he pushed the hood of her robe back with great care. Enovese kept her head lowered. Tears shimmered on her cheeks. When he wiped them away, he felt her heartbreak through his wet fingertips. She loved him so much she died to protect him. Now, she was willing to let him go. Rather than making the choice for him, she would leave everything up to him. She could not have given him a greater gift.

He clasped her cold hand and drew her to the head of the table.

She looked at the narrow space above the virgins' pillows.

Effortlessly, he lifted her and placed her upon the padded white surface.

Enovese gasped in surprise.

After a moment of hesitation, she settled back into the proper pose. Radiant with delight, she was far more stunning than any woman he'd ever known. Even without enhancements, her clear beauty dazzled his eyes. Her hair sparkled in the crystal light, reflecting every harvest color, displaying her indigo starburst eyes to perfection. Most pleasing of all, her truculent nose tilted above her coral lips, which curved into a joyous smile.

He cupped her knees with hands now absent of scars. He

slid her forward and parted her thighs. When the rough fabric of her robe clung to her legs, he whisked it aside impatiently. Meticulously shaved and glistening, her coral lipped sex parted eagerly for him.

Enovese flashed him an impish grin.

In that singular moment, he fell irrevocably in love with her all over again. She understood him. She accepted him. She soothed his pains, blessed his needs, aroused his every sense, and accepted his foibles along with his strengths. She knew him down to the very vestiges of his most miserable self. Despite it all, she still loved him.

Chur placed her left foot on the hilt of his sword, lifted her right foot up to his shoulder until her leg was almost straight against his chest. Breathless with anticipation, he pushed the elaborate codpiece aside. In spite of the *umer* and the *estal* oil, he felt every pulsing inch of his cock. By proximity, he felt her wet heat longing to smooth around his sex.

Upon a deep breath, he tasted the tangy sweet of her arousal, which only hardened him further. Flowers and spices infused her scent. If he did not possess her, he would go mad. Pheromones filled the room, but nothing enticed him as profoundly as her bouquet. Only Enovese would ever soothe his wanton needs.

In the ancient tongue, he uttered, "By might of the blade I claim that which belongs to me." He paused just long enough to cause worry to flitter across her face, then added, "I claim you as my bondmate."

Enovese lifted her face and spoke in the same language, "I freely give myself to you as my bondmate."

Plunging deep within her silky passage compelled a shared groan to erupt between them. His miraculous transformation offered him no protection from his insatiable lust for Enovese. She fit around him as if she had always belonged to him and forever would. Her pulse matched his. Her breath paced his. Gazes locked and he lost himself within her commanding stare.

Her foot lifted from the hilt of his sword and moved around to his back, clutching him closer. He lowered her other leg so now she held him tightly between trembling thighs as he clutched her bottom. Digging his fingertips into her flesh, he yanked her close, pounding into her with a need to be deeper. Something told him he must merge with her fully or lose everything. Sweat pushed through the oil coating his skin, heating him as if *Tandalsul* beat down upon his back.

When she leaned up, clasping his shoulders, she tightened around him. His cock pulsed to bursting and he trapped a scream of passionate surrender in his throat.

She nestled her mouth to his ear and whispered three simple words.

An orgasm started at his extremities, blazed along his nerves, built to a bundle at the center of his body, then erupted with such power he shook the table below her writhing form. Repeatedly, he pumped into her body until he collapsed against the edge, spent and shaking. In that moment, he touched the divine essence the gods bestowed upon him. He understood everything from the light, the changes, the struggles—everything made a perfect, wonderful sense. He was not meant to change the prophecy by continuing its traditions; he was designed to change the world by his relationship with Enovese. For even though there was no outward sign, the gods had blessed Enovese far more profoundly.

Below him, still panting from her pleasure, her pale skin gleamed with the pure brightness of the finest crystal. Her light jade eyes had deepened to the color of the Valry Sea in storm. The starburst of deep indigo in the iris blazed with intensity. Coral peach lips parted with gasping breaths.

"I love you, Enovese."

He had not known how desperately she needed to hear him speak the words until he did. Knowing the sentiment as truth in her heart was not the same as hearing him say it.

"I love you, Chur."

Wrapping her up in his arms, he pulled her from the table, and then suddenly became aware of rumblings from the sacrifices. He had forgotten them all in his drive to possess Enovese. He set her on her feet and then smoothed her robe.

When she moved to pull her hood up, he stopped her. "Do not cover your face ever again. No bondmate of mine will hide her beauty." Whispering to her ear, he added, "Let them gaze upon you and seethe with jealousy."

She cast him that delightful impish grin as she lifted her truculent nose. "What if they fall at my feet? Will you still allow me to dazzle them with my beauty?"

He chuckled. "Worship you they may, but to touch you"—he clasped his blade—"will result in the loss of a limb."

Placing her hand upon his, she said, "Understand the same applies to you. Women may look, but there will be no touching, except by me."

He readily agreed. He didn't want any woman to touch him but Enovese. There was no weakness in this, only strength. He saw through the prophecy, saw clearly how indoctrination shaped his views. Sex did not weaken him. Only sex without love could diminish his spirit. Merging with Enovese transcended the physical. With her, he went far beyond a lover or the mechanical Harvester. In her arms, he became the man the gods meant him to be—strong, secure, utterly at peace.

Whispered babble grew louder as the virgins waited for the ceremony to commence. Those at the south end of the table had no idea what had happened, so those at the north end were whispering that the Harvester had chosen his bondmate. Sacrifice by sacrifice, the information traveled to the end of the table. A myriad of emotions crossed their faces including relief, sadness, annoyance, bitterness, and even betrayal.

Clearing his throat, Chur said, "I have chosen my bondmate. Another Harvester will attend you shortly." He took Enovese's hand. "Come, we must tell the guards to call the magistrate."

She squeezed his hand, conveying her fear of reprisal.

"Don't worry. None would dare to thwart my will in selecting you."

Crushing his hand in panic, Enovese gasped, "You cannot fight them all."

Drawing a breath that puffed his massive chest, Chur laughed. "You said yourself that I was a god. Do you think any of them can harm me?"

Demure, Enovese lowered her head. "They would not dare to harm you, but I think they would seek to destroy me. You know what Clathia said."

"Ah, Enovese!" He laughed. "You are beyond me!" Her frown of confusion softened his tone. "How could you not have surmised the most basic truth of who you are? Think of the carving on the door and on the chalice box. Male and female Harvesters entwined. Merging so fully you can't tell where one ends and the other begins. What comes of that union?"

"A *paratanist*." Her voice was soft. Shock widened her eyes.

"I think, if we dig deeply enough into the past, we will find the ancients revered *paratanists*. Somewhere during five thousand seasons, jealousy forced them into servants. If I am a god, then you are a goddess, and you have been one from the moment of your birth."

A frown creased her brow as the wheels turned in her mind.

"Think of why, from the moment you could walk, you were covered in a robe and trained only to speak when spoken to. It was to protect others from your allure."

Her lips parted with surprise, but her eyes narrowed with disbelief.

"Everything that happened to us, the connection, the power

in our union, all that has sprung from you, from the supremacy inherent in you. The gods didn't transform me. You did. So that I would match you in power."

When she moved to argue the point, he pushed the moment of clarity into her mind, causing her to sway on her feet.

Lifting her chin, Enovese adjusted her robe as if the most regal color enshrouded her. A new light glowed from her face as she removed her bound hair from hiding and spread it proudly over her shoulders. The last time she had left this room her dreams had been in ruins and tears blinded her vision. Now, she would exit this room with more pride than the empress. Chur smiled at the vision she made. Their lives would never be the same, but neither would anyone else's.

At the doors, she turned, leaned close, and said, "We will change the world."

"Of that, I have no doubt."

33

Outside the Harvest room, Chur argued with Ambo Votny while Enovese hid behind his bulk. Never had she shown her face to any but Chur. Exposed, she felt almost naked while standing in the hallway with palace guards, servants, and members of the elite milling about. For all her bold posturing, this unveiling terrified her. All those eyes glaring, seeking out weakness to exploit . . . She resisted the urge to cover her face with the hood only by drawing on Chur's conviction that she was a goddess.

Swaying a bit, his normally florid face pale, Ambo sputtered, "You cannot pick her!" He pointed at Enovese without looking directly at her, as if even glancing at her would turn him to stone. His thrusting finger trembled and he quickly withdrew it. Almost of its own accord, his finger found its way to his nose. After a deft picking, Ambo wiped the contents on his trousers.

Enovese wasn't the only one who cringed. Hearing Chur speak of this compulsion wasn't the same as actually witnessing it.

"According to the prophecy, I can select any sacrifice presented to me." In sharp contrast, Chur was perfectly calm, his voice a low rumble of far-off thunder. His beautiful bronze skin glowed despite the dim lighting crystals.

"She is a *paratanist.*" Ambo twisted the word around his ugly mouth until she sounded like the vilest expletive.

Enovese had to bite her lips to remain silent, then chastised herself for holding to rules that no longer applied to her.

Summoning her strength, she stepped out of Chur's shadow and said, "My station has no bearing on his selection."

"Silence," Ambo snarled. "None has asked you a question."

An unnatural hush fell over the people clustered about the Harvest room doors. His dismissal of her caused Chur to grip the hilt of his ceremonial sword.

Placing her hand on Chur's arm to stop him from chopping Ambo's head off, Enovese moved close to Ambo, so close he had no choice but to see her. Ambo's watery eyes darted across her face, then held to a spot just over her shoulder. He couldn't miss her resemblance to Arianda Rostvaika, not when the woman herself stood just beyond their frozen tableau. His labored breath, ripe with wine and decayed meat, conveyed his terror. Despite his rude behavior, Enovese felt sorry for him. Ambo had never expected such a drastic and irrevocable change during his reign as magistrate.

Lifting her chin, Enovese calmly offered, "Having undergone the Harvest ritual, I am now a fully recognized citizen and I will not be spoken to in that manner."

Ambo stepped back, as if she reeked of corruption, and bellowed, "A *paratanist* speaks when spoken to! You are nothing, nothing! Do not dare to—"

Silver sharp, Chur's blade tip caressed Ambo's quivering chins. "Choose your words carefully, Ambo. I will not tolerate you addressing my bondmate as a servant."

Ambo sputtered but wisely held his tongue. He glared at the palace guards, as if willing them to action. Enraptured by events, they didn't move from the Harvest room doors.

Chur lowered his sword. "You will perform the bondmate ceremony."

"I won't."

They stood at impasse until Clathia stormed down the hall toward them. Everyone parted, allowing the empress access to the small group by the door. Enovese had never seen the empress up close. Her tawny skin glowed and her eyes sparkled with a thousand torments. Clathia examined her critically, then realized quite suddenly that Enovese was not only a *paratanist,* but that she looked familiar.

Clathia shot a glance to Arianda.

Arianda arched her brows and lifted her truculent nose, as if daring the empress to make a scene.

Clathia straightened her shoulders, then turned her penetrating gaze onto Chur. Surprise widened her eyes. She took a moment to take in his transformation, then her gaze narrowed as her face hardened. He had not done as she demanded, but she couldn't very well upbraid him in front of so many witnesses. Clearly, Clathia realized something beyond the ordinary had occurred. Resignation and a weary futility dulled her flashing gaze.

"I see you have chosen, Harvester. May she bring you nothing but happiness."

To Enovese it sounded like a threat, but Chur exhibited his diplomatic skills.

"Thank you, my lady." Chur bowed. "However, the magistrate refuses to perform the ceremony."

"Such would be an abomination!" Ambo snapped at Chur. He gripped his distended belly protectively.

"Once the Harvester has made his selection, there is no undoing it." Clathia spun on her heel. As she strode away, she said over her shoulder, "Perform the ceremony, Ambo, or I will have you executed."

There was no time for Enovese to retrieve her dress so she bonded to Chur wearing her ceremonial robe. She didn't care. Ambo probably wouldn't have let her wear green anyway since her true family color was black. The details mattered little. Even Ambo's snarling disgust couldn't dampen her joy. Since she had no preference for the type of ceremony, Chur selected a traditional Ampirian ritual. They faced each other during Ambo's short speech with hands clasped. When he finished, they embraced. Short, sweet, and they were officially bonded.

Ambo's discomfort amused Arianda. Once he left, she graciously invited them to her suite of rooms for an impromptu celebration.

Enovese felt a little tongue-tied, for what does one say to a mother one has never met? A warmth and generosity of spirit flowed from Arianda. No awkward silences descended upon their trio, but they passed plenty of wistful looks and perplexed smiles. Arianda accepted Enovese without any explanation other than she was her daughter. Their startling resemblance left the matter unspoken but no less true.

Arianda's suite was similar to Chur's rooms and decorated in the same uncomplicated but luxuriant style indicative of a Harvester. Frilly plants filled her rooms, and a myriad of soft touches feminized the severe furniture. Rather than a bathing unit on the north wall, Arianda had a small waterfall that tumbled into a pond. As Enovese stepped close, a dozen black fish with red spots bobbed to the surface with their mouths agape.

"Would you like to feed them?" Arianda handed her a glass jar filled with green-brown pellets. "Just sprinkle some across the surface."

As soon as the fish saw the jar, they shimmied against each

other, jockeying for position. When Enovese lowered her hand to sprinkle the pellets, a few jumped out of the water.

"Greedy creatures," Arianda said with a laugh. "But harmless." She turned to her kitchen area to prepare refreshments.

Chur leaned close and whispered, "I like your mother very much, but I must go."

"Go where?"

A pleased smile lifted the edges of his mouth. "There is a commotion in the training rooms about who the next Harvester will be."

On the tip of her tongue was a question about how he could know such a thing or why it seemed to please him. She didn't ask. The transformation had given him extraordinary insight and somehow he'd become aware of a situation there. She pressed a kiss to his cheek, then waited for her mother.

Arianda placed a tray with food and drinks on the low table between the two couches. She looked about then lifted her brow to Enovese.

"A problem he must attend to."

Arianda nodded and sat with fluid grace. After a moment of silence, she said, "Ask." When Enovese hesitated, she said, "I can tell you have a thousand questions on your mind. Just like me, a little line appears over the bridge of your nose when you are pondering something."

"Why did you withdraw from the Harvester competition right before your sixth year?"

Folding her hands into her lap, Arianda idly rubbed the pad of her right thumb across the nail of her left thumb. "I fell in love. He was the most stunning man I had ever seen. He was kind, sweet, gentle—everything any woman could ask for."

Judging by her discomfort, the relationship had ended badly. Enovese did not wish to cause her mother any pain. "You don't have to tell me."

"No, I don't mind, it will likely explain your other questions as well." She sighed and glanced over at the fish. "For many seasons we tried to have children and couldn't. Since he had children with other women, we knew the problem did not lie with him. I began to wonder if something in the Harvest ritual had damaged me."

"The cylinder to remove your eggs," Enovese guessed.

Arianda winced and nodded. "I didn't know at the time, of course, or I would have stopped much sooner. Most female Harvesters perform only two seasons, so the fertility drugs and the procedure cause no lasting damage. I performed five ritual harvests; that left me infertile."

A tender camaraderie infused Enovese, for she knew exactly how it felt to discover such a truth.

"When I realized the exact purpose, that they took my children from me to create *paratanists,* I confronted Clathia." Fury straightened her shoulders. "I thought she would be as horrified as I to discover the truth, but she laughed because she had always known. To comfort me, she said that children were more curse than blessing."

Enovese did not know what to say.

"I became obsessed with destroying the ritual and finding my children, which only served to push my love away." A tear fell down her cheek. She didn't bother to wipe it away. "Once he left, my zeal escalated, and Clathia's daughter Kasmiri grew close for her time at Harvest. Since Clathia had taken my children from me, I vowed to take her child from her."

Enovese blurted, "That's why you—" then suddenly didn't know how to finish.

"You see, I told you it would answer your other questions. What we did was for appearances; our relationship never went beyond that. Kasmiri had her own motivations, but in the end our scheme worked too well. Clathia was enraged. She still refused to give me access to the *tanist* house but then embarked on a campaign to have me killed."

Realizing her mother had known about Clathia's plans, she offered, "Chur never would have harmed you."

Arianda nodded agreement, then proudly lifted her chin. "You have chosen well. He is a strong man to stand up to the empress." She sighed. "Clathia's panic over Kasmiri forced her to command Chur to select her during the Harvest, which I think is what Kasmiri wanted. Never have I met a more manipulative child."

After what Chur had told her of Kasmiri, Enovese had no desire to defend that statement. "Clathia told Chur to pick Kasmiri or she would destroy his chosen."

"And again, he defied her." A smile of triumph radiated from her mother's face. "I cannot express how much it pleases me to know both their schemes have failed and mine has succeeded."

"But you didn't take her daughter from her."

"No, but that's not what I truly wanted. Now, at long last, I have found one of my children." Arianda reached for her hand, clasping it firmly between her own. "Finding you has rendered everything I suffered bearable."

Enovese tried to keep the quiver from her voice but failed miserably. "For a long time I believed you had given me away."

Arianda moved to her side. "I never would have given you away."

When she wrapped her arms around her, tears flowed unfettered down Enovese's cheeks. She had waited her entire life to feel her mother's embrace. Unconditional love wrapped her in a haze of joy that completed her soul. A thousand questions about what would happen next for her and Chur fell silent. They would change the world. Not overnight, not in a season, but now Enovese firmly believed she had the strength to see those transformations through.

EPILOGUE

Chur proudly flung open the door and ushered Enovese inside their new rooms. He'd had a chance to inspect them while she talked with her mother and couldn't wait to see her reaction. This suite was twice the size of the Harvester rooms and far more lushly appointed with lavish furniture, statues, and a multitude of plants. Fading light from *Tandalsul* filled the space with a soft orange glow. Even the cavernous kitchen had enormous windows that faced the Onic Mountains.

Enovese turned slowly, taking in the space and the spectacular view. "These are our rooms?" She trailed her fingertips over the back of the huge animal-hide couch.

"Clathia was exceedingly generous." Chur knew she acted from fear, not munificence. No fool, Clathia knew she could not stop the coming changes. She was attempting to inveigle herself into his good graces by showering him with a multitude of gifts, including a fine living space.

"What did she ask in return?" Enovese moved to his side and began the laborious process of removing his gear.

He stayed her hand. "You don't have to act as my servant anymore."

A smile lifted her lips. "I'm acting as your bondmate. But too, I have personal motivations in stripping you of your gear and your clothing."

"Ah, would this impulse involve the lewd arts?"

"Perhaps."

It was a race to see who could get the other naked first. Chur won because Enovese wore only her ceremonial robe. Once he freed her from it, he tossed it aside.

"You will never wear that again."

She dropped to her knees and removed his boots. Glancing up at him, she lifted her brows and asked, "You intend to keep me naked?"

Pulling her into his arms, he nuzzled her neck. "I intend to clothe you in the finest fabrics, the most spectacular gems, and then strip you bare."

Her laughter tickled his shaved head. "And what will you wear?"

"Whatever I want. Who would dare to dictate fashion to a demigod?"

"Don't get too enchanted with yourself." She laughed. "No one likes an arrogant man, demigod or not."

"Well, I always have you to keep me humble."

"Hmm. Humble? Somehow I can't picture you as such." Enovese pulled back and glanced at the gear strewn about the floor. "Where is your ceremonial sword?"

"Safely with the next Harvester."

She stiffened and drew away. "I thought we were going to put an end to the ritual?"

Sighing, he pulled her back into his arms. "We are, but we can't change everything overnight. The ritual stands, but there will be no harvesting of the Harvesters. That I have already stopped." He nuzzled his lips to her hair. "There are a thousand details we must attend to, but not tonight. This night we will wallow in decadence, for tomorrow we will attend the celebration ceremony for Kasmiri's bonding."

"The new Harvester selected her?" Incredulous, Enovese shook her head. "Does he even know who she is?"

"Oh, he does, but I don't think he realizes exactly what he's in for in choosing her." Chur had some idea of the road ahead for his friend. If he stood by Kasmiri, he would find his destiny, but it wasn't going to be easy.

Tracing her finger around his nipple, Enovese asked, "Why are we going to a party for that spoiled child?"

"Diplomatic reasons. And too, in the coming season, we will need their help." Chur could see into the future, but dark shadows obscured pertinent details. Before Enovese could start with her endless speculations, he captured her mouth and lifted her into his arms. "Wait 'til I show you the bed."

Her eyes went wide when he pushed open the door. "Are you sure that bed is only for us? It looks big enough to hold twelve people!"

"I assure you, this bed is only for two." He deposited her on the sinking soft covers, then climbed between her thighs. "Now, how does that go? Ah, yes, by might of the blade I claim that which belongs to me. I claim you as my bondmate."

Lifting her hands over her head, Enovese said, "I freely give myself to you as my bondmate."

He sunk into her heat with a sigh of contentment. When their eyes met, he pushed a vision to her mind. Her standing next to him, their entwined hands cupped lovingly to her swelling belly.

"You see this in our future?" Hope animated her face and she blinked back tears of joy. "How could this happen when they sterilized me?"

"Because the gods are kind. When they asked of me to perform their work, I agreed, but only if they granted this in exchange."

Her lips trembled. "You could have asked for anything, something for yourself, but you chose to give this gift to me?"

"Because I love you." He kissed her tears away. "And, of course, I'm not entirely altruistic since this gift benefits me as well." At long last he would know the joy of holding his child in his arms and watching his child nurse at the breast of his bondmate.

Wrapping her legs around his hips, she pulled him as firmly into her body as she could. "My mother said I had chosen well."

"A very astute woman, much like her daughter." Chur moved gently atop her, careful to keep his weight from her and his eyes wide open. "Now, let's see what we can do about fulfilling that vision."